MW00912200

SOMEWHERE EVERY DAY

To Bonnie with
fondest regards.

Herm Gatten

Somewhere Every Day

Verne Patten

iUniverse, Inc.
New York Lincoln Shanghai

Somewhere Every Day

All Rights Reserved © 2004 by Verne Patten

No part of this book may be reproduced or transmitted in any form or by any means, graphic, electronic, or mechanical, including photocopying, recording, taping, or by any information storage retrieval system, without the written permission of the publisher.

iUniverse, Inc.

For information address:
iUniverse, Inc.
2021 Pine Lake Road, Suite 100
Lincoln, NE 68512
www.iuniverse.com

ISBN: 0-595-31404-X

Printed in the United States of America

Acknowledgement

Profound thanks to my dear friends Patti Anderson and Annie Sporn, without whose research, assistance and encouragement this book may not have happened.

Foreword

This story begins and ends "somewhere every day" in America. While this particular story started a little earlier than those of the majority of our current street dwellers, their problems and the causes are the same. The story has many beginnings but too often the same sad ending.

This book is about people. These people could be your children or mine. The men in this story had parents, families, neighbors, and teachers, who were too busy, too ignorant and tolerant or too intolerant and abusive, too drugged, drunk, or absent to provide them with the life skills that would have made them productive citizens rather than outcasts.

It is not only circumstances, but other people that make them what they are. Their numbers are increasing daily. Ignoring the problem will soon exceed both our social and monetary ability to face the cost. It is a national shame that we continue to passively watch them suffer and die along our streets and highways.

PROLOGUE

▼

Corky's heart rate doubled when he saw the pair of huge boots sticking out from under the brush pile he called his "castle."

Fear ran like a great hairy spider up his backbone to the straggly hair hanging over the collar of his ragged jacket. Cautiously surveying the situation, he carefully placed the sack of vegetables and scraps he had gleaned from the day's rounds of the alleys and dumpsters on the ground and laid a couple of loose branches over it.

Slowly he began to recover from his initial fright, and it was gradually replaced by anger and frustration. All his efforts had gone for some big dirty stranger.

He began to consider his options. He knew he could outrun the interloper should it become necessary, but after all the work he had done in building and placing his hideout, and so carefully concealing its use all summer, he decided he was not going to surrender it without some objections. Winter was approaching, and he had nowhere else to go.

He thought at first of setting fire to the pile and running but quickly discarded that idea, because he had grown quite fond of the place. Besides, the few useful possessions he had were concealed inside. He stood there puzzling over the situation, and his mind drifted back over his summer's activity.

Corky Hackett was a derelict—one of those outcasts whose home was the street and the dark corners, where his only acquaintances were the winos and bums who had become his special "nationality." Corky had never in his thirty-seven years felt himself a part of the mainstream of the human species. Born in an old converted railroad utility shack near the Chicago stockpens and railyards, he had lived all his life on the run from other humans. The only talent he had, which had enabled him to maintain his life and his freedom, was his ability to run.

Corky had greasy red hair, beginning to gray, and bright blue eyes. One of these never focused on anything but wandered aimlessly back and forth even when the other was still, and with an occasional upward glance and pause. He carried about a hundred and twenty-five pounds on his tiny five-three frame, and all the clothes he owned were on his back except for some old boots and other odds and ends concealed under the floorboards of the "castle." These things were mostly for winter wear; he wore tennis shoes as long as the weather allowed it.

Corky had never been outside the Chicago area and knew nothing about the rest of the world except what he heard on the street. The only world that really mattered to him was the approximately ten-square-mile area he roamed on the outskirts of the city. He lived daily from hand to mouth, like an old boar coon, a loner whose fear and distrust of people kept him always on the outside, even with the street people.

He had spent a very bad winter competing with the other street people for handouts and warm places. They were, almost without exception, stronger and more aggressive than he. Corky, therefore, had to survive on his wits and speed. The only people he had ever been able to intimidate were an occasional woman or teenager also caught in this flypaper existence.

One chilly spring evening, behind an old warehouse, he had found a very large cardboard box with styrofoam packing in it. He dragged it down across the tracks to a railroad tool shack about a mile from the mainstream junction of the many incoming rail lines. He was afraid to use the box where he had found it, because some other bum or wino would surely take it away from him.

He placed it against the wall of the shack out of the wind. Climbing in and curling up with the packing bunched around him, he pulled the cover down to shut out the cold and was soon asleep.

He did not know how long he had been sleeping, but he heard the train whistle and the crash at about the same moment. The screech of steel on steel and the thumping vibrations running through the ground made him immediately concerned for his own safety. He sprang upright in the darkness like some weird jack-in-the-box, more afraid for himself than concerned for anyone else's tragedy.

After climbing out of the box, he dragged it around behind the shack, out of sight, then went cautiously down the track to see what had happened. Before he had gone a hundred yards, sirens began to scream, and police cars, ambulances, and fire vehicles came in a carnival of flashing lights.

A sleepy driver piloting a huge truck that pulled two cattle trailers had failed to see the locomotive approaching. It was his last mistake. An ambulance crew was already extracting his mangled body from the bent and twisted truck cab, while police officers played cowboy, trying to control the few surviving cattle. Two other officers began walking about, firing their specials at the heads of crippled and dying cattle.

Corky stood in the darkness outside the lights of the nightmare activity and watched, fascinated. Over a period of four or five hours the chaos returned to quiet except for the forlorn bawling of one itinerant steer that had escaped down the tracks and then returned, apparently drawn by the scent of dead companions. The carcasses had all been removed, as had a large part of the wreckage.

In the cold gray dawn, Corky and the steer were for a few minutes kindred spirits, and Corky was momentarily lost in his feeling of companionship for the poor creature.

Oh, well, he thought, if the goddamn butchers don't get him, the trains prob'ly will. No good me worrying about him.

Watching carefully for any returning officials or curiosity seekers, he cautiously approached the crash scene to see if he might find something he could salvage for his own use. One great fender and a part of the hood of the truck still lay beside the track. Scattered lumber and metal from the trailers lay about, although the main body of the wreckage had been hauled away by the wreckers.

Approaching the spot where the ambulance crew had completed its gruesome task, Corky found several coins lying in the gravel.

"Thanks, ol' man," he mumbled. "I know you didn't leave it for me, but thanks anyway."

He pocketed the coins and was strolling slowly around the rubble-strewn area, concentrating on the ground, when a sudden upward glance noted a dark heap in the field on the other side of the track. Looking more closely, he suddenly grinned.

"Hot damn!" he almost shouted. "They missed one o' them dead cows."

Grabbing his old dull pocketknife from his jacket, he ran toward the carcass. After a long winter of mighty slim pickings, his mind's eye saw mountains of T-bones free for the taking.

He dashed up to the carcass and had already cut one great chunk of meat from the torn hindquarter when he thought suddenly, What the hell am I gonna do with it? I can't go around with chunks of raw meat in my pockets. It's cold enough out so's it would last several days if I had a place to put it. Goddamn, what a waste. What am I gonna do?

Taking the one piece he had cut, he walked back to his box by the tool shack. He laid the meat in a corner of the box and stood thinking. Almost crying in frustration, he walked slowly back to the wreckage and then aimlessly strolled on down the tracks.

As he cursed softly to himself, he noted the pile of brush the gandy-dancer crew had cut off the right of way a few days before. Frustrated, he kicked a Budweiser can that lay by the track and watched it bounce and roll down the grade. Watching the can tumbling away, he suddenly noted a large depression in the ground about 30 yards off the tracks and short way from where the rail workers had stacked the willow brush.

Inspiration seized him, and he fairly flew to the spot. Some old rough edges of stone foundation jutted from the ground on each side, and charred wood scraps lay about.

An old tool shack burnt up, Corky thought.

The hole was about three feet deep and eight to ten feet across both ways. A thin grass cover already grew on the sloping sides and ran down to a gravelly bottom.

"Damn, if I only got time!" he suddenly exclaimed aloud.

Then he thought, Jeezus, I think yesterday was Saturday. Maybe I do got time! The sun won't be up for another hour. If I hump my ass a li'l bit, I might make it before them nosy bastards get back.

After running back to the carcass, he cut several more chunks of meat and wrapped them in his jacket, then returned to the brush pile, where he raised the edge of the branches and hid it out of sight. He trotted back to the wreckage and began making a pile of all the longer pieces of lumber from the trailers.

Once they were collected, he seized an armload and, moving quickly, returned to the hole. Taking the shorter pieces first, he laid them side by side in the bottom of the hole. Once this layer was complete and about four by four, he turned the longer pieces the other way and laid a second layer. Working rapidly, he soon had a firm floor completed.

"Now the hard part," he said to himself. "Wonder what that big sucker weighs."

He just got back to the torn truck fender when he noticed two cars coming down the road toward the crossing. One was a police car and the other a light tan sedan with some kind of markings on the door.

Shit, he thought in sudden despair. Them buggers goin' to work on Sunday. There goes my plan to hell just like always.

Instead of running as he normally might have done, Corky ducked his head and slid in under the fender. Crouching there, he waited to see what would happen next.

The three men began walking about and looking over the area. They made marks, took measurements, and generally searched the ground all around the scene. Fortunately for Corky, they rarely even came close to the fender.

Once one of the officers spoke suddenly, quite close to where Corky crouched in hiding. "Hey, Sam, I see they missed one of them dead cows over there. What about that?"

Sam answered, "Aw, hell, it ain't gonna rot today, cold as it is. We'll call County Health when we go in, an' they can come pick it up tomorrow. Shit, man, I wanna get back an' see that ball game."

Great, thought Corky. They ain't staying, and I can maybe finish what I started.

Then suddenly he heard more conversation.

"Hey, guys, look over there in the brush. There's a live one. Ya think that's one from the truck?"

"What the hell ya think, Sam? Shittin' cows don't fly, and they don't hitch in here on no freight either. Mrs. Murphy was the last one allowed to raise cows in Chi, so it musta come off the truck."

"No need to get smartass," the other returned. "Think we oughta try and round it up?"

"Christ, man, it's Sunday. An' I ain't no goddamn cowpuncher. Anyway, what the hell would ya do with it, tie it to the black-and-white and drag it down to the precinct. Let the guys from the yards get it later if the trains don't knock it off first."

Listening, Corky thought to himself, Sons o' bitches got jobs and homes and televisions, but they don't work near as hard as me just to stay alive, and I got nothing. Can't win, can't even get a job. Hell of a world. Why don't they just get the hell out of here and let me work if they don't want to?

After a few more curses and comments and some rattling and banging of trunk lids and doors, the cars circled and left. Corky stood up quickly, and grabbing the open curved edge of the fender, he pushed upward to turn it over. He pushed it up to arm's length and then, straining as hard as he could, raised up on tiptoe. The balance was still against him, and it would not turn over.

He grabbed the flattened end of it and tried to drag it, but the jagged metal kept digging into the ground, and he could not move it except inches at a time.

Finally he gathered up several lengths of shattered two-by-fours lying about and built a small platform by crisscrossing them alongside the open side of the fender. Standing on this, he tried again and finally succeeded. It tipped over with a crash and lay there teetering back and forth like a giant tortoise on its back.

Corky seized hold of the narrow end and raised it so the rounded side of the fender was all that contacted the road, then began backing away toward the brush pile, laboriously dragging the load. By the time he reached the hole, his legs were shaking, and sweat dripped from his forehead, running in small streams down his back in spite of the cold sharp wind that blew across the tracks.

He sat down for a few minutes to rest and, after positioning himself, glanced up to the tracks. A large collielike dog stood sniffing the air on the edge of the grade.

<u>God, I got to hurry</u>, Corky thought. <u>All the frigging dogs in the Midwest gonna be on that cow.</u>

He picked up a couple of rocks and ran toward the dog. It pricked up its ears and stood its ground for a minute. When Corky fired a rock toward it, it turned and trotted off in the direction it came, stopping every few seconds to look back. As soon as Corky went back to his work, it turned and began working its way slowly back on the other side of the track.

Corky pulled and jerked and bounced his prize into position on the brink of the hole. Then, seizing the outside edge, he flipped it over on top of the floor he had made in the bottom of the hole. Straining and pushing and rearranging the floorboards, he finally maneuvered it to a position to one side of the floor so that it shaded one whole side.

Using an old tin can and hands and feet, he dug, kicked, scraped the ground, and packed dirt all along the flat edge of the fender. At one place where it was torn, he laid short boards up against the hole and packed dirt on the outside of the boards.

Then he returned to the crash scene and got the large flat strip of metal, which he thought might be a part of the truck hood or some part of one of the trailers. He really did not care where it came from; it would serve his purpose.

He leaned it up against the open side of the fender so that it covered the rest of the floor in lean-to-fashion. He then packed dirt against the lower edge of that piece so it bent over against the fender nearly all the way across except the lowest end, where it left a triangular opening to the space underneath.

As quickly as he could and watching all the while for intruders, he transferred the brush pile, laying the branches carefully over the metal hutch until it was well concealed. Where he intended to enter, he sloped the branches carefully upward so as to leave a small opening for a crawl space. He then covered this with one large branch that he could easily raise to get in.

By this time the sun was quite high in the sky, and a steady stream of traffic had begun to flow along the freeway about a half-mile away. An occasional car or truck went by on the crossing where the accident had occurred. Each time he saw a vehicle approaching while he was working, he had hidden in the brush near the site or crouched down behind the brush pile that was his newly built home. Finally he had transferred the entire brush pile to roof his hideout, and no sign of the original pile or of the depression was evident to the casual observer.

Feeling extremely pleased with his accomplishment, he retrieved his jacket and the meat from the edge of the brush, where he had hidden it while he worked, and crawled into his castle. When he moved up to the far end, he found he could stand almost straight up in the high curve of the fender. Sitting, he could lean against the curve and feel quite comfortable.

It was very dark inside at first, but after a few minutes his eyes became accustomed to the dim light, and he could see fairly well. For someone his size it was a very adequate living space and as fine a home as he had known for more years than he cared to remember. Not only that, but it belonged to him alone, and as long as he was careful, no one was likely to find it.

After resting for half an hour, Corky began thinking about what else he must do. His stomach began telling him that he had not eaten since yesterday. Kneeling down, he crawled back out the exit and peered carefully around before coming all the way out. He stood up and strolled casually away toward the tool shack.

Hearing a snarling sound from the direction of the dead steer, he moved several steps to his right up the grade and saw two large dogs—the one that had been there earlier and another yellowish shepherd type—facing each other over the carcass. He shouted and threw a rock at them. The one that had retreated earlier did so again. The other turned toward him, with lips rolled back in a snarl and head down, and advanced a few steps in Corky's direction. It growled viciously deep in its throat.

Corky almost panicked and ran, but discretion guided him. He took several careful backward steps to the edge of the grade, heart beating wildly, and ducked down out of sight of the dog. Pausing for several seconds to see if the dog was going to follow, he stayed in a crouched position, then walked quickly away toward the shack. After a few steps he turned to look back. The dog had returned to the carcass, more interested in eating than pursuing the man.

After retrieving his box and the chunk of meat he had left there, Corky looked about for traffic, then retreated rapidly to the castle, taking care to stay below the edge of the grade in order not to disturb the mean dog again. Using his knife, he cut the box into flat strips and dragged them inside.

He spread the Styrofoam packing on the lumber first and laid the cardboard over it to form a smooth and fairly comfortable couch. He then fashioned a small platform on the other side of his room on the upward slope and covered it with a piece of clean cardboard. Here he stacked his supply of fresh meat.

Smiling happily at his marvelous turn of luck, he thought, Jeez, I got nearly thirty pounds of meat and a warm place to sleep. With any luck at all, I can get some more meat too. I bet I can hole up here all summer. Gotta watch it though. Can't let no one see me comin' in here. Sons o'bitches would move me right back out in the cold, they found out how good I got it.

His thoughts again turned to something to eat. He left the castle again and in the same manner, went back to the crash scene, and found an oblong strip of stainless steel that had torn off the truck. Back at the brushy area near the castle, he gathered some medium-size rocks and fashioned a small hearth. Breaking dry branches in small pieces, he started a fire.

While the branches burned down to coals, he returned to the castle and sliced several thin strips of meat. Taking this and his steel strip, he returned to the fire, placed the steel across the rocks, and soon had meat sizzling deliciously over the coals.

Ain't never had it so good, Corky thought. When am I gonna wake up?

After finishing his meal, he wiped off the steel and broke up his hearth, placing the stones back under the bushes where he had found them. Then he carefully scattered the ashes and spread dead leaves over the spot.

By this time the dog had gorged himself and left the carcass. Corky went back and, taking his time, skinned the back area out, cut around the backstrap, and removed both tenderloins. It was in several ragged pieces, but he had secured at least twenty pounds of the choicest meat anywhere.

Over the next three or four days Corky swapped meat around the street for an old soup kettle, a down-filled vest, two blankets, and several odd cans of vegetable, pork and beans, and soups.

All of these memories passed through Corky's mind as he stood looking at his castle, which had suddenly grown a pair of feet. He felt sad, angry, helpless, and threatened all at once. His castle, his home, had been discovered—and not just discovered but taken over. After only two months his retreat was lost.

Whoever this guy was, he knew he could not force him out without destroying the place if he did not want to go. Thinking back, he knew that nearly every challenging encounter he had ever had with another man had ended with Corky on the run. Sometimes there was victory in flight, but this could not be the situation now. How could he deal with this situation and keep his home, his first semblance of permanence and comfort for many years?

While he stood there, his mind in turmoil over strategies, the big boots suddenly jerked, then separated, turned toes upward, and accompanied by grunts and growls, slowly became legs, a torso, and finally a whole body. It kept coming and coming until a black beard and huge head finally appeared. Great brown owl like eyes blinked at the sunlight, and a big hand brushed back a shag of hair from the dirt-stained forehead. Suddenly his eyes focused on Corky, and he grinned.

"Hi-ya, ya ugly little shit!" he roared. "Your place?"

"Yeah," Corky snarled. "Who da hell invited you anyways?"

"Hey, man, don' get sore, hey. I was tired, and I was tryin' to rest on the grade this mornin', and I saw you sneak outta here. I couldn't figger what was up when I saw ya rise from the brush pile, so I thinks, 'I'll just check 'er out.' Quite a pad ya got, the real ham and eggs. How long ya been here?"

"Since spring," Corky replied sullenly. "I put a lot of work in there, and everything in there's mine."

"Hey, ya little fartblossom, no call to get grouchy. I ain't took nothin' but a nap." The big man grinned.

With a staggering lurch he rose to his feet. Even standing down on the slope of the depression, he looked down at Corky, who was standing on the highest lip of it. He reached in his coat pocket and brought out a quart of wine, about three-quarters full. He tipped it back and took a long drink. Corky noticed that the bottom and neck of the bottle were all that was in view behind the huge hand. He lowered the bottle suddenly and wiped his mouth with the back of his hand. Smiling, he reached to extend the bottle toward Corky.

Taking a quick step back, Corky shook his head and frowned. He looked down at the toe of his shoe and said apologetically, "I don't drink."

"Bullshit," the big man roared. "A Bo that don't drink. You not just ugly, you a liar too!"

He laughed and laughed until Corky thought he was going to pass out.

Finally the giant took a couple of deep breaths and grinned at Corky again. "What's you name, ya lyin' ugly li'l shit? I'm Chimp. Chimp Stronski. Come on, have a drink with Chimp. I ain't gonna hurt ya. I only stopped to take a nap. I'm just hoboing through, an' I ain't hanging around to give ya no problem. Just thought we could share a drink and shoot some shit for a while. No call you should be scared o' me. C'mon, have a drink."

The whole speech was given in such an apologetic and coaxing tone that Corky felt quite relieved. He began to think maybe his fears were groundless, but still cautious, he maintained his distance.

"Corky Hackett, that's me," he replied, "and I ain't lyin'. I don't drink. It makes me sick."

This matter-of-fact statement knocked the big man out again. He laughed and choked and laughed some more. He fell back on the brush pile and roared and kicked and waved his great arms and laughed harder than anyone Corky had ever seen.

He felt himself smiling for the first time in years. A pleasant feeling of companionship came over him. He reached out, grasped the big right hand, and helped Chimp to rise from the brush pile. Without releasing the hand, the giant reached his other hand around behind Corky and grasped the whole back of the clothing in one great clutching grab.

Corky knew a second of panic, but wrapping his other log of an arm over Corky's shoulder, Chimp pulled him up against himself in one quick powerful bear hug and then stepped back, smiling, with soft brown eyes twinkling.

"You n' me goin' be great frens, li'l buddy. How'n hell you ever grow up anyhow? You skinnier than shit and too ugly to love. You mother musta run like hell when she seen what an egg she laid."

Corky had been listening to such cruel comments all his life, from his neighbors, from his schoolmates through the fourth grade—which was all he ever went—from his teachers, from his father's friends, and even from his father. Just as Chimp said, his mother had disappeared sometime in his early childhood. She ran, as Corky had been forced to do ever since.

Still, from this giant friendly outcast, each ugly slur sounded somehow complimentary. For the first time in his life, Corky had a friend.

CHAPTER 1

▼

Mondays were always bad for Ed Hackett. Even when it meant that his weekend in Cook County jail was over, Monday was still a bad day. He almost preferred the weekend incarceration to the long week's drudgery at Gordon's Mobile Station.

Nothing Eddie did ever suited Old Gordon. If he came in ten minutes early in the morning, Gordon immediately began pointing out things Eddie had not done to his satisfaction the day before. He would close by saying that coming in early was not going to make up for yesterday's screwups.

"And don't think your going sneaking out of here early tonight 'cause you got here early either," he would growl.

If Eddie came in three minutes late, Gordon waited half and hour before even acknowledging Eddie was there.

He would then wait for just that moment when Eddie was involved with a customer or there was at least one stranger in hearing, and he would suddenly shout, "How the hell do you get off, sneaking in here fifteen minutes late every day? Well, you ain't getting' off with it, ya know. You can hang around and clean the grease rack after five! I ain't paying you for part-time work, you know. If you ain't careful, I'm turning you in to the court."

All day every Monday, Eddie's mind was on the cold beer he would have after work, and a few games of pool with the guys at the Whistle Stop. Weekends were unbearably dry in Cook County, and by the time he was through work on Monday, every inch of his skinny frame was screaming for a cold beer.

Before the judge had taken away his weekends for that stupid hit-and-run, it was not so bad. Eddie could slip over to the Whistle Stop for a couple during lunch hour then, but now he no longer dared. Old Gordon was just waiting for an excuse to throw him out or turn him in for drinking, so for the next three weeks he just had to sweat it out.

Even though Eddie did not love his wife and often wished he had told her to work it out on her own instead of marrying her, he felt he owed her something for sticking by him when everybody else was trying to get him put away. She had come to court and asked the judge to go easy on him so he could keep on working. Eddie never knew whether it was her tearful plea or her very apparent mother-to-be appearance that swayed him to pronounce the eight-weekend work release instead of the one-year sentence.

Fortunately, the hit-and-run was his first adult offense, which also probably had something to do with it. With his juvenile record of three previous DWIs, he had panicked and run when he rammed that old drunk. He was lucky the guy had not croaked.

Janet set the bag of groceries on the sink cabinet, flipped the grubby coat off one shoulder, and took the last can of Hamm's beer out of the fridge. Heaving a big sign, she went across the room and fluffed the two pillows against the backrest, then sat against them on the Hide-a-bed, which she had not bothered to fold away this morning.

I've got to get my shit together and straighten this place up, she thought. Eddie will be home tonight. I hope he comes home early before he gets drunk. Weekends get awful long around here with no one to talk to.

She took one big drink from the can of beer and then, settling back against the pillows, sipped the rest.

Getting' kinda hard to manage, luggin' a sack of groceries and this kid too, she thought. How the hell will I make it after he's born? Since Eddie lost the car, we gotta lug everything. Maybe we can get a stroller with a basket. I know Eddie ain't gonna help me shop unless he's out of beer and I tell him I can't carry it all. Guess I'll just hafta see that he's out of beer when I'm ready to go shopping. She giggled softly to herself at this thoughtful strategy.

Janet had always been a plain-looking girl. She was petite and slim, with red-blonde hair and tiny freckles. She had started early in high school to make herself popular with the boys. She was always ready for a party, particularly if there were more boys than girls. Outgoing and quick-witted, she found it much easier to share the beer and banter with the boys than to compete with the girls in their fashion-crazy, cat-fighting world of teasing, cutting, petty little games. Boys were a lot less complicated.

She was very good at keeping relationships on a casual level. Only twice all through high school had she gotten involved with boys beyond the kissing and rubbing stage. Her first sexual encounter was with a passing stranger, when a handsome, laughing, dark-haired boy who was visiting a cousin in the neighborhood took her heart, her virginity, and a large measure of her self-confidence in one cyclone week, then disappeared forever in the aurora-bora neon of greater Chicago.

She had reclused herself for two weeks in her bedroom until her mother became so concerned that she threatened to take Janet to the doctor for a "complete examination." Frightened that her mother would thus find out about her new "status," she began to act like her old self, and in about two weeks she was.

In the last half of her senior year she met Eddie. He was a great dancer, lithe and quick, only a little bigger than herself, and great fun to be with. He was a couple of years older than the rest of the group but looked younger. It was a bit of a joke with the crowd that Eddie, who was twenty, was challenged everytime he tried to get beer at the Seven Eleven, when several who were seventeen or eighteen were able to buy it by the six-pack or case with equal facility, no questions asked.

One Friday night Janet had gone to a dance with Eddie. They danced every dance together and made more than the usual number of trips to the car for beer. Both of them were quite tipsy by the time the band quit, and instead of taking her home. Eddie drove straight to his little one-room house.

He opened the car door for her, and when she stood, he quickly bent down, picked her up in his arms, kicked the car door shut, then turned and carried her all the way to the door. She opened the door while still cradled in his arms.

He staggered across the room, dumped her in the middle of the open Hide-a-bed, and fell on top of her. After a very hot hour and final cold beer, they both fell asleep and woke up in each other's arms with the sun in their faces the next morning.

"Christ, Eddie, what am I gonna tell Mom?" she squealed as soon as full realization of her situation struck her.

He grinned and said, "Tell her I drove you over the Indiana border and then told you to put out or walk, and you walked. Mothers'd rather believe anything than their darling daughter's been shackin' up with some guy. Go in with one shoe in your hand and tears on your face, and everything will be hunky-dory."

Eddie dropped her around the corner from her home, and everything went exactly as he said, although her father was pretty skeptical, especially since she still had a little money left.

"There's a thousand phones at least between here and Indiana," he said. "You could have called me. I can still find my way around after dark, and I ain't stupid either. I know what you been up to."

Her mother had come to her defense. "Leave her alone, Dan. The poor thing has been through enough already."

Janet had a hard time to keep from laughing out loud when she got in her room, to think how well Eddie had figured her mother's reactions when he had never even met her. They spent many evenings after that in Eddie's place. It was great fun just lying around naked, making love and drinking beer, and talking about things and stuff.

When she graduated from high school, she was two months pregnant. She was pretty nervous for a while, but then she finally told him, Eddie looked at her for about thirty seconds and then grinned.

"Well, you're eighteen, ain't ya?" he said. "We can get married if you want to. I like you a lot, and you'll still be my girl, married or not. You wanta tell your folks, or shall we just get someone to stand up for us and tell 'em after?"

The whole thing was so spontaneous and upbeat, if not too romantic, that her heart and her spirits both jumped a mile. She grabbed him around the neck and, lifting her feet from the floor, hung there and cried for happiness. Later she recalled it was one of the few really happy moments she could remember in her life.

CHAPTER 2

▼

At first everything went along pretty well for Janet and Eddie. They had gotten married by a justice of the peace and then told her parents afterward, not saying anything about her pregnancy.

Her father became extremely angry and told Eddie not to bother coming around, because he never wanted to see him again. He even went to their family minister and tried to get him to intervene and talk Janet into getting the marriage annulled. The minister had come to their house twice to talk to them, but when Janet finally told him she was pregnant, he advised her father to let well enough alone. Janet occasionally went home to see her mother for a few hours, but Eddie was pleased to satisfy her father's wishes, and he stayed away.

They were married a little over a month when Eddie had his twenty-first birthday. Two of the boys at the service station took him to a corner tavern called the Whistle Stop to celebrate. Janet had cooked a real nice meal, gotten him a set of socket wrenches for a birthday present, and spent the whole day cleaning and prettying up the house.

It was nearly three in the morning before Eddie finally showed up, dead drunk. His friends brought him to the front steps, sat him down, and left. That was where Janet found him, curled up on the porch, at daylight. She dragged him inside and did not speak to him for two days.

His evenings out with the boys became more and more frequent as Janet's waistline got bigger and bigger. She was in her sixth month when Eddie came dashing in the door late one night as white as toilet paper and almost as limp. Instantly alarmed, she ran to his side.

"What's the matter, Eddie?" she cried. "You look like a dead man!"

"God, Jan, don't say that," he said with a shudder. "I may wish I was before this night is over."

"But what happened?"

"I think I killed a guy! Some old drunk stepped off the curb right in front of me. I hit him, Jan. I hit him hard with the fender. It's dented in, and I think someone saw me."

"Jesus Christ, Eddie! You didn't run, did you?"

"Hell, yes, I ran. I got three tickets before for driving drunk, and the bastards will lock me up for years if the guy's dead!"

"Eddie, you better go back, "Jan said gently. "They'll get you anyway, and it will be better if you go back!"

"Goddamn, Jan, I'm scared. I can't go back!"

They spent the rest of the night arguing until Eddie became sober, exhausted and worn down in will as well as in spirit. Finally Jan persuaded him to walk with her to the telephone booth on the corner. She dialed the police desk, and Eddie turned himself in. They went back to the house and sat on the sofa with their arms around each other to wait for the squad car.

"Janet, you're great, kid," Eddie cried. "I never thought before how much you mean to me, and I ain't been much of a husband. If I get out of this, everything will be different. I'll hafta start acting like a man ought to act."

She did not have time to reply to his comment, because they both saw the flashing red light pulling up to the door. She hugged him and cried, and the little life inside her stretched and jumped. A shudder ran through her as she suddenly realized who she was and where she was, and what this meant to her baby and herself.

They read Eddie his rights, standing on the doorstep. Jan held onto his arm every bit as hard as she had at their wedding and listened to the officer's solemn words. Eddie turned to kiss her good-bye, and panic suddenly hit her.

"Please, Officer, can I ride along?" she asked, sobbing. "I can't stay here alone. I just can't."

One of the officers smiled kindly and answered, "Sorry, ma'am, it's against the rules, but we'll drive slowly if you want to get in your car and follow us in. Otherwise, we'll hafta send someone back for the car anyway. It's evidence."

"Christ, Officer!" Eddie squealed. "They're not gonna take my car, are they? Anyway, Jan can't drive."

"That's gonna be all up to the court," the bluecoat replied. "Hey, Joe, you think it'll be okay if you take Mister Hackett, and me and the little lady'll follow along in her car? I'll drive, and that way nobody will have to come back for it. She can come back in a cab or somethin'."

"Okay with me," the other answered.

Jan hurriedly washed the tears from her face, combed her hair a little, and silently followed the big fatherly officer to Eddie's old Ford. On the way to the station, she alternately sobbed out her anxieties and listened to his friendly counsel and advice. He said the old man Eddie had hit was still alive, and his condition was not considered critical.

He told her if her folks would not take her back in, that she better contact County Welfare as soon as she left the jail and 'make some plans with them folks, 'cause you're gonna need help, missy! They might have your husband locked up for a while. He's in big trouble. Sure sorry these guys don't think first instead of later. Smartest thing he did, though, was to call us before we come lookin' for him. I'll bet you had something to do with that, didn'cha?" He smiled.

Jan glanced at him with her tear-filled brown eyes and smiled shyly. She felt suddenly better, able to face up to the world again.

In just four days it was all over. A public defender got the judge to hear Eddie's guilty plea, asked him to hear the wife's statement, and then they all sat silently while the judge lectured Eddie.

He told him he could be released for the weekend, but, "Young man, you are not to drink, drive a car, or be out after nine in the evening until I have time to review this case and decide sentence, you understand?"

"Yes, sir," Eddie answered solemnly, "and thank you, sir."

They took a cab home.

That weekend everything was back like it had started. They talked and ate, loved and flirted. Eddie even lay for a while with his head on her stomach, listening to the baby thump and twist around. After four days of sweating it out, he in jail and she at home, no less locked up and isolated than he, it was a true celebration of life for both of them.

For that one weekend they were truly in love, but hard times and poverty have a way of knocking love about that kills the dreams and shrinks the pleasures until all that remains is an occasional warm memory to hold things together. Monday's mail brought a notice for Eddie to report for sentencing on Wednesday.

When Eddie told Mister Gordon, his boss at the station, that he had to be off on Wednesday, Mister Gordon smiled pleasantly and said, "Great. I'll just pay you off on Tuesday evening, and you needn't bother coming back."

"Please, Mister Gordon, I've got a wife, and a baby on the way, and I just can't afford to be laid off," Eddie begged.

"Why didn'cha think on that before you went helling around runnin' over people?" Gordon replied. "Anyway, you ain't laid off, you're fired. There's a difference! Gimme any more shit, and you can leave today instead of tomorrow!"

Eddie worked through Tuesday and collected his little bit of cash that night. He gave all but five dollars of it to Jan when he got home.

On Wednesday the judge sat and solemnly looked at the young couple for a few moments, then said, "Mister Hackett, you have carelessly endangered and very nearly taken another's life. I have your juvenile record in hand, and you have a history of driving and drinking. Is that not correct?"

"Yes, sir," Eddie said submissively.

"You know, you are extremely lucky, Mister Hackett. But for the grace of God you might now be sitting in front of a jury on a manslaughter charge. Well, I don't believe that you can be trusted to drive any longer. I am suspending your driver's license for one year, and I am keeping your car in impoundment until you can make arrangements for its sale or storage. If not sold or stored within thirty days, it will become the property of the State of Illinois, to be disposed of at their discretion. Understood?" he almost shouted.

"Yes, sir," Eddie answered quickly.

"For the very serious charge of hit and run, I sentence you to one year in the county jail, but considering your family circumstances and the fact that you turned yourself in, I suspend the sentence for one year. However, I cannot let you off for so serious an offense. I know you have a job, and for that reason I sentence you to serve eight weekends in the county jail.

"You will be released on Mondays in order to go to your workplace, and you will report back on Friday evenings to serve your time. During this time you are to refrain from drinking. You must not drive a car, even to move it at work, and you must keep reasonable hours and stay out of trouble. I think that I have been very easy on you, Mister Hackett. Do you understand all I have said to you?"

"Yes, sir," Eddie answered. "But sir, can I serve all sixteen days at once, sir, 'cause my boss fired me when he heard I got in trouble. That way, I can find another job sooner."

"What!" shouted the judge. "Before you had even been in court, he fired you?"

"Yes, sir," Eddie answered.

"Officer Conrad," the judge said, addressing the big cop who had befriended Jan earlier, "This is still America, and a man is still innocent until proven guilty. I want you to have a word with this man's employer and see if you can't convince him that since he has not been harmed by this young man's indiscretion, a little charitable intention might save him some trouble—that is, in finding a new employee, you understand." He winked at the officer with a sly little smile.

"Mister Hackett," he continued, "you report back to your workplace at the usual time tomorrow, apologize to the gentleman for missing work, and offer to make it up an hour at a time if he wants you to. I have a feeling he'll probably be more favorably disposed by tomorrow. Any questions?"

"No, sir," Eddie replied again, "and thank you."

"Don't thank me," the judge replied. "Thank God you did not kill that man, and don't ever let me see or hear of you again." He then addressed Jan. "Mrs. Hackett, do you understand everything that has occurred here today?"

"Yes, sir," Jan replied. "Thank you."

"Very well," he said, smiling. "Good-bye and good luck, and when you do things, try to do them together. That's what marriage is all about, and it will save you many heartaches. I know." He winked. "I have been married for forty-two years. Court adjourned!"

For two or three days Eddie kept to the judge's instruction. He sold the car on Monday two weeks later, to a customer at the station. He and Jan went to the second-hand stores that night, and after much shopping around, they bought a crib and a stroller at the St. Vincent De Paul store.

Eddie called a cab to take them home. On the way he told the driver to stop at the Safeway grocery. He told Jan to wait in the car, and when he came out he had a case of beer. Janet frowned at Eddie as he got in the cab but did not say anything, because the cab driver was listening.

When they got home she said, "Eddie, I wish you wouldn't. You know the judge said no drinking until your work release is finished."

"Listen!" Eddie shouted as he popped the first can open. "If a man can't have a beer in his own house, what the hell kind of life is that?"

It's only for a short while," she said, "and I don't want to see you in more trouble."

"There won't be any trouble," Eddie snapped, "unless you're gonna call the cops on me again."

Janet burst into tears. "Eddie, that's mean. I didn't call the cops, you did!"

"Yeah," he snarled, "but you kept at me for six hours, till I didn't know what I was doing. Now I got no car, I'm a weekend jailbird, and I can't even get a car for another year. What kind of a wife turns in her old man anyway?"

"Eddie, you know I didn't" and she lapsed into tearful silence.

He drank seven more beers in the next hour and a half, pacing like a caged animal all the while. He dropped the seventh empty in the middle of the floor and gave it a kick that sent it spinning into the corner. Then he put on his jacket and left without a word.

Janet went to the window, and with tears streaming down her cheeks, she watched him disappear down the street into the darkness. She sat there at their tiny table for a few minutes and drank a beer. While the beer tasted good, it would not wash away the big hard lump in her throat, and her anxiety grew as she sat there.

She dropped her head on the table and sobbed quietly, the empty room echoing the sound back to her. Finally she rose and lay down, fully dressed, on the unopened couch, where she fell into a restless sleep.

She did not know what time Eddie came home. She heard the door open and close. She heard his drunken mumbling as he got undressed, and suddenly her head was spinning from the rap of hard knuckles on the back of her head. She jumped quickly, wrenching her side with the heavy load of her child.

"Why the hell ain't this bed opened?" he growled. "Lazy bitch, don't you know I gotta work in the morning?"

Ignoring her, he flopped the Hide-a-bed open, fell drunkenly into it, and in two minutes was asleep. Janet stood there for ten minutes looking at him and occasionally rubbing the back of her head where he had hit her. In order not to disturb him again, she turned on the little work light over the sink and got a drink of water.

Noticing his pants in the middle of the floor, she lifted them and carefully searched the pockets, then his shirt. He had left home with over two hundred dollars. He had thirty-seven dollars and some change left. She took twelve dollars and put it in her purse.

Opening another beer, she sat down at the kitchen table in a kind of shock and stayed there until dawn woke her from her stupor. Her lower legs and feet were numb, and she nearly fell when she stood up. She made a pot of coffee and poured a cup for Eddie. Shaking him gently, she finally got him awake.

'How the hell did I get home?" he asked her.

"I don't know," Janet said. "I was asleep."

"Christ, I feel like a one-eyed Chinaman shit in my mouth. Gimme a beer, will ya?"

"Eddie, I got hot coffee," she said. "You gotta go to work, you know."

"Goddamn it, Jan, don't tell me what I gotta do. That's what started this whole thing. I don't gotta do nothing I don't wanta do."

He went to the refrigerator, grabbed a cold beer, snapped the top, and drank it down.

He shuddered, walked over to Jan, and putting his hands on her shoulder, said, "Sorry, Kid, I don't know what the hell gets inta me sometimes. I know I acted like a shithead.

He sat down and took a sip of black coffee.

"You want some breakfast?" she asked gently.

"No, I'll just drink this. I'll get a roll at the station."

Then he dressed quickly, kissed her a quick peck on the forehead, and left.

Things went on in this manner for a couple of months. Eddie finally finished his weekends in jail. That, however, did not improve Janet's life in the least. Ever since he had lost his car, Eddie could not seem to get past the Whistle Stop on his way home. He would either come home drunk late at night or bring beer home and finish getting drunk there.

Jan got bigger and bigger and more sad and unhappy each week. Pride would not let her walk out. Eddie treated her well during the day, seldom hit her when he was drunk, and they always had enough money to pay the rent and oil bill and to eat reasonably well, but he spent everything else on beer and the pool tables.

One cold snowy night early in December, Janet walked the floor nervously. She had been apprehensive all day and did not fully understand why. She had fixed a very nice supper and hoped against hope that Eddie would come home early. By six o'clock she knew that was not going to happen.

When the first pain hit her, it was surprisingly strong. She put both hands on her sides tightly and lifted to try to ease the downward pressure.

She sat on the sofa for a minute to get her breath and thought, <u>I've got to get to a phone.</u>

She was struggling to put on her shoes when the second and third contractions hit her. She stood up when they eased off, and she had taken three steps toward the door when her water broke, soaking her legs, shoes, and the front of her skirt. Panicking, she started to run for the door, slipped in her own fluid, and fell headlong in the middle of the floor.

Baby Boy Hackett was born there on the cold linoleum, unassisted and unattended. Janet had passed out from fright and the shock of her fall. She woke to the screaming of her newborn son, and the panic was still with her.

Struggling weakly to her feet, she picked up the baby and shuffled to the sink, where she took a kitchen knife and cut him loose about six inches from his stomach. He was slippery, wet, and cold, and she almost dropped him. With a clean cloth she washed him in warm water, dried him off, wrapped him in a clean towel, and went to the bed, where she leaned against the backrest and nursed him.

For a while there did not seem to be any milk there, and she was concerned that she would have nothing to feed him, but finally the flow began. He ate hungrily and soon became warm and full.

After covering him with a blanket, she turned on the overhead light, then cleaned herself and the rest of the mess as best she could. Feeling weak and sick, she went back to bed and, lying close by the little boy, fell into an exhausted sleep.

That is the way Eddie found them two hours later. Quite drunk, he also knew a few moments of panic when he saw all the blood and his wife's still silhouette on the bed. Thoroughly frightened, he woke her gently, and as she turned toward him, he noticed the stirring bundle next to her on the bed.

"My God!" he exclaimed. "What the hell happened?"

Smiling weakly, she said, "Your son got in a hurry," and added after a pause, "I think we should go to a hospital."

CHAPTER 3

▼

Eddie dashed from the house, slipped on the fresh snow on the sidewalk, and still under the influence of the beer, scrambled frantically to keep from falling into the snowbank between the sidewalk and the street. Slipping and sliding, he dashed down the block to the phone booth, crashed in, and dialed the first ambulance number he could find in the book.

"What is the name, please?" a soft female voice asked him.

"Name...name," Eddie stammered. "I don't know! We haven't named it...him yet."

"Calm down, please, sir," the voice cooed. "Your name, sir. It's your <u>name</u> we need."

"Oh, yeah. My name is Hackett, Edward Hackett, and I need an ambulance, right now!"

"Okay, sir, will you please take a deep breath and calm yourself and tell me the circumstances and your address, so we can help you?"

With considerable difficulty and waste of time, Eddie finally succeeded in providing the required information and directions to his house.

He staggered back to the little one-room house, somewhat more calm. He went in immediately to his wife's side. Taking her hand timidly, he kissed her gently on the forehead and noticed how dry and hot she was.

She woke, smiled, and squeezed his hand.

"I'm glad you're here, Eddie," she said. "Did you get somebody?"

"Yeah, honey, the ambulance will be right here. You have to get ready."

"Christ, Eddie, I'm a mess. What'll I do?"

Suddenly embarrassed for her, he stood silent for a minute. "Goddamn, Jan, these people are used to this kind of thing. Just stay like you are. I'll find something clean and bring it along, and you can change after they clean you up."

"Oh, hell, Eddie, I'm so weak, I don't care what they do with me right now. Hey, did you look at the baby?"

She reached over and lifted the blanket from the tiny red body. Stirring from the sudden draft, the tiny hands jerked upward and rubbed the sharp little chin.

"Good God, Jan!" Eddie cried. "I've bought bigger bodies than that at the chicken market. You think he's all right?"

"Well, he's got a helluva appetite," Jan said, grinning. "What will we call him?"

Just then the ambulance light began blinking hysterically through the curtain, and Eddie went quickly to the door. Two white-coated attendants came to the door, and Eddie ushered them in.

"What time was the baby born?" the smaller of the two asked Eddie as his companion approached Jan on the sofa bed.

"Jeez, I really don't know," exclaimed Eddie. "You'll hafta ask her." He hurried to his wife's side and asked, "Jan, honey, what time did the baby come?"

"Jeez, I really don't know," she said, echoing his words of a moment before. "Sometime between ten-thirty and one-thirty, I think."

One attendant began writing notes on a small pad while the other briefly examined mother and child and recited pulse, blood pressure, and such to him.

"Your wife has a fever," he suddenly said to Eddie, "over a hundred and two. We better get her to the hospital. What hospital we going to?"

"Christ, I really don't know," Eddie replied.

"Well, who is her doctor? Didn't he give you any instructions?"

Jeez, Eddie exclaimed, "she's been healthy as a horse. She ain't been to no doctor that I know of. Jan, honey, do you have a doctor?"

"Hey, Eddie, you know we couldn't afford a doctor," she said, then laughed softly. "Hell, I don't think we can even afford the baby!"

The two attendants looked at each other and then surveyed the shabby little one-room house.

"I guess we go to emergency at General, huh?" one of them said.

He went quickly to the ambulance and returned with a stretcher. Easing Jan gently off the bed, they bundled her and the naked little boy up and carried them out.

When they were all loaded and about to leave, Eddie went to the one on the driver's side. "Any chance I can ride along?"

"Why, hell, yes!" the driver said. "I thought you were going to follow us."

"Don't have a car," Eddie mumbled.

"Well, jump in the back with your family, kid, and let's get the hell out of here."

When they arrived at the hospital, nurses, doctors and attendants quickly surrounded mother and baby, and the two of them were whisked from sight.

"Just have a seat, Mister Hackett," one friendly face said. "Someone will be out to get some information from you soon."

CHAPTER 4

▼

After several hours of thumbing through reception room magazines and pacing the halls, Eddie's patience began to wear thin. Tossing his magazine to the nearby table, he went to the nurse's station and cornered a pretty blonde nurse who was passing.

"I have been waiting for hours to find out about my wife and kid," he said. "Can you find out anything for me?"

"Give me your name and a few minutes, and I'll try," she said pleasantly.

In a few minutes she came back carrying several papers. As she approached Eddie, she smiled and said, "Mister Hackett, I am sorry to tell you, but your wife is quite ill. She has developed a bad infection that is going to take several days to clear up, and she is going to have to stay here for a couple of days at least. Your little boy is fine, and healthy as can be. Now, we have some papers to fill out here, and I need a lot of information from you."

"Oh, no, thought Eddie. Here it comes. They're gonna sock it to me for the medical bills.

Aloud he said, "Well, we might as well get right down to facts. How the hell much is it gonna cost?"

"Oh, don't get yourself all worked up. You'll get your bill much later. I just need some basic information for the records." She said. "Your baby is worth it, isn't he?"

"I'm not so damned sure about that," Eddie replied. "What I seen of him, he sure didn't look like much."

"That's a terrible thing to say!" Miss Burns scowled at him. "He is a really nice baby, and by the way, we might as well start with him. We still don't have a complete birth record on him. We show he was born at about one o'clock a.m., December fifth. Is that right?"

"Hell, I don't know. I wasn't there, thank Christ," Eddie growled.

"Mister Hackett! You're attitude is awful. He is your son, and he deserves your love and attention."

"Hey, don't gimme no lectures," Eddie flipped back at her. "Anyway, I was just kidding around to get you stirred up. You're pretty when you're mad."

At this the nurse rolled her eyes and looked away in disgust. Deciding to give it one more try, she said, "Mister Hackett, we do not have a name for his birth record yet. Surely you and your wife have picked a name for him."

"Call me Eddie," he said with a smile. "And yeah, we decided to all him 'Accident.' Ain't that great!" He laughed aloud.

"Look," the nurse complained, becoming quite agitated, "I have other things to do, and I need this information. Now, what is his name? Really!"

"No, that's not it either," Eddie said, grinning mischievously. "Tell you the truth, we're calling him C.Q."

"Now this is not another one of your silly jokes, is it? What kind of name is that?"

"Seriously," Eddie said, still grinning, "my wife's father is name Charlie Quinn, but neither of us likes the name Charlie. We wanted to name him after the old man, so we just decided to call him C.Q."

Miss Burns looked at him for a long minute and finally decided he was serious. Sighing, she duly recorded C.Q. Hackett on the worksheet. After another thirty minutes of back-and-forth bantering and turning down several "offers" of varying nature, she finally completed all the forms.

"Okay, Mister Hackett," she said finally, "your wife has been pretty heavily sedated and will not be able to talk to you for several hours. Why don't you go home and get some rest and come back in the morning? Feel free to come and see your son anytime during the visiting hours posted there on the wall, okay?"

"What time do you get off?" Eddie asked. "I'll come and see him about that time."

Miss Burns turned and stalked angrily away without replying.

Eddie took a cab from the hospital to the Whistle Stop. It was only two in the afternoon, but he knew that if he went to work, old Gordon would just start raising hell with him for being late, and he did not feel up to listening to that. The tavern was empty except for an old man and the bartender.

"Hey, Gus!" Eddie yelled at the bartender. "Guess what! My kid was born last night while I was screwing around down here. I got a boy!"

He grinned, thinking all the while that his announcement ought to be good for a free beer or two anyway.

"Sure enough, Gus said, "Hey, all right, congrats!" and he set up a large draft, saying at the same time, "Where the hell is my cigar?"

Jeezus Christ, man!" Eddie hollered. "I been sitting around the damn hospital since three o'clock this morning. I ain't been out shopping. I'll bring you one later."

"What did ya name him?" Gus asked.

"Wait till you hear this." Eddie laughed. "I know Jan is gonna be pissed, but I conned the hospital into putting his name down as C.Q."

"C.Q.?" Gus exclaimed. "What the hell kinda name is that?"

"Oh, it's just a joke, really," Eddie said, still laughing. "It just struck me. This nurse was hassling me about a name, and my wife is so doped up, she won't wake up till day after tomorrow, so anyways, we never talked about a name, and the kid is such a scrawny little shit, only five pounds. I just told her to put C.Q. My last name's Hackett, and it come to me that with the start he's getting', he ain't got a prayer of amounting to anything, so I dubbed him C.Q., short for 'Can't Quite.' Get it? Can't Quite Hackett! Ain't that great?"

"Hey, that's pretty good, all right," Gus growled. "If you really did that to your kid, you got a sense of humor like a rabid skunk. I wouldn't be bragging around about nothing like that if it was me."

"Shit," Eddie grinned. "Lots of guys have only initials instead of names. Won't hurt him none to be C.Q. Sounds just as good as Gus to me."

"Okay, have it your way," Gus replied, "but I won't be surprised if a lot of people don't think you're a bit of an asshole when you go laughing around about it."

<u>Goddamn world is getting full of soreheads</u>, Eddie thought. <u>First there was that silly-ass nurse, and now a bartender lecturing me. What the hell kinda world we got here anyway?</u>

Aloud he said, "he's my kid, and I'll worry about whether his name fits or not. If my friends weren't coming in a little while, I'd take my business someplace else."

"Hey, feel free," Gus replied. "You ain't spent no money here anyway. It sure won't break my heart or my cash register neither."

Eddie picked up his beer and turned to the other man who was sitting down the bar from him. "Hey, Mister, wanta shoot a game of pool? He asked. I'm tired of listening to sorehead bartenders."

"If you don't shoot pool any better than you pick names," the man replied, "it won't be much of a game."

"Goddamn!" Eddie shouted. "The world is getting frigging chock full of preachers and do-gooders. What the hell became of fun and games?"

He was about to continue with his tirade when Pete and Willie, two of his usual Whistle Stop cronies, came in.

"Hi, guys," Eddie said. "Am I ever happy to see you. This place is about as cheerful as an emergency room after a fire in the old folks home. Guess what! I'm a daddy, and wait till you hear what we named him"

Laughing all the while, he explained the naming of his son again.

Both of his companions laughed appreciatively, and Pete said, "You won't never change, will you, Eddie? You'll be laughing when they put you in that eight-foot box!"

Willie bought all three of them a beer, and they went together into the pool room.

Janet woke up in a cold sweat, feeling weak, sick, and disoriented. Her breasts were tight and sore, and she felt like someone had been beating her. Suddenly she realized where she was and why.

"My baby!" she exclaimed. "Where is my baby?"

Then she started remembering about waking up on the floor at home and the nightmare of trying to look after herself and the baby.

Her second thought was, <u>Where is Eddie?</u>

Looking around, she noticed the call-light button by her bed and pushed it.

A very pretty young nurse promptly appeared and, smiling pleasantly, said, "So, you finally come out of it. How do you feel?"

"I feel awful," Janet replied. "How long have I been asleep, and where are my baby and my husband?"

"Little C.Q. is doing great," the nurse replied, "and I imagine your husband is too, although I only saw him for half an hour yesterday. He hasn't been back today. You have been asleep, or knocked out, for about twelve hours, more or less. Would you like to hold your baby?"

"Oh, yes!" Jan exclaimed. "Can I?"

"I'll go right down and get him, and you try to get some of that pitcher of water down you while I'm gone. You have a rather serious infection, but you seem to be improving. You are going to have to drink a lot of liquids and take some medication for a while. Be right back!"

She went bustling out and came back a few minutes later with the baby held out, lying flat on her spread palms.

"Meet Mister C.Q. Hackett," she said with a smile. "Oh, thanks," Janet said. "We have already met…but why do you call him C.Q.? What's that mean?"

The nurse looked puzzled and said, "Well, your husband and I had quite a discussion about that, but he insisted that you had talked it over and named him C.Q.—after your father, I believe he said."

"I really don't understand," Jan replied with a puzzled frown. "We never talked about names, and C.Q. doesn't mean a thing to me."

"Well," Miss Burns replied, "I sure hope there isn't some mistake, because you will have to go to court to change it now. It was filed yesterday, you know."

"I wonder what Eddie was thinking of," Jan exclaimed. "C.Q. is an awful thing to call someone. I wonder why…you must have misunderstood."

"Oh, no, I understood, all right. He went to great lengths to get me to put it on the certificate, and I tried to talk him out of it," Miss Burns said.

"I sure hope it isn't one of his dumb-ass jokes," Jan said. "He is never serious about anything. I wish he was here!"

She began looking the baby over carefully, checking finger, toes, knees, and quietly chucking his tiny chin with her finger.

"Can I feed him when he wakes?" she asked. "I feel like my breasts are going to pop."

"I'm sorry," the nurse replied, "But with your infection and the medications you are taking, the doctor doesn't think that would be a good idea. You can give him his bottle later though, if you feel up to it."

CHAPTER 5

▼

Leo Stronski was the uncrowned king of the heavyweights in all the coal-miner-crowded bars and clubs and around Johnstown, Pennsylvania.

Born of a Russian father and a Serbian mother, he had immigrated to the United States in his early twenties. After a year or two of drinking and brawling his way through New York's waterfront district while working as a part-time stevedore, he was persuaded by a one-night beer-drinking buddy to come to Pennsylvania and work in the mines.

He was assured that, "Biga strong man like-a you get good job in mine."

Sure enough, the first week after his arrival in Johnstown, he was underground with a curious assortment of Serbian, Croatian, Russian, Italian, and Irish crewmen, mostly first-generation immigrants.

At six feet five and nearly three hundred pounds of solid manhood, there were few men who cared to challenge Leo in feats of strength. He was a quiet but sullen giant who was very loyal to those who succeeded in making friends with him. He was also quick to accept a physical challenge from any who dared try him. Off the job, his two great loves were drinking and carousing through the pool halls and beer bars, and at home, listening to classical music.

Darkly handsome, with huge brown eyes and a full-grown beard, he was a passably good operatic baritone himself. He knew many songs from classics and bellowed them out as he worked in the hot, dark drifts and tunnels of the mines, enjoying the way the echoes fed back through the dust and clamor of the underground.

He had met his wife on one of his trips to the opera. She was the daughter of an investment broker who was also a Serbian immigrant. Tall, plain, and heavy-boned, she was twenty-six the evening she slipped into the opera seat next to the giant young Stronski. As she was well past the age when most girls of her day were married and raising families, her father and mother were constantly introducing her and guiding her into "situations" with eligible bachelors in their socially prominent group. They were anxious that she make a good marriage but had about decided she would be an old maid.

As Juliana sidestepped down the row of seats to the empty one beside Stronski, their eyes met for a long moment, and an undefined but strong communication passed between them. She seated herself, placed her handbag beside her feet, and began stripping off her gloves. As she removed the right one, it hung momentarily, then snapped elastically from her hand and flew across in front of him to fall between the seats. He reached and retrieved it, then handed it back to her.

For some unknown reason, perhaps some sixth sense, she offered her thanks in the Serbian language, and he replied in the same. After some minutes of whispered small talk, they began exchanging views on the performance, speaking in the old language. When the opera ended, he asked her whether he might buy her a cup of coffee. She readily agreed, and they went to a small restaurant near the opera house. Before they finally said goodnight, they had three cups of coffee, a sandwich, and a date to attend a movie.

For several months young Stronski was a different man. He did not go to his usual haunts, and the only drinking he did was an occasional glass of brandy in his small apartment. He went with Juliana to her home several times during the first few months of their relationship. She lived in a relatively luxurious twelve-room colonial in a quiet residential area. He called for her there often and was occasionally invited to dinner.

Juliana's father did not like Leo, or rather, did not like the fact that she was keeping steady company with a common workman. Her mother and brother like him and usually persuaded him to sing for them as Juliana played accompaniment on the big old piano in their living room.

When Stronski finally asked her father for permission to marry her, his answer was no answer at all. Showing neither anger nor voicing any objection, he looked long and steadily at Stronski. Then suddenly he took his hat from the wall peg over his desk and, picking up his briefcase, left the house.

In Stronski's old country education in family formalities, there was no definition of how to deal with such a development. His upbringing demanded that the father be asked first.

<u>Well</u>, he reasoned to himself, <u>I asked him, and he did not say no, so I'll ask her.</u>

He knew she was sitting in her mother's sewing room.

After knocking formally on the door jamb, he stepped in and said, "Juliana, I asked your father if I could have you for my wife. He did not say yes or no, so now I ask you if you will do me the honor to be my wife."

She smiled at him pleasantly, put down the piece of cloth she had been measuring, stood, walked over to him, and placing her left hand on his chest, raised slightly on her toes and kissed him.

"Papa probably did not answer you, because I told him last night that we would be getting married soon."

"How could you tell him that when I no ask you yet?" he exclaimed, switching to his heavily accented English.

"Oh, I knew when you asked me to go for coffee after the opera that first night that we would be married someday," she said matter-of-factly. "The only question was when."

Stronski suddenly seized her in his great arms and began a wild Russian dance all through the house, swinging her wildly about and shouting, "Ham and eks, Juliana! You da real ham and eks!"

Her mother and brother came running from their rooms to see what all the commotion was about.

Her mother exclaimed, "Oh, my God, I think Stronski and you father have big fight! What you crazy kids doing?"

When Juliana explained, her brother went to the cabinet and took down a bottle of their best wine. He opened it and poured four glasses full, and they drank a toast to the happy couple.

Through the following years Juliana's father never once indicated approval or disapproval of the relationship. He often spoke calmly and cordially with Stronski. He paid for the wedding and gave Juliana a sizable dowry on the big day, but was never openly friendly to or accepting of the young miner.

Their wedding was a quiet affair. Only her relatives and a few friends of both attended.

CHAPTER 6

▼

The second day after her baby was born, Janet was seated on the upraised hospital bed, leaning back on her folded pillow and feeding the baby, when Miss Burns came in and told her that Eddie was waiting to see her.

"Please bring him right in," Janet said.

Eddie came in grinning. He looked tired, disheveled, and red-eyed. Janet smelled stale beer on his breath as soon as he approached. He leaned over to kiss her but she lowered her eyes and presented her forehead, which he pecked tentatively.

"Eddie, you have been drinking," she said.

"Come on, Jan, don't start crabbing at me. A guy don't have a kid every day, and I ought to be able to celebrate a little."

"Well, okay, but we are going to need more money now. Baby food, diapers, and the hospital bills besides. So we ain't gonna have much to waste.

Eddie scowled but did not reply.

"Have you been back to the house?" she asked.

"Christ, no" Eddie said. "I couldn't face the mess. I slept over at Pet's place and then came here."

"You haven't even looked at the baby," Jan said softly. "Do you want to hold him?"

"Oh, no, that's okay," Eddie replied quickly. "I can see him good enough from here. Sure is scrawny, ain't he?"

Tears came to Jan's eyes as she realized the rejection in his voice.

"You must care about him a little," Jan said. "You named him all by yourself, and the nurse said you gave really good reasons for his name."

"Oh, hell, she didn't tell you about that, did she?" Eddie blushed. "Why the hell can't people mind their own business?"

"Eddie, come on now. I know what you named him. Now I want to know why. I have been wondering for hours now what you were thinking when you named him C.Q.. What's that mean?"

Eddie kept on blushing but grinned. "Oh, Jan, it's just a little joke, really!"

"Eddie, I don't know what you are thinking, but I don't want my son's name to be a joke. Now tell me what it's all about."

"Okay, what the hell? Our name is Hackett, right? And he was so nothin'-looking when I seen him that it just popped into my head. This kid ain't never gonna hack it in this world. Christ, when I first saw him, I thought he would be dead by now, so anyways, when I seen him here later, I thought again, this feller can't quick hack it, so then I put it together with our last name and thought it was a pretty good joke. Can't Quite Hackett, Jan. No one's gotta know what the C.Q. part is. That can just be our joke."

"Eddie, you're an ass!" Janet snapped. "It may be a joke to you, but people's names shouldn't be no joke, and I ain't calling him C.Q., and don't let me hear you tell anyone your stupid joke either. As soon as I get enough money, I'm gonna go to court and get that changed, and don't try to stop me."

By this time she was crying. After taking the baby and laying him gently aside, she turned on her side with her back to Eddie.

Angrily he stomped out without a word.

It took her three more days to recuperate to the point that her doctor thought it safe for her to leave. He gave her a supply of medicine, as well as several pamphlets on care for herself and the baby, and told her to come back in two weeks, or sooner if she had questions or problems.

As soon as she was dressed and had the baby wrapped up, she went to the desk, where she asked to use the phone. She called Gordon's Service Station and asked for Eddie.

"What you want with him?" the old man growled at her.

"I am being released from the hospital," she said, "and I don't have no money to get home."

"Well, he's working on a guy's car right now," Gordon said. "Gimme your number, and I'll tell him to call you back."

She gave him the desk number and sat down to wait. Gordon hung up the phone and began immediately waiting on customers and forgot, or intentionally neglected, the message to Eddie.

Jan waited for an hour and then suddenly burst into tears. She went to the desk again and asked the charge nurse to call her a taxi. When the taxi arrived, she gave her mother's address and, holding her baby tightly, she squeezed herself into the corner of the back seat, feeling sick and lonely and more abandoned than she had ever felt in her life.

When the cab pulled up in front of her parents' home, she asked the cabbie to wait, climbed the steps, and knocked tentatively on the door.

Her mother opened the door after a few moments and, when she saw Jan, exclaimed, "My God, child! What is wrong with you...? <u>The baby</u>! My God, you had the baby!"

Jan, tears streaming down her face, said, "Mom, can you pay the cab, please?"

Her mother ran to get her purse and told Jan to get in out of the cold. When she came back from dismissing the cabbie, she found Jan sitting on the floor in front of the sofa, sobbing hysterically. The baby lay on the sofa behind her.

"Mom, everything is gone to hell," she said. "I think Eddie left me, and I know he hates the baby, and I have no money, and I don't know what to do."

Her mother put her arms around her and lifted her gently to her feet. "Come on, Jan. You know your father and I can still help. Dad might not be real happy with you, but he won't see you and the baby on the street either. Come on, let me see my grandchild. What do we have, boy or girl?"

Gently she lifted the tiny bundle and began unwrapping him.

As soon as she had the little face and shoulders exposed, she exclaimed, "He's a boy, huh? Just look at that red hair," and she stood gently rocking him back and forth.

Jan soon got herself under control and began telling her mother all about it.

"Jan," her mother said, "most of this was unnecessary, you know. If you would only stay in touch and ask us when you need help, we are still your folks, even if times are a bit hard. There is no use trying to make it on your own if that kid you married is no good."

"I didn't say he was no good," Jan said defensively. "Maybe he didn't get my message."

"That is stupid, Janet," her mother scolded. "If he hasn't been to the hospital but once in a week to see his wife and new son, then he ain't much. What kind of father wouldn't even come to bring his first child home from the hospital?"

"Mom, I don't want to talk about it. He is probably trying to find us right now," she said angrily.

Her mother, sensing that she was pushing her headstrong daughter too far, took a conciliatory approach. "Now, honey, let's not fight. You are safe and comfortable here. I'll look after you and the baby till you get back on your feet. You look terrible. Why don't you go lie down?"

The strain had been too much for Jan, and she willingly conceded.

Eddie had been thinking all day about Jan, and feeling quite guilty about not having checked on her for three days. When he got off work, he went straight home.

Gritting his teeth, he got out a bucket and some soap and water and cleaned the little one-room house thoroughly. As soon as he finished, he washed himself and put on his best shirt and slacks. He took his pay check, went to the drugstore a few blocks away, and cashed it, then went next door to a flower shop, bought a small bouquet, and called a cab.

When he got to the hospital, Miss Burns was at the desk.

Grinning widely, Eddie said, "Hi, hot stuff. I brought you some flowers."

She looked at him for a long moment, trying to make up her mind if he was serious. She knew his wife had been gone since eleven o'clock that morning.

Hoping that she was wrong about his intentions, she said, "You must be nuts, Mister Hackett."

Seeing that she was irritated, Eddie changed pace. "Hey, don't get all steamed up. I just came to cheer up my wife."

"Don't you ever go home?" Miss Burns snapped.

"What the hell is ailing you?" Eddie shot back. "My private life ain't none of your business!"

"Well," Miss Burns replied, "if you had gone home, you would know that your wife and baby checked out of here hours ago."

"You're shittin' me!" Eddie exclaimed, amazement showing sharply in his eyes.

"No need to get vulgar," she said. "Yes, I am serious. They went home this morning."

Eddie broke out in a cold sweat. If she was not at home or in the hospital, where was she?

Christ, he thought, *I'll bet she went to her folks, 'cause I was so damn careless about visiting. Damn, I don't wanta hafta go talking her away from Mama again.*

He went down to the waiting room and sat there stunned for some time. He finally talked himself into going to her folks' house. He knew if he let it go, he would probably never get up the nerve to do it, and he held a healthy respect for his wife for having put up with his nonsense for so long. He had a fear of being "on the street" and knew that if he let go of the stability of his house and wife, his circumstances were uncertain at best. Reluctantly he called a cab and went to her parents' house.

When he knocked, her mother came to the door, scowling disagreeably.

"Is Janet here?" he asked timidly.

"Yes, she's here, and I hope she has the good sense to stay here."

"Can I talk to her?" He smiled nervously, switching hands with the bouquet so her mother would be sure to notice them.

"Not now, you can't. She's sleeping, and I ain't going to bother her for the likes of you."

"Well, can I come in and wait for her to wake up? I can't afford to be running back and forth in taxis, and there's no place around to wait," Eddie pointed out practically.

"Yeah, I know," she said, "but if there was a bar handy, you'd be happy enough to wait there, wouldn't you?"

Eddie discreetly kept himself under control and did not answer, but he did blush a deep red.

Relenting, her mother finally invited him in and told him he could sit in the living room and wait, but cautioned him to be quiet and let Jan and the baby sleep. It irritated him considerably that she did not offer to take the flowers or to give him a cup of coffee. Or even a comment or two. He sat there holding the flowers in uncomfortable silence for nearly two hours.

Suddenly the baby began to cry in some distant part of the house, and in about two minutes Janet came into the room in her mother's robe and slippers, looking tired and disheveled. She started in surprise when she saw Eddie.

"What are you doing here?" she said suddenly. "I thought you didn't want us."

"Hey, did I say I didn't want you, Jan?" he exclaimed, jumping to his feet. "You know I never said that!"

"No, you never said it," snapped Jan, tears starting in her eyes, "but you sure didn't act like you cared one way or the other. You wouldn't even look at the baby and never came to see us. Besides, you knew I didn't have any money to get home, and you never returned my telephone calls or anything. You just left me! What the hell was I supposed to think?"

"Jan, I am sorry," he said. "I never knew you called. Who did you talk to?"

"I talked to that grouchy old bastard you work for," she almost shouted, "and he said he would tell you as soon as you got out from under a car."

"Honey, I really am sorry, but he never told me, and you wouldn't talk to me when I did come up, so I thought you didn't want to see me!"

"What about the baby, Eddie? How come you won't look at your baby?"

"Jeez, Jan," Eddie said plaintively, "I ain't never had nothing to do with kids. I guess it scares me a little. Go get him. He's hollering his head off. I'll hold him if you want. You take the flowers and quit glaring at me, and I'll hold him the rest of the day if you want. Just give me a break, will ya?"

Relenting, Jan went down the hall and returned with the little one. He had stopped crying the moment she picked him up.

Cringing mentally, Eddie effected the exchange of flowers for child and stood there holding him stiffly as though he might break before his eyes. The baby, sensing the difference, started crying again.

Jan placed the flowers on a nearby table and told Eddie, "Sit down and hold him a little. He'll stop crying. You hold him till I get his bottle."

Eddie settled down in the big old settee and, for ten or fifteen minutes, listened to his son's hunger call. It was the longest time he would spend with little C.Q. for the remainder of his life.

CHAPTER 7

▼

Leo Stronski and bride rented a modest apartment near the downtown area. She worked as a free-lance window decorator and had regular contracts with several downtown department stores in the area, so it was to her advantage to be close to her work.

Leo continued to work in the mines, and as soon as the novelty of coming home to his new bride every night wore off, he began to spend occasional evenings with his old buddies in the taverns—however, now in a more reserved and serious manner.

He became acquainted with the supervisors and union leaders and occasionally joined them for a drink when he encountered them, conducting his enjoyment hours in much more moderate fashion than before he got married. He avoided the loud and raucous bars and people, drank only moderately, and always came home reasonably early.

Juliana did not mind, relishing the quiet evenings by herself to plan her work and sew for herself and Leo, or taking the opportunity to visit her folks.

Leo was bright and ambitious and worked very hard in the underground. Within the year after their marriage, he was promoted to shift supervisor. Happily singing as he arrived home that evening, he shouted at Juli as he came through the door.

"Hey, woman, look out you now! You husband make big boss! Big ham and eks in mine now! Maybe you daddy gotta love me now!" and he roared with laughter.

Seeing what a great frame of mind he was in, she suggested that they go out for dinner to celebrate. She was very proud of her man and loved being seen in the nicer restaurants with him. Everyone liked them both, and his size alone dictated respect and prompt service from the proprietors and workers alike.

She never knew why, but Leo had a special taste for ham and eggs. He often told her how he loved this particular dish and almost invariably ordered it whenever they went out to eat together—breakfast, dinner, or supper. This special taste was catered by their favorite eating places to try to entice them to support particular places. They began competing for his business and enormous appetite by dressing up his favorite meal, increasing portions, adding condiments, and such until his special "ham and eks" dish became legend. Further, it extended into his vocabulary for other things, so that anything that pleased him greatly was described as "ham and eks."

After dinner on this particular evening, they began discussing what had lately become an obsessive topic, raising a family.

"We get married whole year now." Leo said. "No baby start yet! What the hell wrong now, Juli? Baby gotta come soon. Big strong man like me can't make baby? Maybe we see doctor. Maybe problem. Maybe we do something wrong."

"Leo, please," Juli said, blushing, "speak Serbian. Everyone is looking!"

So they went on discussing and decided they should both visit a doctor.

She discussed it the next morning with her mother, who recommended an old family friend who had been Juli's doctor for years. After giving them both thorough physicals, he called them in for a conference.

"You are both young and strong and very healthy," he said. "Frankly, I see no reason for your not having children. I also see no reason for you to be worrying about it so soon. Sometimes there is a lot more to it than just wanting it to happen. Maybe one or both of you are too tired, or too busy, or you are hurrying too fast with your loving. Slow down, relax, take it easy. Drink a glass of good wine or brandy at bedtime. And don't worry. When it's time, it will happen."

Had they known what the result of their desires would be, they would not have been so anxious. They enjoyed more than three fun-filled years together before Juliana finally found herself pregnant. Almost immediately she began to have problems.

CHAPTER 8

▼

Janet went home with Eddie from her mother's, quite against her mother's will and advice. For a couple of days Eddie gave her some love and attention, but contrary to his earlier attempt at her mother's home, he deliberately ignored the baby, except to grouch whenever he cried or whenever Janet gave the child more than necessary attention.

His old pattern of activities began again almost immediately and, if anything, got worse. He got drunk nearly every night now, and there was no money for any of the necessities of child-raising.

Janet, in desperation, finally went to the child-welfare office and managed to convince them she was an abandoned mother. They provided her with food coupons and a little money. They also informed her they would assist her in finding part-time work and free child care. She never told Eddie any of this, because she was afraid he would take her money from her and drink it up.

A few weeks after she went to the welfare department, she got a notice from them in the mail to go for a job interview at a little restaurant about a mile from where they lived. Although she was somewhat apprehensive about how she would manage with C.Q. and a job as well, she felt good about the possibility of a change in her life. She laughed and sang to the baby all the rest of the day.

Her interview was scheduled for ten o'clock in the morning the next day, so she dressed in the very best she had, having trimmed and set her hair the night before. She looked quite presentable when she left home for the interview. She bundled up C.Q in the old stroller they had bought when the car was sold, then walked to the restaurant.

The owner of the restaurant was a disabled veteran of Italian descent whose wife did the cooking and general managing of the business. The restaurant was an old railroad car, or had been built to look like one, Janet could not decide which. The front steps were constructed of wood, and heavy cast railings ran down to the dirt walk from the street.

She left the baby in the stroller next to the rail and went in. There were mostly middle-aged men in working clothes at the counter and at several of the tables. All of them looked at her curiously, and she was suddenly struck with stage fright. Her mouth became dry, her knees trembled, and she was about to turn and run out when an enormously fat and greasy-looking woman stepped out of the doorway behind the counter.

Wiping her hands vigorously on the full-length apron she wore, she shouted, "Hi-ya, sweetheart! What you doin' in a dump like dis? You gotta be lost or awful damn hungry one."

She smiled broadly and gestured with her left hand toward a counter stool.

Janet timidly edged over to the stool but remained standing, clutching her handbag with both hands.

"I'm supposed to be here for a job interview," she almost whispered.

"Interview, hell!" the big kindly lady shouted again. "If you can find your way to dis joint, you hired. Anybody else come lookin', they just too damn late!"

Comments echoed all around from the men in the rough but clean little dining car.

"Atta girl, Rosa!"

"All right, Rosa!'

"Way to go, Rosa!"

"See dere, honey, you just passed the toughest interview you ever gonna get. If dese jokers want ya, they got ya. You ready to go to work?"

Janet, vastly relieved from the tension and concern that she would not measure up, suddenly burst into tears. Rosa, shocked by this reaction, seized her in her big fat motherly arms, and hustled her through the door into the kitchen.

"What the hell is wrong, honey? Did I say somethin' wrong? I didn't mean to scare ya! What's your name anyways?"

"I'm Janet Hackett, and I'm sorry, but I was just so happy to get the job so easy that I couldn't believe it. You don't even know anything about me."

"Hey, baby, I know you got guts enough to walk through a forest of friggin' bums to get to this place, and that's good enough for me. Now, you ready to go to work, or you got someplace else to go? I need you bad. These stevedores runnin' my fat old ass off here, and my helper left for Georgia with some fast-talkin' trucker. Can ya wait tables?"

"I suppose I can," Jan smiled timidly, "but I never tried before."

"Hell, if you can walk and swing a table mop, you'll do," said Rosa. "I'll show ya the how-to's in about five minutes. Grab one o' them aprons there, and I'll introduce you around to the regulars out there. Just call me Rosa, or 'Mom,' whichever suits. Lotsa people call me Mom."

"Jeez!" Janet exclaimed suddenly. "I almost forgot. I can't start right now. I got my baby boy in a buggy outside the door!"

"Well, Mother o' Christ, girl," Rosa said with a grin, "go bring the little fart in here 'fore some damn derelict takes him for somethin' ta eat."

Jan ran quickly out and pushed the stroller up close to the building, then bundled up C.Q. and carried him back inside.

"Well, let's have a look at this little pecker!" Rosa bellowed. "Goddamn red hair. Ain't he a corker! What's his name?"

Janet giggled. "You almost got it right. My husband tacked some awful family name on him, so I just call him Corky."

Actually, she had called him only motherly nicknames like "Sweetie" and "Pumpkin'" ever since she had brought him home, refusing to dignify Eddie's joke by using his given C.Q. "Corky" felt somehow comfortable when her new boss had brought it to mind by her comment, so Corky he became to Janet from that minute on.

Rosa had an old sofa and a desk back in a corner next to her storeroom, and she invited Jan to make the baby comfortable there.

"And come on, doll. Let's feed these baboons 'fore they all take off for da jungle."

Under Rosa's loud but friendly and expert guidance, Janet soon became a first-rate waitress. She loved the job, and her old teenage habit of free and easy banter with the boys served to make her a welcome and valued addition to the "feed lot," as Rosa jokingly called her place. Jan was amazed by how quickly her tips added up to a respectable wage aside from her regular pay.

Janet explained her home situation to Rosa in explicit detail soon after she began working. Rosa listened patiently without comment, except for an occasional cuss word when Jan mentioned that Eddie sometimes hit her and that he did not like the baby.

When she was through with her story, Rosa commented, "Honey, if I was you, I'd flat move out on the son-a-bitch and not even tell him where you goin'. Or better yet, invite him down here some Saturday mornin', and we'll kill the son-a-bitch and serve him for breakfast. These shitheads can't tell doughnuts from dog turds after Friday night anyways. What the hell is wrong with men anyways? Beer and broads is all they think on. I've had more goddamned waitresses talked out of their shorts in this place, and not one of them Romeos is ever around, comes time to pay the piper. Oh, well, what the hell? But look, honey, that guys gets too rough, don't buy none of his crap. You and me can make some kinda better deal than that. Don't you worry your pretty head."

From that day on, Janet felt better about her situation. She and Rosa conspired very carefully on her work hours, and Rosa even made do sometimes when she needed Jan very badly, so that Eddie would not find out that she was working.

She was able to successfully conceal her situation from Eddie for several weeks, but her new-found independence was short-lived, because she became careless in not asking him for money on those rare occasions when he was sober enough to remember, and in letting better food and clothing for herself and Corky become obvious in their little one-room shack.

One spring evening, quite unexpectedly, Eddie came home sober in the middle of the afternoon. Janet was not home, and Eddie went immediately to the refrigerator for a beer. There was no beer, but there was a small steak Janet had expected to cook for herself as soon as she got home, and also a sack of several apples.

<u>What the hell?</u> Eddie thought. <u>It has been two weeks since payday. Where the hell did she get money for steak and apples?</u>

CHAPTER 9

▼

It had been a good day for Jan. She had made twelve dollars in tips besides her forty-three-dollar check which Rosa had cashed for her at the restaurant. She had gone out of her way to stop at the Seven-Eleven store on her way home to pick up a six-pack of beer, some bread and eggs, and some baby food items for Corky.

I will get these all out of the bags and put away before Eddie comes home, if he comes home. That way he probably won't notice, she thought.

Brief apprehension made her pause and frown, wondering what Eddie's reaction would be if he found out she had become almost self-sufficient without telling him.

Oh, well, she thought, at least I can eat my little steak and have a cold beer before I need to worry. He hardly ever comes home before ten anymore anyway.

With that, she dismissed all concern. After loading some of her stuff around Corky in the stroller and carrying the rest, she strolled home. Enjoying the sunshine and counting her small blessings.

She stopped the stroller in front of the steps at home, gathered her packages in her arms, left Corky sitting in the stroller, and took her provisions inside. She opened the door and walked straight across the room to the table, where she started putting down her purchases. With a start, she noticed two empty beer cans on the table and several more on the sink stand.

Suddenly afraid, she turned quickly to go get Corky from the stroller. She almost screamed when she saw Eddie leaning against the wall behind the door. He had a sneering grin on his face and an almost-empty pint Whiskey bottle in his hand.

"So, you goddamn tramp, what did you do, get yourself a boyfriend?" he rasped. "Or you out whoring for it?"

Thinking to sidetrack him, she said, "Eddie, what are you doing home so early? I just went out and got you some beer and a few groceries. Why are you so mad about that?"

"You ain't answered my question, bitch," he stated flatly. "I know you been gettin' extra money. When I seen that steak in the fridge, I knew you had money, so I went snooping around here in the dresser, in the closet, and in the fridge. How much money you got, and where you gettin' it?"

"I only got a little, Eddie," she pleaded. "I had to do something. The baby was hungry, and he needed some things."

"See, he snarled, "you do have money. Now, how much?"

"I'll share with you Eddie. I been working some part-time, and I'll share."

"Share, my ass!" he shouted, slapping her viciously across the face. He dashed for her handbag, lying on the table. He was drunk and lost his balance trying to stop. He ran into the wall and put out both hands to catch himself.

Janet, suddenly defensive, grabbed the purse and turned to run for the door. Eddie, completely out of control between being drunk and in a rage, grabbed the back of her jacket with one hand and her hair with the other. Jerking her backward with both hands, he slammed her against the wall and, when she turned, hit her across the forehead with the whiskey bottle.

Fortunately, the bottle did not break but went spinning across the room, swooshing the little remaining bourbon across the floor. Janet fell to her knees, stunned. She dropped her handbag, and Eddie quickly snatched it up, tearing it open. He seized all the bills and wadded them into his pocket.

"I can't believe this bullshit!" he shouted. "All these months I been breaking my ass at that station to keep this place for you and that useless kid, and you go get a job and don't even let me know. You're a sorry-ass wife! Turn me in to the cops, make me lose my car, and then keep all this money for yourself! Well, you can forget that! This is my share of what you already got, and I better keep on gettin' my share, or your ass is cold meat."

With that he pitched the handbag overhand directly into her face, bloodying her nose, and stomped to the door. As he started down the steps, the stroller was partially blocking his path. After pausing momentarily, he aimed a tremendous kick at the side of the stroller and sent it spinning across the yard.

On about the third turn the stroller tipped over, toppling the baby, screaming, into the dust of the yard. He stood there glowering at the crying child for a moment and then staggered off down the street in the direction of the Whistle Stop Tavern.

Janet came running from the house when she heard the baby scream. Blood was streaming down the front of her blouse from her bloody nose. She picked up Corky and cuddled him, brushing the dust, dirt, and weeds from his clothes and blanket. After righting the stroller, she brushed the dirt out of it as best she could.

Carry Corky, she went back in the house and sat crying for a few minutes on the edge of the sofa, while she patted and comforted him. Blood and tears spattered the linoleum between her feet as she sat there shaking from fear and hurt. She began thinking over what had happened and had almost decided that the whole thing was her fault for not telling Eddie all about it in the first place.

Then she thought, <u>I don't see why he has to beat us though, especially the baby. Corky didn't have anything to do with it. Why would he try to hurt a little baby?</u>

With that thought she was suddenly angry instead of frightened. The more she thought about it, the madder she became.

Going quickly to the sink, she cleaned herself off and examined the bumps on her forehead where he had whacked her with the empty bottle. This self-inspection only served to increase her anger. She took a large shopping bag from the storage space under the sink, gathered up clothing items for herself and Corky, and loaded the bag and all of the items she had purchased earlier back into Corky's stroller. Carrying Corky and pushing the stroller she headed back to the restaurant.

It took Rosa only a glance to see that all was not well when Janet came back into the diner.

"Christ, baby doll, what you been doin', bumpin' heads with the Southbound? Get the hell in here, and let Rosa tend to you."

Taking the baby in one arm and wrapping the other protectively around Jan, she hustled her into the back, away from the curious eyes of her customers.

"Now, tell Mama what the hell happened."

In as few words as possible and in an angry tone, Jan explained her confrontation with her husband.

"I don't know what the hell to do now," she said after explaining. "I have only about six dollars in change left. He took my pay and most of my tips. It was his payday too! Now he has all his pay and most of mine, and I can't even pay my rent!"

"Don't get your temperature up sweatin' that horse's ass, sweetheart." Rosa nodded firmly. "We'll see to him."

Without further comment she went to work spreading out the sofa bed and making it up.

"There, Jan, you and the baby just relax there. I'll be closing dis joint up in about half an hour. I'll leave you the key, and you and the babe can spend the night right here. Fix yourselfs somethin' to eat for supper and breakfast both. We'll worry about the small stuff tomorra or next week, no matter. Just get you and the little one cleaned up, and make yourself to home."

She stood looking down at Jan's forlorn and bruised face for a minute and then said, "Just sit there a minute, babe, and pick the little one up and love him a while. Don't worry about a thing."

She turned, went to the front of the kitchen, and leaned against the door frame, looking into the diner. After waiting there a few minutes, she caught the eye of a big trucker who was having a cup of coffee and talking to some friends. Motioning with her head, she called him up.

Quietly she said, "Hey, Cholly, come back and get a look at this, will ya?"

Like she was really soliciting advice, she stopped with him in front of Jan, who looked small, beaten, and pitiful, sitting there with her baby, bloodstains plain on both their clothes. Taking her small face in one big pudgy hand, Rosa turned her so the light shone on her bruises.

Looking at Charlie, she said, "Wot you think, Cholly? We ought to take this little lady to the doctor?"

Charlie, suddenly quite concerned, looked at her injuries carefully and said, "Naw, I don't think it's anything dangerous. It'll heal up in a day or so. No need blowin' good money to have some sawbones tell ya the same thing. Naw, no doctor. What happened anyways?"

This was just the opening Rosa had been waiting for. "Aw, hell, Cholly, don't go telling it around, 'cause it might embarrass the little lady, and I know you like her as much as I do. Jan here got a husband with a mean streak a yard wide. Too much booze, and no brains at all. He been knockin' her around. Banged the kid around too. A real champ, dis guy!"

"What the hell ya tellin' me!" exclaimed Charlie. "Some guy been beatin' up this little doll here an the baby too? What kind of animal we got here anyways?"

"Okay, okay, Cholly," Rosa said. "I just wanted to be sure she din't need doctorin'. Thanks for lookin'," and she hustled the big man out.

When she had him back in the diner and had taken care of a couple of late customers, Rosa locked the front door, got herself and Charlie cups of coffee, then went over and joined him in the booth. Speaking quietly so she knew Jan would not hear, Rosa began thinking out loud.

"Goddamn, Cholly, dat's the best little waitress I ever had in here. Everybody likes her. I can't unnerstan' some son-a-bitch kickin' her around. Somebody oughta teach that mongrel a lesson. Took all her pay too, which I jus' give her this mornin'. What a lousy bastard! I hear he hangs aroun' down at that Whistle Stop Tavern by the junction. If I was a man, I'd shuffle down there and sharp up that boy's educations some. Imagine, Cholly, the bastard took a kick at the baby when it's just layin' there in the stroller. Yes siree, Cholly, I'm tellin' ya, somebody ought to pay Mister Eddie Hackett a visit one of these nights.

"Well, Cholly, I gotta clean up this dump and get home and get the old man some supper. The little lady is scairt to go home while that cheap li'l bastard is drunked up, or he might really hurt 'em next time. I tole her to stay here for tonight. Maybe she can chance goin' home tomorra. Wish it was me 'stead of her. I bet he wouldn't kick my ol' Guinea ass around. Well, g'night, Cholly. Thanks for the advice and help, even if it ain't goin' to change anything for that poor little doll in there."

Without waiting for comment or acknowledgment from Charlie, Rosa began bustling around, putting her business to bed for the night.

Charlie thoughtfully finished his coffee and strolled to the door. He leaned against the door frame, watching Rosa for several long minutes, then smiled.

"Rosa," he said, "every down-and-outer in the friggin' world oughta have a guardian angel like you. You'll do, mama. You'll do. G'nite."

CHAPTER 10

▼

Eddie was having a bad run on the pool table. He was too drunk to play well and half thinking about Janet keeping secrets from him. He had lost about thirty dollars in an hour or so of playing. He had just won a game but was still cursing his luck as he chalked his cue and waited for the big man who had challenged the table to finish racking the balls.'

When he stepped back from the table. Eddie said, "What we playin' for?"

"Well, I don't usually play for money," the big man answered.

"What'sa matter, 'fraid you might lose?" Eddie sneered.

"Well money don't come none too easy these days, and I got me a wife and kids to look after." He looked Eddie straight in the eye and frowned a little.

"Hell, Eddie said, "if ya wanta play social games, ya oughta go down to the Y. Everybody here plays money pool."

"Okay, kid," he answered, "I'll go you for five on this game only. What's your name?"

He stuck out his hand in a friendly gesture.

"Eddie Hackett." Eddie shook hands quickly and walked to the break end of the table.

"Just call me Charlie," the big man said. "I normally drive a truck, but tonight I thought to try my hand at somethin' new."

Eddie broke the balls and said, grinning, "Well, I'm the teacher here. Five bucks a lesson."

He dropped the nine on the break and ran four balls without pause, then missed his position and his shot. Charlie took over and dropped two quick shots,

Then after some delay of walking around the table and carefully considering the lay of the rest of the balls, he played a slow roller toward the corner pocket.

He missed but left the cue ball sewed tightly in a cluster of balls that included the all-important eight ball. From this lay of the table, Eddie had no choice except to break the cluster with an off chance of sinking the eight out of turn and losing, or making a deliberate scratch shot, which would give Charlie control and advantage.

Eddie eyed the possibilities carefully and surveyed it from every angle. He shook his head in frustration and glanced suddenly up at Charlie, who was looking directly at him and grinning broadly.

"Smart son-of-a-bitch, hey," he said angrily, and riding the tip of his cue on the edge of the table, he made a one-handed break of the cluster of balls and sent them flying in all directions.

Surprisingly, the eight ball was only nudged slightly by this action. It rolled slowly down the table and hung precariously in the corner pocket. One of his own and two of Charlie's object balls fell from the playing field, leaving Eddie with one ball on the table and Charlie with three.

Charlie chuckled out loud and said, "You did say we were playing call shot, didn't you?"

"Yeah, it's call," Eddie sneered. "Go ahead and shoot."

Charlie lined up his seven-ball shot and said, "Two rails in the side."

As he began his stroke, he seemingly miscued. The seven went rolling gently down the table and off one corner of the pocket and stopped, blocking the eight ball neatly, about one inch out so there was not sufficient room for a clear shot at the eight.

Suddenly serious, he said, "Phew, I thought I had it that time. Looked like that eight was goin' down."

Eddie, suddenly confident again, said, "Looks to me like you blew it, mister. How the hell you gonna make that seven with the eight blockin' the pocket?"

He grinned jeeringly at Charlie.

It was Eddie's turn to shoot, and he had a difficult shot to make his only remaining ball, as Charlie had left the cue ball sitting against the end rail, toward the corner where the eight-seven romance lay.

I'll bank it in this corner," Eddie said, and tapped the pocket to his left.

He stroked the cue cautiously several times and released his shot too quickly and too hard. The ball hit the corner of the called pocket and ricocheted wildly across the table, into the side pocket.

Charlie took over again and looked carefully at his three remaining balls. One was near a corner pocket and not a difficult shot. The two ball was almost directly in the center of the table, and the third was the tightly blocked seven ball, which would be very difficult to move without sinking the eight. He bent over that corner and eyed the situation carefully.

"Hey, kid," he said suddenly, "Straighten me out on your local rules, will ya? If I call a 'safe' on this ball here, do I hafta hit a rail and the ball, or just the ball?"

Eddie grinned broadly. "I told you, ya screwed yourself on that shot, mister. You might as well gimme my five bucks. I don't care if you hit a rail or not, but ya gotta hit the ball, or you lose, and you ain't gonna do it without sinkin' that eight."

By this time several bystanders were watching the game, and all nodded in agreement with Eddie's loud assessment of the situation.

Charlie shook his head in a discouraged attitude and went up the table to where the cue ball lay. He lined up his shot, made the three in the corner pocket, and watched solemnly as the cue ball came off the rail and rolled up the table to stop directly behind the two ball, leaving a dead-straight shot in the side pocket, which it would take a blind man to miss.

Chalking his cue carefully, Charlie glanced up at Eddie, his eyes fairly sparkling, and bent over the shot. Aiming high on the cue ball, he quickly stroked the shot in the side pocket and chuckled aloud as the cue followed like it had eyes and dropped in behind the two ball.

Eddie just stood there and stared at the table, shock on his face, as he realized how he had been neatly tricked into reciting the rules aloud to trap himself. Only two balls remained, the eight and Charlie's seven. It was now his turn to shoot, and it was totally impossible to hit the eight without first hitting Charlie's ball. He could not play a "safe," having already announced it was necessary to hit the ball. Either way, he was the loser. He turned pale with anger, and he shook his head as he dug out a crumpled five-dollar bill.

"I seen some shit pool in my time, Mister Trucker," he said, "but that one beats 'em all. You don't care how you win, do ya? Well, that ain't the end of it, 'cause we're goin' to play for ten this time."

Charlie laughed again. "I heard all's fair in love, war, and pool games, and I met some mizzerable bastards in all three. No need getting' all bent outta shape. I told you just one game, and I meant it. I gotta go. Tell you what though. No hard feelin's. Hey, look, I got a jug of good bourbon whiskey out in the rig. Walk out with me an' have a drink, an' I'll show you my rig. I admit I smoked ya on that one, but I feel like I owe you a drink to make up for it. Come on, have a drink."

Eddie was still angry, but the calm voice and pleasant manner of the big trucker, plus the prospect of a free drink that he badly needed, was too much to pass up. He threw his cue on the table and followed Charlie out the door.

Charlie's semi was parked clear on the back side of the cinder-and-gravel, weed-grown parking lot. There were a few cars and no people about as they crossed the area in the dim light cast by the neons in front of the Whistle Stop. Eddie stumbled a few times and almost fell trying to keep up with Charlie's long, sure strides. As they approached the truck, Charlie steered Eddie to the back of the trailer and brought out his keys to unlock the door.

"Jeezus Christ," Eddie panted, a little apprehension in his voice. "If I knew we were goin' halfway to Indiana for that drink, I woulda bought my own in the bar. What the hell we doin' in the back of the rig anyways?"

"I never keep no drink in the cab," Charlie explained. "Inspectors in my business is too damn rough. They find an open bottle in the rig, an' you're all done. C'mon, jump up in there."

Eddie, reassured, scrambled over the tailgate and stood weaving on the edge. Charlie followed and flipped on a small spotlight in one corner. He walked to the back, reached behind the heavy padding that hung on the walls, and drew out a partially empty fifth of whiskey. He walked halfway back toward the doors and stopped, holding the bottle out to Eddie, who grinned in anticipation, stepped forward, and took the bottle.

Charlie stepped quickly past him, swung the trailer doors shut, and dropped the inside latch in place. He stepped back and turned toward Eddie. As Eddie handed him the bottle he took it with his left hand and raised his right as though to scratch his head, then suddenly came back with a crashing backhand slap to the side of Eddie's face that dropped him to his knees on the trailer floor.

Charlie quickly set down the bottle, and clamping Eddie's ringing head between his knees, he bent over and grabbed a double handful of Eddie's jacket and shirt. With a powerful jerk he stripped them off so that Eddie knelt there naked to the waist. Spreading his big hands over his head and brought them down in a tremendous stinging double-hand slap on both sides of Eddie's bare back.

Eddie, totally in shock and distinctly more sober, screamed in pain at this unbelievable attack.

Charlie stood back watching him for a moment or two and pulled out a pack of cigarettes.

"You want a smoke before or after we finish this?" he asked mildly.

"You goddamn crazy or something?" Eddie sobbed. "Let me out of here."

"You was supposed to be the teacher in there on the pool table," Charlie answered calmly, "but you're in my classroom now. We're goin' to play a little game of question-and-answer here, and everytime you give a wrong answer, you're gonna get a real bad mark."

"What the hell you talkin' about?" Eddie shrieked frantically. "I'll turn the cops on you for assault"

"Now that's one o' them wrong answers," Charlie stated matter-of-factly.

Stepping quickly sideways, he laid another powerful open-handed slap on Eddie's bare back. Then suddenly he reached out with both hands and, grabbing Eddie's shock of red-blond hair, he jerked him to his feet and gave him a slight push, followed by a wicked backhanded slap to the side of Eddie's chest that sent him spinning against the wall.

"Okay, son-of-a-bitch," Charlie, no longer patient, snarled at him, "Let's discuss the cops. You got a wife and a baby, both of them little, right? And you beat hell out of them today, right? Now what you think is gonna happen to you if you call the cops and press charges on me, and I tell them about you?"

"Hey, what the hell has my family business got to do with you?" Eddie cried, tears streaming down his face.

"Wrong answer," said Charlie, delivering another backhand.

Eddie, thoroughly frightened and almost sober now, began crying in earnest. "Yeah, I got a wife and kid, and yeah, I did hit her this afternoon, but she been holding out money on me. She had it coming."

"Wrong answer," said Charlie and delivered a series of sharp, stinging slaps with his big callused hands wherever a patch of bare skin offered itself.

"Yes, hell, yes, I slapped her around and the kid too! What the hell business is it of yours? You her boyfriend or somethin?"

"No, said Charlie. "I'm just a friend who thinks your wife is one of the nicest and hardest-working little sweethearts ever sold me a bowl of chili, and I ain't standing by and watching while a useless bastard like you turns rattlesnake on her. I don't like this no better than you, but some fellas take a lot of teachin', and I ain't got much time."

With that he grabbed Eddie again, whirled him to face the wall, and began slapping again, keeping time to Eddie's sobs and screams as he raised great red welts across his bare back with his work-rough hands.

Finally Eddie could stand it no longer and passed out in a heap next to the wall. He woke up there about half an hour later in unbelievable pain. He pushed himself stiffly off the plywood floor and gazed about, shivering.

Charlie sat, seeming unconcerned, against the wall with the bottle of bourbon in one hand and a cigarette in the other.

"Well, hero, did you learn anything in lesson one?" he growled at Eddie.

Eddie, completely subdued, put his head on his knees and cried softly to himself. He heard the big man moving toward him and raised his hands, palms out in front of him.

"Want a drink?" Charlie asked, offering the bottle.

Eddie shook his head slowly, fright displayed in every move.

"How about a cigarette then, 'cause lesson two is about to begin."

"Jesus, man, don't hit me no more," Eddie sobbed desperately.

"What you think about a man that would beat and rob a woman and kick a baby when she been standing by him all the time while he drinks up all the money and acts like a first-class asshole?" Charlie asked.

"He ain't much good," Eddie answered promptly.

"Now we getting' somewheres."

He hauled Eddie to his feet once more and watched as he stood there shivering and shaking with fright.

"And when is this tough shithead goin' to beat his wife and baby again?" Charlie asked crisply.

"I won't never do it again," was the quick response.

Charlie brought his face down close to Eddie's and, looking him square in the eyes, said in a loud whisper, "Mister Eddie Hackett, keep this in mind. It ain't gonna happen again, or Charlie's comin back. By the way, this one's for the baby."

He crashed a big fist squarely on the bridge of Eddie's nose, dropping him to his knees once more. He stood there shaking his shaggy head solemnly as the blood spurted from Eddie's nose to join the tears running down his cheeks and chest.

Picking up Eddie's shirt from the floor, he said, "Wipe yourself down and get that on. I'm taking you home."

He waited while Eddie shivered and shook his way into his shirt and jacket.

Then, picking up the bourbon, he asked, "Got any of your wife's money left besides the five I already got?"

Eddie reached in his pocket and pulled out a wad of crumpled bills. Charlie took it without counting and stuck it in his own pocket. After jumping down from the truck, he reached up and helped Eddie down, then escorted him to the passenger side of the truck and helped him get in.

"Where you live?" he asked.

With Eddie silently pointing the way, he drove the few blocks to the deserted little house behind the warehouses. Charlie jumped from the truck, hurried around, opened the door, and helped Eddie to the ground again. Eddie's eyes were nearly swollen shut by now, and his nose was twice its normal size. He hurt so badly from head to toe that he silently wished himself dead.

Charlie walked to the door with him and waited while he fumbled to open it.

Handing him the half-full bottle, he said, "Here, you're gonna need this in the morning. So long, kid. I hope I don't hafta call on you no more. I don't care what else you do, but if you hurt either one of them again, you gonna hear from me!"

With that he hurried back to the truck and, cranking the wheel hard right, he jumped the curb, then made a wide sweeping turn through the empty lot past the warehouse and disappeared into the night.

CHAPTER 11

▼

Julie was sick. Her stomach churned, and her head ached. She had stayed home from work, because she did not feel quite so bad as long as she stayed lying down, but every time she stood up, she became nauseated. She had retched all morning.

She called her mother and told her about it, and her mother suggested the possibility she might be pregnant. Julie did not think so, but then she had been so busy, she had not really been keeping track of days. She knew she should go to the doctor, but she felt too bad to go by herself. When Leo came home from work, she was still resting on the sofa, looking so pale and hollow-eyed that he was immediately alarmed.

"Juliana, you look like you dying!" he exclaimed. "What make you sick?"

"I really don't know," she replied, "but I would like to go to the doctor. I have never felt so bad in my life."

Leo bundled her up and, half carrying her, helped her to the cab he had called a few minutes earlier.

After about an hour in the doctor's office, where Leo had summoned him for this after-hours visit, Julie and the doctor came out. She still looked pale and ill but was laughing with the doctor, so Leo felt much relieved.

"Mister Stronski," the doctor said, "I have started several tests on your wife, and I won't know what the trouble is until I get the results. I think it may not be trouble at all, but blessings, you know what I mean?" He winked at Leo.

When they got home, Leo was so excited, he could hardly contain himself. He went to the cupboard and brought out two glasses and a bottle of wine.

Julie was very reluctant to start celebrating.

"What if it is only the flu or pneumonia or something?" she asked skeptically.

"You heard doctor say blessing, Julie. Doctor knows flu is not blessing. What the hell you think? Come on, small glass of wine make you feel better anyways."

Julie tried bravely to drink a celebration glass of wine with him, but after a couple of sips had to run for the bathroom again. When she came out, she hugged her husband's great shaggy head for a moment and went to bed.

Leo put some classical music on his player, sat down to drink the rest of the wine, and indulged in happy daydreams about the coming days with Julie and their son. That he might have a daughter never entered his mind.

When he finally rolled into bed beside her, he gave her a gentle squeeze and whispered, "I love you, Juliana. You gonna have fine big son, and tomorrow you be happy and feel better."

The next two days were the same. Julie would feel reasonably well and rested on waking, but immediately after rising, she became violently ill. On the third day the doctor called to confirm that she was, indeed, pregnant.

Leo was ecstatic! He was so jubilant that he completely overlooked his wife's worn and haggard condition and insisted they go immediately to her family's home to share the good news. They arrived at her home, and her mother became quickly concerned about hr haggard appearance.

"My God, Julie, you look awful!" her mother exclaimed. "Have you been to doctor?"

Julie managed a half cheerful laugh. "Yes, Mama, I have been to the doctor, and he says I'm pregnant, but I surely hope pregnancy doesn't keep one sick for the whole nine months. I don't know if I could stand it."

Her mother smiled, extremely pleased. "Oh, don't worry. Sickness lasts only short while. Soon you feel marvelous, and I know you very happy."

"Happy not big enough word!" Leo cried emphatically. He gave Julie a one-armed hug. "We goin' have big fat baby boy. Elias, like my papa. Maybe own coal mine, not have to work there. Buy really nice house for Mama Julie."

Everyone laughed at Leo's enthusiasm.

"Wait a while, Leo," her brother Bernard said. "Maybe you will have a pretty little girl. You better wait and see."

Leo put on a thoughtful scowl.

"No, he said finally, "we having big boy. Be biggest, strongest man in Pennsylvania someday. Leo Stronski knows."

This declaration was so firmly delivered that Julie felt a sudden chill and the premonition that she would indeed have a big baby boy. The strength of the impression made her feel suddenly lost and cold, as though she had no control over what her future would be. Suddenly sobered, she sat down in her mother's big living room chair and, folding her long legs up beside her, she crossed her arms in a protective self-hug, lapsing into thoughtful silence while her mother, Leo, and Bernard laughed and chatted over another bottle of wine.

For the next three or four months, things got steadily worse for Julie. She lost seventeen pounds, and she had not been overweight to begin with. She continued to be plagued by nausea. She was so often sick that she could not properly look after her contracts and had to let most of them go.

With this came concern for money, because she wanted as many of the good things for Leo and the baby as it was possible to attain. Leo made enough so they could live well for the time, but it did not permit any savings or investment, which her father had taught her everyone should have.

Between her health and her concern for their future, she began having periods of severe depression and spent long hours when Leo was not home, just sitting and staring out the window or at a single page in whatever book she might be reading at the time. Sometimes she managed her housework okay and usually had a good meal ready when Leo came home, but sometimes she would become so lost in her half-world of depression that she would be sitting there staring like some great gray ghost when Leo arrived from work.

When Leo was around, things were a little more alive and pleasant. His enthusiasm for the coming event, his big plans, and his love of music, which he always put on the player or radio as soon as he came home, made evenings and weekends a little better for her. She would cuddle up under his big arm on the sofa, and they would chat after supper, or sometimes just sit and listen to the music.

After the baby started moving, Leo was fascinated by the feel of the rubbery pushes and bumps it made on her stomach and sides. He would sit for long periods with one big hand on her stomach and smile and joke to his son.

Julie got bigger and bigger around the middle, but her arms and face became thinner and thinner. It was as though the baby was some great parasite within her, sapping her strength and nourishment. She realized that all was not well with her, but Leo hardly seemed to notice.

The nausea continued into her seventh month, and the doctor became quite concerned about her weight loss. He prescribed pills to ease the nausea and told her to eat lighter but much more often, which would provide nourishment while hopefully reducing the intensity, if not the duration, of her upsets.

Julie was constantly snacking now. Orange or apple juice and the heavy dark rye bread that had always been a favorite with her family became her constant diet, because They were the things that upset her the least. Her doctor told her that her problems were probably the result of her being past thirty years old and in her first pregnancy.

She suffered through the summer and into the fall. As the leaves began to change on the oaks and elms along the street, she became more and more a prisoner in the house, waiting for the big day that would be the end of her suffering and the beginning of all the great plans for her and Leo and their son.

One evening in late October, she and Leo were sitting discussing the cancellation of several coal contracts by the big steel companies. Leo did not know what was behind it, but he was concerned. That day the mine owners where he worked had passed the word to the supervisors to start picking those persons who would be laid off if production had to be cut.

"I got all real good men, Julie," he said, worried, and most got kids. How I gonna tell man with kids he not work no more? I rather not work myself, but I can't do that. Elias got to have his chance. I hope I not have to do this thing."

They had been listening to the radio music. As he finished speaking, an announcement came on the radio that several major banks in New York and Washington had closed early that day and that the stock market was falling rapidly. Within the next week, disaster struck the entire nation.

Leo and Julie went to her parents' home that weekend to ask her father's advice on whether they should take their small savings out of the bank. They had accumulated nearly five thousand dollars over their four years of marriage and were quite concerned about losing it if the bank closings continued.

When they got to her home, her mother met them at the door. "Leo, Julie, come in and talk to Papa. I think he sick. He been home all day and won't come out from bedroom. I think he sick."

She wrung her hands nervously.

Julie went to her father's bedroom door and knocked softly. When there was no answer, she went in quietly to find her father sitting in a big chair by the window and staring out at the quiet street. She went to him and put her hands on his shoulders from behind. He reached up and touched her fingertips with one hand, but did not move or speak.

She finally asked softly, "What's wrong, Papa?"

He still sat there as though in a trance, until Julie became extremely concerned.

She brought one hand around under his chin and, raising his face, asked anxiously again, "Papa, what is wrong?"

He looked at her for a few moments, and two big tears started from his eyes.

In a dry and cracked voice he asked, "Is Leo with you, my darling?"

"Yes, Papa, Leo's here. What's wrong?"

"Leo is a good and a strong man. He will look after you. Stay with him, and don't worry. Tell Leo I need to see him alone…and keep Mama out of here."

With that he turned back to the window. Julie stood looking anxiously down at him for a long moment and then went out.

When Leo came to his side, the older man looked at him sadly for a few minutes, then said in his careful English, "Leo Stronski, I have never appreciated you…no, that's not true. I have not done a man's duty to show how I appreciate you, because I resented a man who had nothing taking my daughter, but I was wrong. You have done well and honorably by my daughter. Now I have nothing to give to show my appreciation."

"Mister Markovic, sir, you have much, but your family, and especially your daughter, are the greatest of your blessings," Leo replied in Serbian. "Why do you say you have nothing?"

"I have lost it all, Leo," he stated matter-of-factly. "I am ruined. A few days ago I was a very wealthy man. I had invested everything in this great country, in what I thought were strong ventures. I am not alone. My partners are ruined also, and it is only the beginning. They have already taken all my money securities, and they will be coming for the house and property. I cannot tell Anna. She would never understand. You must promise me you will look out for Anna and Julie if anything happens to me. You are young and strong and used to living poor, so you know what to do. I have never been poor, and I don't think I want to be. Please take care of them, Leo."

As though ending a business conference, Mister Markovic stood quickly, gave Leo a strong handshake, picked up his briefcase, and walked out.

Leo stood there staring out the window, thinking to himself and trying to absorb everything he had just heard. It did not make a lot of sense to him. The man had avoided him for over four years, speaking only when the occasion left no other route. He had treated him as though he was the conquering hero he had heard about in his long-ago school days.

He was suddenly shaken from his reverie by voices in the hallway. He stepped out of the room to find Julie and Bernard and her mother and father standing by the outside door. Mister Markovic still held his briefcase, and his wife looked upset.

As Leo watched, the father shook hands with his son, set down his briefcase, held his wife tenderly for a moment, then turned to Julie and said, "Good-bye, Julianna, sweetheart."

He held her hands lovingly for a moment, patted her on the stomach, and smiled. Then he picked up his briefcase, waved to Leo, and left.

"What is happened?" Leo asked, bewildered. "Where you papa go?"

"He said he has to go on a business trip and he will be gone for a while, but he didn't say where or for how long." Julie replied, seeming outright confused by it all. "What did he say to you?"

"He tell me I am good man and I should look after everything. Sound like he not come back right away quick. Maybe you and me go home now, Julie."

After they got away from the house, Leo put his arm around her and walked in silence for a while.

"I am much worried for you papa, Julie," he said. "I can't tell you what he say, but I need to talk with him more again. Did you ask him about the money?"

"No," Julie replied, 'but it was really strange. Like he knew what I was thinking. He told me after he came out of the bedroom that we should be at the bank when it opens Monday and take our money out and keep it at home."

Who can say why people do the things they do? Mister Markovic had been a well-respected businessman and professional in his community for many years. He had taken great pains to learn English well and never failed to come to the aid of friends and associates when he was needed. He never discussed business with his family but was a stern and caring father who always took particular pains to see they were well cared for, properly educated, and acquainted with the right people. He should certainly have recognized that the true value of life lay in the love of his family and respect of his community, and not in the material things around him that, once collected, could be collected again.

In any case, the next morning just after sunrise, Mister Markovic canceled all his worldly obligations with a swan dive from his office window to the sidewalk four stories below. He left behind a letter to his wife, apologizing for leaving and telling her to go to Leo and Julianna when the court came for the house. He gave the family much-needed legal advice, including moving any of the smaller furniture and valuables from the house to Leo's apartment before Monday morning.

Julie and her mother both broke down completely as soon as the news about her father was received. The selection and moving of whatever could be salvaged was left to Leo and Bernard. They did not have a lot of extra room in their apartment, so many things that Leo felt extremely bad about leaving had to be left, for purely practical reasons.

Bernard walked about the house as though in a daze. Whenever Leo asked him whether to take this or that item, he would stand and stare and finally reply in uncertain sentences like, "Mama and Papa got that for their anniversary," or, "Papa loved that," or, "Mama gave that to Papa at Christmas one year."

This was no help to Leo and left him with a heavy burden of guilt for several years, especially whenever his mother-in-law would wistfully comment on something she "used to have when Papa was alive." Bernard could probably have salvaged a few more of her belongings, but the whole process seemed a nightmare that he could not bring himself to face.

Julie was in the hospital, under heavy sedation. Her mother had been spirited away by a couple of old and trusted lady friends. She was so grief-stricken that any contact or question from the rest of her family sent her into hysterical sobbing.

Leo, the gentle giant, worked quietly into the early morning hours of Monday, trying to sort sentiment from practicality in this disaster his father-in-law had laid upon him. Bernard finally walked away to join his mother in hopeless mourning over the loss of his father and all the fond memories that formed the cement of their family life.

When the task was finally done, Leo pulled down the window shades and left the keys to the house and workshop on the dining room table. He stood quietly in the entrance of her father's study and mumbled a few words of prayer in Serbian as a farewell to the father-in-law he had never really known. He went home, leaving the front door unlocked to the unkind world that would soon come to relieve his wife and her family of all that remained of a lifetime of selecting "the good things."

He never returned to "Julie's street" again as long as he lived.

CHAPTER 12

▼

Leo arrived home that Monday morning, very sad and very tired. He was extremely concerned about Julie, so after making himself a quick cup of coffee and some toast, he hurried to the hospital.

He met Julie's doctor at the nurse's station as soon as he arrived. He was busy talking to a nurse and writing instructions on a chart.

Leo did not wait for him to finish, but burst in with, "How my Julie doing, Doctor? Is Julie and baby all right?"

The doctor looked at him worriedly for a minute, then said, "The baby is all right so far, Leo, but if your wife doesn't do something for herself soon, he won't be."

"What you mean, Doctor?" Leo shot back. "What she not do?"

"She has not eaten anything since yesterday morning, and worse yet, she won't drink anything. She has cried so much that she is getting dehydrated, drying out, and the baby must have fluids. I have been trying to find you for hours. Where have you been?"

Seizing Leo by the coat sleeve, he hurried him down the ward and into her room. "You must talk to her, Leo. For the baby's sake, if not for her own, she must drink."

As soon as he saw Julie, Leo became extremely frightened for her. She did not even look like his wife, but like some grotesque skeleton, only with big, staring, grief-stricken eyes that showed no sign of recognition. He went quickly to her. She reached one hand to him and began sobbing hoarsely, but without tears. He put his big right hand gently to her cheek, which felt hot and dry.

"My God, Julie," he cried out fearfully, "you cannot do this! You killing our baby. You papa gone! He make hisself dead. We can no help Papa, but baby we can help!"

He slid his hand under her neck and back, lifted her bodily to a half-sitting position, seized the almost-full water pitcher that sat by her bed, and put it to her lips.

"Leo Stronski say you drink," he demanded. "You drink, or you choke. You not can do this. You need water. Baby need water. Now <u>drink</u>!"

She sat inert for a long moment as the cool water began to pour into her mouth and back out again, down the front of her gown. The dazed expression in her eyes changed quickly to one of startled amazement. She had never seen Leo angry before, and for a brief time it actually came to her that she might indeed drown if she did not drink. She gagged slightly at first, because her mouth and throat were so dry, but then she managed two long swallows, and Leo quickly relented and took away the pitcher.

He stood there and looked at her and smiled. He kissed her gently on the forehead and eased her back onto her pillow. Reaching back to the nightstand, he picked up a water glass, filled it, and handed it to her.

"Now, you do what doctor say. Drink and eat, or I have to make you drink. I feel bad for Papa too," he said gently, "but you must think now of baby Elias. I go now and get his money from bank. Elias never going to work in mine! I come back soon, but you do right thing and think about baby, or Leo get mad again."

He patted her stomach gently and kissed her. His eyes met the doctor's for a second as he turned to go. As he opened the door, Julie raised herself on one elbow and drank the glass of water.

Leo nodded at the doctor and left.

CHAPTER 13

▼

Eddie awoke in a cold sweat. His mouth was dry and cottony, as it always was when he woke anymore, but this morning was different from usual. He had slept, but he felt like the sleep had done him no good.

He tried to open his eyes, but only a slit of light appeared for his effort. He had the impression his eyes were stuck shut, and then suddenly the real nightmare of the previous evening came back to him. He raised his right arm to rub his eyes, and the motion made him groan aloud. His back and side felt like they were on fire.

When he touched his fingers to his face, he winced at the pain, both from raising his arms and the tenderness of his face. He tried again to open his eyes, but with the same effect. Everything seemed blurred, and his eyes just did not want to open.

Finally he sat up on the side of the bed and, shielding his eyes to what suddenly seemed like blinding light from the window, stood up. Staggering slightly, he made his way to the small mirror over the kitchen sink. He tried to see in the mirror, but everything was still a blur. He felt that his eyelids were very puffed up. With some effort, he raised both arms, and using his right hand on his lower lid and his left on his upper, he pulled his left eye open.

What he saw in the mirror made him retch. He stood there for a moment wondering whether he was going to vomit. Then he repeated the experiment with his right eye. He just could not believe what he was seeing.

A line of bruises formed the outline of three huge fingers on his left cheek. His nose was swollen to nearly twice normal size. Both eyes, from his brows to well past the outline of the lower edge of his eye socket, were dark purple, an the lids were so swollen that he could not hold his eyes open by the usual muscle control but had to pull them open manually with his fingertips.

Jesus, he thought, I can't work like this, and Gordon has just been begging for an excuse to fire me. Goddamn trucker. Goddamn Gordon, and double goddamn Janet. What the hell am I gonna do now?

He soaked a washcloth with cold water and, holding it to his eyes, stumbled back to the sofa bed. When his knees came up against it, he turned and sat down. He came down hard on the fifth of whiskey Charlie had left and which he had not even thought of until then. He tipped his head against the sofa back to keep the soothing cloth over his eyes and forehead. Groping blindly, he opened the whiskey, tipped it back, and shuddered as a long swallow burned its way to his midsection.

"What the hell's the use?" he mumbled. "I wasn't never meant to be no husband and father anyways. How the hell I get inta this in the first place? Screw Gordon! I'll go back to work when I get damn good and ready."

He took another drink, and another and another, until the last of more than a pint of whiskey had disappeared. The empty bottle hung from his fingertips for a little while, then clattered noisily as it slid out of his hand to roll across the worn linoleum and bump against the open closet door.

It was nearly six in the evening when he woke again to the sound of someone beating on the door.

He thought, My Christ, Janet has come back, and I look like some skid row dog.

He jumped to his feet and staggered toward the door, then thought, Can't be Jan. She wouldn't knock.

He fumbled for the doorknob and pulled the door open. His friend Pete stood there in his dirty work cloths, half a bottle of beer in one hand.

He stared at Eddie for a minute, then said, "Christ A'mighty, Eddie, what happened? I never seen ya aroun' this weekend, and I stopped by Gordon's to pick ya up. He said ya never came in today, so I thought I'd check ya out. What the hell hit you anyways? You look awful!"

"I don't look half as bad as I feel, Pete," Eddie cried. "I been wishing I was dead since Sunday night. A couple goddamn bums jumped me on the way home and kicked the hell out of me. I was too drunk to help myself, and they worked me over good and took everything I got except a few cents change. Come on in, Pete. It's really good to know I got one friend."

The lies came so easily and answered so well for his condition that he kept right on with it.

"My wife ran off with some big asshole trucker, and I got nobody to worry about but me now. Good ol' Pete! Sure glad you showed up. I'm hungry and half froze to death. I tried to light the heater last night, but I couldn't see, my eyes was swole up so bad, and I was so shook up anyways, I couldn't light a match. How about lightin' the damn oil stove, will ya?"

Pete was really concerned. He lit the stove and rustled around and found a can of beans, which he heated up. He got out some bread and butter.

"Who the hell was it hit you anyhow, Eddie?" he asked as Eddie began to eat slowly, not sure he was going to be able to keep it down. "Did ya never see 'em before?"

"Hell, I never even seen 'em comin'," Eddie lied. "It was down by the corner, just before ya turn into warehouse row. I turned the corner, and there they was. One of 'em grabbed my arm as I went by, and the other one hit me. Both of 'em was big too. I don't even know if they was white or black. They musta kicked me around for a good ten minutes. I gave 'em all the money, but they still beat on me after."

"Soon as you finish eatin', I'll run you down to the hospital, maybe you got broke ribs or somethin'," Pete volunteered.

"Hell, no," Eddie answered. "I'm just bruised up. I ain't got no money to blow on friggin' doctors!"

"Christ Eddie, at least let's go run down a cop and report it. Maybe somebody seen somethin' and reported it. Might be you could get some of your money back anyways."

"Screw the goddamn cops too!" Eddie growled. "Cops is the last thing I wanta see today. Have I got a beer left in the fridge?"

Pete checked for the beer. "Eddie, you ain't got nothin' in here but some peanut butter and a couple eggs. If them guys got your money, how the hell you gonna eat till payday?"

"I don't know," came the quick reply. "I'll figger that out later. Right now I gotta have a cold beer, or I'm gonna die."

"Well, the place is startin' to warm up. I'll run down and pick up some beer. You just take it easy, and I'll be right back."

Pete picked up his jacket and left.

In about twenty minutes he came back carrying half a case of beer. He opened two, and they sat on the edge of the bed and drank them.

They discussed Eddie's situation for a few minutes, then Eddie asked, "Hey, Pete, how about doin' me a favor?"

"Sure," Pete replied. "If I can, hell, yes!"

Eddie rubbed his bruised face to create as much sympathy as possible. "Them guys really worked me over. Could you go by Gordon's and tell the old bastard I got rolled and I'm bad hurt, and I can't make it in for a few days? Just stop by there on your way to work in the mornin'. Lay it on good, and maybe the heartless ol' bastard won't fire me, okay? I should be all right in a couple days."

Pete agreed and did his best. However, when he came back on Tuesday evening, he brought Eddie a case of beer and a sack of groceries.

When Eddie met him at the door, Pete shook his head in a discouraged manner. "Me and a couple of the guys kicked in and got you a few things to get by, Eddie. Old Gordon had some new guy, just a kid, working on the pumps and grease rack. He was doin' the tune-ups hisself. He said you got your pay when you left the other night, and he don't care if them guys got both arms and your balls he don't wanta see you no more."

CHAPTER 14

▼

When Rosa came back to the diner the next morning, Jan was still asleep with lit-tle Corky curled up beside her. Rosa kept her kitchen noise down as long as she could, to give her a chance to rest.

One of the first customers to arrive for breakfast was Charlie, Rosa's trucker friend.

"Mornin', Charlie," she called cheerfully.

"Mornin', Mama," Charlie said with a grin. "How's the li'l doll doin' this mornin'?"

"A hell of a lot better than she would be if she went home, I'll bet," Rosa answered. "Tell ya the truth, I ain't sure. She's still asleep. Her and the baby both. How was your evenin'? Anything new goin' on in town?"

"Hell, yes," Charlie said with a grin. "I tried a coupla places last night. Got in a hell of a pool game at one place. Met this raggedy smartass what thought he knew somethin' about the game of pool. Wasn't really much of a player though, but a hell of a talker. Nice friendly feller when we got acquainted. Made a real nice donation to the widders and children's fund."

Charlie reached in his pocket and brought out a wad of bills.

Close to a hundred there, Mama." He chuckled aloud. "Right generous young feller, once I explained how tough it is tryin' to raise kids these days. He must love that little gal a lot."

"Somehow I knew you was a public relations man, Cholly." Rosa laughed. "You plumb wastin' your time with that damn truck. Maybe I'll rent ya an office, and ya can run fundraisers and stay home and raise some kids your ownself.

Thanks, ol" buddy," she said and gave him a friendly hug. "That li'l lady is goin' to be your friend for life."

When Janet woke up half an hour later, Rosa insisted on giving her breakfast and made sure she had plenty of time to see to the baby and feed him. When she was finally satisfied that both were okay and well on the road to recovery, she called Janet aside.

"Look Kid," she began, "I don't want ya to think I'm tryna adopt ya or anything, but you're welcome to stay here just like last night, for as long as it takes to get yourself squared away. By the way, this might help a little."

She slipped the roll of bills into Jan's hand.

Janet dropped it like a hot potato. "Jeez, Rosa, I can't take that. You already paid me, and if I lost it, that's not your problem!"

"Wait now, Missy. Don't get your li'l ass all in thunder there. That's your money. One o' my friends went down and had a little chat with your ol' man last night, and he was real reasonable. Seems he agreed he been a bit of a shithead and gave your money back. Said he was sendin' along a little extra to help with the rent."

She grinned and winked, and Janet could not believe her ears.

"Eddie sent me extra money?" she exclaimed. "Rosa, you're making this up just to get me to take it, ain't you?"

"No lie, honey. Honest to God, come out in the diner, and I'll let my friend tell you hisself."

With that she took Janet by the hand and led her out to where Charlie was halfway through a huge stack of hotcakes.

"This here's Cholly," she said. "You know Cholly. You been serving him off and on for weeks. Cholly, tell the lady how her husband said it was all a misunderstanding and sent her money back."

Charlie stood up, and Janet had to tip back her head to meet the big man's eyes.

"Sure, kid, me and Eddie had a game of pool and a nice long chat. Real reasonable feller for a redhead! Once I explained a couple things to him, he come right around. Said he would be right careful to control his temper when you and the little one is around too. I told him I thought that was a right good idear. You could probly patch things up now if you was a mind to, but I'd let him stew for a few days if it was me doin' it."

Janet could still hardly believe what she was hearing, but both Rosa and Charlie were so sincere that she had to accept it for fact. Though she made no immediate attempt to return home, she went that evening to the realtor's office, where she paid her rent and apologized for being late.

CHAPTER 15

▼

When Leo arrived at the bank, it was still more than an hour before opening time. He was a little surprised to find there were already several people there. Most of them were strangers to him, and they were individually walking nervously back and forth, not saying anything.

Two men from the mine where he worked were there leaning against the brick wall near the door, talking in low voices. As Leo approached, the nearer one pushed away from the wall and held out his hand in greeting.

"Hi, Stronski," he said. "You got the warning too, huh?"

"What you mean, warning?" Leo answered. "All I know, my wife papa kill hisself this weekend. He say to my wife get money from bank quick, early. He say his money gone, and then he jump from window. I can't know how rich man lose all money in one day, but Stronski goin' get money when bank open!"

"Boy, I don't know," Murphy answered. "I seen people waiting in front of the Penn State Bank when I come down a while ago, and Wilanski tole me last night he thinks the gov'mint goin' to close all the banks today. I hope you know how you goin' to get your money if they don't open."

"Bank got Stronski's money, and bank will open!" Leo said confidently.

"Sure hope you're right, big fella," the Irishman answered.

They turned then to discussing the work situation, Leo's father-in-law's suicide, and what it all meant.

Kerrigan, the other worker, put in the view that, "Hard times is here, men! There's goin' to be the devil to pay 'fore it gets better, mind you. I feels it in me bones."

With that he settled back against the wall, and they lapsed into quiet waiting.

The crown in front of the bank continued to grow, and the mutter and grumble of conversation became increasingly louder as opening time for the bank came and went. Five minutes…ten minutes…twenty minutes…and the crowd was becoming more agitated by the minute.

Finally the banker's black limousine pulled up to the fringe of the crowd. When the door opened, however, it was not the banker who got out but a big Irish police officer, club in hand. He was followed by another equally surly-looking uniformed officer. They crossed their nightsticks, and using them and their sturdy bodies, they backed the waiting crowd a few steps away from the car.

Finally the banker appeared, looking pale and tired and very concerned about the large crowd. Pushing and ordering, "Make way there," the police escorted him to the top step in front of the bank.

He stopped and held up his hands, palms out, in a gesture for quiet. "Ladies and gentlemen, this is a stable and strong institution, and there is no cause for concern. Your money is safe with us, and there is no need to be rushing in for your money. The government of the United States is behind us, and believe me, your money is safe. Now, if you will all go home and think about this, I'm sure…"

That was a far as he got. The crowd surged forward, and as if on signal, a thunderous "No!" echoed against the bank front, rolling down the street to echo back again in the still morning air. The banker, a small gray-haired man in a dark blue suit and patent leather shoes, looked at them for a few moments and suddenly his shoulders sagged in resignation.

Holding up his hands again, he said, "Please, friends, I will open the bank, and I will get your money for you, but if your intention is to withdraw all your money, please reconsider. Take what you need, as usual. No bank has all of its depositor's money on hand all of the time. We simply cannot pay everyone all of their money. I will open now, but please think about what you are doing!"

His plea was just as well left unspoken. The crowd in front of the bank continued to grow.

Leo and his friends had not moved from their position near the door. As the banker put the key in the lock, they swung in behind him and were the first three in the door. Neither of the Irishmen was willing to challenge Leo for first place, so he was the first one to arrive at the cashier's window.

The banker had opened the rear door immediately and let in his two clerks, then locked the door again. The policemen stood just outside of the main door, vainly trying to keep people from pushing and shoving. Calling out in loud voices, "One line, ladies and gents," they did their best to keep order. After several minutes of bustling around inside the bank, the cashier finally opened the window.

Leo pushed his passbook through the grill and said, "Give my money, please!"

"How much do you wish to withdraw, Mister Stronski?" the young man asked pleasantly, although he did not smile, nor look like he felt like smiling. In fact, Leo had the distinct impression he was already aware of the answer before he asked.

Leo said quickly, "All. I want all my money. Close out the book."

The clerk looked momentarily as if he might argue the point, but then he shrugged. Taking Leo's passbook, he computed the interest and showed the resulting figures to Leo, who nodded. The young man had Leo sign the book and a withdrawal slip. Leo watched carefully as the clerk counted out five thousand two hundred twenty-three dollars and twenty-four cents.

Leo said, "Thank you," folded the bills carefully, put them in his coat pocket, and shouldered his way out through the waiting crowd. He learned later that day that the President of the United States had ordered all banks closed until further notice.

He went home, hid the money away in the apartment, and went to work. Everyone at work was talking about the financial situation of the country, and many men did not come to work, because they were at the banks trying to get their money. Leo was extremely pleased with himself when the news came in midafternoon that all the banks were closed. He felt badly for many of his friends who had not been as lucky. He was also very concerned because, as a supervisor, he was being kept aware of all the orders the mines were losing because of the sudden financial problems.

That was the first of a string of very bad Mondays for Leo.

CHAPTER 16

▼

Janet stayed on at the diner for the rest of the week. She thought often of going back to the little house, but caution kept her away. She was certain that Eddie had not willingly surrendered that much money for her and the baby, but she was afraid to ask for the specific details of Charlie's and Eddie's meeting. Charlie treated her with friendly respect whenever he came into the diner and usually asked about the baby, but he never volunteered any further information.

The week went by quickly. She felt comfortable and at home with Rosa. The only problem she had was Rosa's hospitality, because she refused to let Jan pay for her meals or lodging, but on Sunday afternoon she had firmly made up her mind that Monday night she was going home, regardless of her reception.

She told Rosa this, and Rosa replied, "Hey, darlin' whatever suits your fancy. I tink you're a damn fool to give that shark another shot at ya. But whatever you tink. I got no problem with ya stayin' here, 'specially since I get more out of ya that way." She grinned, but added, more seriously, "Do ya tink it's safe fer the kid?"

Janet considered that for a time and finally said, "He was mad at me and drunk besides. The buggy just happened to get in the way. Maybe he didn't even know Corky was still in it when he kicked it. He never tried to hurt him before. I think it's okay."

"God bless, little lady," Rosa replied. "Just can't tink bad about anyone, can ya? You're a real jewel, and I don't want nothing bad to happen to ya, hear me?"

She patted Jan's face kindly, then seized her in a tremendous bear hug that made Jan feel all comfortable and warm inside.

With tears in her eyes, she said, "Rosa, I don't know what I would do without you. I think you're the best thing ever happened to me and Corky."

Just before closing time, as she was cleaning up a table that some customers had just left, one of them came back into the diner and said, "Hey, kid, some skinny bum outside the door said he wants to talk to you. He said ask you to please come outside. You wanna talk to 'im, or you want me to run 'im off?"

Puzzled, Jan pocketed the tip from the table, left the dirty dishes behind the counter, went to the door, and cautiously peeked out. For a moment she could scarcely believe her eyes. It was Eddie—but an Eddie she had never seen before.

His thin red hair was straggly and uncombed. His clothes were dirty, and one leg of his trousers was torn out at the knee. There were great dark circles around his eyes, and he looked gaunt and ill. She could hardly believe it was him. She had been away for only one week. She knew he had not been the same Eddie ever since the booze had taken him by the hand, but she could not believe the change in just one week. He looked like a whipped dog.

She just stood there and stared. Eddie stared back for a short while and then dropped his eyes and stared at the ground. He looked so vulnerable and pitiful that she could not contain herself. She went quickly down the steps and took him by the arm. Still he did not look up.

"Jan, I'm really sorry I hit you. It was a stupid thing to do." He mumbled.

"Eddie, what's wrong?" Jan asked. "You look terrible!"

"I was wondering if you would help me out a little," he replied in a subdued voice. "I know I ain't worth it, but I'm in a real fix. I got no money, Old Gordon fired my ass, an' I ain't had nothing to eat since yesterday morning. Can you just get me a san'wich, please? I'm real hungry. I won't ask you for nothing else, honest. I been tryin' to bum some money on the street like these other guys, but I ain't got the guts for it when I'm sober, an' when I'm drunk, I use the money for something more to drink. I know I look like shit, so I won't even come inside. If you could just get me an egg san'wich or somethin'—please!"

He looked so forlorn and pitiful and such a shadow of the happy-go-lucky kid she had married that her heart just went out to him.

"Sure, Eddie, I'll get you something," she said. "Just wait here. I'll be out soon."

So began a new phase in the marriage of Janet and Eddie Hackett. She brought him the sandwich he asked for and more besides. She also gave him two dollars.

"Here, Eddie," she said. "Try not to use it for booze, okay? I'm comin' home tomorrow night, and I'll bring a few groceries, what I can carry, and we'll talk, okay?"

Eddie readily agreed but still would not look up at her. She had a difficult time reconciling this new meek and weak Eddie with the old carefree, happy, and to-hell-with-the-world Eddie she had married. He ate almost silently, thanked her, and then went shuffling off into the darkness toward the warehouse district, still looking at the ground.

Jan was good for her word. When she got home to the ramshackle little house, Eddie was not there.

She was a bit shocked by the condition of the place when she went in. There were empty bottles and cans everywhere. A broken plate was scattered over the floor in front of the sink, and odds and ends of clothing hung on the two chairs and the sofa bed.

She put Corky on the sofa and blocked him there with the chairs, then started in to straighten up the place. It was really more untidy than terribly dirty, and before long she had it as neat as such living quarters could be.

She put away her groceries, put Corky on the floor where he could crawl about, as he did quite well these days, and started to get something ready to eat. She had brought five pounds of potatoes, a few cans of baby food, an onion or two, some eggs, and a polish sausage. Although she had to crowd her purchases tightly around Corky in the stroller in order to manage it all, she had carried a six-pack of beer in one hand and pushed the stroller with the other all the way from the junction, down warehouse row.

She had boiled some potatoes and the sausage when, to her surprise, Eddie came to the door, knocked lightly, and let himself in.

She smiled shyly at him, but instead of answering with the old easy banter, he dropped his eyes to the floor and mumbled, "Hi, Jan. Sorry I left the place in such a mess."

She put down the spoon she had in her hand and went over to him. When she was cleaning up, she had moved the only two chairs they had to the little dining table. Taking him by the arm, she led him over and sat him down in the chair. She opened a beer and set it in front of him, then sat down in the other chair. He took a long drink from the beer and just sat there, eyes on the table. For several minutes they sat like that, neither speaking.

Finally Jan could handle the silence no longer.

"Eddie," she said, reaching out and patting the back of his hand, "I really appreciated you sending back the money. I'm sorry I didn't tell you about the job, but I really needed the money. I know you were drunk, but if you had given me half a chance, I was going to tell you. Anyways, thanks for giving it back."

Eddie looked up at her briefly, and his eyes flashed momentarily. She thought he was going to be angry, but his shoulders suddenly slumped, and he looked back down at the table.

"S'all right, Jan," he replied finally, and he fingered the purple bruises that still adorned his eyes and his right cheekbone.

When the meal was ready, Jan served him and herself and opened a beer for both of them. She went and got Corky from the crib, where she had put him when Eddie came in, and seated him in her lap. She fed him small bits of mashed-up potato and short drinks from his bottle as she ate her own meal. Eddie sat silently, only occasionally glancing at her as she talked, and never once looking at the child.

'I really like my job, Eddie," she said. "Rosa is a real jewel. She treats me just like I was her daughter, and she just loves Corky. There is lots of nice people come in there, and I make pretty good on the tips. We can get by okay for a while, till you get another job. I can talk to some of the guys I know. Maybe one of them can use some help on his truck or somethin'.

"And some of them are stevedores, and I heard them say they work by the day an' get paid every day. They get called by waiting in the union hall, and whenever a train comes in that needs unloaded, a crew boss comes in and calls out for guys who want to work. Maybe you can get a few days in like that. I think they pay pretty good for loadin'.

"Hey, you know that guy Charlie—the one you sent me the money by—well, he's a real nice guy. He said to me that he thought you were a real nice cooperative guy. Maybe he'd help you find somethin'. Want me to ask him?"

Eddie sat there and stared at her for a few minutes, again looking like he was going to be angry, but finally he shuddered and looked away. Jan thought for a moment he was going to be sick. He swallowed hard a few times, tried to take a drink of beer, and almost choked. Then he broke out in a cold sweat. His face turned very pale, and the bruises were suddenly very apparent.

Jan, for the first time, realized that the dark circles around his eyes and the streaks on his face were bruises.

"My God, Eddie!" Are you all right?" she exclaimed. "Have you been in a fight or something? Why didn't I notice before? You're all bruised up! Did old Gordon whip you when he fired you or what?"

Again Eddie looked incredulously at her. From previous experience he knew she was not the devious type. He finally decided that she was really innocent and did not actually know about the terrible beating he had taken from Charlie. However, whatever else Charlie was, he had been a good teacher. Eddie's outlook on life had taken a drastic turn, and never again would he take an aggressive step against anyone who might possibly retaliate.

Using the same subterfuge with which he had sidestepped Pete's questions, he finally said, "Naw, I'm okay. Some guys rolled me on the way home from the tavern last week. I don't even know who they were."

With that, he lapsed into silence again. He slowly finished his meal, then took the rest of the six-pack under his arm, went to the door, and stopped to look back at Jan.

"Thanks, Jan," he said. "The dinner was good."

His eyes fell back to the floor, and he turned and left without another word.

Sometime after two in the morning, Eddie came back. He entered very quietly, sat very gently on the edge of the bed, and removed his shoes and socks. Carefully he eased himself back on the pillow and, fully dressed, fell into a drunken sleep.

Jan had awakened when he first stepped up on the porch, but not knowing quite what to expect, she pretended to be asleep. For a little while she puzzled over in her mind about Eddie's sudden change in personality. The thought came to her that she might even be able to get away with hitting him if she wanted to. Whatever had come over him, she decided it was better than having him beating on her and the baby, so she kept her peace and soon drifted back to sleep.

CHAPTER 17

▼

As the days wore one, Corky became more and more active. He was able to pull himself up to a standing position next to the furniture and would walk sideways steps along the sofa. Sometimes he would watch his mother at work, and whether at home or in the kitchen area of the diner, when he knew she was watching him, he would do a rapid little dance and smile happily up at her.

Jan had been noticing for a couple of months that there was something strange about Corky's right eye. Many times when she was on his right side, particularly when he was standing, she noticed that it was hard to tell if he was looking at her. The eye seemed to wander out of control at times, and independently of the other one. It made him look as though he were half drunk, especially when he laughed.

Corky was a very quiet child. He made baby sounds to himself when he was moving about exploring things, but he seldom ever cried. He was curious about everything and moved rapidly about, but stayed out of the way with amazing ability. He seemed purposely to avoid making loud noises that would attract attention to himself.

Janet took good care of him, she was not a demonstratively loving mother. She kept him clean, fed him when he was hungry, and otherwise approached him only when he needed changing or when she was dressing or undressing him to go somewhere or to bed. Not to say that she was neglectful or uncaring, but she had so much more to worry about in supporting herself and the baby—and lately Eddie—that unless he demanded attention, she just took the child very much for granted.

It was Rosa who first really brought her attention to the fact that something was wrong with his eye. Rosa was the only person in Corky's life who ever took moments aside to give the child a little loving just for love's sake. Every once in a while when he was crawling about in places where he was in the way, or where he might be in danger, she would pick him up and give him a big squeeze, chuck him under his tiny chin with her great fat finger, and kiss him noisily. A little of this was readily accepted by Corky, but if she tried to retain control of him or hold him for any period of time, he would struggle and kick and squirm his tiny body to get away.

After she would release him, he would take his distance from her a little way and stand or sit and smile at her as though to say, "Thanks. You are a nice fat lady, but I don't want to be held."

This particular afternoon when he looked up at her, he laughed aloud, and his right eye strayed way off to the side, while his left stayed focused squarely on her. He was definitely not a pretty child. Even at ten months old, he had some very pronounced freckles on his face, which was thin and high cheeked. His tiny nose was pointed, and his mouth straight and thin-lipped. His eyes, very bright blue, and his tangled curly red hair were the most noticeable of his features. Except when he was smiling or laughing, which was not often, he looked like an ancient Irish gnome or leprechaun who would be right at home on some forest toadstool.

At this moment he looked so comical that Rosa could not contain herself. She roared with laughter and scared the smile right off of Corky's face. Clapping her hands noisily, Rosa laughed and laughed.

Finally she called to Janet, "Hey, Jan, honey, come in here and look at this little clown. What the hell you give him in that bottle anyways, straight scotch? I think da little pecker's drunk as a skunk. Just look at 'im. What th' hell is wit his right eye anyways?"

Suddenly she plumped her great round body on the floor beside him and, leaning close, looked right into his eyes.

Jan had come running when Rosa roared, expecting something serious had happened. When she saw the two of them, great fat Rosa and tiny little Corky, eyeball to eyeball in the middle of the kitchen floor, it was her turn to laugh—but Rosa was no longer laughing.

"Hey, kid, I don't tink this is any laughin' matter," Rosa said seriously. "The little bugger got some kinda problem with this eye here. It staggers aroun' like some Beeler-street bum. You ever notice that before?"

Jan became suddenly serious. "Yes, I been noticin' lately, but I thought at first it was just he hadn't got full control of it or somethin', and maybe it would clear up."

"Know what I tink, honey. I tink he got what folks call 'lazy eye.' I've knowed several guys was afflicted like that. I don't think they's much ya can do about it, and it don't really hurt 'em any, except they always looks peculiar-like. I don't know if they see real good from it neither. Maybe ya oughta see some eye specialist with him." She looked questioningly at Jan.

Jan, a worried frown on her face, squatted beside Rosa and rubbed the baby's little red head.

"What you think it would cost?" she asked quietly. Rosa spread both big round arms, hands palm out and fingers spread, and shrugged her neck clear down out of sight. This, combined with the chubbiness of her face, rolled up about four extra chins and made her look like the great Buddha in the flesh.

She never answered the question, and Jan never asked it again, of Rosa or anyone else. She hardly had money to feed herself and Corky. It never entered her head to ask public assistance if they could help. So, like many poverty-oriented people, she merely accepted it and forgot it.

CHAPTER 18

▼

Julianna's outlook did not improve over the next week or so. She was more deeply depressed then ever and cried continuously all the day of her father's funeral.

Perhaps if she had been well enough to attend, she might have shared her grief with her mother, brother, and husband and gotten some of it out of her system. As it was, she continued to mourn whenever Leo was not there to comfort and console her. Activities at the mine were such that he was unable to take off, for fear of jeopardizing his job.

Her poor health and grief became double burdens for him. He spent his entire Sunday with her the weekend after the funeral. He brought her a great bouquet of red roses and white carnations. He talked and laughed with her. He even sang her a couple of songs as quietly as was possible for him, until a nurse asked him to please not disturb the other patients. Although he really did not feel all that happy, he managed to convince Julie the world still had something to offer, and when he left that night, she was more relaxed and cheerful than she had been for many days.

He kissed her lovingly and told her, "I love you, Julianna. You da real ham and eks. You an' me an' baby gonna be real family soon, okay?"

He held her hands tenderly for several minutes, then patted her stomach, stroked her hair, and left.

That night at eleven-twenty, she went into labor. It was mild and routine for several hours, so the nurses just kept track of her condition and kept her informed of what her progress was and what to expect overall. She went at it with a good attitude in spite of her tired and weakened condition and felt really relieved that it was going to be over at last.

However, as the hours wore on and her pain became more intense, it began to seem that the whole nine months of dreary unreality had suddenly culminated in one dreadful nightmare of pain. She was unbearably thirsty and could not drink. She was unbelievably tired but could not sleep. Her tortured body acted independently of her mind, stretching and pulling and contracting without conscious volition from her.

By nine the next morning she had not progressed noticeably with the birth process but had so exhausted herself that her doctor became very anxious about her condition. He tried to contact Leo but found that he had left early that morning for the mine and was underground somewhere working out a maintenance problem with some of his crew.

Failing thus in finding her husband, he called a fellow physician for consultation. After an hour of discussion and examination, they decided the child was either very large or delivering breech, or both.

The consultant advised, "I think she is going to be too exhausted to deliver normally if you let her go on. I think you should give her something to slow her down and let her get some rest."

"But then she will have to start all over again, and her mental condition may not handle that. It might be better to let her continue. She was badly dehydrated just a few days ago, and she is losing a lot of fluid. Whatever else we do, we have to get her to take some fluids."

For the better part of an hour, they discussed the situation back and forth, and Julie's labor intensified. By the time the consultant decided he had done his bit and departed, her doctor became engrossed in encouraging her to develop a rhythm to her work, and to take water.

One thing led to another, and the hours slipped away, and no decision for procedural change was ever made. Had either doctor firmly suggested surgery, it might have been accomplished at the time of consultation. By the time her doctor decided it should have been done, it was too late for one of them, mother or child.

On Monday, when Leo finally arrived at the hospital, the doctor guardedly told him of the situation and advised him that they might have to make a decision to save mother or child. Leo could not believe what he was hearing. His mind would not accept that such a decision was necessary, and he would not have made the decision in any case. To decide for life between his wife and his child was unthinkable.

"Doctors save people, not kill people!" he exclaimed incredulously. "You take care of my Julie and my baby. We are family, not two, we three people, Leo, Julie, Elias. Leo no goin' say Julie, not Elias, Elias, not Julie. You doctor! You take care of wife and baby!"

With that he put both hands on the doctor's shoulders, turned him toward the hallway, and gave him a firm push in that direction.

After the hours of exhausting work and concern he had already put in, the doctor simply could not face this giant with any more such discussion. He continued back to the labor room, his decision heavy on his mind.

However, in not making a decision, he made one. Within the hour Elias Stronski entered this world with twelve pounds, thirteen ounces of screaming, bawling vigor. As he entered the world, his mother Julie left it, without ever hearing her son's lusty claim to life.

The doctor took much more than the usual time tending to details in the delivery room. He picked up odds and ends, supervised details that normally would have been routinely handled by nurses and orderlies, and took many minutes completing the necessary paperwork. All of this he did because he was extremely reluctant to face Leo.

Finally he approached an older nurse who worked with the newborns and told her to get baby Elias and bring him along. The three of them went to the waiting room. There Leo stood to one side of the room, anxiously awaiting the news of his family. They walked up to Leo without any evidence of the good cheer usually attendant with such an occasion.

The doctor reached up and lifted the blanket from the baby's face. Poking a chubby arm up alongside his head, the baby stretched and squawked aloud as he squirmed sturdily in the nurse's arms.

"This is your new son, Mister Stronski," the doctor announced solemnly. "He is a fine, healthy boy."

Leo reached down and, putting both hands under the child, lifted him gently against his own chest.

He looked steadily at the baby for a few moments without comment, then said softly, "And my wife, doctor. What about Mama Julie?"

The doctor stood silent. Leo, sensing the answer, shuddered and held the baby a bit tighter as two great tears started from his eyes and rolled down into his shaggy brown beard.

"Doctor, I wish to see my wife," he demanded suddenly.

In confirmation of the terrible truth, the doctor replied, "Do you think that is a good idea, Mister Stronski? She does not look very nice right now. It would be better when she looks more normal in a day or two."

"Now, doctor!" He roared. "I will see her now!"

The baby jumped and cried out. Leo, tears streaming down his face, reached with his free hand and grasped the soft little hand in his.

The doctor turned, afraid not to comply, and led the trio quickly down the hall. Julie now lay fully covered on a gurney outside of the delivery room. The doctor stopped just before it and leaned heavily against the wall.

Leo looked quietly at the still outline under the sheet. Suddenly he turned, thrust the baby into the nurse's arms, reached down, and turned the sheet back to chest level on his wife's body. He looked with sorrow on her, wiped the moisture from his cheeks with a crumpled handkerchief, and as though completely alone in the room, he began talking to her softly. After removing a pocket comb from his jacket, he slid a hand under her head and combed her hair. He wiped a drop of moisture from her mouth with a corner of the sheet and gently closed and straightened her mouth with the tips of his fingers.

"Julie," he moaned softly, "what I do now with baby? I know nothing of babies. You not even say good-bye to Leo."

Sobbing hoarsely, he slowly rolled the sheet back over her face, then turned away and leaned, face forward, against the opposite wall of the narrow hallway.

The nurse and doctor stood there, uncertain of what to do for several long minutes, until suddenly the huge man in front of them tipped back his head, raised his eyes to the ceiling, and let out a thunderous roar like a dying lion. Raising his huge right arm almost to the ceiling, he slammed a closed fist into the wall, knocking a six-inch hole in the plaster. Then he turned abruptly, took four or five rapid strides to the door, and without even pausing to turn the knob, walked right through it.

Glass shattered from the panels, and the latch ripped from the wood, scattering wood splinters and plaster out into the waiting room. Without looking back, Leo Stronski disappeared, roaring, into the night.

He never knew how long he walked the streets that night. He stopped occasionally in bars along the way, skipping one, entering the next. Sometimes he would have a drink or a beer, either of which he tossed quickly down, without regard to volume or content. Sometimes, as though in a trance, he drank two or three. In each place he acted the same, never speaking except to order, and often not paying for what he drank.

During a period of four or five hours, no bartender challenged him for the money if he did not offer it. Most knew him by sight from his old days of rowdy good times and knew what he was capable of when aroused. Realizing that clearly all was not well with him, they let him pass and heaved a heavy sigh of relief when he would suddenly depart without paying.

Finally, after several hours of venting his anger and sorrow on trash cans, stray dogs, and other loose objects on the streets, he found his way back to his apartment. He let himself in, leaving the key in the lock and the door standing open, and went to the cabinet in the living room, where he brought out a full bottle of brandy. After taking a small glass from the china cabinet, he poured it full and downed it, poured and downed it again.

Suddenly he threw the glass with tremendous force into the far wall, knocking down a picture and scattering glass over the whole length of the room. He seized the brandy bottle, tipped it back, and drank it down, then threw the bottle after the glass and staggered back to the street.

He stumbled through the now-quiet street like a blind man, mumbling and growling as he went. Anyone whom he happened to meet moved rapidly and quietly from his path and let him pass. One couple was so convinced of his madness that they took time to call the police and give a full report of what they had seen.

He passed several clubs and taverns before finally, just at closing time, he steered his stumbling steps into one where several people were sitting quietly at the bar sipping their nightcaps. Leo ran into a table on his way to the bar and knocked it crashing to the floor. Without a sideways glance, he clomped onward to the end of the bar.

The bartender, who had been thankfully cleaning up his back bar and finishing out a tiring evening, was suddenly jarred from his thoughts of home and bed. He came quickly to meet Leo at the end of the bar. He was a young man, and not a very large or strong one, and when he came face to face with Leo, his hands became wet and shaky and his throat very dry.

"Brandy!" Leo croaked hoarsely.

"I am sorry, sir," the young bartender replied. "The bar is closed for the night."

A wild light began to glow in the owlish brown eyes that glared down at him.

"Brandy!" Leo croaked again.

The young man stood his ground, although it took all the courage he could muster.

"I am very sorry, sir," he said in a quavering voice. "You have already had too much to drink, and as I said, the bar is closed. Come back tomorrow night, and I will be glad to serve you."

The bar was at least twenty feet of solid mahogany, anchored well in the hardwood floor. It might as well have been balsa wood floating in a swamp. Seizing both sides of the near end of the bar in his tremendous hands, Leo gave a yodeling roar and began rocking violently back and forth.

At the first couple of jerks, the bar shook enough to alarm the closest couple, and they slipped off their stools and stepped quickly away. Bracing his left foot against the bottom of the first stool, Leo heaved mightily, roaring and screaming like a jungle ape. The glue and wood screws holding the bar in place began to give. Rocking rapidly back and forth, he began to tear it loose, and all the drinks remaining on the bar went crashing to the floor.

By this time the entire tavern was in pandemonium. People were ducking and dodging to avoid the raging giant, and ran into each other and the furniture while trying to escape.

Suddenly the bar came loose from the floor. Leo moved quickly down to about midway of the bar, leaned his great frame into it, and sent it crashing forwards to the floor. As it went over, he lost his balance and would have fallen but caught himself with one hand on one of the now-free-standing bar stools. It tore loose from the floor and teetered sideways but held sufficiently for Leo to recover. He then started down the row of the bar stools, plucking them from their mooring like a child picking mushrooms in the forest, and tossing them aside as he went.

He had just pulled loose the last one, and was holding it by the shaft in one hand and was mopping sweat from his forehead with the other, when the first cop came through the door. The second one came in right on his heels, but the first one had stopped so suddenly, he almost knocked his partner to the floor.

"God A'mighty, Mike," he said with a gasp. "What the hell is it?"

Leo stood there in front of them, hair standing wildly from his head, great brown eyes staring, and sweat and tears streaming down his face. Panting and weaving, with the bar stool hanging from his huge right hand, he looked like a gigantic Neanderthal waiting to battle some prehistoric monster from his cave.

Mouths open, the two officers started backing carefully toward the door.

"Easy, big fella," one of them said. "We don' want no trouble." Then quietly he told his partner, "You watch 'im. I'll go get some more of the boys."

"You crazy as hell," the other said. "Let 'im have the place. We'll both go for help."

With that they backed out into the night.

When six of them returned, about ten minutes later, Leo was seated in a stupor at a table in the middle of the room, crying softly to himself, an almost-empty whiskey bottle on the table beside him. As the officers approached cautiously, the great head lolled sideways, and the sorrowing giant, Leo Stronski, slid quietly from the chair to the floor. It took four of them to carry him out.

The remaining two surveyed the bar for a moment.

As both shook their heads in disbelief one of them remarked, "I seen one o' them tornadoes out in Ohio one time, an' it din't do this bad. Sure glad that guy wasn't after nobody. Wonder what got into 'im anyways?"

"Whiskey, I think," said the other, and followed his fellow officer out to the waiting paddy wagon.

CHAPTER 19

▼

Eddie took to the street completely. He made no attempt to find work of any kind. He bummed from his former buddies as often as he could without alienating them completely, and when they were very liberal, he still acted his old part, telling jokes and laughing at theirs.

He seldom bothered to eat breakfast or dinner, and if not too drunk to care by that time, he usually made his way home just in time to eat the evening meal with Jan and Corky.

He was always quiet and passive at home and expressed his appreciation for the food to her, but was otherwise very impersonal. He seldom ever touched her anymore. If he did, it would be only a pat on the arm or shoulder or a quick squeeze of the hand. Ever since she had come home after her week's absence at the diner, he was more like an occasional boarder than a husband and father.

One thing remained the same. He displayed a resentment and thinly screened hostility whenever Corky was awake and moving about. He often made unkind comments about Corky's appearance, and if he referred to him at all in conversation it was as "that kid" or "Ol' Can't Quite."

Although this upset Jan and grated on her nerves considerably, she mostly kept her peace as long as no one else was listening. Eddie never stayed long enough to be a real burden. He did not eat that much, and it was a relief to know that he was not going to beat her or Corky anymore, so she tolerated him and his drunkenness, although she did not understand why he was as he was.

After several months they became like old friends who meet occasionally for a chat and the assurance that the friendship is still intact. Sex was never mentioned or approached by either of them. Jan was tempted more than once, when he was not too drunk, to seduce him after supper, both because she missed the physical closeness of sexual contact and because she wondered if she could not in this manner entice him to change his lifestyle.

A few times she started to make some leading comment in this direction and suddenly thought better of it. It bothered her to be tied to a man she could not be intimate with, but she also feared that intimacy might again give him the upper hand. As it was, she was very much in control, and there was safety in that, for her and the child, so she went along, hoping something would happen to change things but never really expecting that they might.

Eddie panhandled his way through the district, drinking up everything he received. One by one his working friends from the old days drifted away or became hardened to his continual quest for money and drinks, and finally they abandoned him. However, he still had an easy charm and fell in rather comfortably with the bums and transients on the - street. He joined their share-and-share-alike drinking society, at first casually and then as a full-fledged member.

Once in a great while, if Jan seemed in a particularly good mood in the morning, Eddie would bring one of his street friends home in the evening. She did not like it, particularly since the presence of another male seemed to spark a little of the old aggression in him, and he would entertain his friends by making cruel sport of his son.

Corky was noticeably agitated when Eddie was around, and she noticed a few times that Eddie's voice would drop to near-whispered conversation and then would be followed by heavy laughter from both him and his friend. At first she thought that they were telling off-color jokes they did not want her to hear. Then she noticed that when this happened, they would nearly always be looking at Corky. Not only that, but Corky would often be visibly agitated by this conduct.

Taking her cue from this, she made it a point to work up close behind them when they huddled in close conversation. In this manner she caught Eddie one evening in the middle of his old recital concerning the naming of his son.

She was suddenly and uncontrollable furious with him. She slapped him across the side of his face from behind with the wet dishcloth she had been using to wipe the table, and as he bent forward on his chair to escape this sudden unexpected attack, she stooped quickly and, with both hands, seized the rung of his chair and jerked it out from under him.

"Eddie Hackett," she screamed, "you are a low-down dog!"

Seizing her broom from against the wall, she began flailing both men with the handle as hard as she could swing. Eddie was the closest and easiest target, since he was sprawled on the floor, so he caught the brunt of the attack, but she paused to surprise the other man with two sudden swipes at him. The short respite gave Eddie the opportunity, and he ran for the door, whining and ouching like a kicked puppy, his friend close behind.

Jan slammed the door behind them and retrieved the chair she had thrown aside. She went and lodged it firmly under the doorknob, then picked Corky up, settled herself in the corner of the sofa and, gently rocking him, held him until he fell asleep. Then and there she made up her mind that Eddie was out of her life forever.

The next day she packed all his clothing and shaving gear in a cardboard box and set it out in front of the house. When she saw him later on the street, she told him to pick up his things and never come back.

Eddie, on the other hand, was not to be dismissed quite so easily. He stayed away from the house but occasionally approached her on the street. The first time he apologized in a wheedling tone, and she completely ignored him. On other occasions he tried the old "pity me" line that he had used at the diner the week after Charlie had beaten him.

Sometimes she complied by giving him money or a sandwich from the diner, but she was as good as her word where Corky was concerned and would not allow Eddie near the child or the house. As time went by, she saw him less and less, but without her knowledge he still remained a threat to the boy.

Corky was just past two years old when Janet had driven Eddie from the house. She continued to work at the diner. Often, after the really hard days, she and Corky would stay on at the diner at night instead of going home.

She had told Rosa the next morning about kicking Eddie out, and Rosa had applauded loudly, then hugged her tightly.

"Hey, kid, I knew you had it in ya," she said with a laugh. "How ya let the sonabitch hang aroun' so long, I'll never figger. I'd o' kicked his ass inta middle o' nex' week a long time gone, was it me. They's enough good men aroun' so's a looker like you don't hafta put up with a do-nothin' drunken shit like him. Don't worry, honey. You'll make out. You're just a young'un. Keep them baby blues blinkin', an' you'll do all right."

She squeezed Jan again after this lengthy speech and, seizing her hand, led her into the kitchen, where she pulled a half gallon of red wine from a cupboard and poured a drinking glass full for each of them.

"Congrats, baby." She grinned. "Here's to freedom. Screw the customers. Today you an' me gonna celebrate an' get snockered."

With that she went out into the diner and announced to the half-dozen truckers who were finishing their morning coffee, "Hey, guys, you gonna hafta hoist your asses into them rigs an' hit da road. Somethin' come up, an' I gotta shut 'er down."

After shooing them quickly into the street, she pulled the blinds, put up her CLOSED sign, and returned to Jan and the bottle of wine. At first Jan tried to talk her out of it, but soon she found that Rosa was not an easy person to dissuade once she had set her mind on a course of action.

They took the wine into the diner, and Rosa set it down on a table in front of the jukebox. She then went to the cash register and grabbed a handful of quarters, a couple which she fed into the slot of the jukebox. She punched out half a dozen tunes and returned to the table.

From a little after ten in the morning until three that afternoon, they celebrated Jan's liberation with Corky looking on. They laughed and danced and told dirty jokes and talked at great length about the shortcomings and virtues of the opposite sex. To an only child like Janet, Rosa became older sister, mother, boon companion, trusted advisor, and benevolent benefactor all in one.

For Rosa's part, Jan became the child she could not have and a sounding board for her own considerable frustrations. Late in the afternoon, when both of them had become quite drunk and the party turned as unruly as a party for two can be, they both became very attentive to little Corky. They took turns dancing with him in their arms, swinging him wildly about, and passing him back and forth. As they tired of this, they sat him down between them and began discussing his merits, his shortcomings, his name, his size, and above all, his looks.

"He ain't really a pretty kid, is he, Mama?" Jan asked.

"Jeez Christ, who gives a rat's ass what he looks like? He's a sturdy li'l pecker, and he'll do all right. Hey, we being downright selfish here, we near killed this jug o' wine an' never give ol' Corky none at all. Le's give 'im a sip an' see what he does."

"I don' know," Jan mumbled. "His ol' man is a real drunk, an' I would'n wan'im to get like Eddie!"

"Hell, a li'l sip won't put 'im on the skids. I just wanna see his face when he tastes it."

"Okay," Jan said, 'but just a taste."

Rosa held her glass out to Corky, and encircling it with both hands, he took a gulp. Without realizing it, they had let the little tyke go most of the day without food or water. After the first taste, he made a terrible face and smacked his lips, and both women laughed heartily. Neither thought how wine on an empty stomach would affect so small a body.

When he reached for it again, they let him have it. He drank so eagerly, and they were so far gone themselves, that they did not realize how much he drank. Before Jan finally seized the glass, he had downed three or four ounces.

"Thass enuff o' that," she slurred. "Reminds me of Eddie. No more for you."

She took him from Rosa and put him back on the floor. He stood quietly looking up at them for a short while but was soon reaching up and clamoring for more. From time to time as they talked, Rosa would reach down and give him a sip from her glass.

Before long Corky was standing in front of the jukebox and jigging up and down with quick little steps. As he got the feel of the wine and the music, he began running in circles in time to the music. Within a few turns his little feet lost control, and he began staggering sideways in his circling.

Suddenly he flopped face forward on the floor, bumping his head quite hard. Pushing himself up on his short little arms, he tried to get to his feet but dived forward once more and shrieked in alarm as he fell.

Jan jumped to her feet and started toward him at a staggering run just as he regained his feet. He raised his arms to her, an as she bent and reached for him, he retched violently, spewing hot wine and bile like a little fountain all over the front of his mother.

As the smell of his warm vomit hit her, Jan, as unaccustomed to wine as he, returned the favor. Together they bathed each other and a wide area of the diner with this ungodly mess as Jan turned and staggered toward the ladies' room.

Rosa, long accustomed to both wine and cleaning up other people's mess, maintained complete control in spite of her drunken condition. After hastily following the two of them into the toilet, she stripped them off and washed them down. She brought a box from the kitchen, rinsed their cloths in the bathroom sink, and put them in the box, then wrapped a blanket around the two of them. She half-carried them to the sofa bed in the back and covered them with the blanket.

After gathering her cleaning materials, she returned to the diner and, for an hour, scrubbed and rescrubbed the floor, then opened the windows to air the place. When she returned to the little room off the kitchen, both Janet and Corky were sleeping soundly, and Corky was moaning softly in his sleep.

For the next several days Corky was not himself. He vomited often, had a brief bout of diarrhea, and suffered a violent headache that kept him crying for most of the next day. He drank small amounts of liquids but was well into the second day before he could keep any solid food in his stomach.

His mother fared little better. However, she suffered bravely through and did her work as usual in spite of the butterflies in her stomach. Both she and Rosa were abnormally quiet for the next couple of days and suffered much remorse each time they looked at Corky's pale little face.

In the long run, perhaps they did him a favor. For as long as he lived, Corky would suffer pangs of pain in his head and a queasiness in his stomach whenever he even smelled the scent of wine.

CHAPTER 20

▼

Eddie's mind became a little warped as a result of his heavy drinking and his subsequent eviction from his home and the lives of his family. He often thought over and, when drunk, talked over his personal situation with his sometime friends on the street.

As time went on, he made Corky the scapegoat for his multitude of personal shortcomings. After all, all of his troubles could be counted from the birth of his son. Before that everything had been pretty good. He had a home, a wife, a steady if not too desirable job, and some good friends who were always there to share a drink and a laugh. Then along came this ugly little kid whom he did not want in the first place, and suddenly he had no friends, no car, no job, and his wife had driven him from his home to the street.

In his twisted thinking, it was Corky's fault that he was in these desperate circumstances. Still wary of retribution from Charlie, however, he dared not do anything too obvious, because he still saw Charlie go by in his truck now and then or observed him at meal times entering or leaving the diner. Nonetheless, in his brooding drunken thoughts Corky was ever the culprit, the albatross in his life. He spent much time considering how to even the score.

As Corky grew and became more active, Jan began allowing him the liberty of going in and out of the diner to play in the sunshine when it was nice. At first she checked on him often and was very strict about the limits of his play area outside. However, as children will, little by little Corky expanded his territory.

He did not have a lot of toys to keep him occupied. Rosa had given him a spoon and a tin cup and instructed him in the science of mud-pie-making, which he enjoyed for a time, but Corky had an active and inquiring mind and soon began exploring. All the stevedores and truckers around knew him, and they let Jan know when they thought he was getting "off limits," or took it on themselves to bring him back to the diner if they thought he had strayed too far.

In spite of the watchful eyes of this extended family and his mother and Rosa, Corky had been clear around the block where the diner stood, and explored every inch of the empty lot behind the diner by the time he was four years old. He had collected all the empty whiskey bottles, wine bottles, tin cans, discarded small car parts and other small objects d'art usually found in empty lots and back street gutters, and added them to his toy inventory.

Not long after his newfound freedom had led him clear around the block the first time. His father just happened by at the right time and discovered Corky playing behind the diner in the empty lot A fiendish excitement gripped him as he saw the little fellow alone and unprotected there. For some perverse reason he decided on the spur of the moment to scare the child.

Looking carefully about to be sure he was unobserved, he sneaked quietly around the corner nearest to where the child was playing. He watched carefully for the moment when Corky was completely engrossed in his game. Raking his hair forward over his face and twisting his face in a demonlike grimace, he crept silently forward to where the little boy squatted, chattering idly to his collection of bottles. Inch by inch he sneaked closer until he was a scant two feet behind the boy. Raising himself slightly from the ground so he had free use of his hands, he extended them, dust-covered, in a claw-like position in front of and to either side of his face and let out a catlike scream.

Poor Corky jumped forward in a mad scramble and twisted his little body in a sideways jump to avoid whatever was behind him. When he turned and saw this nightmare figure paused to leap at him, he gave a scream or two of his own and, crying with fright, ran with unbelievable speed for the front of the diner.

Eddie, completely overjoyed with the results of his twisted attack on the child, beat a hasty retreat straight across the empty lot and around the corner of the nearest warehouse. There he crouched in a doorway at the end of a loading dock and laughed and cried and laughed some more until he became nearly exhausted. He was so pleased with the results of this demented entertainment that he immediately began plotting future activity to "get even" with the little interloper who had put him on the street.

As for Corky, he ran screaming into the diner in such a state of shock that he could not immediately tell his mother what had occurred. As a matter of fact, he did not know what had frightened him. In his child's mind, there had been a monster out there in the weeds, and no amount of persuasion on the part of his mother, Rosa, or any of their friends could encourage him to show them what had happened.

Jan and two customers went outside and made a thorough search to find "the thing" that had caused the child so much fright. Of course, no evidence of anything could be found.

In the wildest stretch of his imagination, the little boy would not have associated this experience with his father, and it was more than three years and several such frightening experiences later before he found out the truth. In the meantime, the experience had so unsettled Corky that his nervous eye twitched and jumped wildly, and he would not venture farther than the front steps of the diner for several days. Actually, his father's cruelty began an education for Corky that would stand him in good stead many times in the hard life ahead of him. Never again, would anyone be able to sneak that close to Corky without some sixth sense raising the hair on the back of his neck, which would cause him to make many a quick move to freedom when he might otherwise have become trapped in serious circumstances.

CHAPTER 21

▼

Leo woke up in jail. His mouth was dry, and his head hurt, and he was plagued with the most tremendous thirst he had ever experienced.

He flipped off the old army blanket that covered him and, with some difficulty, struggled to a sitting position on the side of the too-short bunk he had been sleeping on. Both of his feet had lost circulation from hanging uncomfortably over the end of the cot for several hours. Likewise, his right arm, from fingertips to elbow, tingled and burned as he rubbed it to restore the blood flow. In complete perplexity at his surroundings, he sat there staring at the dim light in the corridor and the growing daylight from the small high windows. He rubbed his matted head and tried to collect his jumbled thoughts. He could not remember how he got here or where he had been. Both hands were somewhat stiff and sore, and he felt as though he had just finished a double shift on the jackhammer in the mine.

Then suddenly the reason for his condition hit him like a hammer.

"Julie, Julie," he moaned softly again. "You not even say good-bye to Leo, and I never see you no more."

He thought of the big soft bundle that was his son, whom he had held so briefly yesterday. Tears sprang to his eyes again, and he bowed his great head toward his knees in misery.

"What I'm gonna do with baby an' no Julie?" he whispered. "How this awful thing happen?"

He stood up suddenly and half walked, half staggered to the door of his cell, seized the bars, and shook the door mightily. The racket silenced the snores from two other cells nearby, and the jailer appeared, walking hastily forward to find the cause of the commotion. Leo focused his big red eyes on the man for a moment and he looked so wild that the jailer stopped suddenly and stepped quickly back, safely out of reach.

"Can I have a drink of water, please?" Leo croaked in a surprisingly mild voice.

Relieved that the man was not going to revert again to the violence described in the charge sheet, the jailer hastened to fulfill Leo's request. He soon returned with a pitcher and a glass. After filling the glass, he extended it to Leo, who ignored it, reached through the bars with one hand, seized the pitcher by the neck, and snatched it from the jailer's hand.

However, the base of the pitcher was too large to fit through the bars. Leo soon solved this problem. Raising the pitcher slightly higher than his head, he turned it sideways so the spout and neck fit through the bars. Leaning forward, he began pouring the water in his mouth and swallowing in great gulps. Much of the water ran over his face, down his beard, to soak into the front of his cloths and splash lightly on the floor.

When the pitcher was empty, he wiped his face with the palms of his hands, then reached for the glass, which the jailer surrendered willingly. He killed the glass of water in two quick gulps and handed that back through the bars also.

"When Leo can leave here?" he asked meekly, in a much-improved voice.

"Well, sir, I don't know that," the jailer replied politely. "You done considerable damage last night from what I hear, an' you're gonna hafta go before the judge this afternoon. Maybe he'll let you off, if you can pay the damage."

When he was called before the judge a few hours later, the bartender and several customers who had been in the bar the previous evening were present as witnesses. By the time they had described in detail Leo's cave-man act of the night before and the officers had added their comments, the situation was looking fairly grim for Leo.

The judge looked at him solemnly and thoughtfully for a short while, then said, "Mister Stronski your conduct yesterday was unthinkable. You have virtually destroyed this man's place of business and severely frightened a number of his customers. You could have seriously injured or killed someone, and such conduct is totally unacceptable. The only saving grace in the entire incident is that you did not injure anyone, and that I cannot find any previous record of misconduct on you. Please explain your behavior to this court. What do you have to say for yourself?"

Leo sat quietly thinking. Suddenly he shuddered so his great frame shook. "I not try to hurt anyone. Sometime man not think right. What I can do? I have to discharge good men who work for me in mine. Then my wife papa kill hisself few days ago, and my wife get sick. Wife Julie get very sick. She going to have baby. Doctor ask Leo who should live, wife or baby? Judge, can you say to doctor, 'I want baby, not wife,' or, 'Wife, not baby?' Leo Stronski cannot do this!"

Again tears started from the big brown eyes of the sorrowful man before him.

Heaving a great sigh, he continued. "I am sorry I cause trouble, but I have trouble no man can fix. Now I have fine big baby son, no wife. I not know how to do for baby. Wife dead! What can Leo do? I guess Leo get crazy like bat—but I not try to hurt anyone but Leo. I have money, I can pay, I have good job, I have nice home, but wife go and not even say good-bye. Now Leo has baby and not know what to do. I guess I am drunk when I do this. Drunk and a little bit crazy. All I know, Leo can't help anyone in jail. Please not leave Leo Stronski in jail until I can say good-bye to wife and bring home baby Elias."

Bravely and solemnly the big forlorn man made this lengthy speech. Tears came, but he did not openly cry. His voice broke slightly at the end, and he leaned forward and covered his face with both hands.

The judge looked at each of Leo's accusers in turn. More than one of them had tears in their eyes, and none would look him squarely in the eye.

Suddenly the little bartender cleared his throat and stood up. "Judge, sir, if it please the court, if Mister Stronski will help me restore my place and pay for the breakage, I will be more than willing to forget the whole incident. I had no idea of the situation until now. Can we forget it?"

Quietly the judge stood and stepped from behind the bench.

He laid his hand softly on Leo's shoulder and asked, "Did you hear, Mister Stronski?"

Again the bowed head nodded.

"Case dismissed," said the judge, and turned quickly to his chambers, lest the gathering of witnesses and officers note the moisture starting in his own eyes.

Leo's bill for damages to the tavern was just under four hundred dollars, plus a day and half of volunteer labor. As soon as he collected his personal items from the jailer, he went to the tavern and formally introduced himself.

The tavern owner's name was Anthony "Tony" Martieri, a first-generation American whose mother and father had both came from Italy via Ellis Island, so Tony was well acquainted with the frustrations foreign-born Americans were apt to encounter. The fact that this Serbian giant should have become overburdened to the point of complete abandon and temporary loss of control was not hard to accept. Being something of a fatalist, he shrugged his shoulders when Leo offered heartfelt apologies for his actions.

"Life goes on, Leo," he said. "I would rather you are my friend than my enemy, and I would be proud such a strong man would be a customer as well as a friend. Perhaps when I open again, we can start on a better note, with a nice antipasto and a cold pitcher of beer and become really acquainted."

Leo was so grateful for this attitude that, in spite of all the personal burdens he had to deal with, he stayed on in the tavern and helped his new Italian friend to begin setting the place to rights. His first action was to bend his powerful back to the task of standing the bar up again and resetting it in its original spot.

Tony at first objected, declaring that, "One man cannot lift so much without hurting himself."

He told Leo afterward that he would have hired at least three men to do the same task. Further he estimated it would have taken them an hour and a half to do what Leo did in fifteen minutes. Leo's helpfulness and willingness to pay the bills and help in the restoration, plus Tony's total lack of animosity for the tremendous inconvenience and expense, served to cement a bond between them that lasted for several years. Tony's place became Leo's favorite eating and drinking place from that day on, and Leo became Tony's favorite customer and friend.

As soon as Leo had done all he felt reasonably obligated to do, he went home. He found the door to his apartment standing open. Glass was scattered over a wide area of the floor, the fireplace mantel, and the window sill. The glass in the picture he had knocked down had shattered, and the frame had broken. Fortunately, no one had bothered anything in his apartment. All was as he had left it, although he could not remember having been there the night before at all.

He quickly went about cleaning up the mess he had made, to the best of his ability, although it was many months later before he and his mother-in-law had finally disposed of the last of the shattered glass. When he had the apartment in as near to presentable condition as he could get it, he called a taxi and went to Bernard's house.

His mother-in-law had been staying with Bernard ever since her husband's funeral. Leo went over and over in his mind what he was going to say to her now about Julianna's death. She had been in such a state of shock after his death and the loss of her home that Leo was afraid she would not survive the further loss of her only daughter, coming so quickly on the heels of the other disasters. He was therefore quite unprepared when it was Anna who answered the door.

"Leo, my son," she said immediately. "Bernard and I have worried for you for hours. We were at the hospital early today. We know about Julianna, and we saw baby Elias. We must accept what God gives. Are you all right?"

Leo was so surprised by her strength of speech, and the contrast between her complete breakdown before and her obvious control now, that it took him completely off guard. Instead of he consoling her as he had expected to do, he hugged her quickly to himself and broke down in sorrow. He sobbed openly and uncontrollably for several minutes while the little old lady, whom he had thought might not endure, loved and comforted him, dry-eyed and calm.

"Papa has someone one to look after and worry about as we must for baby Elias," she said at last. "Doctor say he is fine healthy boy, and we must bring him home soon. Papa said I must stay with you and Julie. Now I will stay anyway, for the baby, if you agree. Bernard has only room for himself, and you still must work, so I will look after Elias as long as I can. Is this as you wish?"

Leo looked at her sadly and nodded his agreement, wondering to himself how she could have been so weak earlier and so strong now. Although he was too sad to express pleasure at her action, he remained grateful for her efforts for the rest of his life.

Further, in many little ways and deeds, her mother kept Julianna's memory alive and fresh for him for all the lonesome years after. She became the one stable influence that made life bearable for Leo.

CHAPTER 22

▼

The months went by, and Janet continued to work at the diner. Rosa often told her how much she appreciated her efforts, and though Jan would not believe her, Rosa often gave her credit for doubling her business over the four years she had worked there.

"Never seen a doll like you could make every muddle-headed truck-drivin' sonabitch in the state of Illinois feel like he's some kind of special like you can," she roared to Jan one morning. "If I had two more like you, I could feed the whole goddamn south side least once every week, an' I'd get so rich I could have my ol' man off to Florida in a coupla years an' jus' let you have this slop chute free for nothin'. Maybe I will anyways. What ya think o' that, sweetheart?"

Jan grinned and shook her head. "No, Mama, I think all these big-talkin' cowboys come in just to hear you cuss them out. They would still be here next year if I left tomorrow. I think you take up where their wives and mothers leave off. If they didn't have you on their ass, they probably wouldn't even be working.

"Anyway, I'm not smart enough to run a business. I'd just like to have a house of my own and a man I could trust, so my kid didn't hafta play by hisself in an empty lot all day. Next fall he's gotta go to school. School is over six blocks from here, an, he's so little. I'm gonna hafta start walkin' him up there once in a while, so he learns how to get there.

"Do ya think that's too far for a six-year-old to go by hisself? 'Cause I ain't gonna be able to take him. That's gonna be right in the middle of breakfast hour, an' that's our best business. I wouldn't mind if there was some other kids to walk with, but there ain't a single kid lives this side the warehouse district but him. I don't think he ever seen another kid except the half a dozen or so that come in here with their ol' man once a month or so. Poor kid don't know no one except truckers to talk to."

"Yeah, I know," Rosa agreed. "I tried to get him to play with that li'l girl in here a week or so ago, an' he went an' hid. It's gonna be hell tryna keep 'im in school. Well, shit, we'll jump that puddle when we come up to it. You still the best waitress I ever seen, an' I'm real glad you're able to keep 'em comin' back without lettin' 'em take ya for a ride. Ain't many gals your age can stick to business with all the road-runnin' Romeos we get for customers. You know, you oughta leave the kid here with me some nights. I could take him home. Carl would get a kick outta him once in a while. He ain't real strong, an' might get tired if the kid was rowdy, but Corky, ya don't hardly know he's aroun'. I wouldn't mind babysittin' once in a while if ya wanta go out an' kick up your heels."

It was odd that after all these months, Rosa should make such an offer at the particular time, because later that morning Janet met a salesman who was to become the new man in her life.

Within the hour after their conversation, a dark-haired, brown-eyed young man, very well dressed to be joining truckers and stevedores in a back-street diner, came in. He seated himself at the counter right next to the cash register and winked at Jan as she was ringing up a trucker's ticket.

As soon as she finished the transaction, he grinned and said, "Mornin', Red. Glad to see I ain't the only Irisher in this joint. You serve coffee an' donuts here, or just Irish smiles?"

He was darkly handsome and had such easy charm that Janet could not resist taking up the banter.

"What part of Ireland are you from, Slick, Rome or Venice? Don't give me that countryman bull. I know a Guinea when I see one." She laughed aloud.

Rosa was at the service window to hear Jan's challenge, and she cheered her on. "Give 'im hell, honey. He looks like my little brother. If his name's Irish, It's cause some Italian broad proposed to his old man. Some Italian broads ain't got no class at all when it comes to men. If it looks Catholic, bring it home."

"Hey, girls, no fair gangin' up. I can handle one at a time, but I don't know any man wants to take on two women at once. Gimme a break, will ya?" Then aside to Jan he said, "Name's Bob McBride, Red. What's yours?"

"I'm Jan, your friendly next-door waitress. Last name don't matter, 'cause that can change overnight."

She grinned impishly at him and walked away to wait on a table at the far end of the diner, leaving Rosa to bring him his coffee and doughnuts. He tried several times in the next hour to start a conversation with her. She made it a point to keep continually busy, but flashed her eyes and a smile at him from time to time.

The next morning, shortly after Rosa opened the door at six, he was back. Again he bombarded her with friendly banter and jokes, and in between scrounged bits and pieces of information about her, he filled in a few times on himself for her benefits. Rosa joined the game from time to time with friendly insults and vulgarities, and openly encouraged the young man to persist. However, although he was certain Jan liked him, he was again unsuccessful in getting further than conversational jousting with her.

When the two of them were closing the diner that night, Rosa suddenly grabbed Jan by the hand and turned her around. "Looka here, li'l lady, I meant what I said. If you wanta go make some whoopee with this Jasper, I'll be happy to take Corky home for the evening. If he comes by again and asks you out, why th' hell don't you go. He's cute as hell, and makes good money, ya can tell by the way he dresses. He's a little too slick for my type, but he's fun, and I can tell he likes ya. If he comes in here tomorrow and asked you out, I'm gonna bust your ass if ya turn him down. It'll do ya good to go out to dinner and dance. No reason you should be slavin' all your life 'cause one man done ya dirt. Wake up and smell the roses, baby. They ain't gonna bloom forever."

Two nights later, Friday night, found Jan nervously waiting at the diner for Bob to pick her up. She had gone home early that afternoon at Rosa's insistence and cleaned herself up, fixed her hair, and dressed in the nicest cloths she had.

She had agreed, or rather insisted, that Bob meet her at the diner, because she was ashamed of her shabby little house and did not want him to see it. He had asked her if she wanted to go dancing on Thursday evening, but because she was going to be off on Saturday, she had put him off till tonight.

She had left Corky with Rosa while she went home to get ready, and was a little concerned that he would make a fuss. In over five years she had never left him alone with anyone else. As soon as she returned to the diner, she brought him into the kitchen and took special pains to see that he ate well, and explained that he was to go with Rosa for the night and she would see him tomorrow. To her surprise, he did not seem at all concerned. In fact, it was almost as though he did not hear or understand what she was saying.

He talked about a dog he had seen that day, asked for seconds of mashed potatoes, which was very unusual for him, and tried to irritate her by repeatedly untying his shoe and asking her to retie it. It was not like him to cause her unnecessary problems, but she was so preoccupied with her own thoughts about the forthcoming date that she hardly noticed.

When Bob finally showed up at the diner, she picked up Corky, carried him out front, and introduced him.

Bob smiled at him, gave him a quarter, and made some comment about, "I thought he might be your kid when I saw him."

Corky took the quarter but turned quickly away from him and began kicking and squirming to get down. As soon as she put him down, he ran to the back room of the diner, where he stayed until after they left.

CHAPTER 23

▼

When Rosa got ready to leave the diner that night, she had to look for Corky. She found him in the men's room, idly splashing his hands in an almost-full basin of cold water.

"C'mon, midget," she said, smiling. "You gonna go home with Mama Rosa tonight."

To her surprise, he turned away from her and pretended not to hear. A little exasperated with his attitude, Rosa reached down, pulled the plug from the basin, and let the water drain away. At that, Corky seized the edge of the wash basin with both hands and, relaxing his knees, hung there under its edge without saying a word.

"Hey, feller, c'mon. Mama Rosa has to go. I will take real good care of you. Let's go."

She took a handful of paper toweling from the dispenser and wiped his hands and face.

"Okay, li'l guy, we gonna go get some supper for Uncle Carl. He's a nice man, an' I know he'll like you. Let's go now."

She lifted him bodily to carry him out.

"Don't wanna go, not gonna go," he shouted, and stiffened himself stubbornly in her arms, kicking stiffly as he cried out.

Rosa was completely surprised by this display. In her experience Corky had always been very quiet and passive and rarely disobedient.

"What th' hell you think your mama gonna say when I tell her you kicked Mama Rosa, Corky? She not gonna like that. Now you be a good li'l pecker, an' let's get outta here."

She put the struggling child back on the floor but maintained a steady grip on his left wrist. He was so small that she had to lean slightly to allow both his feet to remain firmly on the floor, and he set his feet so that every step forward he made was forced by the pull on his wrist. For the whole two and a half blocks to her apartment, Rosa half carried, half dragged the protesting Corky.

"I wanna go my house! Don't wanna go Rosa's house. Where's my mom? I wanna go my house."

As big as she was, the walk home was a strain for Rosa at any time, and she often took a cab. By the time she got home this night, she was nearly exhausted and cursed softly to herself as she unlocked her door.

"How th' hell a li'l shitheel like dis can be such a handful, more than I can figger."

"Hey, Carl, c'mere, honey, an' meet this li'l wildcat I caught. He got me plumb wore out."

"Corky," she said to the still struggling boy, "this here's Carl. Carl, meet Corky."

While she was talking, she closed and locked the door.

Corky watched as the crippled Carl's wheelchair kept rolling closer and closer. As it approached him, he put both hands up to cover the lower half of his face and, backing against the wall next to the door, slid slowly down the wall until he was sitting, feet folded, under him on the carpet.

"Looks like he's a bit shy, Mama," Carl said.

Rosa bent and kissed her husband affectionately on the forehead. "Thought you guys'd be good company for each other, but this little character got hard-headed all on a sudden. He ain't never ack like that before. I can't believe it's the same kid."

While they discussed him back and forth, Corky sat unmoving and without a word.

"You go on an' get something ready to eat, Mama. I'll see if I can't get acquainted," said Carl, and leaning over from his chair, he ruffled Corky's red hair with a friendly hand. "Hey, guy, we ain't gonna eat ya, you know."

Carl smiled at him. "We don't get many kids vistin' here, but I'll bet ol' Carl can find ya somethin' to play with."

Backing his chair in a quick circle, he drove off down the hall and into a far doorway.

As soon as both Carl and Rosa were out of sight, Corky stood and, reaching up, grasped the doorknob and tried to open the door. It was a good thing Rosa had the forethought to lock the door, and Corky would surely have been on the street and gone in a flash. When Carl returned from the bedroom, he was still trying to open the door.

"Hey, Red," Carl said in a friendly voice, "you ain't goin' nowhere tonight. Look here what Carl got for you."

He bounced a head-sized rubber ball off the door next to Corky's shoulder and caught it as it returned. Corky flinched back and turned half toward Carl but would not let go of the doorknob. He watched as Carl bounced the ball several times, but kept on twisting the doorknob back and forth in silence.

For thirty minutes or so, Carl tried his best to attract the boy's attention or get some interested reaction from him. All the reaction Corky displayed was stubborn silence and a determined wish to be out the door and away.

Finally Rosa had Carl's dinner ready and came back to the living room where Carl was carrying on his one-sided conversation with the child.

"C'mon, Corky," Rosa growled in her throaty bellow, "we gonna go out in the kitchen an' visit with Carl while he eats he's supper."

She picked him up, sling fashion, by clasping her hands over his stomach from the rear. This time he did not fight, but neither did he respond. Swinging him gently backward and forward, she carried him into the kitchen. She sat him on a kitchen chair and pushed him up to the table.

Carl rolled his wheelchair to the table next to him, and Rosa pulled up a chair for herself and sat on the other side of him. Rosa mumbled a Catholic grace, and the two of them began eating.

After a few bites she offered a bite to Corky, but he stared his defiance and refused to open his mouth, although the food smelled rich and delicious.

"Should Rosa get you a plate, an' you can eat with us?" she asked.

Corky leaned his forehead on the edge of the table and would not answer.

Rosa, believing firmly in her cooking ability, said to Carl, "Hey, I'm gonna fix up a plate fer the li'l bugger. When I got it there in front of him, I bet he eats." She rose to follow her hunch.

She returned in a couple of minutes with a small plate of Italian noodles covered with a rich red sauce, which she sat in front of Corky's forehead where he still leaned forward against the edge of the table. To her surprise, he still did not react at all.

"Oh, well," she said to Carl, "he can't be hungry anyways. He's mama fed him 'fore she left the diner, so he jus ain't hungry. Never seen a kid turn down good food before though. Wonder if he'll eat a cookie?"

Getting up again, she brought some soft brown raisin cookies and tired to put one in Corky's hand, but he crushed it indifferently and pushed it out on the table with his right hand.

"Jus let 'im be," Carl said finally. "His curiosity will get up after a bit, an' he'll come aroun'."

Rosa and Carl sat there and visited over supper as they usually did and pointedly ignored little Corky. About fifteen minutes later he slipped quietly to the kitchen door, where he stood briefly watching Rosa. Carl winked at her and shook his head slightly, and they kept on talking. In a moment he disappeared into the hallway.

"I tole ya he'd come around'," Carl said, chuckling to Rosa. "When we get through, I'll bet he'll be playin' with that ball I gave him."

"Hey, hon," she replied with a smile, "too bad we can't have no kids. You'd o' made a great papa."

When they returned to the living room, they were both dismayed to find Corky leaning face forward against the door, stubbornly turning the knob back and forth.

"By God," Rosa exclaimed, "didya ever hear such a kid? He don't laugh, nor cry, nor beg, nor eat, nor play, but he sure'n hell makes his point. He ain't gonna do nuthin' but what he's gonna do. Guess we'll hafta just make do."

With this practical assessment, they settled down for the evening and did their best to carry on as usual, but it was hard to ignore the forlorn little figure who would not give up his position by the door.

After a considerable period of twisting the doorknob, Corky finally resigned himself to his prisoner status and slid down the wall to sit once again on the carpet. When Carl and Rosa finally decided to retire for the night, she got out a pillow and blanket and fixed a spot for him on the sofa where she laid him down.

"Poor li'l pecker," she whispered sympathetically. "Looks to me like you got a helluva tough row to hoe in this life. You the hardest-headed li'l bugger ever I see. Hard to believe for such a dinky feller."

After patting him gently on the head, she turned out the light and retired.

When Carl and Rosa awoke in the morning, they talked quietly lying in bed for fifteen minutes or so.

"I didn't hear no racket from the li'l fella durin' the night," Rosa commented. "I guess he slept okay."

"Yeah, kids manage fine when they find out how things are an' they can't do nothin' about it," Carl replied.

"Well, I guess I better roll my big ass out an' head for the diner," Rosa groaned. "It's gettin' nigh five o'clock, an' those truckers don' like bein' kept waitin' for their mornin' coffee."

She rose and stretched and headed out into the hall to the bathroom.

As she stepped into the hall, she came to an abrupt stop. "Holy shit, ol' man, will you get a load of this? I tole you that was the stubbornest kid I ever seen."

There on the floor in front of the door lay Corky, sound asleep.

"You'd think he was a prisoner of war or somethin'. Looka the strained look o him, like he was gonna scrunch hisself through that crack. Pore li'l bugger, his mama will never let him go home with anyone again if I tell her this one. I shoulda paid more mind to see he was asleep 'fore we dusted off to the sack las' night. What th' hell ya make o' that, Carl?"

By this time Carl was in his chair and sitting just back of Rosa, quietly shaking his head.

"Hard to figger some kids, Mama," he said. "Li'l feller ain't been much away from home, I guess, 'sides which I think he don't like people much. Well, he'll be a'right when ya git 'im back to the diner where he knows what's happenin'."

Rosa knelt beside Corky and shook him gently awake. He did not start or seem frightened or upset.

"C'mon, li'l guy," she said gently, 'we gotta get down to the diner. Then Rosa will get you some breakfas', an' it's goin' be the best damn chow you had in months too, okay?"

Corky did not answer but sat up next to the door. Rosa bustled about getting things organized as she always did, so that Carl would have minimum problems getting his own lunch and managing for himself until evening. Soon she returned to the living room and, being almost ready to go, she took the apartment key from her bag and unlocked the door. She put her handbag on the table and went to her bedroom for her coat.

When she picked up her purse on returning, she said, "C'mon, kid, les get outta here."

She turned toward the door, and her heart jumped frantically. The door was standing open, and Corky was gone.

Quickly throwing her coat around her shoulders, she ran from the apartment and down to the street. At this hour of the morning, there were not many people about. The traffic was thin. Seizing an old black man who was waiting at the bus stop by the arm, she spun him half around and asked him whether he had seen a little red-headed kid on the street. He shook his gray head and looked at her like he thought she was crazy. He jerked away from her and turned his back without answering.

She tried unsuccessfully to flag down a passing taxi. Extremely concerned now, she paused to consider her options.

Poor li'l pecker, I can't be sure even which way he mighta went. He never been down this way before, much as I know he coulda gone any old direction. Christ A'mighty, what th' hell to do now? She asked herself.

She stood there shaking her head, perplexed.

Li'l fart must move like greased lightnin' to get outta sight that quick. What's he's mama gonna say to me if sumpin' happen to him? Chris', what a fix.

With that she started walking as rapidly as was possible for her in the direction of the diner.

When Corky saw Rosa unlock the door, only one thought crossed his mind. The road home was open, for the moment.

Quickly and quietly he opened the door as Rosa disappeared into her bedroom, and he made his dash for freedom. Quite used to finding his way on his own, he had not been just fighting Rosa all the way here last night. He had also been observing and cataloguing the landmarks along the way—an overfull trash can here, a particularly bright drugstore sign across the street, a crabapple tree shedding its tiny fruit on the sidewalk. These and many more things he had noted.

He wasted no time heading away at a flat-out run for the diner, where he had last seen his mother, the only person in the world he really trusted. In spite of the fact that he had perfectly routed the return in his mind, it was not without hazards. While he had made trips around town many times with his mother and been told many times about watching for traffic when crossing the street, today the only thought in mind was the quickest, most direct route to the diner. Three intersections split his route, but he paid not the slightest attention in his frantic run home.

At the first cross street there was no traffic, and his light was green, so he crossed without incident. The second was a four-lane street, and the light was red, but Corky pounded relentlessly into the traffic. A trucker approaching the intersection saw him coming before he left the curb and braked down cautiously to allow him to pass.

A man in a car, driving alongside the truck in the curb lane, had no view to his left because of the truck and was no more than twenty feet away when Corky streaked across in front of him. Fortunately for Corky, the car brakes were good and the driver's reflexes excellent. He hit the brake with all the power in his leg and swung the front of the car sharply to the right.

All four tires screamed as they grabbed the pavement. The car swung violently sideways in the street, the rear end missing Corky by inches as it came around. His front wheels jumped the curb, and the bumper made crunching contact with the signal pole on the corner.

Corky might have been totally alone in the world. He paid no attention to the hubbub caused by his dash through the traffic, except to speed up a little. The dazed car driver sat there in dismay and watched the child disappear up the block. The trucker had jumped from his cab and came running to the car to see if the other man was okay.

He opened the car door and said, "You okay, old-timer?"

Instead of commenting on his own situation or the condition of his car as might have been expected, the accident victim exclaimed, "Fastest goddamn kid for his size ever I seen. Where th' hell you think he's goin' at five o'clock inna mornin'?"

The trucker shook his head and grinned.

"I sure as hell don't know," he said, "but I bet he's already there. Sure ain't scared of nothin', is he?"

They stood there for several minutes gazing in the direction Corky had gone and discussing him. The entire conversation was on Corky's speed and agility, and what he might be doing there at that hour and in such a hurry.

They were still thus engaged when Rosa came panting through the intersection with a frantic look on her face.

"Hey, guys, I see you got your own troubles," she told them, "but did either one o' you see a li'l bitty red-headed kid go by here?"

They both laughed out loud.

'Christ A'mighty, lady," the trucker said. "I hope you don't think you're gonna catch 'im, do you? He came by here so fast, his breeze stopped my truck dead an'blew this gent right off the damn highway. You spectin' to catch him, you better rent you'self a motorcycle."

Rosa was so relieved to find that Corky was headed in the proper direction that she did not even ask for any further details, but said "Thanks," shook her head in a puzzled manner, and hurried on after Corky.

The two men looked after her for a moment.

"Tell you what," the car driver said. "If a woman that big was chasin'me, I bet I could burn up the cobblestones for a block or two my ownself."

They both had another chuckle or two over that, then got in their vehicles and went about their business. Corky got to the diner without further incident but, of course, found it locked and dark. He tried the door once and stood for a short time on the steps, trying to think what to do. Not one to wait around for something to happen, he made a complete circle of the diner and, not seeing any lights or people around, started off up the street again at a dead run toward his house.

When he got to the little house on warehouse row, Corky quit running as he rounded the corner in front of it. Head down and apprehensive about what to expect here, he scuffed his feet in the dew-damp dirt from the curb to the warped wooden steps. Standing on tiptoe, he turned the knob and opened the door, which had never had a lock.

"Mom! Mama!" he called. "I'm home. You here?"

Silence greeted him, broken only by the creak of the old refrigerator in the corner. The house was cold and quiet. In spite of the fact he was used to being alone and pretty much on his own, his mother had always been available in the vicinity when he needed something. Now he was completely alone. She was not at the diner nor here at home where he had been certain she would be.

He had been extremely uncomfortable at Rosa's last night, as it was the first night he could ever remember that his mother had left him. He did not understand why his mother had left with the dark-haired strange man, nor why he had been made to go to Rosa's home.

He liked Rosa but did not like being dragged away to her house without his mother. He did not like the man who had taken his mother away, and he was certain he was going to find her either at the diner or here at home.

Suddenly he felt completely abandoned. He did not like the quiet of the empty house, but he was even more afraid of what might await him on the street. At the third intersection he had crossed after leaving Rosa, a man had leaned out of his car window and yelled at him because he had to brake sharply when Corky dashed in front of him. The outside world was a cold and hostile place. Now this little quiet and lonely house did not seem so comforting either.

At first he left the door open, but the sounds of traffic in the early morning quiet reminded him of his frightening dash for home. Reluctantly he closed the door and began wandering slowly and aimlessly around the gloomy little room, touching this and that as he went.

"Where's my mom?" he questioned softly. "Why can't I find my mom?"

Suddenly overcome with loneliness and discomfort at being alone and cold and uncertain, he gave himself over to despair. Tears rolled down his little red cheeks. Sobbing heavily, he rolled himself up onto the sofa bed, where he wrapped a blanket tightly about himself, pulled a pillow over his head to shut out the world, and cried himself to sleep.

Rosa arrived at the diner a good fifteen minutes after Corky had left. Two of her usual customers were standing out front smoking and chatting as she hurried up.

"How long you guys been here?" she queried sharply.

"Only a couple of minutes or so," one replied. "What's up?"

"My waitress, Jan. She left her kid with me last night, an' the li'l shit ran off from me this mornin', an' I don't know where he went. I can't open this place till I know he's okay."

"Hey," the other man said, "you mean Corky?"

"Yeah, Corky," Rosa replied. "Ya seen 'im?"

"Yeah, I was sittin' over there on the lot in my truck waitin' for you to open, an' I seen him come tearin' down the street. He stopped here a minute an' tried the door, an' when he seen it was locked, he went gallopin' down the street there." He pointed the way Corky had gone.

"Well, I'm gonna be in the deep dog dirt with his mama for lettin' him go home by hisself," Rosa said with a sign, "but he been walkin' that route ever day for the las' five years or so. If he can find his way to here from my house after only bein' there once, I guess I needn't worry bout him now. His mom will be lookin' out for him by now, an' she's due in to work at seven anyways. Guess I might as well feed you buzzards 'fore you go huntin' a new joint. Christ, that li'l bugger give me a scare this mornin'. Shore hope Jan ain't too mad at me for turnin' 'im loose."

Still concerned but satisfied that Corky was by now safe at home, she opened the diner and started her chores to get ready for the morning's trade.

CHAPTER 24

▼

Elias Stronski was too much for his grandmother to handle from the very day Leo brought him home from the hospital.

He had remained a few days longer at the hospital than was usual, and had become the favorite baby with all the attendants, nurses, and doctors. When Leo checked him out of the hospital, he was twenty-nine inches long and weighed over thirteen pounds. He was an even-tempered and happy baby, and his growth rate was phenomenal.

Leo was very proud of the boy but at the same time could not shake off a vague feeling of antagonism and resentment. He had loved his Julie very much and knew it was wrong to blame the baby for her death. Nevertheless, there was a nagging feeling of guilt in the back of his mind, because, like it or not, the resentment was there.

Because of this, the major tasks of the little boy's upbringing fell to his grandmother, who, in turn, gloried in her new role. It gave her something to live for and keep her occupied after the double tragedies of her husband's and daughter's unexpected deaths. She loved Elias enormously and pampered and spoiled him as only a grandmother can.

By the time he was nine months old, Elias had more than doubled his weight. If he struggled at all when she picked him up, Anna could not hold him. Fortunately for her physical health, he began walking early, so she did not have to lift or carry him for very long.

By the time he was eighteen months old, he was bigger than some four-year-old children in the neighborhood and stronger than most. He was extremely active for so large a child, and Anna was physically and mentally exhausted every night by Elias' bedtime.

Leo took a very passive part in raising Elias. He would hold him occasionally while relaxing with his music in the evening and was usually the one to chastise him if a major confrontation arose between baby and grandmother.

Times became progressively rougher for almost everyone in the area as the depression settled in. The mines had ground to a halt except for local production for heating requirements. Leo managed to stay on the payroll but no longer as a supervisor. Because of his broad knowledge of the maintenance problems in the mines and a natural bent for mechanical things, he took on the tasks, on a smaller scale, of several less fortunate men who had been laid off over a period of months. He worked long and miserable hours for considerably less pay than he was making as a supervisor, but at least he was working.

Between the loneliness of his widower's life and the pressures of his job, Leo's old drinking habits returned. He drank far more than was good for him but mostly at home in the late evenings. In fact, Anna usually had to turn off his music and wake him from a drunken stupor to get him to go to bed at night.

Many times her pleas for him to retire went unheard if the bottle he usually brought home still contained a few more drinks. He never became abusive or obnoxious with her or the baby. He was passive and polite but very set in what he was going to do or not do. Therefore, she never badgered or criticized his drinking. She accepted this fault as a necessary excess in a life otherwise filled with blessings, the greatest of which was her enormous and cherubic grandson.

As Elias grew and learned, he became more and more difficult for the aging lady to keep up with and control. She often remarked to Leo during the evening meal, "I don't know how long I keep up with him. It is too hard to try to raise big active boy in little city apartment He already owns the street!"

Leo would always nod and comment, "We must do the best we can with him."

Thus the real burden always came back to her.

For Elias, life could not have been better. At three years old, he was king of the neighborhood. Anything he needed or wanted was promptly provided by his grandmother, and from old and young acquaintances and admirers he met in the one or two-block area around where they lived. His size and strength, plus an extraordinarily friendly and happy demeanor, won him a devoted following wherever he went. All he had to do was laugh and clown a little bit, or do some little feat of strength that he learned very early, to fascinate people. If he was not rewarded materially with goodies and coins, he was always rewarded with applause and friendship.

The one exception was his father, whose attitude was usually stern and gruff in response to Elias' clowning. He laughed occasionally at some of the more comical antics but was more often than not critical of his actions.

Elias was awed by his father's size and strength as well, and he adored him. He could never get as close to him emotionally as he would have liked, though he was always trying. He loved to hear his father sing, particularly when Leo would soften a little and hold him at the same time. The songs Leo sang these days were mostly of a melancholy strain, and mostly done after a dozen beers or a bottle of brandy had taken their toll on him.

Elias was also very curious about the things his father was forever drinking from those large brown or green bottles. Whenever he tried to taste it on the sly, however, he was firmly rebuffed.

"No, Elias, you must never drink Papa's medicine," he would say. "It very bad for little boy an' make you very sick. You never see grandma drink this stuff, only Papa. You don't touch, or Papa get very mad, okay?"

Elias would nod and back away from these stern lectures, but the curiosity remained. He often hung around when his father was drinking heavily, listening to his drunken rendition of the operas and other classical melodies and waiting his opportunity.

His grandmother was pleased that Elias liked the music, and encouraged his attempts to mimic his father, remembering the old days when Leo sang to Julie's piano accompaniment. Though she did not play the piano herself, she often opened the cover and encouraged Elias to tinker with the keys.

One evening when his grandmother was in her room busily sewing, as she often did after supper, Elias came in from the street and watched her at work for a few minutes. They chatted briefly about what he had been doing outside.

She hugged him and told him what a good boy he was and to, "Go play now, but no more outside tonight, okay?"

Just at that moment they both heard the music start up in the next room, and Elias told her, "I'll go hear Papa sing, okay?", and he dashed quickly from sight.

It was a Saturday, and Leo had worked only half a day. He stopped at Tony's Tavern and drank two pitchers of beer before coming home to supper. He brought home a sack with six beers and a bottle of brandy. He drank a couple more beers while waiting for his supper and asked Anna to pour him a glass of brandy as soon as he had finished supper. Feeling very mellow and comfortable, he traded small talk with the old lady for a few minutes. Then, taking his newspaper and the remaining beer and brandy, he went to his room.

When Elias slipped quietly into the room, Leo was leaning back in his favorite chair, newspaper folded under his hands, which were crossed on his stomach, and his eyes were closed. The radio was softly playing Leo's favorite evening program of classicals, and he was humming the tune quietly to himself.

Elias had watched this scene innumerable times and knew what to expect. He became suddenly and pleasantly excited. Very cautiously and quietly he eased himself up to the other side of the small table that stood beside Leo's big chair. More than half a bottle of beer and the open bottle of brandy sat on the table. Slowly, carefully, he seated himself on the carpet with his back against the wall in the shadow of the chair and waited.

His father's humming continued off and on for several minutes, broken intermittently by vocal snatches of song. In a little while the humming stopped, and the breathing became more audible. The great fingers relaxed, and little by little the big right arm slid downward until it lay alongside him on the chair arm. His face relaxed, and his mouth fell slowly open. Soft snores became the accompaniment to the classics emanating from the radio.

Smiling happily and so excited he could hardly control himself, Elias eased himself quietly to his feet, tiptoed across the carpet, and left the room. He peeked cautiously into his grandmother's sewing room, where she still plied her needle deftly in and out of the piece of material she was working on.

Satisfied that she was not going to surprise him, he sneaked back into his father's room. Again, tiptoeing quietly, cautiously, he slipped up directly behind his father's chair and picked up the half bottle of beer.

He smelled the bottle first and, finding the odor not unpleasant, he tipped it back and took a sip. The fizzy malty taste engulfed his tongue and tickled his mouth and throat, and he almost coughed aloud. Startled, he set the bottle quickly back on the table.

Tears came to his eyes as he swallowed the unfamiliar fizzy brew, and for a moment he almost retreated, fearing that his father would wake and catch him; but the soft snoring continued, and his original excitement returned. Pleased with the taste, he seized the bottle again, and knowing what to expect this time, managed a larger swallow.

He put the bottle back on the table and went again to check on his grandmother. Seeing that she was still busy with her sewing, he ventured again behind the big chair. He picked up the bottle and, crouching in the shadow, drank all that remained in it over a period of about ten minutes.

Very pleased and excited that he had finally tasted Papa's "big medicine" and gotten away with it, he turned and skipped from the room. Grinning happily, the big little boy returned to his grandmother's room and stopped just inside the door.

"Papa is gone to sleep, and' I'm going back outside," he announced in an unusually loud voice.

Anna answered quietly, "It's too late and getting dark now. You must stay in house."

"No!" Elias announced emphatically. "I'm going out."

"You mus' go in bed soon, Elias. You cannot go out."

"Papa is sleeping, you are sewing, an' I got nothing to do. I'm going out!"

Each exchange became progressively louder.

Irritated, Anna finally said, "Okay, go out, but only just in front, an' you mus' come in when Grandma calls."

By now Elias was feeling the effect of the several ounces of beer he had drunk, and he was seized by an elation like he had never known before. He ran recklessly down the steps at the front of the building and began running circles on the sidewalk. He felt wild and happy and excited, as though he could fly if he wished.

As this thought struck him, he extended his arms like wings and ran full speed away from the apartment down the sidewalk. When he came to the corner, he tried to stop but lost his balance, tripped, and fell full-length on the walk in front of a lady who was just turning the corner.

"Whoa, little man! Did you hurt yourself?" she asked as she helped him to his feet.

Leaning over him, she brushed the dust from the front of his clothes. He was sweating profusely and laughing happily. He jerked his arms away from her and began jumping backward in short hops away from her.

The lady stood looking after him for a moment with a puzzled expression on her face, then stepped from the curb and started across the street. Suddenly in mid street she stopped, disregarding the approaching traffic, and looked back where Elias had disappeared into the darkness.

"I swear," she mumbled, "if I didn't know better, that child smelled like beer, and he acted drunk. He couldn't be more than six years old."

Shaking her head, she continued on her way.

Actually, Elias was just past four, and his first experience with alcohol had been a happy one. For more than an hour he ran swiftly up and down the block, the artificial excitement pushing him on until his grandmother finally caught him as he ran by, took him in, bathed him, and put him to bed. She noted his extraordinary activity but failed to note the beer scent as the lady on the street had done.

Thus began an often repeated experience for Elias that led him into a heavy drinking habit before he was ten years old.

CHAPTER 25

▼

Robert and Janet had gone to a club where there was live music. At first they only sat and sipped a couple of beers and became better acquainted.

Bob was a salesman for a drug company and traveled extensively in the North Central states working out of Buffalo, New York. He was only a couple of years older than she, and they soon found they had quite a bit in common. He had been married, but his wife sold everything they owned and ran off to New York City while he was on one of his sales trips. He had never heard from her again.

He was, like Jan, an only child. His mother hated his wife. He said they had tried at first to get along with his family, but his mother had made life so difficult for his wife that they had not even seen each other in three years.

One of his mother's big complaints was, "The girl is a no-good tramp, an' you're goin' to come home someday and find her gone."

Bob told Jan, "Maybe she was right, but I feel like she did her very best to make it be true, an' I ain't going to let her know she was right. If she finds out, okay, but I won't give her the satisfaction of hearing it from me."

Jan laughed out loud when she heard this.

"Sounds too close to home for comfort," she said. "My mom and dad live just a couple of miles away, an' they ain't never even asked me for my address, so I ain't seen them in several years either. Funny, ain't it, how your folks can raise you up an'then drive you right out like you never belonged there in the first place. Hell of it is, I know my dad was right. My husband turned out to be nothing but a mean little drunk. I ain't gonna go back an' give them the satisfaction of telling me I told you so!"

They chatted for an hour, had a light dinner, and then lapsed into a prolonged period of thoughtful silence.

After fifteen or twenty minutes of this, Jan finally looked up and grinned at him. "We're a hell of a fun couple, sittin' here dreamin' about how it oughta been different. Let's cheer up an' have a good time. Do ya dance?"

"Ever meet an Irishman who couldn't dance?" He laughed. "C'mon, I'll show you how!"

For the next four hours they hardly missed a dance. They were both light on their feet and very capable dancers who complemented each other well on the dance floor. Many times during the evening other dancers voluntarily opened a space for them to show off. They were both smooth and quick and moved like they had been practicing together for years.

When they finally announced the last dance, Bob picked up both their jackets and said, "Let's make it on out of here, so we don't get caught in the rush."

"I can't remember ever having such a good time with anyone," Jan replied, and she linked her arm into his as they made their way to the door.

They headed across the darkened parking lot to his car, and he unlocked the door to let her in. Instead of stepping back to make room for her, he threw both their jackets into the back seat and, turning quickly, wrapped both arms around her waist and lifted her off her feet. She responded in kind, pulling his head down to meet her lips. They stood there for several minutes tightly wrapped in each other's arms.

Finally he released her, and she slid into the seat. When he got in on his side, he reached over, put his hand behind her head, and pulled her toward him.

Looking soberly into her eyes, he said, "I never was one for makin' love in a car, kid. Where we gonna go from here?"

Jan's heart was beating so fast, she could hardly speak. "I made you meet me at the diner 'cause I was ashamed of my place' Bob, an' I still feel that way—but Corky went home with Rosa, an' there's no one there, so if There's nowhere else, that's what it's gonna be."

"Hell, I ain't broke, sweetheart, an' I wouldn't take you nowhere you weren't comfortable. I can find us a decent hotel room for the night."

"Okay," Jan said, "But I gotta be careful, 'cause I sure can't afford no more kids."

"You picked the right man this time." Bob laughed. "Play it safe and date a drugstore supply man. I knew you were smart when I first saw you."

Jan flushed with excitement. "Oh, yeah, one more thing. I promised Rosa I'd be in by seven, so we gotta be up early."

"That's gonna be easy," Bob said. "The way I feel, we'll probably be still awake by then."

He was almost right. The pale blue glow of dawn in the eastern sky was contrasting with the man-made cloud above the city when they finally fell asleep in each other's arms. They slept like there was no "rest of the world" anywhere but right there in that bed.

C H A P T E R   26

▼

"Can I play your music for you, Papa?" Elias asked as Leo made his way into the living room with his bottle and his evening paper.

"Hey, you getting' to be big boy now. You like good music too, huh?"

"I like your music you play, Papa. Show me how to do it, okay?"

Leo was pleased by the boy's active interest in the music, so he laid the paper and bottle aside on the table, lifted Elias to his knee, and for twenty minutes coached him on how to turn the radio on and off and where to locate the stations that played classical and operatic music.

Elias learned quickly and made very careful mental note of exactly where the dial-pointer stood for each of the three stations his father indicated would have good music. When Leo was satisfied that Elias could find them on his own, he stood the boy back on the floor, spread his paper open on his lap, opened the brandy, and took first a sip and then a long drink. Elias watched his father's face, eyes sparkling mischievously.

"Is that good, Papa?" he asked.

"It is good for me, "but for little boys, no good. Now Elias, you go play now, okay?"

"Can I smell it, Papa?" Elias asked curiously.

"No, you not smell, an' you not taste, Elias. This is for Papa only, you unnerstand."

"Please, Papa, I just want to smell it, okay?" He grinned impishly.

Irritated but thinking to end the encounter the easy way, Leo took the cap from the table and held it under Elias' nose. Elias sniffed and made a face as though to indicate it was no too pleasant.

"See," Leo said, laughing, "I tole you, no good for little boys. Now run an' play while Papa read he's paper."

Elias rubbed his nose and thought to himself that the scent was not unpleasant at all. He then ran quickly from the room, but his mind was busy with a plan.

In the kitchen, where his grandmother was doing the supper dishes and cleaning up the table area, he stood watching for a minute.

When she picked up a glass to put it in the cupboard, he said, "Papa wants me to bring him a glass."

"Oh, Papa must think you grown up. Little boys could hurt theirself with glass. I will bring it."

"No, no Grandma. Papa asked me. I'll be careful. Please, Grandma."

He seemed so anxious to do this for his father that she finally relented but watched him to the doorway and then followed as he gave the glass to his father. Satisfied, she went back to her work.

Elias returned to Leo again, who was about to rebuke him when Elias said quietly, "I brought you a glass, Papa, so you don't have to drink from the bottle."

"Ain't you the real ham an'eks to think of Papa, Elias? Thank you," he said, instead of sending him away as he had been about to do.

Elias just smiled and went back to the other room. He stood for some time outside the kitchen door, watching his grandmother. As she finished the last of her kitchen chores and picked up her sewing box, he walked quickly to her side.

"Grandma," he said, "Papa wants me to bring him a beer."

"My, my," Anna answered, "you big helper for Papa tonight—but you must be very careful not to shake it or spill it, okay?"

Elias nodded excitedly and watched carefully as Anna went to the pantry and got a beer, found a bottle opener in a drawer, and opened it.

"Here now, carry it with both hands and be real careful," she said, then turned toward the door and went back to the dining table for her sewing basket.

Elias went quickly from the room but stopped in the shadows just inside the living room door. He watched until Anna disappeared into her little sewing room. Being very quiet so his father would not hear or see him, he waited several minutes for his grandmother to become involved in her work. He then set the beer down by the door in the darkness, tiptoed out, and peeked around the door to be sure she was busy.

As soon as he had assured himself that she was engrossed in her work, he returned quickly to the living room, retrieved the beer, and tiptoed to his room. Standing alone in the darkness, he drank about half of it in ten minutes or so, then set the half-full bottle inside his closet door and went back to the doorway of Anna's sewing room.

"Grandma, I'm going out for a little while," he said.

She looked up, smiled, and replied, "Good boy, Elias, but just out front, and don't stay too long, okay?"

He repeated the adventure of a few nights earlier and for half and hour ran happily and madly up and down the block, clowning and showing off for anyone who would stop to watch. Very soon, however, he found himself thirstier and thirstier. He ran back in the house and stopped by the sewing room door.

"Hi, Grandma! I'm back!" he shouted happily.

"That's a good boy, Elias," she replied, "but be quiet, won't you? You Papa prob'ly sleeping."

Slipping silently into his room, he sat down next to the wall and drank the rest of the bottle of beer. Then he crawled and spun and danced about his room while the fuzzy euphoria of the beer fueled his antics. He laughed and played and talked to himself for nearly an hour.

Realizing suddenly that it would not do to be caught with the empty bottle, he sneaked quietly back into the hall and, checking first to see if his father was still sleeping, which he was, retrieved the bottle from his room.

Again stopping outside Anna's door, he held up the empty bottle. "Grandma, Papa finished his beer, an' he's sleeping. I'll put it in the kitchen, okay?"

"You such a good helper tonight, Elias," she said. "Thank you very much."

This experience began a long-time practice of trickery, deception, and subterfuge that kept Elias first with a ready supply of beer and then, later, stronger drink, with no one the wiser for many months.

CHAPTER 27

▼

Jan awoke in a panic, with the sun streaming in the window and reflecting on her face. She jumped from the bed and ran into the bathroom, washed herself and combed her hair quickly, and shouted Robert awake as she began hurriedly putting on her clothes.

"Jesus, guy, I'm hours late for work. It's twenty minutes to nine, an' I was 'supposed to be there at seven. Rosa is gone be sore at me. C'mon, hurry up an' drive me to work."

"Hey, not so fast, honey," he replied. "You're already late. Hop back in here, an' let's start the day right."

"We already did that from two until five this morning'. You're gonna have to get by on that till later. I can't afford to lose my job! Now get the hell out of there, <u>please</u>!"

She leaned over, kissed him quickly, and went on with her dressing.

Reluctantly Robert rolled from the bed. He stretched and headed for the bathroom.

"Shake it a little faster, will you, love? I don't want Rosa mad at me, and I'm sure Corky already is. Besides, Rosa ain't gonna have time to worry about him and the customers too. She's got to cook, wait tables, an' ever'thing."

By the time she was finished with this speech, she was already talking to herself, as Robert had disappeared into the bathroom and locked the door. When he came out fifteen minutes later, Janet was leaning against the door, clutching her handbag to her chest.

"Sit down and relax, Irish," he said. "I'll be ready in a few minutes. Christ, what's the hurry?"

"I already told you, Bob, Rosa's gonna be mad."

"Hell, let 'er be mad," he replied. "It ain't gonna be the end of the world. That's one thing I love about my job. I got no schedule to keep. Drugstores are always open, an' I can call on 'em whenever I get good an' ready."

"Yeah," Jan replied, "but what about Corky? What if he ain't had any breakfast yet?"

"Now, don't worry yourself so much about that kid." Bob said as he casually straightened and buttoned his shirt. "He's always seemed to manage pretty good, what I seen, an' you know Rosa. She wouldn't let a stray dog go hungry. She told us to have a good time, an' I think that's what we oughta do. Why don't you just take the rest of the day off, you're so late already?"

"Jeez, Bob, you know I can't do that. C'mon, let's get out of here."

She finally got him headed down the hall toward the desk and stood waiting with the lobby door open while he paid the bill.

When they finally arrived at the diner, Jan already had her coat off before she got to the door. She went straight to the kitchen when she saw that Rosa was not waiting tables. She found her rolling buns for the lunch menu in the kitchen.

"God, Mama, I'm awful sorry I'm late. I'll work later this evenin' to make up," she offered anxiously.

"Hi, sweetheart. Don't worry yourself about that. It ain't been that busy. Did ya have a good time? An' how's Corky doin? The li'l fart near scared me into a heart attack when he took off this mornin'."

"What do you mean, how's he doin? Where is he?" Jan cried, suddenly concerned.

"You mean he never came home?" Rosa exclaimed, sudden shock and worry plain on her face.

"Came home?" Jan exclaimed. "Rosa, I ain't been home! You mean he ain't here!"

"Goddamn, I knew I shoulda sent someone down to check on the li'l pecker. He ran off from me this mornin', right from my place. Some guys seen him stop here an' then head out on a run toward your house. I figgered he was with you. Jesus, that was five hours ago, an' he been on his own all that time. Hurry up, Jan. Go make sure he's all right. I'll tell you all what happened later."

Jan grabbed up her coat and handbag and ran for the door. She did not even think to ask Bob, who was sitting at the counter waiting for coffee, whether he might drive her, but took off at a run for home.

When Rosa came from the kitchen looking after her, Bob said, "Where the hell is she goin' so fast?"

"Her kid ran off this mornin', an' I figgered he went home, so I din't worry, 'cause I thought she was home. Now I find out she wasn't even there. Can't ya go drive her? It's near a mile where she lives."

Bob went quickly out as Rosa followed him to the door.

"There she goes, clear down Warehouse Row already. Catch her!" she shouted as Bob ran to his car.

She was more than halfway home before Bob pulled up beside her and blew the horn.

"C'mon, jump in here, kid," he said. "I'll get you there in a jiffy."

She got in, and they sped the other few blocks home. Jan jumped quickly from the car.

"Wait here," she ordered, and ran up the rickety steps.

She burst into the room, and there was Corky, sitting all curled up in the corner of the sofa bed with his blanket pulled around him and wrapped right up to his eyes. When he saw Janet burst into the room, he pushed down the blanket but said nothing. He just sat and stared blankly at her.

"Corky, honey, you okay?" Jan finally asked.

He dipped his head once in acknowledgment but did not move or change expression. Still very concerned, Jan ran to his side, picked him up, and held him tightly to her. Slowly his little arms snaked up around her neck, and tucking his pale little face against her shoulder, he began to cry silently, his sobs shaking his whole body.

Jan stood there for several minutes while the distraught Corky soaked her shoulder with his tears. She whispered softly to him, and hummed a comforting sound in his ear.

Suddenly they were interrupted by the sound of Bob's voice.

"C'mon, girl," he said from the doorway. "I got to get goin', an' your work is still waiting too." Then, rather as an afterthought, he added, "The kid, okay, is he?"

At this, Corky suddenly lifted his head, swiveled in his mother's arms, and gave Bob a stare of pure hatred.

"Jesus," Bob said, as he realized the fire in the boy's eyes, "if looks could kill, I'd be a red-hot cinder right now! He's gonna blame me for the whole thing."

Wiping his tears from his cheeks with the back of her hand, she said to Corky, "Shall we go to Rosa's an' fix you somethin' to eat?"

Corky looked at her and nodded, but from the moment she had entered the room until she asked this questions, he had not spoken a word.

When they arrived at the diner, Rosa came hurrying to meet them. Corky was standing close to Jan, holding onto her skirt with one hand.

As Rosa approached, she said loudly, "Hi, li'l feller. Boy, am I glad you're okay. Come up an' see Rosa."

She extended her arms toward him as she bent to pick him up.

Corky's face contorted, and he turned and ran out the door and down the steps, where he stopped and stared defiantly at her. Rosa was shocked by his reaction and stood there for several minutes trying to coax him back into the diner, but he would have none of it.

Jan interceded by picking him up and carrying him into the diner. She tried to hand him to Rosa, but to her amazement, he went wild, kicking and screaming and trying to get away.

Rosa was dumbfounded. "What you gonna think of me, Jan? He ack like I been beatin' him or somethin'. Honest to God, I ain't tried to be nothin' but nice."

"I know you have, Rosa," Jan replied. "He's just scared and upset 'cause I went an' left him."

Bob said, "Hey, you know what you oughta do is turn him up an' whack his little ass for him. Let 'im know who's boss."

Both ladies gave him a cold stare, so he hunched his shoulders in resignation and said, "See you later, kid. I gotta go to work."

As soon as Bob was gone, Jan carried Corky into their little private area and seated him at the table that served as Rosa's desk—their mutual break area, dinner table, and what have you. She sat there with him for a minute and talked to him.

"Rosa was worried about you, Corky. You shouldn't have ran away from her. Mama didn't leave you. I only went out with Bob for a while. Are you still hungry?"

Again Corky nodded.

"What do you want to eat?" she asked him, but Corky would not answer. He just stared resolutely at the table in front of him.

Finally she told him, "Wait right here, an' Mama will fix you something."

She went quickly into the kitchen and made him some scrambled eggs and toast. After filling a large glass with milk, she went back to find Corky still sitting there, head dejectedly cradled in his arms on the edge of the table. She placed the milk and food in front of him and rubbed the red fuzz on the back of his head.

"Here's your breakfast, Corky. I'm sorry it's so late. I woulda been here earlier if I knew you needed me. C'mon, eat your food."

Corky looked at her for a minute, then took his fork and started shoveling eggs into his mouth rapidly. He paused for an occasional drink of milk or bite of toast but finished it all in record time.

"Do you want more?" Jan asked when she noticed he was done.

"No," Corky replied.

"Hey, that's great. Feed you a little bit, an' you learn to talk again." Jan grinned at him.

To her surprise, Corky did not seem annoyed by her comment but stared accusingly at her.

"Why you leave me, Mama?" he asked. "I don't like Rosa's house."

"I didn't leave you, an' Rosa is a nice lady," Jan said gently. "She wouldn't hurt you. You are getting to be a big boy now. You have to start school soon, so you have to learn to be away from Mama sometimes."

"Don't like school either," Corky replied shortly. "Don't like school, an' don't like Rosa."

With that he slid from his chair, wiped his mouth on his shirt sleeve, and made his way to the front of the diner, where he leaned against an empty chair and stared solemnly out the window.

Rosa soon noticed him standing there and stopped behind him.

Patting him gently on the head, she said, "Mama Rosa din' treat you so bad. You shouldn't run out on me like that."

Corky did not even look up at her but reached up with his free hand and slapped at her hand as she ruffled his hair. Ducking down away from her touch, he again ran down the steps to the street.

It was several days before she was again able to get a word or smile from him, and she noted that he would never stay in a room alone with her, no matter how nicely she treated him.

Later she commented to Jan, "That li'l feller got a build-in dislike for people. Lord knows he prob'ly got good reason, but it sure seems uncommon for one so young. I bet school is gonna be hell for him."

CHAPTER 28

▼

Jan and Bob did not get together again for some time, but it was not for lack of interest on either of their parts.

Bob was away for several days, but when he came back, he came into the diner and, with his laughing, joshing manner, tried repeatedly to commit Jan to another date. She would have been very pleased to accept, but each time he had her almost persuaded, she thought again of the difficulties Rosa had with Corky the first time, and she would end up making some excuse.

After one such occasion, Bob suddenly turned serious. "Look, Jan, you know an' I know the problem is the kid, right? You're gonna have to quit thinkin' of him as a baby. He's had the experience of staying a little while by himself, an' it ain't hurt him none that I can see. If he's too hardheaded to stay with Rosa, let 'im stay by himself sometimes. We can wait till he's sleeping an' then don't stay out too late. He'll never miss us. He ain't gonna go runnin' around outside after dark anyhow with no other kids around to keep him company."

Surprisingly, Janet offered no immediate objection to this suggestion. She thought it over for several minutes before she answered.

"I don't know Bob," she said finally. "He seemed so scared after last time when I came home and found him all alone. He wasn't the same for a couple of days after. He wouldn't talk or go outside or nothing'. He still won't talk to Rosa."

"Sure he was scared," Bob replied. "You would have been scared too if you got dragged off to a strange house an' locked up overnight, then turned loose in the early mornin' to make your way a mile an' a half through morning traffic by yourself, then find out your people weren't where you expected them to be. First

experiences scare everybody, but now he knows you ain't
leave him in his own house where he feels comfortable,
Christ, girl, he's gonna be going to school in a couple of
sit in class with him, are you?"

"You know that ain't the same thing, Bob," Jan replied. "There'll be all kinds
of people around then, teachers and kids. He'll be too busy to be scared."

"Don't you believe it, kid," was Bob's quick reply. "People scare that kid more
than bein' alone does. I think he likes bein' alone. He hides every time a new kid
comes in the diner, or hadn't you noticed?"

This comment from Bob made a serious impression on Jan. It was the second
time in as many days that someone had pointed out that Corky was afraid or at
least shy of people. This made her think of the problems involved in getting him
started in school.

"My God!" she exclaimed to Bob. "Why did I hafta get stuck down here in the
warehouse district to live? I can't afford to move where other people live. Eddie
told me that house used to be an old section house where the track super worked
out of. Eddie took it 'cause no one else was using it. I guess he put the cabinets
an' stuff in there. It wasn't never meant to be a real home in the first place—but
it ain't that bad for just a couple of little people like me an' Corky. I can afford it
without goin' in the hole, an' it's close to my work. What the hell would you do?
It sure don't do much for a kid. No one to play with, how the hell is he ever
gonna learn about people? Kids learn from other kids, but I can't afford to send
him to nursery school, and he doesn't know a single kid in this world by name, to
talk to or to play with."

"Oh, I wouldn't get all in a tizzy over it, Jan," Bob replied. "Kids learn fast.
Once he gets in the situation, he'll adjust quick enough."

"Well, I'll tell you one thing. I'm gonna start walking him up there about five
or six times before school starts, so he learns the way an' it won't be so strange to
him when he has to go."

"Okay, Jan," Bob said, "let's get back to the original conversation. When we
gonna go out again?"

"Gee, Bob, I'd love to," she said, and smiles, "but I jus' don't feel right about
leavin' Corky."

"Well, then, what about if I just come to your house? What's to be embarrassed about? At least we can spend some time together. I've already been there. It
didn't look so bad to me, so why worry about it. We both know how it is, an' if
that's the best you can afford, and it's clean an' comfortable for you, then don't
worry about me. I'm easy."

Okay, you win," she agreed finally. I'm not working Thursday afternoon. Why don't you come over early, an' we'll walk Corky up to the school together? Then I'll cook dinner for the three of us."

"Sure, I'll come," Bob replied, "but I ain't much on walking, an' Corky don't like me much. It would probably be better if you introduce him to that school yourself. Anyway, I have a couple of calls to make Thursday afternoon. I'll just come here when I'm all through."

Jan hesitated a moment before replying. A note of caution sprang to mind as she realized the similarity between Bob's reply and some of the comments Eddie used to make whenever she tried to get him involved with his son.

"Well, okay," she said finally, "I'll walk him up there myself. Maybe you could just come by and pick us up when I get off at one o'clock an' drive us home. Then I can start supper before we go for the walk."

"It's a date, sweetheart," he replied cheerily. "See you Thursday, if not sooner."

CHAPTER 29

▼

Leo Stronski was worried. Very often lately he found himself extremely short of breath, and he had developed a heavy, hacking cough. Sometimes when he had been working for long periods in the underground, he would fall into a heavy spasm of coughing which would, after five minutes or so, become very painful. He was more worried because of the blood spots he was finding mixed with the black sputum on his handkerchief after these coughing spells had left him weak and dizzy.

He worked many overtime hours and had a reasonably good income as a result, but the work was dangerous and dirty. He often had to lie on his back for hours under some coal-dust-covered piece of heavy equipment, breathing in the heavy black dust that constantly billowed around him as he disturbed it with his movements and his tools.

The supervisors at the mine relied on him heavily, and he never complained at the extraordinary work load they heaped on him, but now he was deeply concerned. He knew he was sick but was afraid to consult a doctor for confirmation. He feared that any prolonged illness or hospitalization would cost him his job, so he made the unconscious decision to try to "tough it out," which was ultimately a self-imposed death sentence.

He knew other miners who had left the mine with the "Black-lung" disease, and he knew also that they soon became invalid and died when they left the mine, so he determined not to let it get him down. He worked on and drank more and more heavily to relieve the nagging pain in his chest. As time went on, he no longer stopped at the taverns and liquor stores on his way home but had both beer and brandy delivered to his home by the case.

Had he realized how this stocking up would affect his rapidly growing son, he probably would not have done it. In fact, he might have done something to fight his own growing alcoholism. However, he let his concern for his own health overshadow his common sense and his concern for his family's activities. After all, Elias was in school now and by his report cards was making good progress. Leo's mother-in-law, although aging, ran his household and kept Elias clean, well dressed, and fed.

Leo continued working and drinking his way toward the cemetery, and no one took exceptional notice except Anna. She realized all was not well with him, but all had not been well with Leo ever since Julie had died, so with old-world fatalism, she accepted her burdens, thanked God for her blessing, and held her council. She often thought, however, about speaking to Leo about his drinking but could never quite take it upon herself, preferring to keep her peace and let him make his own decisions without interference.

Anna was concerned about Elias' activities though. She had been waiting for several weeks for what she considered an opportune time to mention it to Leo. Elias was missing school a lot. Often she had difficulty getting him up, he dragged himself around and was so unpleasant to her that she could not understand it. He was like a chameleon, all fun and laughter and full of mischief in the evenings and like a grizzly bear with a splinter in its paw in the mornings.

Elias was seven years old, nearly five feet tall, and well over a hundred pounds. He was also very smart. He absorbed his lessons in a no-nonsense manner, and it was seldom his teacher ever had to explain anything to him a second time. As a consequence, she had a very difficult time keeping him constructively occupied. While she worked with the slower children who needed extra coaching, Elias was into everything.

All the other children loved him and admired him, first because he was the biggest and by far the strongest of his class, and second because his mind was constantly searching for new and exciting activities. When he had first started school, she observed how quick and bright he was, and she pampered him to a certain extent. He was a very handsome boy, as well as being pleasant, outgoing, and boisterous.

Now, in his second year of school, she was beginning to have problems with him. He was often late to school and seemed unpleasant and out of sorts for the first hour or so, but usually right after morning recess, he was an altogether different person—jovial, boisterous, and so full of mischief that she could not keep up with him.

Besides tardiness, it had become a habit lately for him to miss at least one full day of school each week. He would just grin and give her some superficial explanation when she would question him about his absences, so she determined to have a conference with his parents at the earliest opportunity.

Elias' problem was alcohol. He had been drinking varying amounts of beer, wine, and brandy almost daily for nearly two years. Like all alcoholics, he was finding that he needed more and more to keep his spirits up and allay the nagging thirst that developed whenever he was too long without it.

He was too young to realize what problems he was creating for himself. He did not know that the headaches that plagued him every morning and the dull brown feeling that made him crabby and mean to his grandmother and teacher were because of what he was drinking. All he knew was that he felt much better whenever he could get a few drinks, so he established his "hidey-holes," as he called them, in various places including the school. He also knew that he always felt much better much faster if the drink he took was brandy than if it was wine or beer.

He had thought himself very clever and enjoyed the result so much after his first few experiences with the beer he had sneaked from his father that he resolved to try the other bottle as soon as possible, so he watched Leo's drinking habits carefully. He noted that he usually drank most of his bottle of brandy within an hour or two after dinner and always fell asleep. He also noted that Leo usually left some in the bottle, which he finished after he awoke from what often turned out to be a prolonged nap.

Having become quite accustomed to how sound his father slept after the brandy, he was no longer apprehensive about getting caught, as long as he made sure where his grandmother was before he made his move. He even took pains to test his father's wakefulness by untying his boots, stumbling over his foot, or patting the back of his hand as he slept. Most times these tests did not even alter Leo's breathing pattern. Elias was certain he could accomplish his trickery without fear of being caught.

His next move was to snitch a small glass from the kitchen, which he secreted away in his room.

Anna's habits he also noted carefully. Most of the time after the evening dinner dishes were done, if the weather was nice, she would put on her bonnet and shawl and go for a little walk. If the weather was bad, she either did odds and ends of housework until Elias' bedtime, or she went into her sewing room and settled down to sew.

Elias had to wait several days before everything worked out to his satisfaction, but his chance finally came. Anna was engrossed in her sewing, and Leo had been asleep for nearly half an hour. As had occurred when he stole his first drink of beer, he was so excited, he could hardly control himself.

When he was positive his opportunity had come, he slipped quietly into his room and got his glass. Back in the parlor, he stood in the shadows as before and watched his father carefully for a few minutes. The only sounds he heard were his father's smooth snoring and the steady tick-tock of the mantel clock intermingled with the heavy beating of his own heart.

Stealthily then, he crept up behind Leo's chair and set his glass on the carpet beside the lamp table. Cautiously he reached under the lampshade and lifted the open bottle of the brandy silently from the table. He bent quickly and poured the six-ounce water glass about half full of brandy, taking great care to leave at least one good drink in the bottle. Just as carefully he returned the bottle to the table near his father's right hand, picked up the glass, and slipped quietly away to the privacy of his room.

Once in his room, he switched on his light and leaned against the door, laughing delightedly to himself. He held the glass up and looked through the clear amber liquid in the light. Then he held it below his nose and sniffed it a couple of times. The fumes tickled his nose and made his eyes water slightly.

Altogether pleased with his accomplishment, he suddenly tipped the glass and took a mouthful, which he started to swallow. What he had not realized was that brandy, when poured over a warm surface like the tongue, tends to rise in fumes into the nose and then down into his lungs, not bubble in the mouth like beer. As the hot-tasting liquid rushed down his throat when he gasped, and upward into his nasal passages as he exhaled, he coughed violently and blew most of his first mouthful in a fine mist across his room.

Thoroughly alarmed by the fiery reaction from this new drink, he almost decided to run into the bathroom and flush the remainder, but he recovered his composure shortly, and the sudden warm flush that came to his face and the rush of exhilaration from his fume-agitated brain changed his mind.

Approaching it more cautiously, as he had done on his second attempt with the beer, he took a much smaller sip and let it run slowly about in his mouth, then swallowed. He realized immediately the more patent reaction from Papa's "big medicine."

He set the remaining brandy on his dresser and danced a little jig.

"Hup, hup, hup!" he cried. "Papa's medicine is the real ham an' eggs. Hi, hi, hi!" and he turned a couple of quick somersaults on his rug.

Then he lay on his back on the floor and kicked his heels up and down, laughing happily to himself. Over fifteen or twenty minutes he drank the other ounce or two of brandy, a sip or two at a time.

After hiding his glass again in the very back of his closet under some toys, he turned out his light and slipped back into the hallway, where he stopped at Anna's sewing room and told her he was going outside. Again, for more than an hour he excitedly ran off the effects of the drink.

CHAPTER 30

▼

As time went on Elias came to realize that Leo did not really know how much beer or brandy he actually drank. The beer bottles he returned to the store, but the brandy bottles were always discarded. It was a simple matter for Elias to retrieve an empty bottle from the alley trash can.

Anna's habit was to return Leo's empty brandy bottles to the case in the pantry until all the bottles were empty and then place the whole case of bottles in the trash. Elias knew this and so watched for his opportunity. When she had replaced the empty case with a full one and Leo had used two or three, he would wait until she made her daily trip to the little grocery store down the street. Then he would quickly substitute an empty bottle for a full one in the case and hide the full bottle.

When he had come to the point of regularly stealing full bottles instead of single drinks, he no longer hid it in his room but found a couple "hidey-holes" outside the house. In this manner he was able to visit these places while outside at play, so his risk of discovery was considerably lessened.

He also made it a habit to pick up his father's empties and dispose of them in the cases as Anna did. He either made sure that Anna saw him do it, or he told her that he had done it, so she would not be surprised to see him carrying a bottle.

Several times he had noticed, when Anna was hugging him or helping him get ready for school, that she would sniff suspiciously.

One time she exclaimed, "Elias, you must be more careful with Papa's beer bottles. You have spilled it on you shirt. Little boys can't go in school with beer smell. Go change your shirt quickly!"

Elias did not argue and hastily complied. From that moment on he was much more careful not to approach her too closely when he was drinking, or to turn his head away from her when she was fussing over him. As much as he loved her and liked the comfort of her hugs and kisses, he was afraid she would discover his secret, so he began keeping his distance, and the pleasant intimacy was lost forever.

A younger and more worldly woman would probably have caught on to his activities much sooner. Although Anna loved him deeply, she was never as physically close or as mentally attuned to his habits or actions as the normal mother would have been. In fact, if Elias had not been much above average intelligence and so very clever, he would probably have been caught within the first three or four episodes.

Fortunately, he never drank to the point of incapacitation, only taking frequent sips to stay "up" when he was feeling hung over or low in spirits. He was such a naturally active child in the first place that he need not rely on the chemical boost of the alcohol. When other children were about, he hardly thought about drinking at all.

The other boys his age in the neighborhood and in school accorded him the same kind of loving attention as would have been shown for a Saint Bernard dog or a pony. He was everyone's pet. At play on school days they invented rough-and-tumble games where Elias was one team and four or five of the more hardy lads were the other.

They played "hunt the elephant" or gorilla games, in which Elias was the beast and the others were the hunters. They would run and chase and tumble, as many as four or five of them being unable to catch and hold him or to knock him off his feet. He would seize one of the smaller ones under one arm, swing another across his shoulder, and run clumsily away with them.

Because of his size and strength, his little friends soon tagged him with the nickname "Chimp," and he delighted in acting the part with his friends hanging on for the ride. He hated to see anything or anyone physically hurt, and it was almost impossible for them to hurt him. Having never experienced the love and tenderness of a mother and having been loved only casually by his father, he extracted every squeeze of adulation he could from his little friends, his teacher, admiring adult neighbors, and his grandmother.

Though he loved the rough physical contact, he tried very hard never to hurt any of his playmates or to displease his adult friends. Somehow he knew it would displease a lot of people if his secret was known. He lived in a quandary. He liked the "buzz" he got from the beer and liquor. Being such an outgoing and friendly person, he would have loved to share Papa's "big medicine" with his friends, but his father's stern warnings weighted heavily on his mind. Somehow he knew that sharing would most certainly bring disaster, so he drank alone. The newest and biggest joy in his life, he could not share. Thus a new dimension in friendships came unexpectedly into Elias' life.

One fall Saturday morning when Elias was approaching eight years old, Anna was not feeling well. She always waited until Saturday to do the bulk of her grocery shopping, because Elias was there to help. Leo had bought him a coaster wagon, and he always went with her. When her order was put together, she relied on him to load it in his wagon, pull it home, and help her put it away. He loved doing it and always persuaded Anna to buy a few of his favorite foods and goodies for him—but today Anna was too ill to go.

When she did not get up to give Elias his breakfast, he fixed his own cereal and milk and some bread and jelly. After hanging around for a little while waiting, he decided to wake her up. To his surprise, she was already awake but looked so pale and sick that he felt immediately sorry for her.

He lay across the bed, throwing his arms around her, and said, "I love you. Grandma. Can I help?"

"God bless you, Elias, my darling. You help Grandma just to be here with me."

"Don't you feel good, Grandma? You look sick."

"Yes, Grandma sick, but my Elias not worry. I be all right soon," she answered.

"What about the store, Grandma? We always go to the store on Saturday."

"Well, Elias, you father prob'ly go when he comes home this afternoon. Grandma can't go today."

"I can go for you, Grandma. Papa is going to be tired. He don't want to go to the store when he been working since seven."

"You never been to store alone, Elias. You big, but you still little boy. You not know how to do shopping."

"But Grandma," Elias objected, "I can read now. I can count money. If you tell me the list, I can write it down. We don't have to buy everything. I won't buy nothing for me. I'll just get what you say, okay? Please let me, Grandma!"

He was so sure and so sincere in his desire to help that Anna finally agreed.

"You get paper and pencil, write what Grandma say, but you must be very careful with money, okay? Don't show money to anyone except cashier, and be sure to bring receipt from register, so Grandma can check everything."

Elias jumped for joy. "You really going to let me, Grandma? I can do it, Grandma. You will see."

He ran to get the paper and pencil and was soon on his way, pulling the wagon down the street.

He felt so good and so pleased with himself that he decided to celebrate with a little drink. He turned down the alley and onto the vacant lot where he had his bottle of brandy stashed. He let go of his wagon and knelt by the old chimney tile, half buried in the weeds and dirt. He reached inside it, pulled out his bottle, and took a couple of sips, then a larger drink. After recapping the bottle, he put it back and folded the weeds and brush back over the end of the tile.

The chemical excitement seized him almost immediately. He grabbed the tongue of his wagon and made a couple of running circles on the lot, then back into the alley, happily buzzing the sound of a shifting truck as he ran. He decided not to go back to the street but continued down the alley to an interconnecting alley that ran alongside the grocery store.

He was still running when he came to the corner. He turned it sharply and had to come to a sliding stop to keep from running into two men who were leaning against the side of the building in the sunshine. Startled, he stood there and stared.

One of the men approached him and stepped one ragged and dirty boot into Elias' coaster wagon. He reached out a big dirty hand and ruffled Elias' thick brown hair. The other stood there grinning and pulled the cork from a bottle of wine he was holding. Tipping it back, he took a drink and handed the bottle to the other man.

"Hey, there, little man," the first man said, "where you driving this truck to so early on a Saturday?"

"I got to go shopping for my grandma. She's sick, sir," Elias answered politely.

"Good man," he replied. "I wish I could still help my ol' gramma, but she would'n even know me now. Hey, Piney, let's drink a toast to ol' Gran."

He tipped back the bottle, had a drink, an passed it to his friend.

"Here's to good old Granny, a real good Jill, an' wherever she's planted, I love her still," he said as his friend took his turn at the bottle.

His laughed loudly.

"Sam, ye're a real kick in the ass. Yer granma was probably Satan's sister and a Scollay Square trotter at that, but I'll drink to the ol' bat anyways."

He took another turn at the bottle.

"Gardamn, Piney," Sam said suddenly, "we ain't been polite at all to our guest here. Mebbe he'll take a taste to Gran too."

Grinning, he turned and offered the bottle to Elias. To both their amazement, he took it, tipped it back, and took a long swallow.

"That's good wine, sir," he said solemnly as he handed back the bottle. "Thank you."

At this the two bums laughed and laughed till the tears came running down their faces.

"If you ain't a jewel, li'l man, I ain't never seen one. What your name is, kid? You the best I seen in this town!"

"I'm Chimp Stronski," he replied, holding out his chubby hand.

The bums laughed again but shook hands with him, introducing themselves as Sam Davis and Piney Woods.

"We're just two gentlemen of the road, waiting for our nex' job," Sam told him. "We pick apples when they's any to pick."

The three of them stood there in the alley, chatting, for twenty minutes or so. The two middle-aged vagrants were amused and at the same time impressed by Elias. Presently they offered him another drink, which he willingly took.

"How the hell a li'l man like you learn to drink like that?" Sam asked him finally.

"I like it," Elias answered truthfully. "It makes me feel good."

The two bums laughed loudly again.

"You ain't but ten years old." Piney said. "How come you drinking like this?"

"I drink a little bit nearly every day." Elias answered, "and I'm not ten years old, I'm seven."

"Don't you folks tell you it's bad for little boys to drink?" Sam asked.

"My papa said I shouldn't," Elias confessed, "but he drinks two bottles every day, and he's the biggest and strongest man in this town. He says I am going to be the strongest man in Pennsylvania someday. Nobody knows I drink this stuff except you guys. I don't drink lots like Papa. Only a little bit, and I do like it."

"Well, boy," Sam said, "your papa is right. Drinking this stuff is gonna cause you lots of trouble. Kids should'n drink nothing but milk an' sodey pop. I started when I was pretty young, but Cheez Chris', I can't believe a seven-year-old that chugs Dago Red like it was sodey pop. You okay, kid, but you headin' for trouble."

"Hey, looka here, we all outta wine, an' you still gotta get Granma's groceries. You're a real champ, kid an' we like you, but you better lay off this strong stuff. See you aroun', li'l man. You're a great guy."

Elias shook hands politely and said, "Glad to know you men. I like you too. Good-bye."

Elias went on to the store, and his two new friends stood looking after him.

"I wonder if he'shittin' us, Sam," Piney mused. "He's too damn big an bright to be seven, an' I can't believe no seven-year-old is chunking Dago Red like a yardbird."

"Anyways, he's a great kid," Sam said. "How many kids tole you they like you in your lazy life, Piney? Really great kid, an' smart an' funny. I'd like to see him some more."

Elias hurried through his shopping. He had done this with Anna many times, so he had no trouble finding all the items on the list, including a case of his father's favorite beer.

When he went to check his items out through the cashier, she told him, "I'm sorry, but I can't sell beer to little boys."

The store manager happened to be standing near and heard the comment. He was well acquainted with Anna and had seen Elias shopping with her on other occasions.

"Where is your Grandma today?" he asked.

"She is sick, sir," Elias answered politely, "and she let me do the shopping by myself."

"Let me see your list." he said.

Elias promptly handed it to him. The beer was the third item on his list.

Turning to the cashier, the manager said, "It's okay, Helen. If his Grandma put it on the list and she is sick, we better let this little gentleman bring it home. I'm sure he will not cause us any trouble. He's a good lad," and he ruffled Elias' hair with a friendly hand.

"By the way, young man, if you are big enough to shop for your grandma and get it home okay, I can find you some other delivery jobs around here, and you can make some spending money for yourself if your grandma says it's all right. Would you like that?"

Elias jumped excitedly. "I can do it, sir," he almost shouted.

"Well, tell your grandma to talk to me about it, and we'll see. Now you better get that stuff home, so she won't be worrying."

Elias thought all the way home about this very eventful morning. He was really pleased that he might have a chance to make some money on his own. He was even more excited about having met men who treated him more or less as an equal rather than as a child. It had really surprised him that there were adults who thought him old enough to join them for a drink, in spite of the fact they had criticized him in an offhanded way for accepting. He was curious about their ragged appearance and rough manner and made up his mind to talk to his grandma about them to see what she would say.

When he got home, he carried the groceries a few items at a time into the house and put them on the kitchen table. He put away his wagon and ran excitedly into Anna's room to tell her about the shopping and the men. He found she had gone back to sleep. Reluctantly but quietly he slipped from the room and went to sit on the front steps and wait for his father to come home from the mine.

He had been sitting there for twenty minutes or so, thinking about the morning's experiences. He was quite pleased with himself and the world in general. He had completed his grandma's shopping all alone, had been complimented by the store manager for doing it so well, and possibly rewarded with a job in the bargain. He also had two new friends with a very special mutual interest. He knew he could not discuss that part with his family, but he could hardly wait for Anna to awake or for his father to come home.

Suddenly he heard laughter and voices from down the block and turned to look. To his surprise and pleasure, there were his two men friends approaching, walking rather unsteadily and laughing as they came. Another wine bottle jutted jauntily from Piney Woods' jacket pocket.

"Well, darn my socks," said Sam as they approached the steps where Elias was sitting, "If it ain't our friend Chimp sittin' here atop the world. This where you live?"

Elias grinned and nodded.

"Didja get them groceries home okay?" Piney asked.

"Yes, sir, I did," Elias answered, "and I'm waiting for my papa to come home from work."

No sooner had he said this than Leo came around the corner and rapidly down the block. Long before he stopped at the steps, Elias could tell he had been drinking.

"Can I help you men?" he asked gruffly as he came up.

Elias jumped up and ran to him.

"Papa, these are my new friends," he said proudly. "This is Sam, and this is Piney." Turning to the two vagrants, he said, "This is my papa, Leo Stronski."

"What you mean, friends?" Leo asked. "How you know these men?"

"Oh, he don't mean he really knows us," Sam said quickly, not wanting to get the boy in trouble. "We just seen him sittin' here an' stopped to jaw a bit."

He stuck out his hand, which Leo ignored.

Leo towered over the other two. He glowered at them and said flatly, "Some-time little boys not know what they do. Elias, you know not to talk to strange man you don't know. Now go in house an' help you Grandma!"

'But Papa," Elias started to explain, but Leo's scowl cut him off.

As Elias reluctantly turned to go in, Leo said, "If you gentlemen lost, maybe I give direction, but I don't want you should hang aroun' here an' bother my family."

He turned abruptly and went inside.

Sam and Piney looked at each other and went off down the street without further comment.

Elias had stopped just inside the door and heard his father's curt dismissal of his friends. Tears started in his eyes as he ran down the hall to his room, where Leo soon followed. He found Elias sitting on the edge of his bed, sulking.

"Elias, you mus' not talk to such men again," Leo admonished. "These men no good. You see they drunk. They got wine in their pocket. They never work. Little boys not supposed to be friend with bums, okay?"

"Papa, they told me they work on farms. They pick apples," Elias said.

"Maybe for one day they work, then they buy wine an' git drunk till money all gone. No house, no food, no family. Elias, these men bums, an' you don't talk to them anymore. Papa goin' be very mad if they come here again, you unnerstan'?"

He cupped his hand under Elias' chin and bored into his eyes with a hard stare.

"Yes, Papa," Elias answered and dropped onto his side on the bed, turning away from Leo.

Leo stood there for a few seconds, hoping he had properly impressed his son with the seriousness of the situation. Had he known Elias' thoughts at the moment, he might have saved his breath.

Elias' mind was heavy in conflict with what he perceived to be the facts of the situation. Sam and Piney had been pleasant, friendly, and giving. His father, in contrast, was gruff, unpleasant, and unreasonable. He could see no harm in these men. Contrary to what his father said, they claimed to work for what they got. As for the drinking, his father drank more than anyone he knew, yet he labeled these men as drunks. This was a contradiction he simply could not reconcile in his bright young mind. He determined to straighten it out with his grandmother as soon as he could get her alone.

From this moment on, for several years to come, Elias' gut feeling was that his father was somehow being less than honest with him. He had been preaching to him as long as he could remember, "Drinking is bad for you," and yet in fact, he,

Elias, got nothing but joy from it. Besides, his father drank constantly, which belied his advice. Further, he named his friends unacceptable because they drank. It was complete contradiction, therefore completely false.

CHAPTER 31

▼

Bob met Jan at the diner on Thursday as agreed and drove her and Corky home. He did not stay at all, telling Jan he had a few more calls to make.

Jan went inside and began preparing dinner. She put a large chunk of corned beef on to boil. She washed and cut her vegetables and tidied the house a little. Then she called Corky into the house. She washed his face and hands, combed his hair, and talked to him all the while about starting school in just a month.

Jan had neglected education matters until the last minute, as many busy mothers do. She had not prepared Corky in any way for the forthcoming change in his life. She had never so much as shown him a book. As a matter of fact, she did not even own one. She had never bought him pencils, crayons, or paper or made any attempt to explain what school was.

Never having had any playmates who might have given him some slight introduction, Corky became increasingly apprehensive about school, which his mother seemed to be constantly bringing up now. She had mentioned it many times recently but had not explained in any detail, only that it was something he had to do.

Now, only a month in advance, she tried to make up for lost time. She talked about reading and writing and playing with other children. She talked about teachers, obedience, and studying, all of which only served to increase Corky's anxiety, since he understood little of it.

Today, when she had Corky all clean and fresh, she took him by the hand and told him they were going to visit this place called school, which became more mysterious and frightening to him each time it came up. As they strolled along in the August sunshine, Jan described the joys of school. She told him what fun it would be, how exciting it would be to have all these new friends, and what a beautiful place school was. She also told him how nice teachers were and what a big help they would be to him.

As she talked, she pointed out the obvious landmarks along the way, a skill that Corky had developed on his own to a much greater degree than Jan could have imagined. She made it plain to him that he would be going to and from school alone after the first couple of times.

"So you better watch and learn, so you can remember your way back home," she told him.

"Mama, I don't like school, so why do I hafta go?"

"Oh, don't be silly, Corky." Jan replied. "Everyone goes to school. In America, everybody goes to school, at least until they are sixteen years old."

"When will I be sixteen years old?" Corky asked quickly.

Jan laughed at this. "You are really something, Corky. You ain't even six yet an' haven't even started school, an' here you are thinkin' when you can quit."

"Well, I just don't want to go," Corky said stubbornly.

They were walking along arguing back and forth about school when suddenly Jan said, "Look, Corky see that fence across the street. Well, inside that fence is the playground, and the school is at the other end. See that big building down there. That's your school."

Corky made his feeling very plain.

'It ain't my school, an' I don't want it," he said emphatically.

Jan laughed again. "Wait until you see it, will you? It's going to be real nice, you'll see."

All that Corky could see was that it was an enormously high fence, and he had no desire to be shut away inside.

The school was an ancient brownstone building set back perhaps eighty feet from the street. There was no exit from the eight-foot-high chain link fence, except into the school building. There were two entrances to the building on the side from which Jan and Corky approached, one inside the fence and the other outside. Both were secured with massive double doors with opaque panels. The chain link joined the building exactly halfway between the two entrances. It ran all the way around the school grounds, which occupied most of one city block.

Walking further around the building, Jan was pleased to see that the fence joined the building again on the back corner, and there was another entrance into the building inside this back fence. One side of the school, across the street, was flanked by the long rows of warehouse buildings that ran for several blocks, the other side of which stood Jan's and Corky's tiny house in the field by itself. It crossed Jan's mind to hunt a shorter route for Corky between these warehouses, but then she thought better of it.

It will be safer for him, she thought, if he keeps to the sidewalks where there are always people watching.

On the other side of the school grounds was a mixture of older residences and office building, which comprised the outward southern edge of the Chicago residential area.

Jan led Corky up the steps, and they stood there for a few minutes looking around. There was a printed sign on the door announcing that registration for school would start on the first of September for all new students. They walked together down the steps, and Jan took Corky close to the fence. Kneeling down to his level, she pointed inside, explaining about the swings and climbing toys, the ball diamond, teeter-totter, and sandboxes.

Corky was unimpressed.

"Why do they have a fence?" he asked suddenly.

"Because, Corky," Jan explained, "it is dangerous to have kids playing in the street, and the fence keeps them where it is safe. It also keeps people who are not supposed to bother the kids from getting in."

Corky had been playing in or near the street and in unfenced areas all his life, and all he could see was that someone was going to try to lock him up again as Rosa had done a few weeks before.

"I'm not staying in no fence," he exclaimed suddenly. "Let's go home."

Jan was concerned about the boy's stubborn refusal to accept what to her was the natural and inevitable course of things. All the way home she did her best to paint a clear picture of the fun and excitement that awaited Corky just one month from now.

When they got home, Jan hugged him and said, "Well, that's not so far, is it? Do you think you can go there by yourself?"

Corky, stubborn as ever, replied, "I don't like it, an' I ain't gonna go there."

Jan shook her head, and as she busied herself with dinner, Corky slipped out the door. Still agitated and apprehensive about what he considered going to prison, he began running, at first aimlessly and then with purpose, around and around the house. As he ran, his mind and his heart both pounded the message in rhythm with his flying feet, "Not gonna go to school...not gonna go to school..."

He was still running when Bob arrived an hour later. Corky went past as Bob came up the path to the steps.

"Whoa there, Corky!" he called. "Where you going so fast?'

Corky completely ignored him and disappeared around the corner, only to reappear amazingly soon around the opposite corner. Bob tried to block his path and stop him, but Corky easily avoided him and kept on running. Bob went inside.

"Hey, Jan," he called in greeting to her, "that kid of yours is running like a damn whirlwind around the house. He's soaking wet with sweat. What the hell is he trying to prove?"

"Oh, don't worry about him," Jan replied. "He always runs when he's mad about something. He'll get over it when he gets tired."

She put down the dish she was holding and kissed him lightly.

"Hope you're hungry," she said. "I made a nice Irish dinner for you."

"Hey, lady, I smelled that corned beef and cabbage before I even got out of the car," he told her, laughing. "How did you know my favorite meal?"

"Just a lucky guess," Jan said and continued to get the dinner together.

They chatted as she worked, and soon the meal was ready.

"Do me a favor Bob, and call Corky," Jan said, "an' then we can eat."

Bob went to the door and waited until Corky appeared.

"C'mon an' eat, little man," he called as Corky went by.

Corky acted as though he were deaf and continued running. Bob called him a second time as he went by again. Still there was no response.

"Hey, Jan," Bob said, "I think your kid is gone bananas."

At this, Jan stopped what she was doing and went to the door just in time to see Corky speed by. She went down the steps and waited. When he came by again, she reached out and caught him by the arm. He made no special effort to avoid her.

She brought him in the house and went through her earlier cleanup routine again. He was sweating so heavily, she might as well not have made the effort. When she had him in reasonably presentable condition, she led him to the table and lifted him into his chair.

Corky was not pleased. He was agitated enough about school, and now his mother was making him eat dinner with a man he hated. He leaned back in his chair and fixed Bob with a cold stare with his good eye, while the other jumped and twitched spasmodically.

During the thirty or forty minutes while Jan and Bob ate, Corky did not move or drop his eyes for a moment. In spite of numerous promptings from Jan to eat his dinner, he continued to hold Bob with an icy glare and ignored his food.

Only when they had finished and left the table did Corky finally begin eating. When he was done, he slid from his chair and went to the far corner of the room. Crouched in the corner, back to the wall, he resumed staring at Bob.

After nearly an hour, Bob became so agitated that he could not concentrate on his and Jan's conversation.

Finally he told her, "Can't you send that kid outside or get him to play or something? I'm beginning to feel like the prize pig at the county fair. What the hell ails him anyway?"

"Corky, stop that!" Jan exclaimed. "Why are you acting like that? Bob is our friend. Now come over here and tell him you're sorry, and be a good boy."

Corky got up quickly and left the house without a word. He did not come back until he saw Bob get into his car and drive away.

CHAPTER 32

▼

August of 1941 went by quickly, and Jan had walked Corky to the school several times during the month. She had given him all the details she could remember of her beginning school days and tried her best to convince him how much he was going to like it. However, the response she got after the first few stories was taciturn silence from Corky.

One afternoon as they were walking toward the school, she noticed that Corky was lagging behind and looking back and across the street.

"What are you looking at, Corky?" she asked.

"That man keeps watching us," Corky said. "Who is he?"

Jan looked carefully up and down the block but saw no one who looked as though they were watching or interested in them.

"What man, Corky?" she asked. "I don't see anyone."

Corky pointed toward an alley that led back through the warehouse district toward where they lived.

"He was there by that building," Corky replied. "He watched us the other day too."

Jan looked again but saw no one. "Well, Corky, I don't see anyone. I think you are imaging things."

They went on to the school and walked completely around the block. Corky still seemed concerned about the man he had seen. When they were going home, she crossed the street so the would pass directly in front of the alley where Corky had claimed to see whoever it was he was suspicious about.

As they approached the alley, she became suddenly apprehensive, because she glanced up and thought she saw someone peeking around the corner from the alley. She moved out to the outside of the sidewalk and approached cautiously. They came to a spot where they could see down the alley, just in time to see someone in an obvious hurry duck around the corner out of sight.

"That's him! Corky cried. "Did you see him, Mama?"

A cold chill ran down Jan's back. She did not want to worry Corky, but she was suddenly very worried about her decision to let Corky go back and forth to school by himself. She was almost certain the shadowy figure she had seen disappear down the alley was Eddie.

"Yes, Corky," she replied, trying to sound confident, "but I think it was just someone who probably works around here. Don't worry about it."

"Okay, Mama" Corky said, "but I know he was watching us."

For the rest of their walk home, Jan coached Corky on the dos and don'ts of talking to strangers and what to do if anyone bothered him on the street. She carefully avoided stating her concerns about who it was. She did not know if Corky remembered his father as far as she knew, Corky had not seen Eddie for over two years, and she did not know if he would remember him. She sincerely hoped he would not. She had no intention of reminding him of his father if there was no really good reason to do so.

Jan mentioned her fears to both Rosa and Bob. She really did not know what to expect from Eddie, and she was not certain it had been him. If it were him, she could see no reason for him to conceal the fact that he had been watching them unless he had some mischief in mind. Call it a mother's intuition, but she definitely felt uneasy.

Bob, said, "What the hell harm can he do? It's a busy street. He's only a bum, and it will be daylight. Why invent trouble?"

Rosa, on the other hand, agreed with Jan. "Why the hell would he run, unless he's tryna hide something'? If you want, I can get one of the guys, maybe Charlie, to give 'im a li'l scare just to be safe. I used to see him on the street once in a while, but I ain't seen 'im in ages. You sure it was him?"

"Almost certain," Jan replied. "I didn't get much of a look at him, but he obviously didn't want me an' Corky to see him. He looked like a street bum, an' he was small an' skinny like Eddie. The more I think about it, the surer I am it was him."

CHAPTER 33

▼

Jan took Corky to school to register him on Wednesday. The school was a hub-bub of action. Children by the dozens were coming and going with their parents—some with mothers, some with fathers, some with both.

It was easy to tell which children were newcomers. They clung tightly to parents hands or hung behind but close to the adults and peeked shyly or apprehensively at each other. Many of the parents were apparently acquainted, quite in contrast to Jan and Corky, who knew no one there, young or old.

This contingent of older children ran scurrying about in the crowd, playing hide-and-seek behind the adults in doorways and halls and exchanging laughing greetings and insults with friends from last year. They had been the clinger and weepers at this time last year but were thoroughly enjoying themselves now.

Corky hung close behind Jan but did very little looking around. Mainly he stared, hard-faced, at the floor as they waited in line where the alphabetical group, G through M, containing Hackett, was being processed.

Occasionally some forward or curious child, usually a second or third-grade student, would come down the line asking the new children their names or where they lived. Those who approached Corky were either treated to a sudden view of his back or a cold hostile stare.

One very pretty little blonde girl, who seemed to know practically everyone in sight, stopped and seized Corky's hand and turned him toward her.

"What's your name?" she asked him as she pulled him around.

He gave her his coldest stare and jerked away his hand so violently that he caused her to stumble forward and run into Jan, who had been visiting with the lady just ahead of them in line. When the little blonde head ran heavily into her thigh, she turned and caught hold of the child to keep her from falling.

The little girl recovered quickly and scowled at Corky.

"What's wrong with you anyway?" she asked angrily.

Corky, not used to the curiosity or company of other children, replied icily, "Don't you touch me!"

Again he turned his back to her.

Indignantly the little blonde put her hands on her hips and shouted. "Who wants to know you anyway? You're ugly!"

The angry tone and loud voice attracted the attention of several other children who apparently knew and liked her. Very soon there were several of them in a half-circle near Corky, whispering, pointing, and laughing.

Jan put up with it for several minutes, ignoring them, but Corky became increasingly agitated. He moved to the opposite side of her so that Jan was between him and the group of mocking faces. However, within seconds, the half-circle began to form on that side, causing him to switch back again. Finally Jan and the lady she was talking with began to take serious note of what was happening, and they scolded the children and told them to go play.

The blonde child was not to be dissuaded. Every few minutes she would dash by with one or two of hr friends and call out, "Redheaded creep!" or "Ratface!" or something similar.

Finally Jan began inquiring of other people nearby whether they knew who the child's mother was. After questioning several adults and children, she was directed to a beautiful blonde, well-dressed young woman who was standing near the wall, talking to two persons who were obviously officials of the school.

Leading Corky by the hand, Jan left her place in line and walked up to the lady.

"Excuse me," she said, "does that little girl belong to you?"

She pointed the child out.

"Yes, she said sweetly. "That's my Patricia. Isn't she pretty?"

"Yes, she is pretty," Jan replied, "but she doesn't act pretty. She has been teasing and bothering my son for some time. Would you please speak to her?"

The young woman scowled, and a slight flush came to her face. She went quickly and brought the child back to where Jan and Corky were standing.

"Patricia, this lady said you are bothering her little boy."

"Mama, I only asked him his name," she said innocently, "and then he tried to knock me down."

Turning her back to Jan, the lady stroked the golden curls and instructed her daughter, "Say you are sorry to the baby boy, darling, and then stay away from him. We don't need to know people like that anyway."

She walked haughtily back to her friends.

Jan's blood began to boil, and she gave serious consideration to knocking the woman out of her high-heeled shoes. However, she soon got control of herself without blowing up, and she and Corky returned to their place in line.

Within a few minutes they were standing in front of the registration table. Registering Corky took only a short time. Jan was given a room number and a teacher's name—Miss Humphrey. The lady at the registration table gave Corky a lollipop and told them to go to the classroom and meet the teacher.

Miss Humphrey was a tall, heavy woman in flat shoes, gray skirt, and dark blue blouse. If told to guess her age, Jan would have made it somewhere between forty and fifty-five. She had graying hair, pulled back in a bun and pinned tightly so it pulled her high forehead as smooth as the world globe on her desk. Jan thought she would look more at home leaning over a scrub board and washtub than in a first-grade classroom.

Her voice was as dark and heavy as her manner of dress as she said, "Hello", to Jan and Corky.

"This is your teacher, Corky," Jan said. "Mrs. Humphrey, this is Corky Hackett, my son."

"Please, it is <u>Miss</u> Humphrey, if you don't mind," she said in her deep-throated purr. "You don't have any other children in this school, do you, Mrs. Hackett?"

"No," Jan replied, "Corky is my only child."

"I thought so," said Miss Humphrey. "I know every child and family who has passed through this school in twenty years. I do not remember any Hacketts. What is the child's proper name?"

Jan flushed and replied quickly, "His name is Corky."

"Come now, Mrs. Hackett, we do not use nicknames here. We try to keep things proper. Part of getting an education is learning the difference between right and wrong and proper and improper." She looked sternly down her nose at Jan.

"All right," Jan confessed nervously. "Corky is a nickname, but he has no given name. His birth certificate reads C.Q. Hackett, but I don't want him called C.Q."

She opened her purse and took out the offending document, extremely sorry at that moment that she had neglected her vow to get it legally changed. She passed it to Miss Humphrey, who gazed momentarily at it and handed it back.

"How very odd. C.Q.," she said musingly. "Why would anyone name a child C.Q.?"

"I don't want to go into it," Jan said impatiently.

To her extreme discomfort, she suddenly found herself sweating profusely.

"I prefer he be called Corky," she said flatly.

"I will take it up with the principal and advise you," the matron growled distastefully.

Jan could sense disapproval in every nerve. It was as though Jan had deliberately challenged her sensibilities with two unacceptable choices. Her intuition told her that the woman would probably call Corky anything but one of those choices.

She showed Jan briefly around the classroom and explained the school's rules on everything from wet pants to recess and lunch, including her personal philosophy on "Immediate and appropriate" discipline for problem children. She emphasized "Problem" and stared directly at Corky as though she had already consigned him to that status in her mind.

After their brief tour for the mother, she challenged Corky directly.

"All right, young man, I want you to be here Monday to start learning. Miss Humphrey does not put up with any nonsense from children. Do you understand?"

She ended up hanging directly over Corky's head like some great gray thunderstorm and emphasizing every word.

Corky's heartbeat was echoing the now-familiar phrase to his innermost self, "Don't like school...don't like school..."

Jan and Corky walked quickly and quietly home. Between apprehensively watching the side streets and alleys for Eddie and pondering the total unpleasantness of the afternoon, Jan could not bring herself to try to impress the boy further with the virtues of school. Corky was preoccupied with his dislike for the little strangers who had mocked and teased him, and with apprehension over the confrontation with the big unpleasant woman who was to be his teacher.

They walked in silence—but for Corky the unpleasantness of the day was not over. When they came around the corner in front of their house, the first thing that caught Corky's eye was Bob's car parked in the dirt next to the doorstep. One car door and the trunk stood open, and Bob, in coveralls, knelt on the top step. Tools of various sizes and shapes were scattered around him.

"What the hell you doing, Robert?" Jan challenged.

"Hi, kids," Bob called cheerfully. "I thought I would surprise you by putting a lock on your door. That way you won't hafta worry when you are gone out, or when you're home by yourself. It will be a lot safer."

"Jeez, Bob, we got by for a long time now with no lock. It's nice you thought about us, but I don't know if we really need it," Jan replied.

"Hey, too late now to talk about it, honey." Bob grinned. "I almost got it done. Besides, if the kid's ol' man is really up to some mischief, it's better you should be able to lock the door."

Jan shook her head to silence him and glanced down at Corky. He was looking up at her with a questioning look on his face.

"What's he talking about, Mom?" he asked anxiously.

"Nothing, Corky, forget it. Bob was only joking with us, weren't you, Bob?" She nodded at him, asking him to confirm her statement.

"C'mon Jan, you mean you ain't goin' to tell him? Let the kid grow up a little, so he knows what the world's all about. How you expect him to protect himself if he don't know what to look for?"

"Damn it, Bob, shut up, will you? I'll decide what's good for him. Let him alone!" Jan almost shouted. "C'mon, Corky, let's go in an' change your clothes an' get something to eat."

She looked down at Corky, who again was staring hatefully at Robert and backing slowly away. Suddenly he turned and took off at a run across the lot toward the warehouses. Jan stood and watched him go with tears in her eyes.

Corky did not return to the house until late that evening. When Bob's car finally started up and pulled out of the yard, Corky came home, scuffing through the dust and weeds of the lot to where his mother sat waiting on the rickety front step.

CHAPTER 34

▼

Elias defied his father and rationalized it by remembering that his father said he did not want to <u>see</u> the men at his house anymore. As long as they did not come near the house, he determined to carry on the acquaintance. He made a concerted search of the streets and alleys of the neighborhood over the next few days until he again stumbled upon his newfound friends.

Sam was lying on top of a half wall under a big maple tree with his jacket as a pillow, not quite awake but not quite asleep either. Piney sat in a sunny spot a few yards away, enjoying the warmth of the fall afternoon. The ever-present bottle of wine stood against the wall within easy reach of Piney's hand.

"Well, kick my shins," Piney announced. "Chimp's done come vistin' agin, Sam. Sit your lazy ass up there an' say hello."

"Welcome to paradise, li'l frien'," Sam said. "What you reckon the rich folks are doin' while we're here slavin' ourselves to death in this hot sun?"

Elias smiled happily and shook hands with both of them.

"I'm awful sorry my papa wasn't nice to you the other day," he apologized in greeting, "but he gets crabby when he's tired, especially when he ain't feelin' too good."

"Don't you worry, boy," the two bums chorused together, "we din't mind at all."

They looked at each other and laughed.

Piney said, "We make it a practice not to give home folks no lip if they don't make us welcome right off."

"Yeah," Sam added, "'specially when he's big enough so's I could take a bath in one of his shoes. Have a drink, kid, an' don't bother yer head about it. In a coupla weeks we'll be on our way to Californy anyhow."

Elias looked suddenly downhearted, but took the offered drink of wine.

When he finished he exclaimed, "You mean you're moving away? You can't do that! I just met you, an' I like you, an' I thought you were going to be my friends."

"Well, Chimp," Piney said, "we're right proud you call us friends, an' we ain't gonna forget you either, but me an' Sam is always moving away, as you put it, but we always move back again sooner or later, jus' like the hands on a clock."

"Yeah," Sam put in, "The last few years the William Penn Bank here an' the Frisco Savings an' Loan in Californy been settin' their calendar by me an' Piney."

Both men laughed heartily and had their turns on the bottle.

"My Papa told me I couldn't talk to you, because you were bums," Elias said matter-of-factly, "but he must be wrong. If you travel that much, you must have money. What do you do? For work, I mean,"

"Your papa is right in a manner of speakin'," Sam replied. "We don't have regular jobs like most folks do, but we do what we hafta do to get by, an' try to stay out of other folks way, an' out of their business too."

"That's right, my friend," Piney said, "we kinda foller the sunshine. If we hang aroun' too long in one spot, it gets harder an' harder to move, but folks like us don't get burdened down with nothin' we can't carry, 'cause mostly home folks don't put out the welcome mat for our kind for very long. We work for what we need if we don't find it layin' aroun' for the takin'. We don't generally need much. Makes life pretty simple."

After that lengthy speech, Piney sighed and reached for the bottle again.

"But don't you have any kids or family?" Elias asked innocently.

"Ol' Piney there has a couple someplace," Sam told him, "but his wife run out on 'im when the banks went bust a few years back. I ain't never had no family since I was your age."

"How old are your kids, Piney?" Elias asked.

"Oh, they mus' be near growed up now." Piney said thoughtfully, "but I ain't seen nor heard of them since twenty-nine. Don't even know where they at."

"Then where do you guys live?" Elias persisted, wanting to refute in his own mind the unpleasant picture his father had painted of these friendly men.

Again the partners exchanged smiles, and Piney stood up to move closer to Sam and handed him the bottle.

"We live wherever God puts us down of an' evenin', kid," Sam said finally, "an' I figger we'll keep right on till he puts us down for the last time."

"Yeah," Piney added, "an' I don't reckon it'll make much difference where that's at neither. The box is gonna be the same size an' the hole jus' as deep as the one they make for folks that stays all their days in one big house packin' their precious stuff in around 'em."

This solemn statement quieted Elias' questioning for a short while, but his little-boy mind was still not satisfied about how and why these men were different from the other people he knew.

"But what kind of work do you do?" he asked once more.

"Well, by Gar," Sam replied, "me an' Ol' Piney'll work at any damn thing comes up if folks give us the chance. We pick cherries an' lettuce in South Jersey in May an' June, fix a porch for some widder or clean out a basement in New York or Boston in July an' August. Maybe help unload or load a ship or a train somewhere else. Then we pick apples an' pears in New York an' Pennsylvania in September an' October, corn in Illinois in October an' November. Then we hightail it for Southern Califorry in December an' pick us a couple Mexican cuties an' hibernate till things start growin' across the Southland agin."

Both men laughed heartily at this, and Elias joined in. When the laugh was over, all three had another drink.

"You about the nosiest kid I ever seen," Piney told Elias. "How come you got to know all our secrets anyhow?"

Elias shifted in embarrassment at this accusation.

"I didn't mean anything by it," he replied, kicking at the dirt with the tip of his toe. "My papa was mad 'cause I was talkin' to you, and I just wanted to know if what he said was right. If I said something wrong, I'm sorry."

"Nothin' you ask is gonna bother me an' ol' Sam, kid. Your pop is right. We probly ain't much count, an' for most folks this probly ain't no way to live. We drink too much, an' we don't get a bath too often. Sam ain't lived in a house in twenty years, an' I ain't for the last seven, but we don't owe no one anything, an' we move on when the mood hits. I guess it's kinda tit for tat. That is, nobody worries or cares too much about us, 'cause we don't have nothin' or no one but each other to worry or care about. Like I said before, it makes life pretty simple."

"Yep, my man," Sam added, "you listen to your pop. Ain't no good can come of you hangin' round guys like us. Jus' keep in mind when you grow up that all the folks that lives in the street ain't bad, an' they ain't all there by choice. I'd rather work for my needin's when I got the chance, but I ain't always got the choice, an' so I help myself to a chicken or a melon if the work don't come. The world is a beautiful place, an' some things just belong to everybody. Ain't gonna hurt anybody to feed a hungry man once in a while, whether he knows he's doin' it or not. Most of us din't git this way by choice, an' anybody on this green earth could end up in our shoes mighty easy."

"Hey, Sam," Piney interrupted, "why we gettin' all serious here? I ain't heered you all wound up like this in years. You gettin' to be a reg'lar flap-jawed ol' woman. 'Sides, the sun's startin' to set, an' we almost outta wine. We gonna sleep in that warehouse again tonight, or you got somethin' else figgered?"

"Okay, Piney, "I'm just tryin' to keep this lad on the straight an' narrow. Look here, son." Sam turned again to Elias. "You're a right fine boy, an' me an' Piney are proud to know you. We'll prob'ly see you around the streets again one o' these days, but you listen to your pop an' don't come lookin' for us. We ain't nothin' but trouble to a kid like you."

"An' pretty quick me an' ol' Sam are gonna hop on another midnight freight an' hit for the Midwest, then on to Californy for the winter," Piney added. "We'll be aroun' for a few more days, then you'll prob'ly never see us no more. Sure been nice talkin' to you, an' when we get back to Ol' Pen-syl-toonia we'll try an' look you up. Keep your eyes peeled, 'cause we apt to be most anyplace. Good luck, kid, an' remember us if we don't see you. We'll be thinkin' 'bout you."

The two vagrants shook his hand heartily and went off down the street toward the railyard, arm in arm.

Elias was nearly in tears on the way home. He felt suddenly very sad and lonely. These two men were like old friends, although he had met them only a few days before and had seen them a total of only three times. They had made a deep impression on him. They were very different from other adults he knew. It surprised and pleased him that they treated him like an equal instead of talking down to him as other adults did.

He had asked his grandmother about the men and why his father treated them so gruffly. She had explained that his father was only trying to protect him from people who might be "Bad." She, like Leo, could not explain satisfactorily why his new friends were not acceptable. She said they drank too much and that they were "bums," just as Leo had said.

When Elias asked her why it was okay for his father to drink, but not these men, she replied, "You not get smart with me an' you papa, Elias. When we say these men no good, you mus' listen. It is good enough if you papa say it. Then you not ask no more silly question. Now go play!"

Now his friends were probably gone, and he would never find out all he wanted to know about them. Their description of their way of life fascinated him, and as he ambled along through the quiet back street toward his home, he daydreamed of catching a freight train to "Californy" someday, where he would find his two friends waiting in the sunshine to greet him.

However, this day was not to bring Elias any of life's sunshine. He smelled supper cooking as he went up the front steps, but as he stepped into the hallway, the house was strangely quiet. He called out to his grandmother as he entered the kitchen. His nose identified the supper as his father's favorite Hungarian stew, but his grandmother was not in the kitchen, nor did she answer his first call. He called again, louder, and became anxious at the heavy silence that followed.

Through the hand-stitched little curtains on the window of her sewing room, he could see Anna sitting in her rocking chair. She appeared to be asleep. He opened the door quietly and tiptoed up to her. Her head was tipped slightly to the side, and a strangely peaceful expression was on her face. He quietly reached up and touched her hand and found it cold and stiff. Her other hand still held a piece of knitting that she would never finish.

Elias looked away as a hard lump he could not swallow came into his throat. Tears suddenly burned his eyes and rolled down his cheeks. His friends had left him, and now his grandmother as well. He knew what was wrong but not how to deal with it. He held the wrinkled old hand in his own for a few seconds but could not stand the cold still feel of it, so he quietly turned his back and tiptoed from the room, closing the door softly behind him.

He went to the front steps and sat down to wait for his father. He watched anxiously for Leo to appear and thought of going to meet him, but something told him he must wait. After forty minutes or so of waiting, he surrendered to his sorrow, put his head down on his knees, and cried.

Leo did not get home until nearly an hour after dark. Poor Elias had been standing his death-watch vigil for over two hours and had not ventured back inside the house, although he was quite cold and uncomfortable by this time. Leo was drunk but still coherent.

"What my man doing waiting outside for Papa?" he asked as he came up to the steps. "Why you not inside with Grandma?"

Elias raised his sad eyes to his father, and tears started again down his cheeks.

"Grandma is gone, Papa," he said, his voice cracking in a sob as he spoke, "an' I couldn't go back in there alone."

Leo was suddenly struck by his son's subdued and sorrowful manner. He took the boy by the hand, raised him to his feet, and opened the door with his other hand. The stench of burning stew immediately buried itself in his senses, along with a sudden premonition of disaster.

He went down the hall in a staggering rush into the kitchen, which was by now filled with smoke. Cursing in Serbian, he grabbed a potholder and a towel, turned off the stove, and seized the smoking pot in the same motion. Dashing through the pantry, he kicked the back door open and tossed the pot into the alley.

He rushed back into the kitchen to find Elias numbly huddled against the wall, staring at nothing.

"Where you Grandma, Elias?" he demanded in a loud voice.

Elias scarcely moved, just raised one hand and pointed across the hall.

Leo flicked on the light as he stepped into the hallway and immediately spotted Anna's quiet figure in the old rocking chair. The enormity of the situation rolled over him in an emotional wave.

"Poor Elias!" he cried aloud. "What happen to my poor son now?"

He did not have to go into Anna's little sanctuary to verify his intuition, but he did. With tears in his eyes he reached out, gently touched the smooth cold brow, and brushed a few strands of hair into place. He went to the little setee by the window and picked up her handmade shawl, which was draped across the chair arm. He returned to Anna and wrapped it gently around the now-shrunken little body as though to warm the life back into her.

"Good-bye, Anna," he whispered. "Give Julie and Papa my love."

He moved heavily but quietly from the room and closed the door.

"Elias, my son," he called, "I am sorry! I not know. Please do not blame Papa."

He went into the kitchen where Elias still crouched against the wall. He ruffled his curly brown hair and leaned over and kissed his forehead.

"This very bad time for you, my son," he said. "Papa very sorry."

He walked slowly into the pantry and picked a full bottle of brandy from the case. Tucking it under his arm, he returned to Elias, raised him gently on one great arm, and dazedly shuffled down the hall into the parlor.

He sat Elias down in his big chair and opened the bottle, from which he took a long drink. He turned on the radio and searched the dial until he found the music he wanted, then picked up the boy again into his arms, settled down in the chair, and held him closely with his left arm as he patted him gently on the thigh with his other hand.

For a few hours, Elias spent the most intimate moments of his life with his father. Neither spoke, nor moved but slightly.

Leo had several more drinks from the bottle over the next hour until it was over half gone. Then he no longer bothered to set it down but held it in one hand resting against the boy's leg.

Finally, Elias reached slowly down, grasping the neck of the bottle, and lifted it carefully from his father's hand. Slowly he raised it and, tipping back his head, took a sizable drink, then set it back in his father's hand. Leo made no move to stop him, nor said a word, but began humming softly with the music and gently rocking the boy back and forth as he held him.

As the bottle went slowly empty, they shared drink for drink until both feel asleep.

In the quiet hours of the late night, Leo roused himself. He got up slowly and gently, still holding Elias, and made his way into his bedroom. He gently undressed the boy, then himself. Again he cuddled him as though he were still a babe, and they slept away the initial shock of Anna's passing in loving silence until long after daylight the next day.

CHAPTER 35

▼

Corky's first day of school was finally here. Jan was very excited about it. She knew that Corky would take it in stride once he got there and began to get acquainted with children his age.

It was something she had been wishing for since Corky had started walking. She had always wished that they did not have to live in the isolated situation they were in, but she had never had the money or the courage to hunt for anything better. Now, at last, Corky was going to have other kids to play with.

Corky was angry. He did not know anything about the world outside of the warehouse district where he lived. He felt that he and his mother were doing just fine as long as Bob stayed away, and he did not want that to change.

When Jan woke him, the first thing he said was, "I don't want to go to school, Mom."

He continued to emphasize that statement with every word and action until they were ready to leave the house. Jan locked the door as they left.

"When you get out of school this afternoon you come straight to the diner, 'cause I'm locking this door, and you won't be able to get in, okay?"

She had made arrangements with Rosa to come in late this morning, because she wanted to be sure Corky got to his classroom all right. She was sure Miss Humphrey would have everything under control once she got him that far.

As they walked the now-familiar route to the school, Corky hung back, scuffing and dragging his feet, a sullen and pouting look on his face.

"C'mon Corky," Jan pleaded. "Don't act like that. You have to go to school, and it's going to be great fun, you'll see."

Corky mumbled again, "Don't want to go to school."

As they neared the schoolyard, there were dozens of children already there. It was a beautiful fall day, sunny and warm. Children were running and laughing and playing, both on the street and inside the fence. Jan could not believe Corky's lack of interest. He stared steadfastly at his toes, ignoring the hubbub around him.

They went up the steps, and Jan opened the huge door and led Corky inside. He turned and watched as it clanged shut behind him, and he wondered how hard it would be for him to open. They walked directly to the classroom.

Jan could see the forbidding figure of Miss Humphrey standing in the hallway, hands on hips, as though daring any of her small charges to do something, anything, to defy her.

"Well, young man," she greeted Corky, "I've been waiting for you."

She said it as though she had some special plan in mind for him alone. Jan knelt down with Corky, brushed his hair back with her hand, and kissed him on the forehead.

"Now you be good, Corky, mind Miss Humphrey, and come straight to the diner after school."

Miss Humphrey tapped her on the shoulder.

"No reason for you to stay around, Mrs. Hackett," she rasped. "It just makes it more difficult to get them settled down. I can handle it from here, thank you."

Jan again felt a twinge of apprehension and wished silently that her son's first teacher could have been someone younger and more pleasant. She watched as Miss Humphrey directed Corky to a desk in the front row next to the window. It was several minutes yet before class was due to start, and Jan considered making another try at cheering him up. She stepped toward the door, but Miss Humphrey was suddenly in front of her, blocking her way.

"He'll be just fine, Mrs. Hackett," she assured Jan in her gruff voice.

Jan's temper flared momentarily, and she flashed her blue eyes at the gloomy old maid who stood between her and her son. Then, thinking better of it, she turned and went quickly from the school.

She walked rapidly, still angry, the nearly six blocks to the diner. As she walked, she thought of how difficult this must be for Corky and wondered how she might have made it easier by taking the trouble at some point to make him interactive with other children his age, but time had gone too quickly. It seemed like only weeks since she had carried the newborn Corky from the hospital.

Mom was sure surprised when I came home, Jan thought. Maybe I should have stayed home, but what the hell did I know then? God, here is Corky starting school, an' Mom hasn't even seen him since he was about a year old. I gotta take him home again pretty soon. Wonder how Mom and Dad are doing.

Thus deep in thought, the walk to the diner seemed surprisingly short. She cut across the empty lot and turned the corner to the front of the diner. She halted abruptly and stared in amazement as she approached the diner steps.

There, chin in hand and a grim look on his face, sat Corky.

"I knowed something was crazy here," Rosa shouted from the doorway. "He been sittin' there for near ten minutes, an' every time I tried to git ahold of 'im, he'd run away. Wouldn't answer no questions or nuthin'. I was getting' pretty worried there. Thought somethin' mighta happened to ya."

"Corky!" Jan exclaimed. "How the hell did you get here?"

She seized his arm and jerked him upright. "What you think you're doin'? You're supposed to be in school. How did you get here?"

"I ran across through the warehouses, Mom. I don't wanta go to school," he whimpered, tears starting down his cheeks.

He looked so pitiful that Jan had to feel sorry for him, but she also knew that she could not back down.

"Rosa," she said, "I'm sorry, but I'll have to take him back to school."

"No sweat, kid," Rosa replied. "I know how it is. Maybe Bob was right, an' you oughta paddle his li'l ass for 'im."

"No," Jan replied, "I'm not going to hit him, but he is going back to school, and he's going to stay there if I have to tie him to his desk and sit there all day and watch so he don't untie the knots. You hear me, Corky?"

With that, she stamped angrily down the street, dragging Corky behind her. On the way, she alternately chastised the boy verbally and the teacher in thought.

How the hell can a teacher just let a little kid take off by himself from the classroom? She wondered. She knew I walked him to school. She knew I had left. How could she let him get away?

To Corky she said, "How did you get out of school?"

"She was talking to a boy in the back of the room, and the door was open, so I just left," Corky replied. "She don't even know I'm gone. Why do I gotta go back there?"

"She certainly does know you're gone," Jan said indignantly. "I'll bet she has someone out looking for you right now."

Jan had no sooner said the words than a dapper little man in a dark blue suit came trotting around the corner. He stopped as he saw Jan and the boy.

"Are you Mrs. Hackett?" he asked tentatively.

"Yes, I am, and I'm taking him back to school," she replied.

"I'm Henry Adams, the principal at your school, Mister Hackett," he said to Corky. "You have 'caused your mother a lot of trouble and worry and made me come looking for you. That's no way to start your first day of school. Mrs. Hackett, if you will allow me, I would like to return your son to his teacher's care. I assure you she will know you're not pleased with what has happened, and it won't happen again. I think he and I need to come to an understanding, and the walk back should be just about enough time."

Jan hesitated. She did not know the little man, but he seemed calm and confident.

"Well, I guess I have to trust someone," she said finally. "I can't watch him all the time, and he has to go to school. Corky, Mister Adams is taking you back, and you're not to leave until they tell you, understand?"

She shook him gently but firmly. "Now you go back with Mister Adams, and don't cause no more trouble."

Mister Adams grasped his wrist firmly and reassured Jan, "We'll work things out on the way back, Mrs. Hackett. Please don't worry. We'll see that he gets settled in this time. Mister Hackett, I think you should tell your mom you're going to be okay."

Corky did not answer but stood quietly looking at his toes.

"You are going to be all right, aren't you?" Mister Adams insisted.

Corky finally nodded, and the two of them and Jan went their separate ways.

CHAPTER 36

▼

Corky was finally returned to Miss Humphrey's care, after a lengthy lecture from Mister Adams about the use and value of education. He extracted a promise from Corky not to run again, and he cautioned Miss Humphrey against relaxing her vigil in the future, which did not make any points for Corky.

As soon as she closed the door, Corky knew he was in trouble. She grabbed him by the left arm and jerked him violently across the room to the desk she had put him in earlier. Still holding him tightly, she grasped the desk by the back rest and hauled it around to the front of the classroom so it faced the rest of the students. She raised Corky from the floor by one arm and dropped him into the seat.

"Class," she called out in a severe tone, "This person doesn't like us. He has run away already before we even get started. Now, I have put him here in front where we can all watch him. Since he does not care to join us, at least we can all help to see that he does not leave us. All right, children, let us get back to what we were doing, introducing ourselves so we all know each other."

Although he was not told, Corky gathered from the next fifteen minutes of listening that each child was supposed to stand and tell the class his or her name, his mother and father's name, and something he likes to do. From time to time, Miss Humphrey would ask a speaker to tell a little more or explain something further about his likes, dislikes, and interests.

It was apparent in a short while that most of the children had already fulfilled their roles in this activity while Corky was gone. Some were quite shy and had to be coaxed. Others had to be told when to quit talking. Although he took no active part, Corky was interested and tried to remember as many of the children's names as he could. Miss Humphrey commented on their little speeches from time to time.

When all of the children except Corky had been introduced, Miss Humphrey walked slowly and dramatically over to the window near where Corky sat facing the class. The room was very quiet, everyone staring expectantly at Corky. As the tension increased in the room, some small voice near the back of the room giggled nervously. Miss Humphrey turned quickly from the window and took two quick steps in Corky's directions, which made the focus on him unanimous throughout the room.

"<u>Now</u>," she announced loudly, "we have not met our little runaway yet."

She paused to let the tension build again. Corky squirmed nervously and put his chin down on his hands, which were tensely gripping the edge of his desk.

After several seconds of silence, the teacher said, "Well, are you going to tell us your name, sir, or do we have to wait all day?"

Corky made no response except to turn his head sideways away from her so that his right cheek rested on the backs of his hands. This prompted a few more spontaneous giggles from the other children.

It apparently irritated Miss Humphrey. She came quickly to Corky's side, locked her left hand tightly in his shaggy red hair, and pulled up his head. Then she dropped her hand from his head to his collar and hauled him sideways from his chair to a standing position beside it.

"We are waiting to hear your name, sir," she said severely, "or don't you have one?"

Corky stood nervously watching his right toe, which was bump-bump-bumping the floor next to his left foot, and still he made no response.

Miss Humphrey now seemed to be taking peculiar delight in her harassment of this helpless little stranger.

"Class", she said, "I know what the problem is. He doesn't tell us his name, because he does not have one. His mother calls him Corky, but he has no name. He has only initials, Mister C.Q. Hackett. Perhaps Mister Hackett can tell us what C.Q. stands for—or must we guess, Mister Hackett?"

Still there was nothing but silence from Corky.

"Have you forgotten how to talk, young man?" she demanded, shaking him roughly by the arm.

Corky shook his head, still looking at the floor.

"Well, I can see we are going to have real problems with you. I guess we will have to call you Corky, whether we like it or not. Oh, on second thought, nicknames are not really proper. Class, we shall call him Mister Hackett. I do not want to hear anyone call him Corky or C.Q. Is that clear? We will call him only by a proper name, and Mister Hackett is the only one we have."

"Yes, Miss Humphrey," the class chorused.

"Mister Hackett, we have wasted nearly half an hour of our time trying to get acquainted with you, and you insist on ignoring us. Would you like to tell us your mother's name, or do we have to guess that too?"

There was no answer.

"Mister Hackett, we are waiting," she insisted.

"Her name is Janet," Corky muttered.

"Did you all hear that?" Miss Humphrey cried. "His mother has a name! Now, Mister Hackett, will you tell us your father's name?"

"Don't have none," Corky replied sullenly.

"What? Your father doesn't have a name either?" Miss Humphrey cried out. "What an odd family. Well, what initials does he go by then?"

"No father," Corky replied, almost in a whisper.

"Oh, I see," Miss Humphrey gloated in a half smile, as though all the secrets of the universe had been revealed in Corky's brief confession. "Mister Hackett has no father. Well, that happens sometimes. Sorry I asked."

She smiles broadly at the class.

Without the least consideration of human kindness, she continued her torment of the little fellow.

"Very well, Mister Hackett, tell us something that you like to do. I have had to pump every word out of you, and you are wasting our time."

Corky, by this time thoroughly agitated but not knowing how to escape her badgering, again declined to answer.

"Now we know, class," Miss Humphrey rasped after several moments of silence. "Mister Hackett likes to do nothing, and there are many more like him in this world. Come on, Mister Hackett, there must be something you like to do."

Finally, in desperation, Corky thought of something he would have dearly loved to be doing at that moment.

"I like to run," he said timidly.

Everyone, Miss Humphrey included, laughed. This final straw overwhelmed Corky completely. He turned his back on the hateful sight of this adult monster and her pet monkeys. He dropped on his knees, face against the wall, and began to cry.

Miss Humphrey ignored him completely. She returned calmly to her desk and proceeded with her twenty-year ritual of "civilizing" children.

CHAPTER 37

▼

Eddie had taken to street life as readily as any wino.

He had found an alley door into a stairwell in one of the warehouses. The stairs led to office space, seldom used, above the storage floor of the warehouse. There was a sizeable dark storage area behind the staircase on the ground level that contained a few old boxes and a large sack of clean rags. It was comfortable and warm, and Eddie was small and quiet.

The street door to the stairway was never locked. Only the door at the top of the stairs was secured to prevent entry to the office area. Over a period of months Eddie had slept there most of the time and had never been bothered. He left his hiding place only after the few people who worked upstairs went up in the morning, and he never returned to it until after dark.

This warehouse was across the street and just down the block from the school where Corky went. Eddie had spotted Jan and Corky walking to and from the school on several occasions during the summer and had immediately felt the old resentment. He accurately assessed the situation when he watched them inspecting the school grounds and building. He thought to himself that perhaps he could find a way to make mischief for them if they did not know he was about, so he endeavored to stay out of their sight.

After Corky had been going to school for several weeks and Eddie was confident he could depend on the boy being alone, he began plotting how to cause him trouble or frighten him as he had done when Corky was alone near the diner. He began spying on Corky's activities and stealthily following his route to and from the diner and the house to the school.

He learned that Corky always went home on Thursday afternoons, Jan's day off, and the rest of the time he went to the diner. By this research he also learned that Jan had a boyfriend who was usually at the house early on Thursday afternoons, and some evenings.

He found that Corky spent nearly all his time outside when the boyfriend was there, and that much of this time was spent in running rapidly around and around the house. Sometimes Corky went south, away from the house and warehouses, to the rail lines that ran by several hundred yards away.

Corky liked to sit in the sunshine on a rock pile close to the rails and watch the trains go by. He entertained himself by throwing rocks at the eagles and mountain goats painted on the sides of the railway cars. Sometimes a friendly brakeman or porter would be standing on the rear platform of the caboose and would throw Corky an occasional piece of candy or a nickel or dime or rail token as the train went clicking by. Corky would wave at these unknown benefactors and scramble quickly to retrieve whatever they had dropped to him.

The track maintenance crew kept the right of way strip along the tracks cut clean, but weeds and bushes grew thick across the empty acreage between the warehouses and the track. Two loading spurs of track to the warehouse district broke away from the mainstream of track about a quarter mile both above and below the little house where Jan and Corky lived. It was easy for Eddie to slip along the raised grade of these spurs and into the undergrowth and observe Corky's actions without being seen. He had to be very careful, however, because Corky never stayed long in one place and had worn trails all over this miniature wasteland with his solitary running and playing.

Eddie was amazed by the animal-like sensitivities of his son. Often when he was hidden nearby watching, and Corky ventured closer than usual to one of his hiding places, he would notice that although he was totally silent and still, the boy seemed to sense a foreign presence and would quickly shift his activities to another part of the lot. Sometimes he would stop short near where Eddie was hiding and, rising on tiptoe, would look nervously about but would not venture off his trails to search for the intruder he obviously sensed was there.

This fascinated Eddie in the same fashion a hunter is sensitive to the activities and peculiarities of wild game. In fact, it kept him sober more than usual, trying to keep up with Corky's activities and plotting how he might do him some mischief. He had no conscious intent to do the boy serious harm but took devious delight in the possibility that he might discover ways to frighten him. Perversely he hoped he might cause Corky to be constantly looking over his shoulder, as he himself had done for months after Charlie's visit.

One beautiful Sunday afternoon in October, Eddie finally chanced on the opportunity, if not the means. He was lying in the shade of a clump of bushes near the railroad spur, watching Corky run like a gopher over the maze of trails he had worn through the brush and weeds of the lot.

Bob's car was parked in front of the house. Corky had gone to the door twice within the hour and apparently found it locked. Each time the boy became very agitated, stamping his feet and bumping the door. Eddie was too far away to hear any conversation, but he assumed Corky was being told to go play. Both times Corky reverted for a few minutes to his habit of running around and around the house, then finally returned to play in the empty lot.

Memory and latent jealousy stirred active pictures in Eddie's mind concerning the reasons for the locked door, and it only served to agitate his perverted resentment toward the boy. He thought that while Jan and her lover were actively engaged inside, he could get at Corky without too much fear of discovery or reprisal...but how?

All through the afternoon he puzzled over the question until his thirst got the better of him and he stealthily retreated to the shelter of the warehouses. As he was walking through the warehouse area toward his favorite panhandling corner, a warehouse worker came out on the loading dock with a very large cardboard box that he pitched carelessly in the direction of an overloaded dumpster near the dock.

Eddie looked curiously at the box for a moment, and suddenly he knew how to carry out his plan. Quickly he seized the box and dragged it away behind the warehouse, out of sight where the trash collectors would not pick it up. It was a heavy, corrugated ceiling-tile box about four feet long and thirty inches square.

He had been without a drink now for several hours so was in no condition to deal with Corky anymore today. He could only hope the box would be there when he returned. Besides, Sunday afternoons, when the churchgoers were out walking after the sermon, were a prime time for putting the touch on people. He did not want to waste the opportunity, as it was usually the best of the week.

He placed a large rock in the box and left it close up against the warehouse, so hopefully it would not blow away.

"If this booger is still here on Thursday," Eddie vowed to himself, "I'm gonna give that brat the scare of his life."

Luck was with Eddie on Thursday evening. He returned to find the box just as he had left it. He was half-canned on cheap wine but still very much in control as he set his plan in motion.

He waited patiently for Bob's car to appear, knowing Corky would be called indoors for supper within minutes of Bob's arrival. At the moment he could see Corky in an open space near the house, throwing rocks at the row of cans he had set up. He knew that he would have thirty minutes or so to get ready while all three were in the house eating, so he waited.

Meanwhile, he stood the long box upright and found that it came almost to his shoulder. He lifted it and dropped it over his head. Just as he thought, he had plenty of room inside, and by crouching slightly he could stand within it as it rested on the ground. He took his knife from his pocket and cut a long narrow strip out of the box at eye level, so he could see out when he was inside the box.

Not long after he had made his final preparations with the box, Bob's car came wheeling across the spur track and up to the front of the house. From where he was, Eddie could not see the front steps, but he saw Bob get out of the car and hear him call some kind of greeting to Corky. The boy completely ignored him and continued his target practice on the row of cans.

If this Thursday went as usual, Eddie knew they would all be in the house for twenty-five to forty minutes while supper was in progress. Then Corky would be banished again to the outside while Bob and Jan had their usual hour or two of privacy. He also knew that Corky would probably run around the house for at least fifteen to twenty minutes after they had locked him out.

When Jan called out to Corky to come inside, Eddie began counting the minutes. He had long ago surrendered his watch to the local pawn shop for drinking money, so he had to physically count down the time for his action. He did not want to spend a long time inside the box, because it was a very warm afternoon. The sun had already sunk behind the warehouse, but still he knew it would be uncomfortably warm in the box. If Corky failed to make his usual run around the house, he knew he might have to stay in the box until dusk to avoid discovery. Furthermore, he would not be able to carry out his plan today.

It was vital he be in position when Corky came out of the house, so prepared to sacrifice comfort for success, Eddie took a final drink from his bottle of wine and hid it in the bush beside the warehouse. After once more tipping the box over his head, he stood straight up inside it and walked quickly out into the open to a spot about fifty yards from Corky's path around the house. Here he crouched down so the box settled on the ground, and he waited.

He did not have long to wait. In about ten minutes Corky came out of the house and immediately began his frustrated routine of running around and around the house.

Eddie's heart pounded in anticipation. No hunter ever became more thrilled on sighting his trophy than Eddie did at that moment. He had to hold himself in check to keep from giving himself away, but he knew the game was his.

When he was sure the boy was not going to take undue notice of the huge box standing in his territory, he began to move. Each time Corky disappeared around the corner, Eddie would raise up and move himself and the box several steps forward. It was slow work, and tiring to his back to stay hunched over in the box.

He did not want to move too quickly because he wanted the surprise to be complete. He had to be sure he was not moving when Corky came around the other side of the house, because from that angle he was looking directly at the box. For the moment the boy seemed completely engrossed in his own thoughts, lost in his activity. Eddie wanted to be as close as possible to the boy before springing his surprise, so the game continued.

Each circuit Corky made, Eddie inched the box closer until finally he was only twenty to twenty-five yards from the house and Corky's path. He was beginning to wonder what had dulled the boy's senses, because it had not taken this long on any previous approach for the boy to become apprehensive and move away.

I hope he wakes up pretty soon and notices this box, Eddie thought. I would like to see him walk toward me before I have to hump. Jeez, I hope them two are right in the middle of their big moment when that kid comes screaming to the door.

Closer and closer he edged to Corky's path. Finally Corky slowed as he came around the far end of the house. He actually watched the box for the whole distance from when he was in sight of it to where he turned the corner going away. His little face was turned back over his shoulder as he disappeared around the corner.

Eddie made one more quick move. This time he was only fifty feet from the path. Corky came in sight again, this time no longer running. He walked forward slowly toward the box, leaving his beaten path. Step by step he approached, one hand up to his little pointed chin, curious about how this thing had gotten here without him noticing.

Suddenly he stopped, apprehensive. He picked up a small rock and threw it at the box but missed. He took a few more steps forward, then bent to choose another rock.

Eddie waited gleefully, invisible, in plain sight. When the boy bent over, taking his eyes from the box for a moment, Eddie charged. He pounded the backs of his hands against the inside of the box and gave an insane scream as he charged at Corky.

Though suspicious and uneasy, Corky had not anticipated anything like this. He jumped frantically to get out of the way, tripped, and fell backward. He completely lost control and wet himself. He rolled frantically to get to his feet and barely succeeded before the huge box was on him. Once on his feet, he was gone in a flash around the corner and out of sight, screaming frantically, not even aware that the box no longer pursued him.

Eddie quickly discarded the box as soon as Corky turned the corner. He ran as fast as he could to the nearest bush and from there made his way cautiously to the corner of the warehouse where he had left his wine. He could not believe how successful and complete the surprise had been.

Only thing better would have been to be around front to watch Jan come running bare-assed to the door, he thought, and he laughed and laughed and took a long drink of wine to congratulate himself.

He watched, and within a few minutes Jan, Corky, and Bob came around the corner of the house. The boy was still crying, and Jan was gesturing angrily. They walked up to the box, Corky hanging back and pulling frantically to get away. Bob kicked the box as though to show it was harmless, then picked it up and tossed it away again. They stood arguing back and forth in excited voices, but Eddie could not hear what they said from where he was. More than pleased with his efforts, he took another drink of wine and slunk away around the warehouse.

As for Corky, he could remember only one time in his life when he had been so frightened. Once before some creature had jumped at him behind the diner, and he remembered it vividly now.

When he had gotten to the door of the house, he was screaming and pounding with both little fists as though to break it down. He was soaked from his crotch to his shoe tips, and he was sure the box was going to get him before his mother got the door open.

Jan and Bob had been lying on the open bed, not completely undressed but not far from it either, when Jan heard the first of Corky's screams. Against Bob's protests, she jumped up and began hurriedly putting on her outer garments. She was heading for the door when Corky began beating on it. She swung the door open and Corky nearly fell on his face in his rush to enter.

Jan grabbed his arm to save him from falling. Reaching with her other hand, she started to pick him up when she noticed he was wet. He was still screaming frantically, so she knelt in front of him and shook him gently to quiet him.

"What happened, Corky? Why are you screaming?" she asked.

Corky did not answer but jerked away from her and turned and slammed the door shut.

"Hell," Bob broke in, "look at 'im. He pissed himself and figures you're gonna raise hell with him. Ain't nothing really wrong."

"Now, Bob, there's more to it than that. Look at him. He's white as a ghost an' shakin' all over. What happened, Corky? Tell Mama."

Corky was quieter by now but still sobbing. He really did not know how to tell her what was wrong.

Finally he said, "That big box came after me."

"What? A box came after you? What are you talking about? Come on and show me," Jan said.

She turned and started to open the door, but Corky quickly slammed it shut again.

"C'mon, Corky," she coaxed. "Boxes don't chase people. You must have imagined it. You got to come show me what you're talking about."

However, Corky steadfastly refused to even let her open the door.

At this Bob became exasperated. "Look, Jan, he's puttin' up a smokescreen, so's you won't whack his behind for wettin' his pants. Throw him back outside, and let him wear them wet. Maybe that'll teach him not to do it again."

Jan came strongly to Corky's defense. "Bob, you stay the hell out of this. Something scared him, an' I gotta find out what."

With that she pushed Corky roughly aside and, grasping his arm in one hand, opened the door with the other. With Corky jerking and protesting behind her, they went down the steps. Bob jumped up and followed.

When they came to the corner of the house, there was the box lying in the yard about fifty feet from the house. Corky squawked and tried to get away from Jan. To stop his struggling, Bob seized his other hand, and all three of them walked out to the box together. Bob kicked it carelessly, and it turned over.

"Just an ordinary big box," he said. "It made noises and jumped at me and chased me."

"Corky," Jan said again, "empty boxes don't chase people. There ain't nothin' to be scared of. It's just an empty box."

"He's just trying to distract you like I told you before," Bob put in again. "Trying to get you to forget he pissed his pants."

They argued back and forth for a few minutes, Bob critical and Jan defensive.

Finally Bob said, "A damn gust of wind, whirlwind, or something prob'ly rolled the box an' startled him. Tell him to go play, an' let's go back in."

He grabbed Jan playfully around the waist and started pulling her toward the house, ignoring Corky completely.

"Wait, Bob. He was awful scared, an' I'm not going to leave him all wet an' worried. You do what you want. I'm gonna take care of him."

She pushed him away and went back to Corky, who was still standing there staring at the box.

"Okay," Bob said, "if that's the way you want it, I ain't hangin' around here all afternoon while you baby this pisstail kid who oughta know better."

He strode angrily to his car, got in, and drove away. Jan stood looking after him for a moment and thought how like Eddie Bob's actions had been.

Finally she shook her head, took Corky's hand, led him inside, and helped him find dry clothes. She reassured him as he was dressing that the incident with the box was only unusual and nothing to worry about.

However, Corky would not let it go so easily.

"Mom, can you help me get rid of it?" he asked.

"Oh, just ignore it, Corky. I'll get Bob to carry it over to the dumpster tomorrow."

"Please, Mom," Corky insisted. "I want to tear it up. Will you help me?"

The two of them spent the next half-hour in close companionship, tearing up the box.

Corky, extremely pleased to be allowed to destroy it, kept making aggressive comments. "You're dead now, you ol' box. Can't chase me no more."

It was as though he were actually destroying an enemy. Jan indulged his fantasy and joined in the game, insulting the box as they worked. Suddenly she noticed the slot Eddie had cut in the side of the box. She stared briefly and stuck her fingers through the hole, feeling its rough edges.

"Corky," she asked suddenly, "did the box tumble and roll toward you?"

"Nope," he said emphatically, "it stood right up and chased me."

When they were through tearing up the box, Corky stayed close to Jan, declining her instruction to run and play.

For several hours after, Jan kept thinking to herself, <u>I wonder what Eddie was up to today? Maybe there was more to it than a windblown box.</u>

She knew Corky was not a timid person who scared easily, and she could see no reason for him to lie. She totally distrusted Bob's judgment that he was trying to cover up for wetting himself. He had not wet himself in over a year. She thought again of the other incident, months before.

<u>Eddie Hackett</u>, she thought to herself, <u>if I ever find out you are responsible for this, you are going to be one sorry drunk!</u>

CHAPTER 38

▼

Anna's funeral had been small and quiet. Only a few family friends and Elias, Leo, and Bernard were there.

After the funeral Bernard came by the apartment and had a drink with Leo.

"I'm sorry to leave you and Elias with so much trouble," Bernard apologized. "I know you are not well, and you will have to find someone to help with the house, but I can see no way I can help in this. I have an offer from my company to move to Cincinnati. There is nothing to keep me here any longer."

He looked sadly at Leo, tears in his eyes.

"You not worry about us, Bernard." Leo answered softly. "We be all right. Elias is big boy. You must do for self. Life is to live the best you can."

Leo poured another drink for the two of them. They touched the rims of their glasses briefly, then joined right hands as they drank a silent toast to better times.

When his drink was gone, Bernard turned and wrapped his arms tightly around his big little nephew, who now stood almost as tall as he.

"Good-bye, Elias," he whispered. "Be a good boy and look after your papa. He is going to need your help."

He shook hands with both of them and left quickly, trying vainly to control the tears. Elias never saw his Uncle Bernard again.

After Bernard left, Elias quietly followed his father as he roamed through the apartment. Leo moved as though in a dream, touching things here and there as he went. Occasionally he would pick up something and stare at it, but as though he were not actually seeing what he held. Each object seemed to hold some memory—a blue vase that Anna had always kept full of flowers in summer, the piece of knitting she had held when she died, the old shawl that still hung over her chair.

He carried his everpresent bottle of brandy with him and took a short drink every now and then as he made his silent tour from room to room. Once he stopped in front of a picture of Julie and stared at it for so long that Elias wondered if he was ever going to move on.

Elias wanted a drink so badly that he could feel the welcome burn of it in his throat each time his father took a drink. Still, even though they had shared drink for drink a few nights before, he dared not ask for one now. He followed quietly, hoping against hope his father would offer. His hopes were in vain.

After more than an hour of silently counting memories, Leo finally broke the silence.

"Mrs. Vukovich makes our dinner tonight, Elias," he said. "Go now an' wash you face an' hands and comb you hair so you look nice. Maybe we ask Mrs. Vukovich to keep our house now sometimes. We mus' do much ourself, but maybe she help us. Go now an' get you ready."

Elias went and did as he was told, wondering all the while how he could manage to sneak a drink. The longer he went without, the more he wanted one, and the more agitated he became.

Mrs. Vukovich was a friend of Anna's and about the same age. A fat kindly lady, she never had any children and had always admired Elias. For Elias' part, he did not like her loving attention. She always ruffled his hair and hugged him, which bothered him immensely, because she was always sweaty and damp and smelled strongly of garlic.

The dinner was excellent, but Elias could not have told anyone ten minutes later what he had eaten. Mrs. Vukovich opened his father a cold beer as soon as he was seated at the table and brought Elias a large glass of milk. He drank it immediately, hoping it would quiet the turmoil in his stomach, but his thoughts were on the foaming glass of beer in front of Leo.

He ate quickly, excused himself from the table, and asked his father if he could wait outside. Sweat was pouring down his face, and he felt weak and sick.

"What wrong with you, Elias?" his father asked. "You not like Mrs. Vukovich's cooking? You must say thank you, an' not run away while we still eat."

Fortunately for Elias, Mrs. Vukovich was more sensitive to children than Leo.

"Let the boy go out, Leo," she said in Serbian. "It has been a hard day for the little man, and he should get some fresh air before he sleeps."

When the door closed behind him, Elias ran as fast as he could to his "hidey-hole" in the empty lot. His bottle of brandy was still more than half full.

He seized it with both hands and twisted frantically at the top. His hands shook so badly, he could hardly open it, but he was finally successful.

He tipped it back and took a long drink, still kneeling in the dirt at the end of the half-buried tile tube. He closed his eyes and sighed as the warmth of the brandy spread from his throat to the pit of his stomach. For a few seconds it was the most wonderful feeling he had ever experienced. His skin tingled marvelously, and his tense face and neck muscles relaxed. He swam momentarily in the heady fumes of the sun-warmed liquor.

Suddenly his system reacted to the unaccustomed deprivation of the last two days, during which he had been unable to get away from the doting friends and family to slake his thirst. His nervous stomach emptied itself in one violent rush.

He nearly dropped the bottle but managed to get both hands on it and save it from spilling. He fouled his right sleeve and hand in the process. He sat the bottle hurriedly in a safe place and, leaning forward on hands and knees, alternately heaved and gagged until he was so weak, he could hardly stand.

In twenty minutes or so the sickness ran its course, and Elias felt much better, but the desire for brandy was still there. He picked up the bottle, looked at it, and wondered if he would be sick again if he drank. He started to try it once or twice, but each time his stomach twitched nervously, and he would shakily lower the bottle. He did not know what was wrong with him, but he knew he could not leave there without a drink.

After several tries he finally managed small drink. This time he kept his eyes open and his head up, and slowly his stomach settled.

He drank again, a larger drink, but now he was drinking on a completely empty stomach. He did not feel like running and playing as he usually did when he drank. Instead he leaned back against a hump of earth, the bottle between his hands in his lap, and every few moments he took another drink.

The sun had been setting as he left the house after dinner. He had no idea how long he sat there in the empty lot. When he finally realized the brandy was gone, he also realized it was full dark. Suddenly startled out of his stupor, he thought about his father and sprang to his feet, took one step, and fell headlong into the dust of the lot.

He tried to stand again, but his feet would not hold him. Alternately crawling and staggering a few steps, he had bruised his face and hands, torn his pants, and dirtied his clothing beyond salvage when he heard his father loudly calling his name. He tried desperately to get control of himself, suddenly frightened at what his father might do to him.

By this time he had reached the mouth of the alley that led to his street. He pulled himself upright against the side of the first building and, holding desperately to the wall, managed to slide along it toward his father's voice. He was afraid to answer but more afraid to stay alone where he was. In spite of having been drinking almost daily for many months, he had never been completely, totally drunk before.

The ground pitched and rolled under his feet, and the building kept leaning crazily away from him. Suddenly the wall tipped clear away from him and he shouted in alarm, expecting it to go crashing down in front of him. He cried out again as the hard gravel of the alley struck him hard on the side of his face. He did not understand what was happening to him, and he lay there and shook in terror.

Leo heard Elias' first shout and wondered at the tone of it as he started in that direction. He began running when he heard the desperation in the second outcry. The next thing Elias knew, his father's great hands were under his arms, and he was pulled roughly to his feet.

Leo immediately smelled the combination of brandy and vomit.

"Elias, you really drunk!" he exclaimed. "Where you get brandy? Papa tell you not drink, an' here you drunk in alley."

He shook the boy violently back and forth. Elias reacted much like a rag doll and would have fallen if not for the support of his father's strong hands.

"Papa, you gave me brandy last week," Elias mumbled.

Leo shook him again. "But I feel sorry then, 'cause you find Grandma dead. I think it help. You know you not supposed to drink. Now you be sorry boy before morning," he declared ominously.

He gathered the boy in his arms and carried him home quickly. He took him into the bathroom and stripped off his clothing while the tub was filling with cold water. When the tub was full, Leo picked up Elias none to gently, dropped him unsympathetically into the cold bath, and began rubbing him vigorously. Using soap and washcloth and occasionally pushing his head under the water, he kept at it until all the evidence of the ordeal was cleansed away.

After about fifteen minutes Elias' teeth were chattering, and the world was beginning to come back into focus.

"Get you out of there," his father suddenly ordered. "I be back in minute."

When he returned, he had clean clothes for the boy and a cheese and ham sandwich on heavy rye bread.

"Get you dressed and eat san'wich," Leo demanded gruffly.

Elias staggered about, mumbling and shivering, but finally succeeded in getting dressed.

"Eat you sand'wich," Leo ordered again. "Walk aroun' an' eat you san'wich. I wait for you."

Elias stumbled up and down the hallway, munching on the sandwich. When his father saw he was done, he went back to the kitchen and returned with a cup of hot tea.

"Drink tea now," he ordered.

Elias drank. Leo took the cup and went back to the kitchen. Shortly he returned with a pitcher full of cold water and a glass. He took Elias by the hand and led him outside. Seating himself on the steps, he put down the pitcher of water and glass and gripped Elias roughly by the arm.

Squeezing hard enough to make sure the boy winced, he said firmly, "We gon' make you sober, so you not drink no more. You not gon' like it, but you will do it, okay?"

Elias nodded numbly, not knowing what to expect.

"Okay, now you run! You gon' run down to corner," Leo said, and pointed, "an then you turn aroun' an' run back to other corner." He pointed in the other direction, indicating the full length of the block. "You not stop till Papa say you stop. Now run!"

He emphasized the order with a firm push that nearly landed Elias on the sidewalk again. Elias ran, stumbling and staggering at first, but gradually improving.

After a few circuits up an down the block, Leo stopped him momentarily and said, "When you thirsty, you stop, an' Papa give you glass of water. You stop for nothing else. You get sick, you still run. You just run till Papa say stop."

Elias' feet hurt, and his legs ached, as did his head. His tongue was dry and sticky too, but he ran on. Once or twice be begged his father to let him quit when he stopped for water, but Leo was relentless and made him run on and on.

After more than an hour Leo finally asked, "You like to have drink of brandy now, Elias?"

Elias looked at him in shocked surprise. Then sensing the trap in the questions, he stated firmly, "No, Papa, I won't drink your brandy no more. Can I stop now, please, Papa?"

"You not drinking anything anymore, only milk an' water, or Papa get very angry. You understan' Papa?"

Elias nodded vigorously.

"Okay, you run now two more blocks, an' Papa let you go to bed, but you never come my house again drunk. Now run!" he shouted once more.

Elias promised and never forgot. He still drank when and where he could find it, but true to his word, he never let Leo see him drunk again.

CHAPTER 39

▼

Eddie continued to keep an eye on activities at the little house. As summer faded, the evenings became uncomfortably cool, but Corky played outside as much as ever.

It was apparent to Eddie whenever Corky was "shut out" of the house, as compared to when he was just out playing. He also sensed that the boy did not like Jan's boyfriend. His mood was obviously different when the man was with Jan than when he was nowhere around. He wondered how he might take advantage of this relationship, but without making himself known to Corky, he could think of no way.

Corky continued in school, but nearly everything he learned was due more to his own observation and listening ability than to any effect on Miss Humphrey's part to teach him. She had quite effectively relegated him to nonperson status in her class. She very seldom addressed him and made no effort at all to teach him, except as part of the group. Any individual attention she gave him was negative. The rest of the children, with few exceptions, followed her lead and consigned him to the very bottom of their social pecking order.

One large and not-too-bright youngster named Wallace availed himself of every opportunity to make life miserable for Corky. He was the ring leader among the children in most mischievous activities that occurred in the class, and often he enlisted the aid of others, mostly boys, to make cruel sport of or play practical jokes on Corky.

On one occasion when Miss Humphrey had left the room for a few moments, Wallace and another boy slipped up on either side of Corky's desk, seized his arms, and raised him from his seat. While they held him up, another boy slipped up alongside and slid three or four thumb tacks onto his seat. As soon as the culprit jerked away his hand, they suddenly released him, and he fell back in his seat.

He jumped back up and shouted aloud when the tacks penetrated his backside, just at the moment Miss Humphrey returned to the room. She came quickly to his side, seized him by the arm, and made him kneel in the corner in front of the class without even questioning the reason for his outburst.

Most of these activities were conducted in a clandestine and furtive manner inside the classroom, and whenever Corky made loud objections, Miss Humphrey would invariably blame him for the disruption. Thus he spent more time in his position of isolation, on exhibition in front of the class, than in his desk as part of the class.

Life in school was not better outside on the playground than in the classroom, except that his size and speed gave him the advantage of occasional escape from the children's harassment. Patricia, the little blonde who antagonized him on his first day of school, often joined Wallace in leading group taunts against Corky, and sometimes physical attacks as well. Whenever a group of them could corner him, they would rough him up, pull down his pants, or pinch and pummel him until he would finally escape or the ringing of the bell would temporarily end the torment.

Over a period of time Corky became very adept at eluding the outside pursuit and capture. He was small, quick, quite wiry, and strong. Even when surrounded by a considerable group of children he could twist, duck, and spin among them until an avenue opened up to permit him to run. Once he was free of their grasp, there was no child in school, even those several years older, who could catch him without assistance.

Up to a point, Corky even enjoyed this activity, because it was the one situation where he was superior and in control. At times, when only two or three children pursued him, he delighted in throwing their taunts and name-calling back at them as he ran easily away.

He preferred to be alone. Most of the time when lunch hour or recess time came, he would attempt to be first out the door. Then he would run quickly to some out-of-the-way corner of the school ground, play by himself, and just rest and watch distant groups of children in their games and social activities.

When the weather was good, he would occasionally see the man he had mentioned to his mother whom he thought was watching them when they visited the school yard. Most of the time he acted oddly, to Corky's observation. He would stumble and stagger around and, on rare occasions, come across the street and peer through the chain-link fence.

Once he was standing there hanging tightly to the fence when Corky went dashing by, pursued by Wallace and two other boys. Corky heard him laugh and call out to the others, but he was intent on escape and continued on his way.

Wallace stopped. He stood looking curiously at Eddie for a moment and then said, "What you want, you ol' drunk?"

He spat at Eddie through the fence.

Eddie grinned and said, "Why you chasin' that li'l kid?"

"'Cause he's a doofus, like you," Wallace answered in a smart-aleck tone.

"What you gonna do if you catch him?" Eddie asked.

"We're gonna pull down his pants and pinch his li'l ass an' show his dinky to the girls."

"What's his name?" Eddie asked.

"Oh, I guess it's Corky, but who cares? He's just an ugly doofus anyways," the little bully replied.

By this time several children had gathered to see what this drunk was talking with Wallace about. Some of them started jeering him and tossing small rocks at him. He did not mind, because the rocks were deflected by the chain-link and never hit him directly. He kept on talking to Wallace.

"You wanna know what that kid's name really is?" Eddie asked.

"He don't got a name really," Wallace said wisely. "He just has initials."

"Yeah, I know." Eddie grinned. "C.Q., right?"

The boy looked surprised and asked, "How did you know that?"

"Oh, I know, all right. I know what they stand for too." He laughed aloud.

"Okay, Mister Drunk, if you know, why doncha tell me?"

"Sure, Eddie replied. "It stands for Can't Quite. The kid's name is Can't Quite Hackett, but don't tell 'im who tol ya, okay?"

Several of the children began laughing and snickering and repeating the name among themselves.

"Hey," one of them said suddenly, "let's go tell 'im we know his name."

Joining hands, several of them went skipping merrily along in the direction Corky had gone. As they skipped, they laughed and sang, "Corky's name is Can't Quite, Can't Quite. Corky's name is Can't Quite. Can't Quite see, and Can't Quite fight. Corky's name is Can't Quite."

They soon spotted him sitting in a corner of the school yard, back against the fence. They stretched out their arms to form the longest line they possibly could with joined hands and attempted to surround him, so he could not escape from the corner, Patricia on one end of the line and Wallace on the other, leading. They advanced singing their taunting chant and new verses as they came to mind.

"Cockeyed Corky Can't Quite!" they screamed at him as they approached, laughing.

Corky did not stir until they were nearly upon him. Then he jumped up and immediately was running near full speed. He ran directly at Patricia, who was nearest to him and the fence. She quickly guided her end of the line closer to the fence to cut him off. Instead of stopping as she thought he would, he speeded up and ran at the joined hands before him, striking the line where Patricia's and the next child's hands gripped together.

They attempted to hold tightly, but their grasp slipped when he hit, and Patricia spun violently around and slammed heavily against the chin-link fence, scratching her arm and tearing her dress. She immediately began screaming in earnest, only this time in tears instead of laughter. She held her bleeding arm tightly and ran into the school as fast as she could.

She burst into Corky's classroom, sobbing. "Miss Humphrey, Miss Humphrey! That stupid Corky knocked me down and tore my new dress. Look at my dress, and he cut my arm too. Look!"

Miss Humphrey quickly put away the remains of her lunch.

"Come here, darling," she said in a soothing voice, "let teacher see. Oh, my, he really did hurt your arm, didn't he? Was it an accident, dear, or did he do it on purpose?"

"On purpose, Miss Humphrey!" She cried. "He just ran right at me and knocked me down and tore my dress and cut my arm. I'm bleeding, and <u>oh</u>, it hurts!" she wailed.

"Don't cry now, my pretty. We will tend to him, but first come in the lavatory, and we will fix it up."

Taking some gauze and tape from her desk, she took beautiful Patricia by the hand and led her into the girl's bathroom where she washed the superficial scratch with soap and water and bandaged it with gauze, sympathizing with her all the while.

When the bell rang, summoning the children to return to the classroom, Miss Humphrey posted herself as usual just outside and to the left of the classroom door. It was Corky's habit, more in self-defense than anything else, to be either first or last in the line filing back to class. Experience had taught him that to be anywhere but at the end of the line subjected him to abuse, both verbal and physical, that he could avoid if he were able to move in at least one direction freely. Once he was in line between two other children, he was trapped. Today he managed to be first.

As he approached the door, Miss Humphrey stepped forward to meet him. Reaching out suddenly, she seized the unsuspecting child by the hair with her left hand and jerked him forward, her grip the only support to keep him from falling on his face. Corky clenched his teeth to keep from crying out, but a squealing sound escaped him in spite of himself. She swung in behind him, still maintaining a tight grip of his hair, and began whacking him with her other hand, alternating between his buttocks and the back of his head with her blows.

Once inside the classroom door, she turned toward the incoming line of children. Holding Corky there on his tiptoes by her grip on his hair, she put him on tortured display to all of his classmates. When all of the children were finally seated, she marched the child stiffly to the center of the room in front of the blackboard, where she finally released her tight-fisted grip on his shock of red hair.

"All right, children, who saw what Mister Hackett did to Patricia outside on the playground?"

Several small hands shot up in response.

"All right, Tommy," she said, addressing one smiling imp who had been in the line of children pursuing Corky, "what did you see?"

"I saw him jump up and run at her and knock her down against the fence," he announced loudly.

"Is that what the rest of you saw?" Miss Humphrey asked, nodding in the affirmative as she spoke.

Several small heads nodded in unison.

"All right, Mister Smart-aleck Hackett," she announced, "you can stand right there in front of the class the rest of the afternoon, so all the children can see what bullies who pick on little girls look like"—this in spite of the fact that Patricia was at least five inches taller and ten pounds heavier than Corky.

From that moment on, for the rest of the day she steadfastly ignored him except to scold him if she caught him leaning against the wall or shifting his position. She had absolutely no interest in his side of the story, so saw no reason to bother asking.

This time Corky did not cry. He stared his blue-eyed defiance to the teacher and the class. He endured the rest of the day, although his legs, feet, and shoulders all ached enormously, and he very nearly wet himself before the final bell rang. Then she finally released him from his torment without a single word.

Corky did not say anything about it to his mother that night at home. Somehow he realized that if Jan knew, she would visit the school, and then future days would be even more unbearable if Miss Humphrey was confronted by his mother.

However, the next day when Jan handed him his lunch, he started off in the direction of school, but as soon as he was out of sight of the house, he changed direction and went down among the warehouses, where he spent the day watching the hum of commercial activity as the big trucks came and went. He climbed on the running board of a huge truck and sat and watched as men unloaded it.

Once a big kindly looking man called out, "Hi, kid," and he smiled and winked at Corky.

Two hours later Corky was sitting on the loading dock, munching one of the two sandwiches his mother had made for his lunch, when the same man walked by. He stopped briefly and asked Corky if he was waiting for someone. Corky did not speak but nodded. The big man smiled again, reached inside the front of his bib overalls, and brought out a candy bar which he dropped in Corky's lap.

Corky smiled at the man and said, "Thank you," for the unexpected kindness.

For the rest of the afternoon he watched the big man work, following a few paces behind him both inside and outside the warehouse. Once he stopped what he was doing and brought a long-handled push broom over to where Corky leaned against a support post in the warehouse.

"Sweep out my truck for me, kid, an' I'll give ya a quarter," he said.

Corky was pleased to accommodate and reported back for his reward in a very short while.

"Lots of these guys unloadin' here might do the same if you was to ask, li'l man," the trucker told him as he paid him off. "The warehouseman might let ya sweep the dock sometimes too."

Again Corky smiled and said thank you and thought to himself that this was a better way to spend his time than waiting to get mistreated in school.

Corky had no way of telling exactly what time it was, and he did not want to be late to the diner and cause his mother to become suspicious. When he thought it was close to time for school to be out, he left the warehouse and went to the corner of the block, where he could see the school.

His estimate of time had been pretty good. He had been watching the school only a few minutes when the shouts and laughter of the other children, freed from the drudgery of class, proceeded with a rush out the gate onto the sidewalk. Here they pushed their way onto buses or, if they lived close enough to walk home, streamed off in small groups in various directions.

Corky watched the scene for a moment, standing close against the building so he would not be noticed. Wistfully he wished he could be part of the laughing, playing, shouting group, instead of hiding here always on the outside. The feeling passed when he thought about how mean they were to him most of the time. Turning away, he ran the few blocks to the diner, where he knew his mother would meet him as usual with a hug and something to eat.

Miss Humphrey did not even mark Corky absent for the day. She would probably have been pleased if he had just disappeared and never come back. When Corky came to class the next day, he went quietly to his seat and sat down. Miss Humphrey did not acknowledge his presence all morning.

At lunch time several of the children again took up the "Can't Quite Hackett" chorus on the school grounds. After lunch Wallace announced loudly to Miss Humphrey that he knew what C.Q. stood for in Corky's name.

"His real name is Can't Quite Hackett, Miss Humphrey. C.Q. stands for Can't Quite."

"Why do you say that, Wallace?" She scowled at him. "Even if he doesn't have a real name, we cannot just make up new ones."

"I didn't make it up," Wallace said, defending his statement. "A man came up to the fence and told me and Patricia and Tommy that he knows Corky, and his real name is Can't Quite. Can we call him by his real name now?"

Miss Humphrey smiled in spite of herself and turned to watch Corky squirm uncomfortably in his seat and stare defiantly at her. Then she quickly became her stern self again.

"I'm sorry, Wallace. I don't care if it is his real name, it is no more proper than Corky, and I will not hear it in this class again. He will be Mister Hackett to us as long as he is in my class. Now, let us get back to our work."

Fortunately for Corky, he was bright and alert, so he learned in spite of his isolation. Because she was so set in her routine of twenty years in the classroom, whenever she gave learning drills, she automatically included Corky. She made small cards with each child's name printed in block letters. These she placed on each desk facing the child, and each day the children were required to copy it until they could do it without the card. Then she substituted the name cards for other word cards.

Several times each day the children were required to pass their cards to the child behind them or across from them. Each of these words was routinely added to each child's word list as soon as the child could spell, pronounce, and print the word. On Friday of each week the child who could go to the blackboard and print the longest word list from memory without a mistake would get some kind of prize. Any child who wished to challenge the champion could do so. If successful, he could claim the prize. Although Corky never challenged, he often felt a sense of personal pride in knowing he could have added words to every list that went up.

Miss Humphrey did similar exercises with numbers, although these were usually on flash cards, and the children worked in twos to drill each other on the exercises. Most of the time when these cooperative activities were in progress, she would seize the flimsiest of excuses to see that Corky was in the "Dunce" chair in front of the class, so he seldom received the benefit of interaction learning exercises with the other children.

Still he watched and learned. Every practical exercise Miss Humphrey gave the class throughout the year found Corky within the top ten performers whenever the tests of her twenty-five students were scored. However, the grade she invariably marked on his papers and quarterly report cards was <u>C</u>.

Whenever life became unbearable in the classroom for Corky, he would take the day off as he had done the day after Miss Humphrey had beaten him. By the end of his first year in school, he was regularly absent at least one and often two days a week. She never recorded these absences or questioned the reason for them.

She would, however, find ways to make life miserable for him the day following his absence. She would pointedly ignore the situation whenever Wallace or other class bullies picked on Corky until things got out of hand. Then briefly she would scold the other participants but would punish Corky.

Jan looked briefly at his drawings and exercises when he occasionally brought one home. Sometimes she offered a small comment or asked him to explain something but seldom expressed any great interest or encouragement.

Somehow Corky endured the first year and started the second. School for him was a torment to be endured. Sometimes he would ask Jan if he could quit school, but she would only laugh and tell him he was not sixteen yet. Somehow she missed the urgency in his terse requests. Engrossed in her own problems of how to make ends meet, she never took it on herself to visit the school or check to any extent on his progress or activities there.

Late in the fall of his second year in school, Corky came home on a Thursday afternoon and found Bob and his mother sitting in Bob's car in front of the house. They had both been drinking beer and were in a relaxed and jovial frame of mind.

Jan called to him as he came across the lot, and when he walked up to the car, she told him, "Corky, Bob and I are gong down to the tavern for a couple of beers. Your supper is on the table. We won't be very long. You can play outside till we get back, okay?"

Corky dropped his eyes, scuffed his toe in the dirt, and did not answer. He was unhappy enough to find Bob there. Now his mother was going to go and leave him alone, so that she could be with Bob. He was frustrated and angry.

"Oh, Corky, don't be like that," Jan begged. "You play outside all the time by yourself anyway. Today is Mama's day off, an' I should be able to have a little fun too."

"I don't want you to go," Corky said sullenly.

"Oh, Jesus!" Bob exclaimed. "Let's not go though this whole damn scene."

He reached into his pocket and pulled out a fifty-cent piece, which he flipped out the window. "There, kid, run up to the diner after you eat and get yourself a goody. Me an' your mom will be back in a while."

With that he started the car, whirled it into the street, and left Corky standing forlornly on the path, dust swirling about him.

When they returned, it was two o'clock in the morning, and Corky had been asleep for hours. After that day the scene was often repeated until Corky found himself alone at school and more alone at home. The only place he found relief from isolation was among the warehouse workers and truck drivers on warehouse row, where at least he was greeted and smiled at by many of the men.

It was there he sought sanctuary during his spontaneous days off from school and his lonely evenings at home while Bob and Janet went carelessly about their own affairs, leaving the diminutive, lonely elf to his own devices.

CHAPTER 40

▼

A few days after Leo had made Elias run off his drunkenness, Elias was wracking his mind as to how to get back in his father's good graces.

Mrs. Vukovich was there, as she often was since his grandma died, getting their supper ready. She called out to Elias, who was sitting on the front steps and asked him if he would run to the store for some coffee. Elias liked Mrs. Vukovich's cooking, if he was not too fond of her, so he readily agreed.

He was just going out the door, leaving the grocery, when he met Mister Schmidt, the store manger.

"Hello, Elias," Mister Schmidt greeted him. "How are you and your papa doing?"

"Okay, sir," Elias answered politely.

"I was so sorry to hear about your grandma," he said. "Is there anything I might do to help?"

Elias almost said no, but then he suddenly thought of Mister Schmidt's offer of a delivery job.

"Yes sir, there is," he said emphatically. "You said once you might let me deliver groceries, an' I think I can do it if you will still have me."

The boy sounded so sincere and ready that Mister Schmidt could not resist.

"Certainly, my lad," he replied. "When would you like to start?"

"I would start right now, sir, but I have to take this coffee home and ask my papa an' get my wagon, but I must ask my papa first, okay?"

Mister Schmidt laughed at his eagerness. "Well, I'm sorry, Elias. We close up in a few minutes, and I have no orders to deliver anymore today, but come back tomorrow after school, and let me know what your father says."

Elias ran all the way home.

He delivered the coffee to Mrs. Vukovich and scarcely paused to hand it to her. He ran into the living room, where Leo sat drinking a beer and listening to the music. "Papa, Papa!" Elias shouted. "Can I go to work? I have a job if you let me. Can I, Papa?"

"Elias, don't shout at you papa. You too young to work. What kind of work you can do anyways?"

"With my wagon, Papa. Mister Schmidt said I can deliver groceries from the store with my wagon in the evening after school and Saturday. Can I, Papa, please?"

Leo was very pleased by his son's enthusiasm about working. He was also surprised. He did not immediately give any thought to why Elias might want such a job. He just felt pleased that anyone would invite a little boy, not quite nine years old, his little boy, to go to work.

Because Leo was so big himself, he saw Elias as little. If Elias had ever brought any of his friends from school to visit, or if Leo had ever gone to the school and seen that the other boys Elias' age were only half his size, he might not have been so surprised. In any case, he was a little skeptical.

"Okay, Elias," he answered finally. "While Mrs. Vukovich finish supper, you an' Papa walk to store an' see Mister Schmidt. If Mister Schmidt say to me, Elias come work, then okay, you work, but I don't think Mister Schmidt give very big job to little boy."

They went back to the store. Leo and Mister Schmidt were old friends, although they had not seen each other for a long time. They shook hands and talked about the weather, Anna's funeral, the economy, Leo's and Mister Schmidt's health, Leo's job, Mister Schmidt's new car, and various other subjects.

Elias stood impatiently by for a while. Then he patted the back of Leo's hand whispered, "Papa, Papa, what about my job?"

Leo stopped talking momentarily and scolded, "Elias not butt in when grown-ups talking. Okay, now you be good boy!"

He returned to discussion of routine things with Mister Schmidt. Finally, when Elias was about to give up in despair, Leo reached out and rumpled the boy's hair with his big right hand.

"How you think about my big boy, Mister Schmidt?" he asked.

"He is a fine big boy, Mister Stronski," the grocer answered, "a fine strong boy. I mentioned to him several weeks ago that I could use a strong, polite boy to deliver groceries to some of the ladies in the neighborhood."

"Well, Mister Schmidt," Leo replied, "he is pretty strong boy, but I think maybe he too young to go to work."

"No, no Papa!" Elias squealed excitedly. "I can do it!"

Leo scowled at him and repeated his earlier comment. "Little boy not butt in when grownups talking, Elias. I think you go run home an' tell Mrs. Vukovich I be home in a few minutes for supper. Run quick now."

He stopped and smacked Elias lightly on the behind.

Elias ran home nearly in tears. He delivered the message to Mrs. Vukovich, but he looked so downhearted that she wiped her hands and hugged him.

"What is wrong, Elias? You look like you are about to cry?"

Elias pouted. "Mister Schmidt offered me a job, and Papa told him I was too young. I used to get groceries for Grandma. I get groceries for you. Mister Schmidt was going to let me deliver groceries for other ladies, but Papa won't let me."

By this time tears of frustration were rolling down his cheeks.

"Maybe if I talk to him, it might help," Mrs. Vukovich offered.

"Oh, please do," Elias pleaded. "I don't know why he wants to be so mean. He knows I can do it."

"Don't give up yet, "Mrs Vukovich encouraged him. "I'll talk to him."

A few minutes later Leo came in, carrying a case of beer. He put it in the pantry and seated himself at the table. Elias was already seated, staring forlornly at his plate. Mrs. Vukovich quietly went about serving dinner, and they all ate without speaking except for brief requests to "pass" this or that.

Leo suddenly pushed back his chair.

He looked solemnly at his son for a few seconds, and then he said, "Young men must learn to be very polite to older people. My son must know when to speak, when no speak. If you work for people, you must be polite, even if you in big hurry or very angry. I will not have people say Leo Stronski's boy not polite. You understand me, Elias?"

Elias stared at his plate, downhearted, "Yes, Papa, but I can do the job. You know I can do it."

"Yes, I know you can do, Elias. I just want to be sure you know <u>how</u> you must do job. Now, when you go to Mister Schmidt tomorrow at five o'clock to start work, you must be always polite, always ready, never interrupt, never argue, and work quick and careful. Mister Schmidt say he give you fifty cents for every delivery. If ladies give you money at house for tip, you may take, but must always say thank you. You must never ask for tip or act like you waiting for tip. If they wish to give, they give. Bring groceries in, be very nice to people. Do extra little job if they ask, but always be polite, so Papa be proud of you."

Elias had been so sure his father had refused him the job that he could hardly believe his ears.

"I have the job, Papa?" he asked incredulously. "Am I really going to work tomorrow?"

"Yes, my son," Leo replied. "Mister Schmidt is very nice man. He thinks you very nice boy. Papa just want to know you going do good job an' not let Mister Schmidt down. If you have problem, you not bother Mister Schmidt, you bring problem first to Papa. You bring Mister Schmidt nothing but money an' hard work, okay?"

"Thank you, Papa," Elias exclaimed. "I thought you told Mister Schmidt I couldn't do it."

"See," Leo replied, "if you be polite an' not butt in, you hear whole story an' not have to worry. I want you learn to be polite if you work with people. One more thing. You not spend all money you get for work. Half you bring to Papa every week. I put it away for you, an' someday you need it, I have it for you. You understand Papa?"

Elias was so happy at that point, he would have agreed to anything. As it turned out, it was fortunate for him that his father cared enough to make him follow his wishes. Elias worked nearly every evening and several hours each Saturday from that day. Mister Schmidt was very pleased with his work and often gave him other odd jobs for which he paid him extra.

Elias no longer sneaked his drinks from his father's stock. Now he bought his own. He often took groceries home at night, and whenever his stock of beer and wine was low in his hidey-holes, he would just buy it along with the groceries his father or Mrs. Vukovich asked him to bring. He would stop on the way home and secret it away and bring only the requested items home. Leo never checked on him with Mister Schmidt, and Mister Schmidt was so kind and trusting that he just assumed that Elias' purchases were for his father.

He was very careful about his drinking. He drank often, but not overmuch. He chewed the strongest smelling gum he could find or sucked peppermints or lemon drops so his father nor his teachers ever caught the odor of the drink. He also religiously avoided close contact with grownups for an hour or so after drinking, but now he drank every day without worrying whether his father would miss the bottles from his supply.

Elias missed the brandy. Mister Schmidt sold only beer or wine, so the only way he could still get brandy was to sneak an occasional drink from his father's open bottle when he left any. He seldom did.

His father insisted that Elias give an accounting of his money each evening after supper and would collect the fifty percent toll from his daily labor. He kept his own personal funds in a covered dish high up in the cupboard. He had never trusted banks since that disastrous week in 1929 when his world began coming apart. Now he labeled another container for Elias and kept it beside his own. He also kept a very exact written record of all he collected from his son, which he kept on his person along with his own account record. Elias kept a mental tab of how much he passed on to Leo, but he could not be sure of the exact amount.

After a few months Elias was sure he was rich. He sincerely wished he had kept his own record in writing, but even so he knew his account was in the hundreds of dollars. He never let his little friends know how much money he had. He did not really buy that much for himself except beer and wine and occasionally cookies or candy bars. He managed to save a major portion of the share his father let him keep, as well.

Spring was in the air again, and Elias had nearly one hundred dollars tucked away in a corner of his drawer in a matchbox. His frugality was not generated by any thought of long-range goals or plans but by the constant concern that some morning he might wake up without sufficient money to buy the beer and wine he needed. In spite of this, there was no real recognition yet in his young mind that the alcohol was a daily need that had to be satisfied before, and without regard for, any other.

His work, both in school and in the grocery, was excellent. He tried very hard to please both his teachers and his employer. He also attended too many small tasks at home without being prompted by Mrs. Vukovich or his father. Also, he remained very popular with the other children in his school.

Over the course of the next year or two, he became more and more involved in doing odd jobs for money. Many of the ladies to whom he delivered groceries engaged him for other small tasks. He mowed the lawns and cleaned basements and windows in the summer and shoveled walks or carried wood or coal in the winter. By the winter of his eleventh year, he was five and half feet tall and one hundred sixty-five pounds of solid bone and muscle.

Leo, on the other hand, seemed to be shrinking day by day. He became less and less able to do his full day's work and often arrived late to work or came home early because he was ill. He seldom ate a full meal anymore. He stopped at the tavern or liquor store going to or coming home from work and remained almost constantly drunk.

His alcoholism was only the outward manifestation of a much more serious problem. He was dying on his feet from cancer and silicosis. He steadfastly refused to seek medical help and became more and more sullen and withdrawn. His ability to do his job deteriorated until his presence at work was just a daily formality, tolerated because of his long and faithful service and because of his illness.

At last the mine superintendent came to him one afternoon as he bent gasping for breath over the wash basin in the workshop.

"Leo, my friend," he said, grasping the once-powerful arm that was now thin and slack, "you must go to the personnel office tomorrow morning and ask for your retirement."

"I cannot retire," Leo growled. "I have bills to pay and son to raise. I must work!"

"Leo, we have been friends for many years," his boss replied, "but you know and I know what is happening to you. You are a walking dead man. Go home and rest. Spend what time you have with your son and make arrangements for what is to come. I love you, and I do not want you to die here in the dust and dirt. You have done your best. Now go home and talk to your priest and your doctor. Fix things as well as you can for your son. I respect you too much to tell you lies. If you need help, let me know, but don't come back to work anymore unless you get well."

He turned Leo gently to face him and thrust out his hand to say good-bye. Leo stubbornly refused both the hand and the gruff but kind advice of his friend and supervisor. He shook his shaggy head and said, "Leo Stronski gave whole life to this place. Work is all that keep me alive, and this you would take from me and make me quit. Friend like you I don't need!"

With tears in his eyes and trembling violently, he made his way to the door without even saying goodnight to the friends with whom he had worked for over fifteen years. He went home, turned on his music, and got completely, stupidly drunk.

CHAPTER 41

▼

Elias had gotten used to seeing his father still asleep as he was going off to school in the morning. He had not been very social with his father over the last several months, because Leo was seldom in a good mood and nearly always drunk. He spoke when he was spoken to and surrendered his savings as usual from each days work whenever his father was sober enough to collect. Other than that, they were as strangers, passing and speaking only briefly.

Mrs. Vulovich had all but given up on their meals, as Leo was seldom home, and Elias worked every evening until odd hours. Elias knew his father was very ill. He often placed his pillow over his head at night and pulled his blankets over that to shut out the sound of his father's wracking, gasping cough, which echoed constantly through the house. Many nights his father could not lie down for long, because he simply could not breathe lying down.

He listened as his father wandered, wheezing and gasping through the hallway, to the bathroom, back to the kitchen for another drink, and back again to his bedroom. Leo staggered his lonely hours through the darkness until total exhaustion demanded he sleep. Often he spent his only sleeping hours sitting in the big chair in the parlor, where he rested somewhat better and a little quieter than in his bed.

Mrs. Vukovich still came by several times a week, did the housework, and occasionally cooked a meal if Leo indicated a desire to eat, which he seldom did. She often remarked to Leo that he should be seeing a doctor, but Leo either answered her sharply that, "Doctor's more like kill people than help them," or, he would just give her an icy stare that said silently, "Mind your own business."

One morning about two months after Leo's last day at the mine, Elias woke early and began getting ready for school. He went to the bathroom and got dressed, strangely uneasy all the while. He did not know what bothered him until he suddenly realized how quiet it was in the house.

He finished dressing and, not really knowing why, tiptoed quietly, softly to the parlor door and peeked in at his father's big chair. It stood empty. More apprehensive now, still tiptoeing, he slipped up to the door of his father's room. The door stood partly open, and Elias looked in to see Leo's still form under the blanket. He listened silently, holding his breath. He heard no snores, moans, or gasps that he had been listening to for months.

He turned quickly, a chill running down his spine, and looked into the glass front of his grandmother's sewing room. The vision of his dead grandmother sitting cold and still in the old rocking chair flashed before his eyes.

Suddenly terrified, he ran to his room, seized his overcoat from the floor at the foot of his bed, and dashed from the house. His mind would not accept what his heart told him was true. He ran straight to the empty lot where his bottle of wine lay waiting in the end of the tile. With trembling hands he pulled it out and took a long drink, then closed the bottle tightly, put it back, and trotted the rest of the way to school.

For the rest of the morning he boisterously played the fool for his class, clowning and cutting up until his teacher was thoroughly exasperated with him. No sooner did she correct him for one prank than he would pull another, keeping the class in an uproar the whole morning. He tried every trick he could think of to keep his mind off what waited him at home.

Mrs. Vukovich, being a good catholic, immediately called her priest. He administered the appropriate rites and called the coroner. Leo's body had been removed from the house about twenty minutes earlier, and she and the priest were waiting for Elias when he arrived home from school.

Elias stopped short when he saw them standing, waiting for him.

"Come in, son," the priest said. "We have something we have to talk about."

The big little boy stood there silently for a minute and, looking the priest straight in the eye, asked calmly, "Have they taken him away already?"

In spite of his long training and considerable experience, the priest was startled by the calm acceptance in the boy's voice and attitude. He came silently down the steps and reached for the boy's hand.

"Come in the house, my boy," he said. "We have much to talk about."

Elias followed him silently. The three of them sat down at the kitchen table.

"Your father has gone to be with God, Elias," the priest said. "He will not be sick or suffer anymore. His troubles are over. Do you understand what I am telling you?"

"Yes, sir," Elias replied. "He was very sick, and he felt bad all the time. I guess it is good he don't hurt anymore."

The kindly priest nodded in agreement. "Now, son, if I am going to help you, I need to know more about your family. Can you tell me if you have any relatives here? Any aunts or uncles we should tell about this, or who can help you?"

Elias thought about it for a long while.

Then he said, "I think I have an uncle. His name is Bernard, but I don't know where he is or if he cares about us. I haven't seen him for a long time. He is the only one I know about."

"Okay, son" the priest answered. "I will see what I can find out. Do not worry. We will see that you are taken care of." Turning then to Mrs. Vukovich he asked, "Do you know his Uncle Bernard?"

"I know of him," she replied. "He left here several years ago, and I don't know where he went. Right after Anna died, he left. I don't know if Elias has any other family."

"Can you make arrangements for the boy tonight?" he then asked.

"Oh, yes, Father," she answered. "He is welcome to stay with me and my husband as long as he likes."

"No," Elias put in. "I want to stay here. All my stuff is here! I can't go nowhere else."

He was suddenly very concerned that if he left with Mrs. Vukovich, he might not be able to get away from her when he wanted to. He just did not want to have to answer to an adult to whom he might have to explain his actions.

"No," he repeated, "I don't want to go anywhere else. Besides, I have to go to the store and work right now."

He got up to leave.

"Wait a minute, young man," the priest said firmly. "No one is going to expect you to work for a few days. I will go to Mister Schmidt and explain. He will not wish you to work after what has happened. You must stay with Mrs. Vukovich. She will help you put some things together, and you can go to her house, where you won't have to worry about anything until I can find out what has been done to take care of you."

"But I want to work. I don't want to take time off, and I want to stay here in my own house."

He made his statement so pleadingly, and so close to tears for the first time, that Mrs. Vukovich felt very sorry and concerned for him.

"Father," she said, "do not worry. If you will stay here for a few minutes, I will go home and let my husband know, and I will stay here with Elias tonight. My husband won't mind."

Elias knew they were trying to help him, but he resented their interference at the same time. Seizing the better of two alternatives, he got up and stood close to Mrs. Vukovich.

"Please, sir," he pleaded, "can't I just stay here tonight?"

Sensing the boy's agitation and proud of him for the brave way he was conducting himself, the priest agreed.

"All right," he said, "but you are going to have to expect some changes in your life. They will not permit such a young boy to live by himself. For tonight you may stay here, and Mrs. Vukovich will take care of you. I will talk to Mister Schmidt and tell him you will not work tonight. Tomorrow we will see what else must be done."

For that evening Elias had his way. Mrs. Vukovich talked to him, fussed over him, and hugged him and told him what a man he was until he was thoroughly fed up with her. He tried not to show how he felt, remembering his father's instructions about being polite to grownups. Finally, when he felt he could control himself no longer, he said goodnight and went to bed much earlier than was usual for him.

He lay there in the darkness for several hours, thinking of his father and the good days when his father was well. He shed a few tears and finally fell asleep but slept fitfully, worrying about how this change would affect his future.

One thought emerged strongly from Elias' first long night alone. He was determined not to surrender his freedom of movement to strangers, no matter how well intentioned they were.

CHAPTER 42

▼

Whenever Eddie sobered up enough to start regretting his situation, he would start thinking about how good things had been when he had a paycheck coming in, a home and wife to go home to, and someone to cook for him and wash and mend his clothes. Invariably these thoughts led to Corky, the symbol of his troubles.

Today he was dead broke. His wine was gone. He had no clothes except those on his back and an extra pair of pants that he kept hidden in the bag of rags he slept in under the stairs at the warehouse. Worse yet, he was both sober and hungry.

This morning he headed out of the warehouse district toward the business area, where he might be able to bum a little cash. When panhandling failed to meet his immediate needs in a long two hours, he headed for the old mission where, in exchange for attending the prayer meeting, derelicts like himself could get a meal and a bath.

The manager had recently begun a new program which Eddie, as well as many like him, resented heartily. Anyone who looked well and strong enough was asked to do a little work in the mission. Sweeping, washing dishes, unloading furniture, peeling vegetables, and other small tasks were made a condition of exchange, particularly for those who might wish to spend the night.

Some of the street people did not mind doing an occasional task, but it often happened that those who readily accepted these little burdens without complaint were asked to do more. Even though this new manager's intention was to teach some of them the value and satisfaction of earning their way, she mainly succeeded in earning herself a "Simon Legree" label and a lot of curses and resentment.

Besides this, those who did work often demanded that little extra which they thought their due, such as two desserts, a second sleeping bag to use as a mattress, or not having to listen to the sermon as a dinner condition. This engendered more complaints and curses from those who did not receive these gratuities.

Eddie usually tried to avoid the mission. After all, he had a warm and fairly comfortable place to sleep, and he had become quite adept at panhandling, particularly when he was reasonably sober. When he did find it necessary to go to the mission, he tried to stay within a group of larger men, so he would not be noticed while the matron's work parties were being chosen. Mostly he was quite successful.

Today he was hungry. It was a gray, windy day, and he had carelessly failed to take account of the weather, so his only jacket lay under the stairs many blocks away. As soon as he became aware of the cold wet wind blowing in off the big lake, he headed directly for the mission, determined to work a little bit if he had to in exchange for a hot meal and a chance to wash up a little.

Unfortunately, today he arrived at the door just a little too late to enter with the group. As soon as he opened the door, he was eyeball to eyeball with the manger. She was a large, buxom, bustling, overly friendly, and very religious woman in her midforties who had held various paid and volunteer management jobs in social service all over the Midwest.

"God bless you, brother," she greeted Eddie. "How can we help you this morning?"

"Well, I was hoping to get a hot cup of coffee and a little breakfast if I ain't too late," Eddie said.

He reached up and snatched the greasy old railroad cap from his head, hoping to make some small favorable impression on her.

"The blessings of the Lord are always available to him who believes, brother," she replied, "but I wonder if you would mind helping me by getting a couple of small items off a truck out back—since you're too late for the sermon anyway."

This last bit was added to try to make him feel a little guilty, at which she was an expert.

"Sure," Eddie said, seeing no easy way to refuse. "I hope it ain't a grand piano." He grinned. "I ain't exactly the stevedore type, as you can see."

"Oh, no need to worry," she said pleasantly. "Just a little old bureau and a couple of kitchen chairs. Won't take us long at all. The driver is out there, and he said he'd help with the bureau."

Eddie followed her somewhat reluctantly to the loading dock out back. The truck driver stood there leaning against the tarp-covered box of the truck, working a toothpick between his teeth. There were about twenty straight-backed chairs and an old five-drawer dresser, scratched and marred, in the back of the truck.

"Okay," the manager said to the driver, "here's your help. If you gents will grab that bureau, I'll show you where it goes."

The driver was somewhat larger than Eddie and looked like he was used to this kind of work. The bureau was not extremely heavy, but it was large and clumsy to carry. When Eddie and the driver came through the door with it, she pointed to a stairway going up at one side of the room.

"It goes up there," she said, gesturing upward.

About twenty steps led upward to a small door at the top, which was closed.

"You want tops or bottoms?" The driver asked Eddie, shifting his toothpick to the other side of his mouth with his tongue.

Eddie's legs were already trembling, and all he wanted to do was get it over with.

"Don't matter," he grunted.

The driver started backing quickly toward the steps. Because he had the lower end, at least three quarters of the weight shifted to Eddie's skinny frame as soon as the driver started upward. He bravely began to struggle up, but before he was halfway, he knew he was not going to make it. The several years of heavy drinking and inadequate food, plus a pack-a-day cigarette habit, had weakened him far more than he realized. The stairs were steep and narrow, and the sudden realization that he might end up at the bottom with the bureau on top of him almost made him panic.

The big truck driver felt the hesitation and trembling and looked over his end at Eddie.

"For Chris'sake, don't drop it, feller," he said loudly. "It could kill ye."

The manager had been watching their progress from the safety of the bottom of the stairs. Seeing the whole situation in a flash, and sensing the urgency in the driver's voice, she dashed up the stairs behind Eddie with surprising agility for so large a woman.

"Bear up! Bear up!" she shouted. "The Lord will share the load."

The stairway was too narrow for the big lady to squeeze by and get a helping grip on the bureau. She did the only thing she could see to do. She cupped both of Eddie's buttocks in her chubby hands and leaned her considerable weight into hoisting Eddie and the bureau the rest of the way up the stairs, calling loudly on the Lord to "strengthen us!"

The whole shebang hit the small landing at the top of the stairs in a matter of seconds. The driver, pushed backward, caught his heel on the top step and fell against the closed door, smashing it open and driving the doorknob through the plaster wall inside the room.

He lit on his back in the doorway with the bureau legs pinning him down. Eddie went face first between the driver's outstretched boots with his pelvis hanging over the top step. The lady's knee hit him square in the ass, driving his private parts against the edge of the landing as she sprawled full-length on top of him, crushing the last of the air from his already-tortured lungs.

Eddie passed out cold, and it took her a long five minutes of rolling, rubbing, and resuscitation to revive him. Meanwhile, the big driver lay where he had fallen, alternately drumming his heels on the floor and squawking incoherently.

As soon as she began to see some signs of life stirring in Eddie, she helped him to sit up, back against the wall, next to the doorway. She then jumped up and hurried to see what damage had been done to the driver. He still lay where he had fallen, making weird squawking noises. She immediately noticed that the legs of the bureau had come down on top of his jacket under his arm pits, pinning him firmly to the floor.

"One moment, brother," she encouraged him. "I'll have you loose in a jiffy."

Hoisting her skirt to her lower thighs, she scrambled to the top of the dresser and slid herself across it into the small storeroom. Ignoring any embarrassment to herself or the driver, she quickly straddled his head and shoulders and raised the end of the dresser, releasing him.

He rolled slowly over and raised himself on hands and knees to crawl out from between her legs.

She then seized the end of the dresser and, pulling and tugging, slid it noisily inside the door, so she could get back out without climbing over again. Highly concerned about Eddie, because he had been unconscious, she stepped onto the landing again to check on him.

Eddie, nearly recovered, sat slouched against the wall groaning, legs spread, massaging his crotch with both hands. His face was pale and greenish, and sweat was running from his forehead and dripping down his nose.

Satisfied that he was recovering, she returned to the storeroom to find the truck driver still crawling in circles on hands and knees and making weird barking noises. She went quickly to him and slapped him heartily a few times in the middle of his broad back. Then, straddling him, she wrapped her arms around his middle and hoisted him to his feet.

"You okay, brother?" she asked.

He nodded and cleared his throat noisily but did not look like he meant it. He, like Eddie, looked pale and sweaty.

"Knocked the wind out of you, did it?" she asked.

The driver finally answered, only now in a high squeaky voice instead of his usual bass. "Swallered me gawdam toothpick, lady," he squeaked, "an' it like to kilt me. Gawd, do I need a drink!"

He headed shakily but purposefully down the stairs to find one.

By this time Eddie was finally up and about. He wiped his dripping forehead with his shirt sleeve and leaned against the doorjamb.

"I don't think I can manage them chairs lady," he said in a begging tone. "I'm not feelin' so good."

"Well, okay," she replied, "but if you can just help me put this bureau over in the corner, I'll get somebody who has already had breakfast to bring up the chairs."

Eddie almost refused this final task but then agreed and was very pleased with himself afterward for having helped her, even though it had nearly crippled him. As they picked up the dresser again, Eddie, still shaky, let it tip forward a little, and the top drawer slid partway open. Staring out at him from the bottom of the drawer was a luminous green monster mask, the ugliest he had ever seen.

When they had the dresser where she wanted it, Eddie leaned quickly down over the end of it as though exhausted. As soon as she turned away toward the door, he quickly seized the mask from the drawer with his left hand, turning his back to her as he came up off the dresser, and poked it quickly inside his shirt.

"Okay," she said, "now, if we can push it just a little further into the corner, I'll see you get a good breakfast. Sorry about the fall, but God bless you, brother. We made it, didn't we?"

Eddie grinned in self-satisfaction, not at earning his breakfast with honest labor but at obtaining the mask, which he saw as a way to make more mischief for Corky, the symbol of his downfall.

CHAPTER 43

▼

Corky saw Eddie watching him from the alley as he left school, but he tried to act as though he had not seen him. He walked rapidly until he reached the first corner, and as soon as he was around it, he cut across the street and ran through the warehouse area and the empty lot to the diner.

Although it was only three in the afternoon, Bob was already at the diner. Corky pointedly ignored him and went straight to the kitchen where Janet was washing dishes.

She said, "Hi, sweetie, how was school?" but kept on with her work, not expecting or getting a reply.

Corky leaned against the end of the deep sink, looking up at her, and she could tell he was displeased about something. She waited for several minutes, but he did not speak, only stared steadily at her.

Finally she could stand it no longer and said in an irritated voice, "Why are you staring at me like that, Corky?"

"What's he doing out there already?" he asked.

"Who you talking about?" she asked, knowing the answer already.

"Bob," he said angrily. "You know who! What is he doing here?"

"Well, he got back early today, and we thought we would eat supper here when we close, and then we were going to go have beer. We'll take you home first."

"He ain't takin' me anywhere," Corky declared. "I'll walk home."

Jan had become quite accustomed to Corky's resentment of Bob, but she was not about to surrender to his wishes.

Whenever she discussed it with Bob, he always told her, "You can't let the kid run your life. If he don't like me, that's tough shit. Why should we give in to him? He'll get used to it by the by."

As the months rolled by, Corky's resentment grew rather than diminished. Whenever their relationship came to a standstill, Bob would attempt to buy him off. He would offer him fifty cents or a dollar to get him out of the way, and he an Jan did whatever their plans dictated, leaving Corky to his own devices.

Now, when Corky bluntly declared his unwillingness to cooperate, Jan just shrugged and said, "well, okay, just wait till I finish these dishes, and I'll make you a sandwich. Then you can go home if you like. You have your key, and if you go to bed before we get home, be sure to lock the door."

Corky was angry, but he did not argue. He waited until Jan had made his small lunch, then ate it and left. It was still early evening, and the weather was not bad, so he decided to go to the warehouse loading docks for the rest of the after-noon instead of straight home.

The strip of warehouses directly across the field from his house consisted of seven great buildings on either side of a wide street. Each warehouse was half a block long and had concrete loading docks on the street side. Railway tracks ran close in front of the docks on both sides of the street. There was about a thirty-foot gap between the ends of the warehouses.

Steps led up either end of each dock, and Corky liked to run the docks. He would run up the steps at one end, then run as fast as he could the length of the dock and down the steps at the other end until he had made a complete circuit of the two-and-one half blocks of warehouse row.

If there were men working, he would stop occasionally to watch. If warehouse doors were open, and no one was paying particular attention, he would go inside to explore the huge buildings. Most of the warehouses contained row upon row of boxes or crates, and the noisy little fork-lift trucks hurried and scurried like giant bugs up and down between these mountains of mysterious merchandise.

One warehouse in particular fascinated Corky. The big man who had favored him with a smile and a candy bar the first day he skipped school worked in this building. The warehouse was filled with huge rolls of paper stacked like pencils, row upon row, against the walls. The rolls were so large that Corky, standing on tiptoe, could just barely look into the center hole of a roll. They were stacked lying down, so when one was separated from the stack, one man could roll it from place to place.

Each roll weighed between one thousand and fourteen hundred pounds. They would arrive at the warehouse in boxcars and go out again on trucks. A fork-lift truck with very long tines would run up under the first roll in a stack, lift it clear of the floor, and back slowly off, allowing the stacked rolls to come down gently one space. Then the warehouseman would block the stack with a large wooden wedge.

At the floor level between these rolls, there was enough space so a small man could crawl easily in between. Corky liked to slip into the warehouse, crawl back in these warm dry places, and play hide-and-seek with imaginary playmates.

The big man who worked here running the fork lift to load trucks and unload trains never objected to Corky's visits.

After the first few times he became quite friendly, often cautioning Corky, "Careful you don't get hurt in there, young feller," or, "Be sure you don't get in the way of this here fork lift. I can't be watching for you all the time."

He did, however, and also often gave Corky the push broom and an area to sweep, for which he paid him a quarter or fifty cents. After a while it became Corky's regular duty to sweep the dock in front of the door nearly every night. The man also got him extra little duties with the other truckers up and down the dock, mostly sweeping or picking up trash.

There was a toilet in one corner of the warehouse where Corky could wash himself at the sink, get a drink of water, or relieve himself when necessary. It was pleasant and convenient, and a home away from home for Corky. In fact, if the truth were known, he was happier here than he was anywhere else.

After Corky's first few afternoons of hanging around, the warehouseman introduced himself as Otto and asked Corky for his name. Once introduced, they became more or less silent companions. Neither spoke much, but each watched for chances to do some slight service or favor for the other. Neither would have referred to the other as "my friend," but a bond of cooperative companionship sprang up between them that lasted for many months.

Today Corky went directly to the paper warehouse. The door stood slightly open, and Otto was nowhere about. Each of the rolls of paper had a wooden block with a small hole in the center stuck tightly in the center hole of the roll. These round wedges kept the center holes from collapsing from the weight when many rolls of paper were tacked on top one another.

Sometimes the warehouseman let a paper roll drop heavily from the fork lift, or if rolled around, the wedge became loosened and popped out of the larger roll. Otto and others who came and went in the warehouse gathered them up and threw them into a large cardboard box that stood near the toilet. Whenever Otto was loading the paper onto the trucks, he would get one of these from time to time and replace a missing one in a roll going out.

Corky invented a game with these small wooden wheels. He would take three or four with him clear to the end of the warehouse and roll them toward the wall at the other end with an underhanded motion like a softball pitcher or bowler might use. At first his object was to make each one go a little farther than the last. Soon he began inventing variations, making them curve, slide, or bank off the front of the paper rolls to an imaginary target far down the warehouse floor from his starting point. Before long his accuracy and his distance improved, until he often surprised himself with some of the things he could accomplish with these uncomplicated toys.

He was thus engaged in sharpening his skills when he noticed someone walk by the partly opened door. The shadow passed quickly, as the door was open only a foot or two. Corky, curious, discontinued his game, ran quickly to the door, and peered out. He was startled to see the raggedy-looking drunk he had seen earlier near the school go down the steps at the end of the dock and head across the street between the two warehouses directly across from his house.

Quite curious now, he watched until the man disappeared around the corner. Then, quickly but cautiously, he followed. He sneaked very quietly up to the corner where the man had disappeared, and he peeked around.

At first he saw nothing. Then a movement in the willow brush near the tracks caught his eyes. Watching carefully, he soon saw that the man was bent over and was slipping along in the brush. At intervals he would pause and raise up to stare intently at the little house in the middle of the empty lot.

Corky followed. Being very small, it was easy for him to stay concealed from Eddie.

For the next hour he played this cautious game of hide-and-seek, watching Eddie make an almost-complete circle of the house. By this time it was approaching dusk, and Corky was beginning to wonder what the end of the game would be.

Finally, as Eddie came near the rear west corner of the house where there were no windows, he raised up and, sneaking rapidly on tiptoe, ran right up to the rear wall of the house and made his way around the corner nearest the kitchen window. Corky reversed directions and ran as fast as he could back along the path he had been traveling to a point where he could see the front of the house.

There was Eddie standing on tiptoe, one hand shading his eyes, peering in the kitchen window. He stepped back after a moment and looked all around, as though he expected someone to come.

Then he went to the front door and tried it. When he found it locked, he shook it angrily, like he might be trying to break in. Corky could hear him mumbling to himself. Suddenly he turned, went quickly back across the lot, and disappeared between the warehouses.

Corky did not know what this was all about, but he was worried. He wished heartily that he knew where to find his mother, but he did not. He was afraid to go home, for fear this ugly man would return. He had acted like he knew the area well, and that worried Corky even more. He even thought briefly of other occasions when weird creatures had tried to attack him when he was alone, so he did not want to be in the house by himself.

He felt more comfortable out in the open where he could run. Reluctantly he made the decision to remain outside until his mother came home.

With darkness came the cold. Though he shivered and shook, occasionally curling up in the tall grass to shield himself from the night breezes, he kept his vigil outside until long after dark. When the welcome headlights of Bob's car finally rounded the corner and crossed the tracks, he still did not stir from his hiding place fifty yards from the front door.

He knew that Bob seldom came into the house after he was gone to bed, and tonight, though he was very tired an cold, he preferred to be cold a little longer than to have to explain to Bob why he was outside. He knew Bob would only call him a liar again and talk against him to his mother—so he waited an eternal fifteen minutes more while they sat in the car and talked.

Finally Jan got out of the car. He heard her say goodnight, and the car door slammed. Bob's car spun quickly about and bumped across the tracks into the darkness.

Only then did Corky rise up from his hiding place and run stiffly toward the porch where Jan was unlocking the door.

She stepped inside and turned on the light, and he notice the alarm in her voice as she called, "Corky," then louder, "Corky, where are you?"

"I'm here, Mom," he answered as he jumped quickly onto the porch.

She turned and stared at him for a moment. He could tell she had been drinking as soon as he saw her eyes, but he was completely unprepared for her anger. Seizing him by both arms, she shook him violently.

"You stupid little idiot!" she yelled at him. "It's after midnight. What are you doing still outside? Look at you. You are half frozen to death. Just because you hate Bob, you don't have to scare me like that. How do you think I felt when I came in here and you weren't home?"

All the whole while she screamed at him, she continued to shake him, and his cold little body felt it would crack in a thousand pieces.

"From now on I better find you in our bed asleep when I get home," she scolded.

Corky longed to tell her the reason why he had spent half the night in a cold empty lot and how frightened he had been, but he reasoned that in her present frame of mind, she probably would not believe him anyway. He did the next best thing and began to cry.

Seeing that he was cold and miserable, and not inclined to argue with her, she relented somewhat. "Get those cold damp things off of you before you catch pneumonia or something. I'm sorry I stayed out so late, but I thought you were home in bed. You know you should have been, don't you?"

She shook him again with one hand, a little more gently this time.

"Yes, Mama," Corky sniffled. "I'm sorry too."

Though he wanted with all his heart to tell her the whole story, he bottled it up with the rest of his frustrations and rejections and never mentioned it to anyone ever again.

CHAPTER 44

▼

Eddie waited until Thursday, although he was eager as a yearling bull to try out his newfound device against his son.

He had made a couple of crude torches by dripping candle wax on two lengths of heavy string and wrapping them tightly on short pieces of clothes-hanger wire.

He had tried the mask on in a gas-station men's room. It was grotesquely ugly. Pale luminous green in color, it had a fringe of fuzzy reddish-orange hair around the forehead piece and down the sideburns. Large pointed ears jutted out from either side of the eye sockets, which were streaked with blood red, encrusted with tiny varicolored sparklers of glass or foil. It somewhat resembled pictures he had seen of the devil, but it had large animal-like teeth painted between its grinning red lips.

The only thing wrong with it had been the elastic string that pulled it tight to the face. It was broken free at one end, but it took Eddie only a few seconds to reattach this, and it was good as new.

Spring in Chicago was unpredictable. The morning had been beautiful. The sun shone, and the birds announced their territorial claims from every elm tree and rooftop in the neighborhood. This evening the weather was changing. Clouds had started blowing in from the lakes in mid-afternoon, and the temperature began dropping.

By early evening as Eddie peered from his place of concealment by the warehouses, he began to wish he had chosen a better day. It felt like rain or snow or both, but so vindictive was he, so eager to vent his frustrations on a child, that he would not abandon the effort. He knew his best opportunity was on Thursdays, and he could not bear to wait for another week to go by.

Bob's car was parked in front, and he had seen Jan leave the diner in early afternoon. He watched from the corner of the warehouse as Corky made his dash through the lot after school. He grinned in anticipation and took a couple of gulps from his bottle of cheap wine.

"Be just my luck them two will decide to sit home tonight, an' I'll spend two hours here freezing my ass for nothin'," he said crabbily to himself.

Finally, at about six-thirty, his patience was rewarded. Jan and Bob came out of the house. Jan paused by the car and waved at the front of the house. Although he could not see the window or the door from where he was, he envisioned the elfin face peering from the house and Corky's good-bye wave to his mother.

"You'll be wishin' you never was born soon's its dark, you li'l bugger," he chortled.

He watched Bob's car disappear in the dusk and then settled down in a sheltered spot to wait for darkness to come.

Considering the weather, he was fairly sure the boy would not leave the house. However, his success or failure hinged on whether Corky turned out the light. Darkness was a must to make his plan fully effective. As fate would have it, Corky never turned on the light.

Jan had made spaghetti and meat balls for supper, which was one of Corky's favorite meals. He had eaten a considerable plateful for so small a boy. He leaned on the window sill for nearly an hour after his mother left, staring forlornly at the spot where the car had disappeared over the tracks as though trying to wish her back again.

He had no great variety of things to play with in the house, because he seldom played indoors. He preferred to be outdoors. However, after what had happened a few evenings earlier he was leery about going out, and his mother had warned him not to leave the house and to keep the door locked.

Jan had turned the heat up on the oil heater before she left, because the weather was acting up, so it was quite warm and comfortable, if lonely, in the little house.

She had told him, "We probably will be quite late, so you go to bed when you get ready, and don't leave the house."

As darkness took away the vision of his mother waving good-bye from the driveway, Corky finally gave up to boredom and loneliness and crossed the room to flop on the sofa bed, which his mother had spread out sometime during the afternoon and had not bothered to fold away again. He took off his shoes and socks, pulled a blanket up over his legs, and was soon asleep.

"This is going to be easier than I thought," Eddie mumbled to himself as he waited. "I'll scare the dog shit out of that brat and have plenty of time to put the touch on a couple creeps before I hit the sack."

He was pleased to be able to get on with it, because the wind was starting to pick up, and a few drops of rain had started to fall. He was determined to proceed in spite of the weather.

"Maybe the wind shaking that shack will add to the effect, and I'll scare him plumb to death. That'd serve her right to come back and fine the brat crapped out."

He laughed drunkenly as he pulled out the mask and slipped it on.

Not even thinking of caution now, Eddie left the shelter of the warehouse and hurried to the house. The front window was on the sheltered side of the house, which suited his purposes exactly. Shading his eyes with his hands on either side of his face, Eddie peered into the half-curtained window. He could not see much inside except the white of the bed sheets and a faint glow under the oil heater by the wall.

In order for his plan to be effective, Eddie had to be sure Corky was awake. He took a rusty nail from his pocket, pressed the sharp end firmly against the glass, and pulled downward.

The piercing vibration scree-ee-eech filled the darkened room, and Corky stirred restlessly.

Eddie noted the slight movement on the bed and squealed the nail once more over the glass.

Scree-ee-eee…!

Then he slapped his palm sharply against the wall next to the window frame. This time Corky sat up quickly on the bed and began peering around to see what had awakened him.

Eddie ducked down and, taking a book of matches and one of his torches from his pocket, lit the torch. Standing again in front of the window, he held the torch next to his chest below the level of the window sill, so it lit up the awful luminous face with a weird flickering glow. Again he applied the screeching nail to the glass, but this time the noise was almost drowned out by Corky's own frantic scream.

Eddie cackled happily at the sound and waved his torch wand back and forth to increase the flickering effect.

Corky stared wide-eyed for a few seconds at this awful creature that had come to get him. He jumped out of bed for a second, then quickly back in again, realizing there was no way to get away except through the door, which was a scant three feet from the monster at the window.

"Get away from here!" Corky screamed frantically.

Seizing the heaviest of the blankets, he pulled it over his head and squeezed himself tightly into the corner next to the arm of the sofa bed. Sick with fright, he lay there trembling, wondering if he had remembered to lock the door. Every second he lay there seemed an eternity, and he expected at any moment to feel the monster's fingernails dig into his body.

The third scream of the nail on the glass told him the thing was still there. Though not wanting to look, not knowing was worse than the awful sight of the face at the window. He raised the blanket and peeked out again. The snarling monster was there briefly, then suddenly disappeared as Eddie's first torch burned out.

<u>Maybe it couldn't see me and went away</u>, Corky thought hopefully.

He felt weak and sick to his stomach, and the sweat dripped uncomfortably down his tiny pointed nose.

Suddenly, with a thump and a growl, the face was back as Eddie got his second torch going. He emphasized his return with a fierce growl close to the glass.

Corky stared, fascinated, unable to escape and too frightened to move.

Eddie had made two slight miscalculations that turned his wicked adventure against him. The first was that while the light from the torch flowed on the window glass, he could not see anything happening inside the room. The second was that even the miniscule mouse, when cornered and frightened, will fight and bite viciously if not mortally wounded.

Corky suddenly got mad. Throwing back his blanket, he jumped from the bed, remembering the groceries his mother had bought earlier that day. They still sat where she had left them on the small counter next to the sink. Seizing a large can of beans firmly in right hand, Corky ran at full speed, screaming loudly, straight toward the gruesome face at the window.

From only three feet away he launched the heavy can through the glass with all his strength. In his anger, his only thought was to do as much damage to this horrible creature with his single weapon as he possibly could. The results were far more drastic than he could possibly have anticipated.

The glass was a very thin barrier and thus failed to cushion the blow in the slightest. The can crashed through the glass, and the base rim of it struck Eddie directly on the bridge of the nose and left eyebrow. It dropped him to his knees in the mud and nearly knocked him unconscious. Worse, the lower edge of the can carried with it a two-inch, razor-sharp shard of glass that penetrated the mask just to the left of Eddie's nose and punched its way clear to the bone in his left cheek, opening a gash that gushed blood like a fountain.

It was the monster's turn to howl in pain and fright. He dropped his torch, pulled the blood filled mask from his face, and began tugging frantically at the spear of glass imbedded in his cheek bone. He cut both his thumb and finger in working the triangle-shaped blade of glass from his face and was bleeding so badly that he was suddenly afraid for his life.

He had no clean cloth to staunch the flow of blood from his face, so he pressed the heel of his hand to his cheek to slow the bleeding. Sick and dizzy from the blow and shock, he ran as fast as he could toward the lighted street, where he might find someone to help him.

Corky, awed at first by the frantic shout that had followed his attack and then hearing the rapid retreat of his tormentor, returned again to his shelter under the blanket. Now he was worried about two things. First, the thought that the monster could now get in through the broken window filled him with dread. Second, he had broken the window, and to the best of his knowledge there was nothing to prove that he had not just thrown the can through the window.

How was he going to explain to his mother? He felt he had been fighting for his life, but he was sure that his mother and Bob would not believe him. Now he was not only worried about the monster coming back, but he was also worried that his mother would punish him for breaking the window—that was, if the monster did not get him first—so he sat in the darkness and kept his lonely vigil until Jan and Bob came home sometime after midnight.

Jan came in by herself, having said goodnight to Bob in the car. When she switched on the single light, she immediately noticed Corky's shock of red hair and blue eyes peeping from the cocoon of blanket against the arm of the sofa. She was feeling a warm glow from the drinks she had consumed over the last several hours and from Bob's warm advances in the car. He had done his best to persuade her to go to a motel for a couple of hours, which she would have loved to do, but because of having to be to work at six-thirty in the morning, and somewhat concerned about Corky, she had put him off until Saturday.

She was shocked out of her euphoria as soon as she saw Corky, wide awake, peering at her as though terrified. He reminded her of a baby raccoon she had seen scanning the world from a knothole on some long-ago day at the zoo with her father.

"My God, Corky, what are you doing still awake at this hour?" she asked.

Corky, both relieved that he was no longer alone and anxious that he was going to be blamed for breaking the window, suddenly burst into tears. Jan, feeling a bit guilty about have left him alone, went quickly to him and picked him up in her arms.

"What's wrong, baby?" she asked. "What is wrong? Why are you crying? Everything is okay."

Corky did not answer but only stared wide-eyed at the window, wondering if the monster was still out there. At least there was someone else now to help fight it, but still he was worried that he would be in trouble for the broken window.

Jan was too concerned about why her son was awake and crying at this hour to notice the window immediately.

"What's the matter, honey? You have been alone before. Why are you crying?"

She begged him for an explanation that would relieve the guilty feeling growing stronger by each minute. Corky still did not answer, but unable to keep it to himself any longer, he pointed to the broken window. For the first time Jan noticed the cold draft from that side of the room and, looking more closely, saw that a full panel of the four-panel window was broken out. A few shards of broken glass littered the linoleum near the wall.

"Corky!" she exclaimed. "What happened? How did you break the window?"

Relieved that the whole thing was going to be out in the open now, Corky began explaining excitedly. "The monster was trying to get in, and he was screaming at me, an' I din't know what to do, an' I was scared, so I hit him with a can of veg'ables."

"Come on, Corky. There are no monsters," Jan chided. "What really happened? We can get the window fixed. I just want to know what happened."

"Really, Mom, there was a monster, an' when I hit him with the can, he screamed an' ran away."

He seemed so sincere that Jan could not help feeling that something had really frightened the child, but she still was not ready to start believing in monsters.

"So okay, Corky, tell me again how the window got broken," Jan said gently.

"When the monster wouldn't go away, I hit him with a can of veg'ables," Corky repeated.

"Then," said Jan, "If I go out and look in the yard, I'll find the can out there, right?"

She thought that by challenging him, she might get the real story.

To her surprise, Corky became quite concerned. "It's still there if the monster didn't take it," he said, "but don't go out there, Mama. He might be still there."

Too curious now to let it pass, Jan replied, "You get up there on the sofa and stay there, Corky. I'm going to just take a look outside. Don't be afraid. I'll only be a minute."

She went to her kitchen cabinet and got a flashlight. After cautioning Corky again to stay inside, she left the door standing open and stepped into the yard. As soon as she shined the light under the window, it picked up the luminescence of the ugly mask, and nearby lay the unopened can of beans Corky had thrown.

Both curious and excited now, she walked to the spot and looked closer. It took her but a minute to gather up the remainder of Eddie's torches, the mask, and the can and return to the lighted room. Not wanting to frighten Corky further, she closed the door softly and, concealing the objects at her side as best she could, went to the sink and laid them out side by side.

Immediately she felt repulsed by the ugliness of the mask and how realistic the streaks of blood down the face were. Not until she spread the mask open did she notice it was soaked with fresh blood on the inside and realize that the streak down the face was real blood too.

Truly aghast now, she began to assemble the situation in her mind.

"Goddamn you, Eddie Hackett," she said softly to herself. "No mask was ever made to picture the monster you really are."

Suddenly overcome with the enormity of what Corky had been through, and thinking back to the other incidents, she began to cry. After a few minutes she got control of herself, returned to Corky, sat down, and gathered him into her arms.

"I'm very sorry I didn't believe you, little man," she said. "Mama was wrong. There really are monsters, and I'm very proud that you were brave enough to fight one, but I know who and what this monster is, Corky. It is only a very mean and ugly man. You remember the man you thought was watching us at the school? Well, that's who it is. I should have told you this before, but that man is your father, and he hates us. That's why he has done all these things to you. I'm sure now that he was the monster who chased you before, and he was in the box that chased you too. Tomorrow we are going to the police, and we are going to see that he never bothers us again.

True to her word, Jan took Corky, and they went to the police early the next morning. They stopped at the diner to let Rosa know what had happened and to make sure she could handle the business while they made their report.

"Told you we shoulda cooked the bastard's goose a long time gone," Rosa exclaimed when Jan told her. "You want I should sick Charlie on 'im again?"

"No, Rosa," Jan replied. "This time we'll let the cops handle it. Eddie hates cops anyway, an' if I can get them after him, maybe he'll go away an' leave us be."

The policeman at the desk was very sympathetic when Jan told him their story. He assured her they would pick him up and charge him and told Jan she would be called to witness if they caught him.

"One thing, ma'am," the big cop said. "If we find your husband an' he has cuts an' all, like you say, that's pretty good evidence, but we need to keep these things to see if the blood matches an' all. You can probly get 'im put away for a spell if it all checks out. In the meantime, I'd keep a pretty close watch on the little feller. If his ol' man's mean enough to do them kinda things, no tellin' what he might try to do to get even now."

Jan did not let Corky go to school that day but kept him close by where she could see him. Several times he asked to go out on the street, but she was firm in her demand that he stay put inside the diner.

Eddie was arrested a few hours later. When the case came to court, Eddie was found guilty of criminal trespass, malicious mischief, and assault on a minor. The judge sentenced him to six months in jail and granted Jan an injunction forbidding him to ever approach his wife and child again, on penalty of further jail time.

This relieved Jan's mind considerably, and she soon returned to her old habits of leaving Corky to his own devices, with only casual concern for his welfare.

As for Corky, it only served to strengthen his distrust of people and raise the wall of isolation behind which he would hide for the rest of his life.

CHAPTER 45

▼

Elias was up early the morning after his father died. He heard Mrs. Vukovich stirring around in the kitchen as he dressed. He washed himself, combed his hair, and brushed his teeth before she even knew he was awake.

"I have made a good breakfast for you, Elias," she said. "Sit down, and I will bring it. Then we will wait for Father to come back. Maybe he has found your Uncle Bernard by now. Do you want to wait here or at my house?"

"I have to go to school," Elias answered quickly. "You don't need to worry about me. I have a job, and I have some money. I can manage for myself, thank you."

Mrs. Vukovich was surprised and a little taken aback by this forthright and mature answer. Still she knew the authorities would not permit an eleven-year-old boy to live alone and fend for himself.

"There is no need for you to go to school for a few days, Elias. Father Francis has told your teacher what happened, and no one expects you to go to school."

"Please, ma'am," Elias answered politely, "I do not want to sit around here. I want to be with my friends. I don't want to get behind in my schoolwork. I can talk to Father Francis when I get home tonight."

Without waiting for reply or argument from her, he quickly got up from the table, picked up his books, and left.

When Father Francis arrived about ten o'clock that morning, Mrs. Vukovich told him of Elias' stubborn refusal to stay home. After she had explained, the priest agreed.

"Perhaps," he told her, "it is better for him to be with his friends and stay busy. Let's just let it be and take it up with him tonight. Don't let him run off to work after school though. I could not find anyone who has any information about his uncle. If we can't find him, we will have to make arrangements with child welfare for foster care or state custody. Do you know if they have any money?"

Mrs. Vukovich knew nothing of their family finances except that Leo had always paid cash for anything she had seen since she had worked for him. They discussed the situation for a few minutes and agreed that Father would make a further attempt to locate relatives and ascertain the state of their family finances during the day, and they would take it from there with Elias when he came home from school.

Elias, quite in contrast to the previous day, spent his day in nervous silence. He slipped away from school at lunchtime to visit one of his hidey-holes and substituted a few sips of wine for his lunch. He was worried and just did not feel like eating.

Contrary to what he expected, the wine did not help and the afternoon dragged interminably on. When the closing bell finally sounded, he left school reluctantly, nervous and apprehensive about his forthcoming conference with Mrs. Vukovich and the priest.

It was a pleasant spring afternoon, and he took his time going home. He visited the empty lot on the way and fortified himself against the coming meeting. He chewed two sticks of gum afterward and spit it out just before he arrived home.

The door was slightly ajar when he came up the steps. He walked quietly and eased the door open when he heard the priest and Mrs. Vukovich talking.

"If the police can't get any information on his uncle," he heard Father Francis say, "The welfare people will put him up for a while until they can find a foster home for him. I know it will be tough on him, as independent as he is, but he simply cannot be left to manage on his own at his age."

"It's a real shame, Father," Mrs. Vukovich replied. "I'd put him up for a while myself, he's such a nice boy, but I got my husband to think about too. We ain't got any kids, and I don't know what my husband would say to taking one in at this time of our lives. I hope you find his uncle, but then, there is no guarantee he would have a place for him either."

Elias' first impulse was to run, but thinking better of it, he stepped backward silently to the door, opened it a little farther, then closed it noisily to create the impression he had just come in. As he walked into the kitchen, the two adults fell momentarily silent.

'Hi, Father," Elias said. "Did you find my Uncle Bernard yet?"

Father Francis shook his head and looked at Mrs. Vukovich, who got up quickly and began fussing around in front of the stove.

"Come in and sit down, Elias," the priest said kindly. "I have found some people who will look out for you until we find your relatives. It is a nice place, and there are many other boys and girls their who will be company for you. It will be just like a new family. Tomorrow a lady will come, and we will talk more about it then."

Elias was smart enough not to object, already making his plans before he had come in to face this meeting.

"Okay, Father," he replied, "but I need tonight to get my things ready. Maybe Mrs. Vukovich can stay and help me pack, and I can sleep here again tonight. Will that be all right, Father?"

"Well, I guess it is okay with me if Mrs. Vukovich doesn't mind one more night away from home," Father Francis replied.

He was quite relieved to see the boy taking it so well, and he had a hard time remembering that this young man, who stood as tall as he, was only eleven years old.

Mrs. Vukovich readily agreed to stay and gave Elias exactly the opening he needed.

"I will be happy to help you, Elias," she said, "and I am sure my husband will understand for one more night. I do need to go home for a while though and get his supper and explain. You can either stay here and start getting ready, or come home and eat with us, and we will come back later."

"Oh, if you don't mind, I'll just stay here," Elias replied, "I'm not real hungry, an' I can fix myself a sandwich."

"That won't be necessary," she said. "I'll be back as quick as I can and bring you a plate of food when I come."

"Well, that is all settled then," Father put in. "Would you like me to stay until Mrs. Vukovich gets back?"

"Thank you, Father," Elias replied, "but I am used to doing things for myself. I will be okay."

The priest and Mrs. Vukovich left, promising to return quite soon. Elias immediately got a chair and climbed up to the cupboard where his father had been hoarding their money. He thought that probably Mrs. Vukovich did not even know about it. Certainly he hoped she did not.

When he opened his father's dish, he was pleased to find it undisturbed from his father's last deposit, as was his own. Though he did not take time to count it right then, he later found that between his father's and his own savings, there was nearly two thousand dollars. He put it all in one dish and climbed down.

He sat the bowl on the table, ran to his grandmother's sewing room, and got two of the flour sacks that she had used to make aprons and dish towels. He put the money in a small paper sack, twisted it tightly shut, and put it in the bottom of one of the flour sacks.

Then he scurried around, quickly gathering things he thought he might need. He took a jackknife his father kept in the kitchen drawer, a fork, and a spoon, then returned as an afterthought for a can opener. A box of stick matches stood on the back of the stove, and he added these to his collection.

Over the next hour he carefully selected a few items of clothing he thought would be most useful. Heavy pants, two cold weather shirts, some underwear, a towel, and a bar of soap went into the second bag, along with a few other odds and ends.

Over the next hour he carefully selected a few items of clothing he thought would be most useful. Heavy pants, two cold weather shirts, some underwear, a towel, and a bar of soap went into the second bag, along with a few other odds and ends.

Quickly he stripped the wool blanket from his father's bed and carefully rearranged the bedspread so it would not be noticed, then spread the blanket open on the floor. He also took one of the pillows from the linen cabinet by his father's bed. In the pantry he gathered three full bottles of brandy remaining in the case, some canned fruit and vegetables, and one loaf of homemade brown bread wrapped in heavy foil.

After laying all of the items in the middle of the blanket, he gathered the four corners and tied them together as he had seen his friends Sam and Piney do many months before. Lacking their long experience, he was soon to find that he had packed too heavy a bundle and that a blanket did not make the world's best backpack. By the time he had his pack all secured, it weighted forty pounds or more. This would prove to be very inconvenient within a few hours.

Hurrying as fast as he could, he took his collection from the house and hid it in the willow brush on the empty lot where he had kept a bottle stashed for many months. There was a few ounces of wine left in his bottle, which he drank when he had his pack safely hidden. Then he hurried back to the house.

When Mrs. Vukovich returned an hour later, Elias had a very orderly array of clothing and towels, soap, and other sundries laid out on his bed. He asked her politely for her advice on other things he might need. For another hour they worked together sorting, folding, and packing these things which Elias was certain he would never see again.

Quite by accident he gained another item that he secreted away at the last moment to take with him. Mrs. Vukovich asked him very practically whether he had ever sewn a button on a shirt. He admitted that he had not but had watched his grandmother do it many times.

She suggested that he might want to do this for himself so, "Maybe you should take a needle and thread."

Immediately he ran to the old sewing room again and took his grandmother's small sewing kit containing needles, thimble, buttons, thread, and both straight and safety pins, which were done up in a foldable packet. When Mrs. Vukovich was not watching, he slipped it into his jacket pocket.

Mrs. Vukovich finally retired to his grandmother's bedroom. Then Elias slipped quietly from his room and listened cautiously at her door for a few minutes to make sure she had actually gone to bed. When he was fairly certain she was settled in for the night, he dressed in the heavy clothes he always wore to work in the store and silently slipped out the pantry door into the alley.

Three hours later, Elias "Chimp" Stronski was in an empty freight car with his weighty bindle beside him, heading south out of Pennsylvania on his first of many such train rides in a lifetime on the road.

"Maybe it ain't gonna be ham an' eks, Papa," he whispered, "but I can't let them lock me up. I gotta look after myself."

CHAPTER 46

▼

The train had slowed many times during the night and once or twice had come to a complete stop. Each time the rhythmic <u>clickety-clack</u> of the wheels changed, it woke Chimp. Once or twice he woke in panic wondering where he was and what was happening, but then he would realize it was not a nightmare and drowse off again.

It was chilly and uncomfortable in the open boxcar, and he was sore and stiff within a few hours. He managed to protect the upper part of his body somewhat by pillowing himself against his pack where it was not too lumpy.

At one stop he heard the <u>crunch-crunch</u> of footsteps on the cinders along the track and low-voiced conversation between two men. Although he could not hear everything that was said, he became very anxious for a few minutes, because it was obvious they were arguing about whether or not they should board the car in which Chimp was riding. Hastily he gathered his bindle and slipped over to stand just inside the open door against the wall.

<u>If they get on, I'm gettin' off real fast</u>, he promised himself.

He did not want to chance unfriendly contact with strangers in the dark. He realized that everything he owned or would ever own for the foreseeable future was gripped in his right hand.

Suddenly, right next to the open door, one man spoke. "Shit, Joe, we don't have a single drop of stuff with us. I ain't taking no cold ride inta Georgia without a bottle. Le's wait an' ketch an afternoon ride tomorrow."

Just about that time the car lurched as the train began inching forward. The sudden movement as the slack came tight on the car hitches threw Chimp sideways, and he nearly fell down. He quickly seized one of the slats on the inside of the car and steadied himself, but seeing that the men were not trying to climb aboard, he returned to the corner and again relaxed against his pack.

The next time he awakened, it was daylight, and sun flickered through the knotholes and the open door as the train click-clacked down the track. Wiping the sleep from his eyes with the back of his hand, he opened his bindle and dug out the loaf of bread he had carried along. He tore a chunk off the end of it and wrapped the rest back up. After making his way to the doorway, he grasped the lock bolt firmly in one hand, while holding the chunk of bread in his teeth, and relieved himself of last night's wine into the cool breeze of the North Carolina morning.

Alternate stretches of forest and farm land rolled by in front of him for an hour or more, and soon he relaxed in the sunshine in the open doorway, his back against the doorjamb and one big foot swinging in the wind of the fast-moving freight.

Chimp had never been away from home or completely on his own before, but he remembered conversations with his friends Sam and Piney about life on the road and thought to himself, If Sam and Piney can make it without any money, I should be able to do okay with all I got. I gotta be careful though, 'cause they said there is lots of bad guys, but there must be more good ones like them too. I'll just hafta learn how to figure out for myself which is which. I'll get off first chance I get an' look around. Long as I stay close to the railroad, I can always catch another ride.

With this thought in mind, he settled down to wait. It was not long before the train began to slow again, and Chimp noticed with some alarm that he was rapidly moving into a large town. He wished he could get off the train before it stopped in town but was afraid to jump while the train was moving because of the likelihood of breaking his brandy. He decided to brave it out and see what would happen next.

The passing scene had changed from farms to row upon row of neat cottages and homes, mostly white, and then changed again to tall office building, smoking factories, and long gray warehouses. As they moved into the industrial part of the city, Chimp noted from time to time small groups of men, usually two to four, sometimes standing but more often sitting or lying down on or near the high banks of the railroad right of way. Some of them had small campfires burning and were apparently making coffee or cooking.

One such fire was in the shelter of an overpass, and the smell of coffee and meat cooking hung so strongly in the air that it made Chimp suddenly hungry for both food and the comfort and warmth of his grandmother's kitchen back in Pennsylvania.

He wondered briefly whether the priest might have set people to looking for him. He knew grownups had the means to touch far-distant places by phone or wire. He had heard detective stories and real-life stories of manhunts that went all across the United States and ended up with the police "getting their man." He hoped that no one cared enough about his situation to go to that much trouble.

He was quite confident of his ability to make it on his own and was determined to try. He was not about to surrender his freedom to live as he wished. Particularly he did not want anyone interfering with his right to have a drink of beer or wine when he wanted it, and right now was one of those times.

The chunk of bread he had eaten had only served to make him hungrier, and now a thirst was building that he felt he must satisfy. Sitting on the floor with his pack beside him, he reached inside and felt around until the smooth cool feel of a brandy bottle fell under his touch. He pulled it out, broke the seal, and worked out the cork slowly with his teeth.

Once it was open, he smelled the bottle briefly, savoring the heady tickling sensation in his nose. Then he tipped it back for a taste. He rinsed the first mouthful back and forth and swallowed it in slow trickles to the back of his throat. Sensing the train slowing to a crawl, and noting many people moving back and forth ahead, he took another hastier gulp, jammed the cork back in the bottle, and slipped it back into his bindle.

He stood up quickly and moved back out of the doorway as the train came to a bumping, jerking halt.

Very cautiously now, he laid aside the bindle and peered out, trying not to be seen until he knew what he had to contend with. He could see the long curve of the train cars ahead, and several car lengths beyond the one he was in there appeared to be a loading dock where men were working, moving bales and boxes of something back and forth.

Suddenly a large black man came down the steps at he end of the dock and began moving down the length of the train, opening and peering into each empty car as he went, and writing something on a pad of paper each time he checked a car.

Chimp hastily reviewed his options. There were two more sets of tracks and then a picket fence about three feet high between him and the edge of the railroad grade. There was nothing beyond that except weeds and brush for several hundred feet, so he thought of making a dash for it, believing the man would not bother to chase him.

The door on the opposite of the car was closed and locked, so he could only guess what lay in that direction. He thought he could jump out of the car and climb out of sight between the cars in the short time it took the man to inspect a car. Thus he would have small risk of being seen. Still he had no way of knowing what lay on the unseen side of the train.

While he was making up his mind, the man had moved two cars closer. Only three more remained between him and the inspector, so he decided on risking being seen on the chance the man would not chase him far, if at all. He watched until the inspector leaned into the next car to look around, then slid quickly out the door. His bindle struck the ground sharply when he jumped, and two of the brandy bottles knocked sharply together. Fortunately, neither of them broke, but the inspector heard the noise and looked around.

Chimp gathered himself and his pack quickly and started trotting toward the fence.

"Hey there, you, hold up!" the inspector shouted, and started running rapidly in Chimp's direction.

Chimp was amazed by how quickly the big man moved. Thoroughly frightened now, he ran as fast as he could, but the pack impeded him, and he had never been a fast runner.

He reached the fence only fifty feet ahead of his pursuer. He tossed the bindle hastily over the fence and heard the unmistakable crash of breaking glass as one brandy bottle contacted a big rock. Too frightened to care now, he put one hand on the fence and tried to vault himself over, but his pants leg caught on one of the sharp picket spikes, tearing his pants and dumping him heavily into the dirt and rock beyond the fence.

Scrambling frantically, he seized his now-dripping bindle and jumped to his feet. As he straightened up, he was looking directly into the big black face and angry eyes of the inspector, nothing between them now but the flimsy board fence.

"You-all bums think you can ride my train fo' free!" he shouted. "Wal, I ain't goin' put up wid it!"

He had started to climb the fence but suddenly stopped.

"Sweet Jesus Chris!" he exclaimed. "You ain't nothing but a shavetail kid. What th' hell you doin' on my train?"

Chimp moved back a few steps, and the man made no attempt to follow, so he did not run, but neither did he reply.

"I know what you up to," the inspector said suddenly. "You a runaway. I seen many others jes' like you. Wal, I'm tellin' you jes' this once, you better find you way outta this town another way. I'm tellin' the cops about you, an' I'm gonna be watchin the trains, so wheahevah you come fum, you better hie you ass back that direction 'fore them cops gets on you trail."

With that he turned and went back to the train. Chimp heaved a big sigh of relief and limped off into the brush to examine the damage to his pack and plan his next move.

He kept moving deeper into the brushy area, hoping that if the railroad inspector did report him, it would be some time before the cops began looking. Anyway, he doubted that they would do much searching for a runaway kid, particularly in this heavy dusty brush.

It turned out he was right. The inspector did report seeing him to the first police officer he saw. The officer nonchalantly agreed to "keep an' eye out" but made no report and forgot about it within the hour.

Chimp soon found the clothes he had on were uncomfortably warm. The midmorning sun seemed much warmer than what he was used to in Pennsylvania. He was soon sweating profusely and became both thirsty and very dusty, struggling through the weeds and brush with his pack.

Quite unexpectedly he broke out into an open space where there was a small pond shaded by a huge hardwood tree that he had been unconsciously steering toward for half an hour. He laid down his pack for the first time since being chased by the inspector and felt very relieved to be rid of the weight. He explored cautiously about for a few minutes.

He took off his coat, laid it on top of his pack, and walked down to the water. He bent down, wiggled his hands in it for a minute, and found it clear and cold. A rim of cattails surrounded the pond on three sides, and near where he stood a small stream ran off into the brush toward the railroad. He splashed a little water on his face and neck, then dipped some up in the palm of his hand and tasted it. It was cool and refreshing and did not taste bad, so using both hands, he dipped some more and drank his thirst away.

When he returned to the tree, he untied his bindle and spread it out. To his relief he found he had only broken one of his bottles of brandy, but most of his clothing items were dampened, and the dripping pack had wet the legs of the pants he was wearing. The bottle he had opened earlier and one full one remained.

He hung his wet items on nearby bushes to dry, sorted the broken glass from the rest of his possessions, and threw it away in the weeds. Then he opened a can of fruit and sat back against the big tree to eat it while his other things dried in the sun.

One very large branch of the oak tree hung quite low and extended out over the pond. When he finished eating the fruit and another chunk of bread, he decided to climb the tree to get a better view of the area. When he was about twenty feet above the ground, he perched himself in the crotch of a large branch to look around.

He found he was in kind of an island of brush and trees between a row of warehouses and factories on one side and the railroad on the other. Considerably beyond the railroad to the east appeared to be more houses. This was the section he had been unable to see from the railroad car when he arrived.

Climbing a little higher, he spotted smoke along the railroad and, after watching carefully for a few minutes, found it to be a campfire, with at least two men moving casually about. They were nearly a quarter-mile away and seemed occupied with their own business, so after watching for a while, he climbed back down.

Exploring more carefully around the area of the big tree, he found a small rock hearth filled with ashes and partly burned sticks. There were also several rusty cans that had been opened jaggedly as with a pocket knife, and an empty wine jug and two wine bottles. He picked them up one at a time and thought wistfully of Sam and Piney.

Wouldn't it be great, he thought, if that was Sam and Piney camping down the tracks? It ain't likely, but maybe after a while I'll go check.

With this in mind, he began putting his things back in order. When he had his now-dry belongings neatly packed back in his bindle, he picked it up and headed down the faint trail that led toward the tracks.

Suddenly he halted.

Hey, this is stupid. Sam and Piney told me to be careful, he thought. What if those are bad guys. I can't run with this stuff in my hand, and I sure don't want to lose it.

He went back to the big tree and reopened his pack. With uncommon foresight for one so young, he took the sack containing his money, placed it in a rusty bean can, went to a nearby bush, raked dirt and leaves away from the roots, and placed the can well down out of sight. Then he carefully covered it with dirt, sticks, and dry leaves. Farther back in the brush, he hid his pack and his coat under two large bushes growing close together.

"Now," he said to himself, "if someone chases me again, I can run, and if they don't think I got anything, they ain't likely to chase me."

Satisfied now that he had nothing to lose, he went to pay a visit to his neighbors down the track. As he left the brush at the right of way, he noted carefully where the trail entered, so he would not miss it coming back, also noting the relative position and direction of the big tree.

It took Chimp about ten minutes to walk to the area where the campfire was. These men had built their fire just off the right of way where a tiny stream trickled down the rocky slope and into a culvert under the roadbed. He heard them talking as he approached their camp but did not immediately see them. The fire was in plain sight, but the men were not.

Moving cautiously, he approached from the open area near the right of way, so he would have a clear route to run if necessary. As he came close to the fire, he noted the blackened and bent old coffee pot sitting on the rocks over the coals, and then the two men who were lounging in the shade of a big bush a few yards away. Both were bearded and ragged, one black, the other white.

The white man saw Chimp first and said in a warning tone, "Hey, Jonesey, us got company."

The black man came quickly to his feet, apparently prepared to run.

After staring for a few seconds at Chimp, he growled, "Shit, Morgan, ain't nuthin' but a kid. What you sneakin' 'roun' here for, kid?"

"I just wondered why there was a fire an' came to see. I thought I might know someone here."

"What make you think you goin' know us?"

"Nothing really, sir," Chimp replied politely. "I meet lots of people, and I thought you might be someone I knew."

The white man broke in, "You ain't fum aroun' here, kid. What you doin' sneakin' aroun' here spying on us?"

"I wasn't, really, sir. I'm staying with my uncle here, and I was just out for a walk and saw your fire."

He made up the lie on the spur of the moment, because he was apprehensive about the men's suspicious attitude, which was directly opposite of the open and friendly approach of Sam and Piney.

"Well, now you seen us, you can be on your way. We ain't in the ennertainment business, an' we ain't invited no company for dinner neither," the black man said.

He bent down and picked up a shiny hardwood stick that lay on the grass near his small bindle.

The one called Morgan walked over within a couple of feet of Chimp and looked him over carefully. He stopped there, and his nose wrinkled a few times as though he was sniffing the air.

"How old you is anyways, kid?" he asked Chimp suddenly.

"I'm fifteen, sir," Chimp lied again, "and I didn't mean no harm. I won't bother you anymore."

He turned to leave.

The two men stood there watching him suspiciously as Chimp retreated back down the track the way he had come. If he had been a little more seasoned to the road, he would have gathered his belongings and beat a hasty retreat from the area, but not being of a suspicious nature and having no acquaintance with men such as these, he returned straight to his own camp, retrieved his pack from where he had hidden it, and sat down under the big tree to wait for darkness.

I'll just hang around here for a while till it gets dark, he thought. Then I'll walk over to the town and find a store or restaurant and buy myself something good to eat and look around a little.

Soon the sun drifted low to the west and shone brightly on Chimp where he relaxed under the tree. The pleasant warmth awoke his thirst, and he pulled the brandy from his pack and took a couple of sips. Instead of putting it back in his pack, he corked it and held it between his knees. Soon his head nodded forward, and his eyes dropped shut.

"See, I tole you, Jonesey," came a growl that woke Chimp with a start. "He on the road jus' like us, an' looka that fine stuff he got there 'tween his legs. Hey, boy, you done lied to us. You goin' share that stuff wif us poor folks, right? I tole you the kid had drinkin' liquor on him. Cain't fool the nose on this ol' houn' dog."

He bent suddenly and seized the neck of the bottle, but Chimp simultaneously grabbed it with both his hands and held on. Morgan jerked it several times but was unable to break Chimp's grip on the bottle. He was a tall man with big bony hands, and as his efforts to remove the bottle from Chimp's grip proved unsuccessful, his eyes turned mean.

"Hey, Jonesey, he pretty stout for a young 'un. Show him what it mean when you impolite to company in the South."

Jonesey, who was small and thin and dirty, was still carrying the knotted oak stick he had held earlier. He suddenly raised it, stepped close, and struck Chimp quite hard halfway between his neck and the point of his shoulder. Chimp's left arm went suddenly dead, and he lost his grip on the bottle with his left hand but still held on with his right.

Switching targets, the scrawny-looking Jonesey rapped him sharply on the back of his right hand with the club, and the battle was over. The two men stood back then, opened the bottle, and had a long drink each.

"Well, now," Jonesey said, "thass some stuff. Bes' drink I had since I 'member when. Wonder what more good stuff our frien' here totin', Morgan. Ought we take a peek in this here pack he hangin' onto?"

As soon as he had lost the brandy, Chimp had seized hold of the knotted corner of his bindle, thinking he would jump and run if they stepped back just a little more. However, now they were closing in again.

"Bes' you han' me that tow-sack, boy," Morgan said, "or I gon' sic my dog on you agin."

"That's everything I own in there," Chimp said frantically. "I got to have that to get along."

Morgan's blue eyes turned mean again. "You get along best you can in this worl', kid. We know you run away from somewhere. All's you got to do is walk up to the firs' cop you see, an' you is set. Plenty food, place to stay, an' all. We-uns ain't got nuthin' an' ain't gon' get nuthin' but hard times, 'cept what we can rustle for ourselves. Now you mind what I say an' pass me that tow-sack 'fore I give you another lesson in manners."

Morgan stopped again and grabbed the edge of the bindle as Jonesey threateningly raised the club once more. Chimp pushed away the bindle and began to cry.

"Don't you set here blubberin' all over our campgroun', boy," Jonesey said. "We tole you a while ago, we-uns ain't invited no company. Now git!"

He kicked Chimp sharply in the butt to emphasize his point.

Chimp was hurt, angry, and frightened all at once. He was on his own in a strange place. He had only a few coins in his pocket, and everything he had kept from home was suddenly gone. He knew it was not likely that these two vicious men would find his money, but he had no idea how long they would decide to stay here, and he had buried it too close to the big tree to chance trying to get it now.

He had run a few steps down the trail when the black man had kicked him, but he was not one to remain frightened for long, and he was certain he could outrun these men if they chased him. He stopped and threw a few rocks at them, hoping to discourage them from rummaging through his pack, but they responded in kind. The black man was too accurate for Chimp's liking, so he retreated.

Discouraged and angry, he went back to the tracks and walked in the direction of town. It was getting late in the evening now, and dusk was upon him. He stumbled along in the half-darkness, alternately crying and talking to himself.

<u>If they stay there a couple of days, I could starve</u>, he thought. <u>They sure are mean men. If they had asked, I would give them a drink, but they wanted everything. I wonder what I should do now. How can I get my stuff back?"</u>

Before long he came to a place where the railroad ran in front of the loading docks and then crossed a street. Looking both ways at the intersection of rail and street, he could see lights beginning to come on in the area to his right, so he walked in that direction. Soon he found himself in a section of town that was mostly gas stations, bars, and small two-story hotels.

A police car cruised slowly by, and Chimp hid in the darkness of an alley next to an old hotel. When it disappeared down the street without pausing, he came out again.

<u>Maybe I should tell the cops</u>, he thought. <u>Those guys robbed me, so the cops could arrest them—but then they would want to know about me, and they'd send me back.</u>

Soon he was standing in front of a small run-down diner, peering in the window and wishing he could get some of the food the people inside were eating. Though he was not yet excessively hungry, the fact that the food was inaccessible made him want it all the more. He stood there for some minutes deeply engrossed in his own thoughts about his situation.

"What the hell am I gonna do now?" he suddenly exclaimed aloud.

"Gonna do about what?" said a deep voice behind him.

Chimp had no idea that anyone was anywhere near him, and he jumped in fright and spun around, putting his back to the wall.

An old black man with white hair and a small battered suitcase in his hand stood there, eying him curiously. He was not quite as tall as Chimp but was nearly as wide as he was tall. His worn shoes and rough clothing told Chimp immediately that here was another man of the road, but this one was somehow different from the pair he had just left.

"Folks call me Wash," he volunteered in his soft bass voice. "Ya'll look like a young man with troubles."

"Yes, sir," Chimp answered immediately. "I am Chimp Stronski. I have been robbed of all my stuff, and I don't know what to do."

"Ya'll can't go to the police, 'cause they gonna know you run away fum somewhere, right?" Wash asked with a smile.

For some reason Chimp could not define, he decided to be truthful with this calm, pleasant man. It amazed him again that everyone recognized him immediately as a runaway, and he could not understand how or why.

"Well, I didn't exactly run away from anyone," Chimp replied. "My father died, and some neighbors were going to send me to a…boy's home or something, so I packed some things and caught a train to here. I got nobody or nothin' back there, and I can look after myself."

"Look to me like ya'll is makin' a poor job of it so far. Who took your stuff, and what did they git?"

"They got all of my clothes and a blanket and some food an' things," Chimp replied. "Their names are Jonesey and Morgan, and they beat me with a stick and took it all."

"One is a tall white trash, and t' other one is small an' black, an' they as mean as they come," said Wash. "How come you to be havin' any truck wit guys like that anyways?"

"I just got off the train this morning, and I saw this campfire. I stopped to see who was there, and they followed me and grabbed me when I was taking a nap," Chimp confessed downheartedly. "I didn't know what kind of guys they were, and I just stopped to say hello."

"You too young and tender to be snoopin' 'roun' these hobo camps, boy," Wash said. "Why, they's guys out there would cut your throat for an ol' pair of shoes if'n they wanted 'em. Those two guys is just that kind too. Tell you one thing though. They is both coyote-yella clean through an' wouldn't look twice at anyone they thought might fight back. How much liquor they git off'n you?"

Again Chimp was amazed that someone knew so much about him without being told but again decided to trust this clever old man.

"I had two bottles of brandy," Chimp confessed. "A little bit was gone from one bottle."

"What you do, use one bottle to wash up wit this mornin'?" Wash asked, and his eyes twinkled.

Although he could not notice it himself, Chimp finally realized that the liquor he had spilled earlier must be evident to anyone who came within a few feet of him. He determined to wash his clothes at the earliest opportunity. For now, he smiled back at Wash and calmly told him of his day's experiences.

When he had finished his story, Wash said, "If you gonna take to the road, boy, they's a sack full of things you better learn real quick. First, you don't trust none of these guys on the street, 'less they sound asleep, dead drunk, or you the one holdin' the club. Second, you can't trust none of these yard bulls. Now it happen this guy that chase you ain't too bad a guy, but they is some of them that is starving-dog mean an' don't mind cripplin' a man to show they mean business.

Now, for today, you just think on them two lessons from Ol' Wash. Now, what you goin' to do about your stuff you lost?"

"I don't know what I can do," Chimp replied. "I can't go to the police, and I can't whip two men by myself. I think all I can do is wait till they leave, and see if they left any of my stuff."

"Well, boy, here's one more lesson for today, an' best you learn to judge fo yourself real quick. Some people is on the road 'cause they chooses to be, maybe like you an' me. Some is there 'cause they are temporary down on their luck, an' they lookin' for somethin' better. An then," he said, and paused before continuing, "an' then they's the devil crowd. They too lazy, too drunk, or too stupid, sometimes all three, to do any different. They don't know nothin' an' don't want nothin' 'cept to live free off other folks. Them is the kind you gotta learn to spot, 'cause they'll do anything for a drink, a meal, or a buck an' don't give one tinker's dam if someone git kilt or hurt in the process.

"Now, these guys took you stuff is drunks. They live an' die for a bottle. It's they best friend an' they worse enemy. By now they has drunk ever drop of what you had an' probly sleepin' it off. Tomorra they gonna be on the hunt for ways to get some more. Was I you, I'd slip on back there an' keep an eye on things. Once they both asleep, you couldn't stir 'em with dynamite. If you right careful, you could slip in there, pack up ever'thing you own, or they own for that matter, an' get on away slicker'n snail tracks."

"But that black guy has a club," Chimp replied. "Maybe If you came with me, they would give me my stuff back even if they are still awake."

"I thought I heered some young fella say somethin' bout lookin' after hisself a while ago," Wash said solemnly. "No, sirree, I ain't gon' near these guys, not 'cause I don't want to help. It jes' ain't none o' my fish fry. Either you can look after youself, or you cain't, an' best you find out right now. Turn out you cain't, you better stop that cop car you see crusin' round here an' tell him who you is an' head back where they's folks can afford to look after you. Ain't nobody I know on the road gonna take on the job. I already help you much as I'm goin' to. If you cain't take it from there, you knows you choices."

He stared at Chimp for a few seconds, then suddenly put his suitcase down on the sidewalk and opened it up. He fumbled among his things briefly and came out with a short heavy flashlight. He flicked it on, then off, and stood back up.

'Here, kid," he said, "I'm lendin' you this. Might come in handy, case those guys let they fire burn out. Getting' perty dark out there in them bushes. Don't want to be walkin' in on them in the dark if they still awake. Jus' be patient.

You'll ketch 'em out pretty quick. Now beat it. You'll find me hangin' 'roun' som'ers close should you decide to return the torch."

"Thanks, Mister Wash," Chimp said quickly. "I'll be sure to return it tonight or tomorrow."

He turned and started away.

'Hey, boy,' came Wash's deep voice again. "Keep in mind ol' Jonesey's club'll fit you hand good as it does his. If you catch 'em sleepin', get the club first, an' they ain't goin' bother you none after that. Good huntin', boy."

He waved a hand and watched as Chimp slipped away into the darkness.

As soon as he got back on the railroad track, Chimp switched on the flashlight. He was suddenly not at all sure he could find the path leading back to the big tree. Things just did not look the same in the dark.

He walked rapidly on the edge of the circle of light from the torch and within a few minutes noted a trail that he thought was the correct one. Apprehensive about advancing on the two mean men alone, he decided to be sure of his ground, so he continued down the track to where he had first seen them. The little stream along the track at this spot reassured him that he was in the right place.

Having assured himself, he clicked off the light, suddenly considering the possibility that they might have returned with his things to their former campsite. Slipping along very quietly, he climbed the slope where he could look down on the spot where he first met Jonesey and Morgan.

Some faint embers still burned from their fire, so Chimp listened carefully for several minutes before risking the light again. He flicked the light back on and shined it carefully over the ground where he had visited earlier. There was no sign of them except the smoldering embers of their fire.

Hurrying, he retraced his steps to what he was now sure was the right trail. He flashed the light briefly up the grade from the tracks to be sure they were not lying in wait for him, then turned it off.

Inching his way carefully in the darkness, he soon came to a spot where he could see a flickering glow ahead of him. Moving, then pausing, moving, then pausing, he inched along, his heart pounding so hard he was sure the men would hear it rather than his footsteps. Soon he heard low musical sounds coming from the direction of the firelight. He crept softly, softly forward.

Soon he was within a few steps of the big oak tree. The campfire glowed brightly in the middle of the small clearing, and Morgan was stretched out on his back within a few feet of the fire. As Chimp watched for any move from the bigger man, a sudden rasping snore echoed across the open space. The man slept soundly as the campfire made flickering shadows jump and waver around the dark perimeter of the clearing.

Chimp could hear Jonesey but could not see him from where he stood. Quietly, carefully he crept up where he could reach out and grasp the bark of the big tree with one hand, saving the risk of losing his balance and crackling dry brush and leaves. With infinite caution he inched his way around the base of the great tree.

Jonesey sat hunched over on a small stump a scant three feet away on the opposite side of Chimp's shelter. He was drunkenly mumbling a ribald song, both elbows resting on his knees and quite unaware of Chimp's presence. His back and left side were toward Chimp, and he faced directly into the light of the campfire.

As Chimp leaned out from his hiding place for a better look, he could see the two brandy bottles, obviously empty, lying on the ground in front of Jonesey. The rest of his ransacked possessions lay much as they had left them several hours earlier.

Glancing down in front of him, Chimp suddenly noticed the smooth polished oak branch that Jonesey had beaten him with earlier. It was leaning against the tree within easy reach of his right hand.

He became suddenly elated and angry at the same moment. With scarcely a thought of possible consequences, he grabbed the knotted club, took three quick steps forward, and whaled Jonesey across the shoulders as hard as he could swing. Jonesey let out a croaking squawk and fell face forward into the dirt.

Morgan ceased snoring briefly, shifted his feet apart a little, but otherwise paid no heed.

Jonesey moaned and groaned, rolled over on his back, and raised his hands and feet protectively above his body.

"Don't hit me, mister. Don't hit me, mister!" he begged in a whining tone.

"Get up and get out of here, or I'll beat you to death," Chimp said in the deepest voice he could muster.

He cracked Jonesey once more, this time on the shin bone to emphasize his point. Jonesey scrambled to his feet and headed into the darkness at a staggering run, breaking a new trail through the brush as he went. Chimp stood and listened for several minutes to the sound of Jonesey's crackling retreat. He heard him fall at least twice, then continue running. He had no doubt the man was in full flight and would not immediately return.

Morgan's rasping snore again echoed through the clearing. Chimp walked slowly up to him, his anger abated somewhat but his heart still beating wildly. It was the first time in his life he had ever attacked anyone. The thought that he had sent a full-grown man running for his life increased his confidence immeasurably. The outcome of this venture had amazed him and at the same time impressed him with the value of attack rather than retreat as a future strategy.

He stood and looked at Morgan, and the thought of beaning him with the club crossed his mind. He decided against it and backed silently away.

He pocketed the flashlight and switched the club to his left hand. Working quickly, he retrieved what remained of his belongings and tied them back in the blanket. The men had eaten some of his food, but the major loss to him was his brandy. Everything else seemed to be as he had left it, except his pack was not fouled with dust and leaves. Slipping quietly into the darkness beyond the big tree, he put down his pack, switched on the light, and went in search of his coat and his money cache.

The money he had buried quite close to the big tree, and it took only moments to find the right bush and dig out this all-important treasure. His coat was a different story. He searched back and forth through the brush for several minutes before he finally found the spot where he had hidden it. Here he learned another lesson he would never forget. Nothing ever looks the same in the darkness as it does in the light, particularly in the woods.

Returning to the clearing he went boldly to where the cantankerous Morgan lay snoring, legs spread, in the warmth of the campfire. He looked at him thoughtfully for a few minutes and decided the man should not go free and unpunished for what he had done to him. Whenever he had done wrong at home, his father had found a way to make him remember not to do it again.

He thought once more of attacking the man as he slept, but that bothered him as being cowardly. Not sure of his ability to fight the big man if he awoke, he decided against it. Instead, he gathered a few small dry branches and sticks and very quietly made a neat pile of them between Morgan's outstretched legs, taking care not to touch him.

Morgan snored on. Smiling to himself, Chimp went to the campfire, selecting a short branch that was burning brightly at one end, then turned and laid it atop the pile he had made. Then he quickly gathered his things and walked as rapidly as caution permitted back down the trail to the railroad. In his right hand he tightly clutched the oaken club which for the next several years became as an extension of his right arm.

Safely back on the railroad grade, he heaved a sigh of relief and smiled to himself, wondering how long it would be before Morgan woke to make a headlong dash for the center of the little pond in the woods.

CHAPTER 47

▼

Corky's second year in school went much the same as the first.

Jan, for the moment, was more interested in her affair with Bob than Corky's progress, or lack of it, in school. Although the school occasionally sent her notices of class activities or conferences, she never bothered to inquire further or to attend.

Miss Humphrey taught first and second grades, so Corky saw no relief from her harassment upon graduation to second grade. He still skipped school at least two days a week and sometimes more. She continued to ignore his absence as she did his presence and dutifully recorded his C average for each grading period.

The major problem for Corky now was that his many absences left him far behind the other students, even though he was brighter than many of them. Because he was often unfamiliar with what they were discussing, he became more and more disinterested and bored and paid less and less attention to whatever subject was being covered that day.

His classmates no longer made such a concentrated effort to torment him. On occasion Wallace or one of the other boys would play some kind of prank or practical joke on him, but it was more an effort to gain attention to themselves than to make sport of him as they had at first. They no longer chased him in groups when outside at play. Once or twice a week some of the faster runners might try to catch him, but usually they quickly gave it up. They were more testing their own skills than deliberately tormenting him.

If they were no longer specifically mean to him, neither were they kind, accepting, or outgoing toward him. He was still an outcast. No one ever invited him to participate in party, play, or conversation, as they did with each other.

When they found him playing his lonely games that he was adept at inventing, they would pause momentarily in their own activities to mock him or despoil whatever aids he might have constructed to enhance the activity. He withdrew more and more from contact with those his own age.

With adults, during his absences from school, his conduct altered somewhat. He still actively avoided social contact with others. However, he kept himself quite busy with the little odd jobs they gave him. Whenever he saw a warehouse worker or trucker doing something that he knew he could do as well, such as sweeping, or the like, he was quick to offer his services for a quarter or fifty cents. He made what was to him considerable money with this odd-job activity. He hoarded it away as though he knew he would have serious need of it someday.

His mother was unaware of Corky's work efforts and would have been surprised to learn that he had nearly fifty dollars put away. The "nuisance" money that Bob often gave him to get him out of the way, he nearly always added to this collection.

He soon found that the working people in the warehouse district were not only friendlier than other people he knew, but more generous in nature and in action. Many of the men who knew him went out of their way to give him little odd jobs and often paid him more than the agreed price for the service once it was done, as well as sharing tidbits from their lunches with him.

When Corky entered third grade, his new teacher was much more interested and concerned with his activities than Miss Humphrey had been. Miss Benson was a direct opposite to Miss Humphrey in every way. She was small and petite and always pleasant. She made a serious effort to become individually acquainted with all of her students and was very concerned about Corky's shortcomings in class as well as his frequent absences.

In his first month in her class, he was absent eight times. She discussed it with the principal and checked his attendance record for previous years. When she found that school records showed a perfect attendance for all of his previous two years, she wrote a concerned letter to Jan and gave it to Corky to carry home.

Corky threw it in an alley trash can on his way home.

When Miss Benson received no reply from her letter, she decided that Corky's mother just did not care about his school activities. Corky was not at the bottom of his class and showed little interest in most classroom activities.

During the second month of his third year, he was absent ten days. Miss Benson wrote Jan another letter and this time mailed it to her instead of trusting it to Corky.

When Jan received the letter, she could not believe what she was reading. As soon as Corky got home from school, she confronted him.

"Corky," she said, "I got a letter from your teacher today, and I want to know what is going on in school."

Corky was surprised. For as long as he could remember, his mother had never received a letter from anyone. The mail service was a complete mystery to him, and he was amazed and concerned that his teacher could reach his mother without sending a note with him or coming to visit in person. He had never lied outright to his mother and did not know what to say, so he stood silent.

"You better answer me, young man," she threatened. "Your teacher says you are the poorest student in her class, and you are absent as much as you are there. Is that true?"

"I don't know, Mom," Corky answered truthfully.

He could not have told her how many days he missed if his life depended on it.

"What do you mean, you don't know?" she shouted. "Do you go to school every day, or don't you?"

"No, Mom," he admitted, but did not elaborate.

"What do you do when you don't go to school?" She was amazed to find the information she had received was accurate.

"I just stay outside and play," Corky said in a matter-of-fact tone.

"Play. Where do you play?" she squealed in exasperation. "When I send you off to school in the morning, you are supposed to go to school. Where do you play?" she repeated, shouting.

"Sometimes I go back to the house and sometimes just in the street by the warehouses."

"Why don't you go to school like you are supposed to?" Jan asked, truly shocked now at the outcome of her inquiry.

"Because I don't like school. Because I hate those kids, and I hate the teachers. School is awful, an' I'm going to quit anyway."

"I told you before, you cannot quit school till you are sixteen years old, and you are only eight. You are going to grow up being nothing. You will be stupid and won't find a job, and you will be on the street just like your father. He quit school when he was sixteen. Do you want to be like him?" Her voice was almost a scream by the time she finished this lecture.

"I don't have no father, and I only go to school 'cause you say so. And I'm almost nine. I don't want to be there, an' I'm going to quit soon as I can."

Jan completely lost her temper. For the first time in her life, she picked him up, laid him across her leg, and spanked him fiercely. He yelled in surprise and then cried briefly. This was a side of his mother he had never seen before. Always before she had been defensive and protective in everything. Now she was acting like everyone else. She had physically attacked him, and because of school, the most hated activity in his life.

As soon as she put him down, she seized him by both arms and shook him. "Now you listen to me, Corky Hackett. You are going to school. I am writing a note to Miss Benson and telling her what you have been up to. I will tell her to let me know if you miss any more school. If you do, I will personally take you to school every day and bring you home again at night. Do you understand?"

She shook him again.

Corky tearfully nodded his head and wondered how he was going to survive if he had to go to school every day.

When he was ready to leave for school on Monday morning, Jan handed him a sealed envelope.

"Now, Corky, this is the note to Miss Benson. You give it to her as soon as you get to school, and if you miss any more, she is going to let me know. Is that clear?"

"Yes, Mama," Corky answered.

As he passed the alley near school, he dropped the letter in the same trash can in which he had earlier deposited Miss Benson's letter to his mother. During the following month, he skipped school twelve days.

Miss Benson thought that if his mother cared little enough that she failed to answer two concerned letters from her, her efforts were probably not appreciated. She did what she could to teach Corky when he was present and made no further attempt to contact Jan.

Jan, for her part, occasionally asked Corky how things were going in school, but since she heard nothing adverse from Miss Benson, she assumed all was well and continued with life as usual.

Just before Christmas his teacher made the mistake of giving Corky his second-quarter report card to carry home. On it was recorded all of his absences since his mother's stern warning and the complete and dismal record of his consequent failure in all of his studies except spelling.

Corky did not even look at his grades. They would not have meant anything to him anyway. He knew it was another message that he could not allow his mother to see. Again he made his casual stop at the alley trash can to dispose of the incriminating message.

Jan, caught up in her romance and the fun, work, and worries of the holiday season, never thought to ask him about his report card. When school resumed in January, Corky, as well as nearly half of his classmates, caught the measles. He was home for two weeks. Jan stayed home with him for the first week because he was quite ill, but went to work each day of the second week.

Corky stayed home by himself the second week, because he insisted he did not feel well enough to go to school. Had Jan known or taken the trouble to check, Corky really did not stay home either. For three of those afternoons he was back on warehouse row, playing and doing odd jobs for the truckers, but he made it a point to be home again before Jan finished work.

It was the end of the third quarter before Jan finally learned that Corky was still defying her instructions. When he did not bring home a report card, she asked him about it. He told her he did not know anything about it. She then asked him if he was doing okay in school, and he gave her an answer that was so vague, she became serious.

"Corky Hackett," she exclaimed, "are you still skipping school?"

She knew immediately by the expression on his face that it was true.

"I don't like school, Mama," he mumbled, looking at the floor instead of her.

Worried and exasperated, she paid a visit to his classroom. In conference with Miss Benson and the principal, she received the disturbing news that Corky had been absent more than half of the period and that he could not possibly be advanced to the fourth grade the following year, regardless how well he might do in fourth quarter. Further, both Miss Benson and the principal seemed to feel it was her fault for not keeping better track of her son's activities.

When Jan got home, she beat Corky again, this time with a small willow switch. It did not improve her guilty feelings in the least and only served to convince Corky that everything about school was bad. Neither his attendance nor his knowledge of school subjects improved in the slightest during the last term of third grade.

When Jan received the letter from the principal that Corky was still failing and still skipping school and would be required to repeat third grade if he returned that fall, she gave up in despair.

Tearfully she consulted Rosa. "I'm about to give up, Mama. I gotta work. I can't keep track of him every day, an' I feel so bad about beatin' him. It's worse for me than it is for him, and he won't hardly even talk to me anymore. What can I do?"

"Goddamn, honey, I ain't never had no kids. I don't know what to tell ya, 'cept the li'l pecker's gonna do what he's gonna do. You know he's independent as a twenny-year trucker. Always has been. His head has jus' growed up faster than his body. He got his own mind an' ain't gonna let no one run him. I know one thing though. Beatin' ain't gonna be the answer for Corky. It don't take no time at all of kickin' a stray dog till he either turns mean as hell or runs off, one. I'm thinkin' kids ain't no hell of a ways separate from dogs in that manner. Maybe pettin' an' persuadin' will bring 'im aroun'. In any case, was I you, I would'n be beatin' on 'im. He's too little. It's only gonna bring you grief an' bad memories."

Rosa patted Jan's cheek and returned to cleaning her grill.

That night at home Jan told Bob all about it. She had not previous mentioned it to him, afraid that he might do something to make his relationship with Corky even worse.

"Hell," Bob said, "I know what I'd do. I'd make a surprise check on the school 'bout three days a week. If he wasn't in class, I'd find him, kick his li'l ass good, an' take him back to school. He wouldn't pull that quittin' bullshit on me but about once or twice."

"Bob, you don't know Corky. The harder you hit him, the more stubborn he gets. Besides, he's too small and defenseless to be beatin' on him. I can't do that."

"Jan, you're just too soft," Bob replied. "If it's that big a problem, hell, my schedule ain't that busy. If you want me to, I can try my hand at correctin' his ways. I bet I'll straighten him out in a week."

"No way," Jan stated emphatically. "I told you before, he's my kid, and I'll handle the problems, right or wrong."

'Okay, kid," Bob agreed, "but I thought you were askin' me for advice. That's the way I'd handle it. I think kids are like mules. You got to get their attention 'fore you can teach 'em anything, and I only know one sure way to do that."

Jan would not hear of it. She cautioned Bob again about letting her take care of it.

'In any case," she said, "school will be out in a few days, and maybe by fall I can talk him into doing it right."

By fall the situation was totally out of her hands.

CHAPTER 48

▼

June and the first half of July went by pleasantly and happily for both Jan and Corky. For a few days they were back on their old comrade terms again. Corky inadvertently let her know that he was making a little money doing odd jobs for people. She was very pleased and told him so. She even told Rosa about it, and good-natured Rosa laughed aloud.

"Told ya the li'l pecker was made of good stuff," she joked. "Hell, I could use a chore boy aroun' here my ownself sometimes. Nex' time he comes in, I'll see if he wants to do some odd jobs for Mama Rosa. We'll keep his bony li'l ass humpin' till he ain't got no time for mischief. Hell of a lot better n' beatin' on 'im, an' if he won't go to school, work'll teach him somethin' anyways."

Jan grinned at Rosa's enthusiasm and agreed it would be nice if he could work there where they could both keep an eye on him.

Within a few days following this conversation, Rosa gave Corky an empty bushel basket and told him she would give him fifty cents an hour if he would gather all the empty cans, bottles, and trash around the diner and dispose of it in the dumpster across the street.

The job took him all of one day and part of the next. He required no prompting or supervision during the whole project.

Rosa was quite pleased with his efforts. She paid him the agreed price, plus a dollar bonus. She also instructed him to check with her every day, because there was always some little chore that needed doing around the diner.

During the next three weeks, Corky became accustomed to helping out at the diner. He swept floors, took out trash, cleaned up spills, helped wash dishes, and even began helping Jan to clear and clean the tables. At nine years old, he was still too short to reach across the tables without climbing on the chairs, and he had to stand on an empty beer case to dump his baskets of trash in the dumpster. However, he undertook any task willingly and seldom failed to complete what he started.

Rosa was so pleased with his progress and work attitude that she made a rather unusual proposal.

"How you think ol' Corky would look all done up like li'l businessman, honey?" she asked Jan one afternoon.

"I don't know," Jan replied. "Why? What kinda crazy idea you got now?'

"Well,' Rosa said, laughing, "he always looks so, well, sorta scraggly. I was thinkin' if we dressed him up like a li'l gentleman an' let 'im seat people, give 'em menus an' stuff like that, we might get someone 'sides stevedores an' truckers in here sometimes. Maybe some o' these guys'd bring their wives an' kids in here if they seen we had a li'l class."

Jan laughed aloud for several minutes.

"What the hell is so funny, Jan? Christ, he's kinda cute if ya look real close, that curly red hair an' all, an' he's smart enough to do the job. I'll bet it'll work."

"No, Mama, you got me wrong. I wasn't laughin' at your idea. It's just I ain't got money enough to buy him decent things for school. He always looks ragtag like that. I don't like it, but there ain't much I can do about it—an' here you're wantin' me to put out fifty bucks for a whole outfit for him. That's what's funny."

"Holy smokin' balls, baby! I ain't ast you to lay out one red cent. If the li'l pecker'll try it, I'll foot the bill for the duds. It'd be worth it jus' to see him all dressed up once, if it never worked a'tall."

"Well, I got no reason to object if you wanta do it," Jan replied, "but you better ask him 'fore you go spendin' the money, 'cause there ain't no way in hell to make him do it if he decides he ain't gonna."

Rosa approached Corky before they closed the diner that night. She gave him a dollar for the odd jobs he had done during the day and then, rubbing his curls with her chubby left hand, said, "How'd ya like to be a regular worker here in Mama Rosa's place, Corky?"

"What do I hafta do?" Corky asked quickly.

"Just' open the door for folks an' show 'em where to sit, where tables already been cleaned, an' give 'em menus an' water. More or less pick up after folks when it gits busy in here. Say good mornin' an' goodnight. Jus' kinda make 'em feel at home. I'll pay you more. Besides, you might earn a few tips like your mama does if you do it right. You think you can do that?"

Corky was a very unemotional child and had always been uncomfortable talking to any adult except his mother. He answered adults' questions in the shortest possible terms and immediately broke contact. He treated Rosa no differently now.

'Sure," was his only response.

"Okay," Rosa replied. "I knew you was a worker. I'm gonna get you some new clothes, so you look nice, an' you can start soon as we get you spruced up."

Corky looked at her and scowled. "Why do I need new clothes?"

Rosa laughed. "Well, I thought you ought to have somethin' new for a change. When people come to eat, they like to see the help lookin' sharp. It'll be nice, you'll see."

The following Monday morning when Jan and Corky arrived at the diner, Rosa was all excited.

"Jan, baby," she shouted, "you ain't gonna believe the outfit I got for Corky. Goddamn, we gonna be knockin' the walls outta this place to put in more table."

She handed a large box to Jan and said, "Here, git 'im sportied up, an' we'll try 'im out on the breakfas' crowd to see if they like it."

A few minutes later Jan did not know whether to laugh or cry, she was so delighted by her son's appearance.

"Corky!" she squealed. "You just can't believe how wonderful you look! You were born to be a gentleman." She called loudly, "Rosa! Come quick an' look at Corky!"

When Rosa saw him, her reaction was much the same as Jan's.

"My God!" she exclaimed. "I ain't even a mother, an' I got everything to fit. Mus' be some kinda damn miracle."

Rosa had really overdone it in her enthusiasm over her idea. She had gotten Corky a three-piece medium-blue suit, a burgundy bow tie, and black patent-leather shoes. As if that were not more than sufficient for a working man's diner, she had topped it off with a coal-black tiny bowler hat. With his serious manner, intent expressions, and pointed elfin face, Corky would not have looked out of place in the office of the president of a large corporation or even on Wall Street, had he been three feet taller. As it was, he was a character straight out of an Irish fairy tale, and his crooked eye emphasized the characterization.

Both women were genuinely impressed by the little boy's unbelievable change in appearance—so much so that neither could have accurately predicted the reaction of other people to this phenomenon. He was neither man nor boy but a fictional apparition, theatrically perfect and totally contrived but personally unprepared for what was to come. Neither woman recognized the hazards to Corky's already-battered self-esteem, so neither took the time to prepare him.

Rosa seized his hand and proudly marched him into the diner.

Several truckers had already come in while they were fussing over Corky and had helped themselves to coffee and sat down to chat while waiting for Jan to take their order. They did not notice when Rosa brought Corky into the front and positioned him by the door.

"Now, Corky," she instructed, "when the next guys come up, you open the door and tip your hat and say, "Good mornin'," then lead 'em to a table. That's all there is to it. Jus' be nice to people, an' it'll be okay."

Corky, somewhat apprehensive, quietly took his place beside the door and waited. Soon four men left the parking lot across the street and headed for the diner.

As the first one came up the steps, Corky dutifully swung back the door, stood in front of it solemnly, tipping his hat with his left hand, and said "Good morning."

The first trucker looked, stepped back, looked again, and then roared with laughter. The other three crowded through the door and joined in as soon as they saw the cause of his outburst. The four men who had already been seated quickly turned to see the cause of all the merriment.

Corky had backed up a few steps, amazed and embarrassed by their laughter. As the other men noticed him, they all came forward, laughing also. In a moment Corky was surrounded by roaring, cackling men, and he was at his wit's end.

Totally overcome, he made a flying dash for the door and jammed himself out between two pillared legs, not knowing or caring whether they belonged to one man or two. His hat fell off and rolled into the dust of the walk, but Corky was at least a hundred feet away and flying in retreat before it stopped rolling.

Jan and Rosa stood in silent consternation, all their plans and dreams for Corky and the business gone in the rolling thunder of male merriment. Tears came to Rosa's eyes as she silently returned to the kitchen.

"Poor li'l pecker," she whispered apologetically to Jan. "Poor li'l pecker, an' it's all my fault. He looked so sweet…an' now he's gonna hate me forever."

CHAPTER 49

▼

Chimp hurried as fast as he could back to the spot in front of the restaurant where he had last seen Wash. He was both anxious that the two thieves might come after him, and elated that he had bested them and gotten his things back. Now the foremost thought in his mind was to get something to eat and then find Wash.

His money was still in the coffee can, just as he had dug it up. He knew it would not be smart to go into a grocery store or restaurant and dig into a dirty coffee can for money to pay for his food.

Guess I'll have to find a quiet place and repack all my stuff, and then I can hold some money out to use and put the rest in my pack, he thought to himself. I just can't let anyone know I have all this money.

With this in mind, he turned into a dark alley and flicked on the borrowed light. Slipping along the alleys and back streets, he looked for a secluded spot where he could get his things back in order.

Within a few minutes he came to a small park. It was heavily wooded, but hardpacked pathways led away from the street. He followed one path for several hundred feet, then turned off into a dark corner, protected on all sides by heavy shrubs and bushes. He reached up into the fork of a tree and hung his flashlight so it shone directly down on the grass.

Again he opened his pack, sorted out as much of the leaves and weeds as he could, that the two vagrants had rolled into his things. Then he reorganized and repacked his bindle. He threw away the coffee can, placed the sack of money inside his pillowcase, and packed it in the bottom of the load. He took out a single twenty-dollar bill and kept it in his pocket. After retrieving the flashlight and returning to the path, he switched it off and walked in darkness back to the street.

By this time it was nearly ten o'clock. He had not eaten anything since early afternoon and had not really had much to eat all day.

I gotta find Mister Wash tonight if I can, he thought. Maybe he can tell me a place to sleep. Besides, I gotta thank him and return his light.

He returned to the restaurant nearest to where he first met Wash and went inside. The smell of food was too great a temptation, and he decided to have something to eat, then hunt for Wash.

When the waitress came forward, she invited him to sit at the counter and teased him briefly about the load he was carrying. He told her it was laundry that he was taking home. Then he ordered a ham sandwich and a glass of lemonade, which he paid for with change he had in his pocket. The waitress was a pleasant middle-aged woman who chattered briefly to him while he ate.

When he was through eating, it suddenly occurred to him that the lady might know Wash. The next time she came within speaking distance, he stopped her.

"Ma'am," he said, "I have a friend around here somewhere that I am looking for. He is about as tall as me. He's black and has snow white hair. They call him Wash. Do you know him?"

"What's his whole name, young feller?" she asked.

"I don't know any other name than that," Chimp replied. "He just said his name was Wash."

"Mos' niggers' names don't mean much to me," she replied.

"I really don't know much about him," Chimp said innocently. "I only met him once, and that's all the name he used."

"Where you from, boy? Anybody from aroun' here callin' a nigger frien' ain't none too bright."

The direct question put Chimp on the defensive, and he stuttered and stammered before explaining that he was "just visitin' here."

"You soun' like a Yankee to me. Know what a nigger is, boy?"

"Not really, ma'am," Chimp replied, becoming more and more embarrassed.

"Well, mostly they's a waste, but jus' cause you're so young, I'll give you a piece of advice. Anybody ain't white's a nigger, an' if you got good sense, you don't go aroun' tellin' white folks hereabouts that no nigger is you frien'. I don't got nothing agin 'em personal, but I can't call none frien' neither. I don't know what you want with this nigger, but I did see a white haired one hangin' out front a while ago. Come nightfall, though, they skitters away to they own quarter mostly. You won't find no niggers hangin' round a white business after dark, 'less they workin' there."

She came out from behind the counter and walked to the front door. Leaning into the bay window next to the door, she motioned to Chimp.

"C'mere, boy…ya see that Texaco sign yonder? Well, if you turn left there and go bout five block, you be runnin' into Niggertown. If I was you, I wouldn' be goin' down there in the dark though, but thass yo own business. I wouldn' be tellin' you if you wasn't so young, but I figgered since you was a Yankee kid, you mightn't know no better. It's your bacon your fryin'. I'm just givin' you good advice, like a neighbor ought."

"Well, thank you, ma'am," Chimp answered politely, "but if I can find him tonight, I think I will."

Back on the sidewalk, Chimp pondered this new problem. His father had never told him there was anything different about black people, and he knew he had worked with more than one in the mines. There was a black man who cut meat in Mister Schmidt's store back home, and he had been a very nice man in Chimp's estimation. No one had treated that man any differently from anyone else in the store. Now this lady was telling him that all blacks were somehow different and not to be trusted after dark.

Well, Chimp reasoned, Mister Wash didn't even know me, and if it weren't for him, I'd probably be on my way back to Pennsylvania by now. He acted like a friend. Papa said all bums were no good, but Piney and Sam were really nice to me. I think I'm just gonna have to make up my own mind who's a friend and who ain't.

With that settled, he started off up the street in search of Wash. As he walked along, he could not help noticing how the appearance of the street changed from clean and busy small businesses—hotels, restaurants, garages—with clean streets and lighted walks into empty weed-grown lots between large, dark, seemingly abandoned houses. Small old hotels and boarded-up business places dotted the spaces between. Here the street was graveled and dusty, and no sidewalks or lights bordered the street.

Then began rows of small cottages, old and faded, some with broken windows, most with unpainted picket fences in front. Here and there a few dimly lighted windows cast patches of light on the dry grass lawns.

Dark silhouettes sat silently on front porches or stood in open doorways. Occasionally a shadowy form passed in front of a light. Chimp had the nervous feeling that he was being closely watched, even though he could see no human form, and he clutched the oak branch he had taken from Jonesey tightly in his hand.

In spite of the overall gloomy atmosphere of the place, and it's poor appearance, numerous smells of home cooking drifted tantalizingly on the spring breeze. Now and again the sound of song or laughter floated forth, cheerful islands of sound in a vacuum of gloom.

Soon he could hear the steady tinkle of a piano. On turning the corner at the next intersection, he found himself in another, much different business district from the one he had left a few minutes earlier.

Here little groups of black people gathered on corners, sat on steps or porch railings, or dashed back and forth from one group to another. Two restaurants almost directly across the street from each other seemed the focal points of most of the activity. Chimp noted a grocery store, two small hotels, a Texaco station with two bare bulbs hanging on a wire strung between two poles, plus the business from which the piano jangled happily. It appeared to be a tavern.

Several young black boys, barefooted with pants cut off at the knees, kicked a ball of twine-tied rags back and forth under the light from the gas station. A cloud of yellow dust sat above them like a great umbrella.

In the light of the doorway from whence came the music stood a circle of six or seven black men. They were laughing and talking noisily and passing a large brown jug from one to the other. Each would wipe the mouth of it with the palm of his hand, take a drink, and pass it along to the next. The bottle scarcely paused in its roller coaster course around the circle.

One of the men was Wash. He was on the far side of the circle from Chimp. The light from the doorway made his crown of white hair glow like a halo, and Chimp recognized the deep bass voice and wide shoulders immediately, though he was still several yards away.

As he approached the group, all suddenly fell silent.

The tall man nearest to Chimp turned to face him and said in a loud and unfriendly tone, "What you want here, white man?"

For the second time that day, Wash came to his rescue. "Nothing but a runaway kid, Poker. Friend of mine. I 'spect he's lookin' for me." To Chimp he said, "Well, kid, I see you got some of you stuff. How'd it go?"

"It was exactly like you said, Mister Wash," Chimp replied. "I got that guy's club an' made him run like a scaredy cat. The other guy was drunk an' sleeping, so I just took all my stuff and came to find you. Here's your flashlight, and I really thank you for helping me."

The man called Poker interrupted. "What kinda white man you found here, Wash, come inta Niggertown after dark by hisself, callin' folks mister, sayin' thank you. He tryin' run some kinda deal on you, Wash?"

"Jus' a brother of the road, friend Poker. He's young, an' he's white, but he'll do, an' for a young'un he's hell for stout. Don't go callin' down on him wifout knowin' what you callin'. Might cause you misery by an' by."

"Okay, brother Wash, if you say so, he's okay, an' I'll go along. Mayhap since he so friendly, he'll take a li'l taste wif us dark folks."

Poker, who happened to be holding the jug at that moment, tipped it back and took a drink, then held it out to Chimp with a jeering grin on his face.

Chimp's tongue had been dry for hours, and his pulse quickened as soon as he saw the men passing the bottle around. Now he could hardly believe his good fortune that these men were willing to share with him as Sam and Piney had done. He failed to recognize that Poker was baiting him and thought to back him into a corner by his offer. Poker would have held it against him if he had refused. His eyes bugged out in surprise when Chimp seized the jug and took a long drink without even wiping the top.

Chimp lowered the bottle and gasped in surprise as the fiery liquid, which he had at first thought to be wine, burned its way though his chest and into his stomach.

He managed to maintain his composure, however, cleared his throat, and said, "Thank you, sir. That's pretty good brandy."

The men howled with laughter.

Finally Poker turned to Wash and said, "You sure right, brother. Any mother's chile can take a strike of lightnin' like he jus' done, an' fum a nigger's bottle, then stan' back an' say thank you, he all right."

The earlier circle broke up, moved a few paces, and reformed, but now with Wash and Chimp in the center. Wash introduced him to all, and they chatted a few minutes about Chimp's misfortune and how with Wash's advice he had gained back all that he had lost.

"I was hoping you would let me buy dinner for you, Mister Wash," Chimp said when their questioning had died down. "I'm pretty hungry myself, and I thought if you would join me. I would be glad to buy whatever you want to eat."

"Well, now, young fella," Wash replied, "thass right thoughty of you. I could use a bite. Whyn'cha come inside here, and we'll see if ol' Whiskey Tom got any grits laid by."

Stepping toward the light, he caused two of the men to yield to either side to let them by.

"You boys go on yarnin' there," Wash said to the group. "Me an' Chimp here goin' inside an' git down on some chicken an' grits. We'll be talkin' to ya directly we gits done."

The two of them went into the honky-tonk and took a seat at the corner table. There were four other people in the room. An old couple sat at the other side of the room in a booth eating. One younger man on a stool at the end of the bar was drinking a glass of beer. The fourth person was behind the bar. He was a tremendously fat man and quite tall as well. All were black. They all fell silent and stared as Wash and Chimp made their way to the table.

An old piano stood in one corner, and opposite, near the corner where Chimp and Wash sat, stood a potbellied wood stove which was not burning. The floor was covered with faded linoleum, worn full of holes. Pedestal lamps with dusty shades stood on either end of the bar, and a single lantern-style lamp hung over the rusty old stove.

Near the booth where the old couple sat, a ragged army blanket covered a doorway, and a single red light bulb glowed dimly above this makeshift curtain. As Chimp watched, one of the men from the circle outside came in, gave the big man behind the bar some money, and disappeared behind the blanket.

The huge black man shuffled slowly from behind the bar and approached their table, wiping his hands on his dirty white apron.

"Brotha Wash, what you goin' have?" he asked in a high squeaky voice. He did not look at Chimp or otherwise acknowledge his presence.

"Well, Tom, my frien' here been so kind as to offer to buy ol' Wash some fixin's, an' he hungry too," Wash explained.

"Don' really git many white folk settin' down to our level, do we, brotha Wash? What you reckon bring him here to bless us wif his coin?"

"Now, ain't no need to be uppity, brother Tom. He only a kid. He feel he owe ol' Wash a favor. If he willin' to eat what we got an' offer to pay up front, where the harm in it?"

The big man looked Chimp in the eye for the first time and scowled. "Well, I got some pone or some grits or some chicken, or if you don' want that, I got chicken, grits, an' pone. Take it or leave it."

He looked Chimp square in the eye as though challenging him to try the standard fare of the black man's house.

Chimp, uncertain of what pone and grits was but feeling the grip of hungry anticipation in his stomach at the mention of chicken, looked at Wash and said, "Whatever they got is okay with me. Mister Wash. I'm hungry."

Wash's eyes twinkled as he told the big bartender, "Bring us a couple plates o' whatevah, brother Tom, an' a beer to go with it."

As soon as Tom turned to the bar, Wash slapped Chimp on the back and said, "Keep on surprisin' these black folks here, you gonna make a name fo youself that you don't want to get back to the white side of town, kid. White people down here ain't gon' like for a white boy to be cozyin' up wif the niggers. Bes' you head back uptown after you eats, 'cause it ain't goin' be good fo you or us if any those white po-lice come lookin' roun. An' they do, boy, believe me, they do. Now tell me bout Jonesey and Morgan."

Chimp eagerly recited his adventures of the evening, leaving out only the part about recovering his money. When he told Wash about building a fire between Morgan's legs, Wash gave him a hard stare and scowled at him for several minutes before commenting.

Finally he broke his silence. "Even though the two of them is bad as they git, I'm disappointed wif you, kid. I know you was mad an' worried an' all that, but they ain't nevah no call to hurt a man jus' to be hurtin' or getting' even. I truly hopes ol' Jonesey come sneakin' back 'fore that man got burnt. They ain't too many rules to be followed when you livin' on the street, Chimp, but I hope you takes a word of advice fum this ol' man. Don't nevah set out to hurt a man agin, less'n he tryin' to hurt you. Then you got to look out for number one, but ever' single man on the road gonna need help one day. If he leave the smell of revenge behin' him when he goes, it gonna be waitin' fo him somewhere up ahead. Do it too many times, an' someday when you gits in a tight, the one man what can save you life apt to be carryin' your scar. Revenge ain't got no reward but misery."

Chimp hung his head, feeling quite ashamed after Wash's sensible lecture.

"I know you are right, sir," he said finally. "I really didn't think about it like that."

"Well, don't worry you head too much bout Morgan, 'cause he's one that has trouble findin' help when he need it for jus' that reason. Lotsa guys on the bum has trouble thinkin' that far ahead, but I feel like you prob'ly smarter'n most. Ain't no use plantin' no crop you can't harvest. Here come our grub, so les' jus' eat up an' forgit it. I think you done jus' fine for a young'un."

Whiskey Tom set two huge plates of chicken, cornbread, and a brown and yellow substance that Chimp assumed to be grits on the table. He returned to the bar and came back with a pair of dripping glasses of beer.

He gave Chimp a cold stare and said, "I understan' you payin', white boy."

"Yes, sir," Chimp replied quickly.

"You owes me one dollar an' fifty cents. Sixty cents each fer the grub an' thutty cents fer the drinks."

Chimp quickly dug into his pocket and brought out the crumpled twenty-dollar bill he had held out of his cash earlier. Whiskey Tom took it and, holding it in both hands, examined it closely on one side, then turned it over and checked the other side. He snapped it loudly between his thumb and forefinger a couple of times, all the while staring questioningly, first at Chimp, then at Wash. When neither commented, he went back to the bar and soon returned with the change, all in one-dollar bills.

"Jus' when I commence thinkin' you smart enough to go it alone in spite of you age, you go an' do something else to make me think you garden plumb full of weeds," Wash said as soon as Tom had left the table.

Chimp, quite unaware of what he had done to upset his friend, did not answer. He returned Wash's steady gaze in silence.

Soon Wash asked gruffly, "Don't see nothing wrong wif what you jus' done, do you?"

Chimp shook his head.

"You know it take a workin' man ten days to two weeks aroun' here to make a twenny-dollar bill. I guess some o' them fellas you seen out front ain't nevah had no ten-dollah bill in they whole life, an' you, a wet-nose kid, gonna pull out a twenny an' wave it aroun'. You jus' askin' for trouble. I ain't goin' do you no harm, but you can't be lettin' no down-an'-outer know you carryin' that kinda money. You gonna wake up one mornin' wif you throat slit all the way to you ass. You got anymore like that?"

Chimp nodded, a worried look on his face.

"How much you got?"

"Quite a bit."

"Look," Wash said, almost in a whisper, "How much you got is gonna make a big difference in where you goes, where you sleeps, who you hangs aroun' wif. I'm tryin' my bes' to help you. I ain't gonna take nothin' fum you, but any advice I give you gonna be on what I knows, not what I guesses. You got a hunnerd? Two hunnerd? How much you got in that tow sack? An' don't lie to me neither."

Chimp was frightened. Wash had helped him a lot, and he seemed sincere, but he was not sure he could trust anyone to know how much he had. He knew it was a lot of money, but he really had no true idea of the value of what he carried. Unconsciously he reached down, grasped his bindle, pulled it closer to him, and laid the club across it in easy reach, but still he did not answer.

"Look, Chimp," Wash said, "ain't nothin' says you gotta tell me. It's you money an' you own business, but if you ain't tellin', I'm all through tryin' to steer you right."

Chimp briefly thought over his options. This kindly, gruff old man had been a good friend so far, and he still was very uncertain what to do next. He knew he could catch another train and keep on moving, but he would have to trust someone sooner or later. Wherever the next stop was, he would still need answers. He abruptly decided on sooner.

"I think I got a little more than two thousand dollars," he said at last, speaking very quietly.

"Sweet lovin' Christ!" the old man exclaimed, so loudly that all in the honky-tonk looked their way. Then in a near whisper he said, "You know you could prob'ly buy ol' Whiskey Tom out for that kinda money. You ain't safe, an' you ain't safe to be wif, if anybody knew. What you do, rob somebody 'fore you lef' home?"

"I'm not a thief," Chimp answered sharply. "My papa had all this money at home, and then he died. There was only him and me, so I think it's my money. Some neighbors were going to put me in a boys' home. They didn't know about the money, so I took it an' ran away."

"Been a sight better for you if'n you went to the home, boy. What you ought to do is bring that money to the bank an' let them worry 'bout it for you."

"My papa told me never to put my money in the bank. That's why he kept it at home, 'cause he said he almost lost all he had one time, 'cause the banks lost everybody's money. Besides, I can't stay around in one place. I have to be able to move with everything I got if someone comes lookin for me."

"Tell you what, Chimp. You can't go walkin' no dark streets tonight wif that kinda money in hand. I got me a li'l place down the street. You can come hole up with ol' Wash tonight. It ain't much, but it's warm and dry, an' nobody goin' bother us. Tomorrow we can think on what to do 'bout you problem."

Chimp was so tired at that point, after the food and the beer and the excitement he had been through, he would have agreed to any friendly arrangement. They left Tom's place, said goodnight to the men still talking out front, and headed down the street into the darkness.

A few minutes later Wash turned off the main street and onto a side street. The third yard they came to was weed-grown, and the fence had fallen down. As they went up the path to the door, it looked like the door and windows were all boarded shut.

Taking Chimp by the arm, he steered him around the house. There was a back porch, and the door here had also been boarded shut. However, on the lower half of the door the boards had been stripped away. Wash reached up under the lower board and turned the knob. The door squeaked open, and Wash and Chimp ducked down and entered on hands and knees.

Once inside, Wash closed the door and flicked on his electric torch. Keeping the beam trained on the floor, he led Chimp to a room and flashed the light briefly on a rusty old bed in the corner. It was covered by a bare mattress.

"Welcome to Wash's palace. Like I tole you, it ain't the best, but it's dry an' warm. Sleep long as you want. Only toilet we got is the back yard. Make yourself at home. I'm right across the hall, an' mine ain't no better nor worse than yours. Better drop that mattress on the floor an' shake some dust off'n it 'fore you lay down, or you won't sleep for sneezin'."

He held the light briefly for Chimp to put down his pack and bump the dust off the mattress. Then he said goodnight and disappeared.

Chimp leaned his club against the wall, placed his pack at the head of the bed for a pillow, and spread his coat out on the bed. It was past midnight, and it took him less than three minutes to begin dreaming his way back over this, his first twenty-four hours on his own.

CHAPTER 50

▼

Corky did not stop running until he got to his house.

He unlocked the door and began undressing before he was inside. The very nice new clothes Rosa had so carefully, lovingly selected, he threw in a pile on the floor and put on the shabbiest pants and shirt he could find. After slipping into a raggedy old pair of tennis shoes, he silently stalked out of the house carrying a folded blanket and a package of uncooked wieners. He left his key in the lock and the front door standing open.

Running again, he headed for Otto's warehouse. Mondays were always busy in the warehouse area. Nearly double the number of trucks were waiting to load or unload as on any other day. Several box cars were usually dropped to be loaded or unloaded as well. Therefore, no one paid much attention when Corky came running down the dock. Many of the warehouse workers and truckers were used to seeing him there anyway.

Corky paused outside the great doors for a few minutes, waiting until all the men in the vicinity were busy and not watching him. Quickly then he slipped inside and ran past the first few stacks of huge paper rolls. Then he squeezed in between two stacks, moved back to the last V-shaped space, dropped to hands and knees, and crawled between the rolls.

Here he spread his blanket, leaving it doubled to be softer. He stretched out on his back and lay there thinking about how everything always seemed to turn out for the worst for him.

After much discouraged mental conversation with himself, he made the decision that from this moment on, he could never depend on another person again if it were at all possible to avoid it. He would not go to school, and would not trust

- 270 -

other people for anything he needed. Whatever he needed, he would get for himself in his own way. This decision made, he lay there, mind more or less blank, until he finally feel asleep.

When he awoke, it was past noon. He could hear the traffic in the street outside and the jovial shouting of the truckers and warehouse workers. After a few minutes of lying there analyzing these sounds, he suddenly realized he was hungry.

He felt around for his package of wieners that he had placed against the roll on the floor a few feet beyond the edge of his blanket. When he got them in hand, he started to tear the end of the package open and found it already was open. This surprised him greatly, because he knew it had been closed tightly when he took it from the house.

It was quite dark between the paper rolls, so he crawled out to the light to investigate. As soon as he looked, he immediately realized his package had been opened and his food shared by a hungry rat or mouse while he slept. Nearly half of one wiener had been eaten and bites taken from the ends of the others.

He was more upset at the loss of the food than with whom he had shared. He had caught and played with mice, small snakes, and gophers before, so he had no fear of wild things. It was the first but far from the last time that he was to share his meager food supplies with rats, mice, and birds.

Carefully he pinched the nibbled ends off the three wieners and pitched the pieces back between the rolls in the next row. Calmly he ate the three damaged wieners, then rolled paper around the rest of them and stuck them in his pocket. He went to the toilet and got a drink of water from the faucet.

As he left the toilet, Otto came driving through the door on the fork lift.

"Hey, Corky," he called, "your mama was out here looking up and down the street for you a while ago. I didn' see you come in, or I would have told her you was here."

"That's okay," Corky replied. "I'll run home pretty soon an' see what she wants."

Otto rolled on back in the warehouse with the truck, and Corky returned quickly to his hotel between the rolls. At the moment he had no intention of returning home, today or any other day.

Rosa and Jan had shared the blues for a couple of hours about Corky's embarrassment and sudden retreat. Finally they decided Jan should go home and get him, so the two of them could try to explain or apologize.

Jan was quite upset and somewhat alarmed when she got home and found the door open and Corky's key in the lock. She immediately began wild imaginings about Eddie coming back to get even with Corky. However, she relaxed a bit when she saw the clothes in the middle of the floor. After a brief look around, she assessed quite accurately what Corky's mood and actions had been.

She picked up the new clothes and dusted them off carefully. She put them in a sack and, after another brief look around, decided that waiting there for Corky would be a total waste of time. She locked the door and put Corky's key in her pocket.

She had never met any of Corky's acquaintances on the row so did not know where to start looking. She was concerned enough about his mental state to at least try. Otto was the third person she talked to in the warehouse area. He assured her he had not seen him but that Corky came there often, so he would send him home as soon as he saw him.

Jan returned to the diner, somewhat relieved but still worried Corky might decide to run away farther than warehouse row. She discussed it with Rosa and returned the new clothes to her.

'I sure hope you will be able to get your money back, Mama," she said to Rosa. "I don't think there is any use tryin' to get Corky to try that again, an' he sure don't need fancy stuff like that for school."

"I think you're right, honey," Rosa replied. "Ain't no use wearin' yourself out chasin' 'im up and down the street. He'll come home in a few hours. I sure felt like a dumb-ass though. I shoulda knowed that dumb idea was too high-falutin' for this dump. Tell Corky I'm sorry, will ya? An' you can take off an' find 'im if ya think ya can. Hell, ain't nothin' happens 'round here in the afternoon any-ways."

Jan decided against looking for him and worked the rest of her shift. She was sorry she had when she got home after sundown and Corky was still not home.

Corky had hidden out all day in between the paper rolls. He kept out of Otto's sight, hoping he would believe he had gone home as promised. Late in the afternoon he fell asleep again on his blanket.

When Otto slammed the big doors shut to lock up for the night, Corky woke up. He heard Otto rattling around on the dock for a few minutes, and then all was quiet as a tomb in the warehouse. It was also dark. The only light came from a row of small windows thirty feet up on one wall. Although there was still two hours of daylight, the windows were on the shady side of the building and admitted only limited lighting on the brightest of days.

Bored after nearly eight hours of hiding and sleeping, Corky began to explore the great building in ways he had never done before, because Otto would have stopped him. At first he ran the L-shaped length of the building in the semidarkness. He tried rolling the wooden plugs as he had done before but soon lost them in the darkness between the rolls.

Then he decided to try climbing the pyramids of giant paper rolls to get up closer to the rapidly fading light. The bottom roll was higher than he, but by placing one of the wooden wedges near a roll, he managed to get up by standing on it. From there he found he could reach over the top of the next roll, but the surface was quite slippery, so he could not get a good grip. The rolls were stacked one-high in front but five-high in back, each roll about three-and-a-half to four feet high. After considerable struggling and kicking, he finally succeeded in getting atop the second roll.

By now he was beginning to get a sense of height, but he ignored it and attempted the third roll. This time, having gained a little experience and confidence, he made it in half the time. After pausing only a moment, he went for the fourth one without bothering to look down.

The fourth roll he managed to scale in about the same length of time it had taken him to make the third. By now he was easily fifteen to eighteen feet above the floor of the warehouse. It was much lighter up here, but now he could scarcely see the floor. As the sun sank lower, it got darker and darker by the minute.

After gazing around over the mountains of paper for a while, he began imagining himself as the only person left in the world. He was king of this desolate mountain range, and he would live here forever, where no one would ever see him or bother him again. He leaned his back against the top roll and leisurely ate another wiener. The trip would not be worth it until he had conquered the highest peak, so still chewing the last of the wiener, he placed his hands on top of the last roll and began scratching, clawing to the very peak of this imaginary mountain.

Twice he slipped and nearly fell from the narrow, rounded ledge of the roll on which he stood before he finally clawed his way to the top of the fifth roll. Once on top of this highest roll, some eighteen feet up, he had no support to help keep his balance and became suddenly nervous and shaky at his sudden lack of control. He at first stood shakily up, but with the immediate sense of height and nothing at his back or under his hands to hold onto, the danger of the situation put butterflies in his stomach and a weakness in his knees.

Spreading his arms and fingers for balance, he bent slowly at the knees until his fingers touched the sides of the paper roll. Now that he had nothing to lean his body against, he was suddenly more aware of how slippery this paper mountain was.

He eased himself down onto his stomach, managed to spread his legs on either side, and then pushed himself to a straddled position near the center of the roll. Leaning forward, he tried to see the floor but could not. Looking up, the windows were only a distant strip of pale light, insufficient to allow him to distinguish anything beyond the next row of rolls on either side of the one on which he sat.

Realization came quickly that this was not a place in which one would wish to spend the night, and having gained a sense of how very slick the paper was, he became frightened. His mouth turned dry, and his heart thumped fiercely against his chest.

I've got to get down from here right now, he thought, and cautiously backed away from the edge of the roll.

When he was near the middle, he turned sideways, rolled onto his stomach, and began easing himself onto the steep slope. He stretched himself downward, trying to feel the next lower roll with his toes. He was tense and stiff, and it seemed that each downward inch he moved thrust his feet farther out into space.

Really quite frightened now, he scrambled his way back to the top of the roll and decided to try going down, facing outward away from the roll. He reached his arms backward as far as he could and, arching his back, began thrusting himself outward on the face of the roll an inch at a time. The heels of his tennis shoes provided some grip, as did his hands, until he reached the point where his heels no longer touched the rounded edge. He felt himself slipping, and it was too late to turn back.

Instead of landing on the edge of the next roll as he had planned, his heels struck further out on the round of the roll and kept right on going. Suddenly he was on an uncontrollable slide downward.

Flup! Flup! Flup! went his back side as it struck each succeeding roll. The distance it had taken him more than half an hour to climb took less than five seconds to come down.

Corky made a five-point landing on the cement floor, luckily missing the wooden wedge he had used for a stepstool. His feet, buttocks, and the palms of both hands came in contact with the floor at almost the same instant. Fortunately for him, he was both lightweight and strong for his size. Still he was badly shaken, and the wind was knocked out of him.

He crawled in small circles for a few minutes, gasping and moaning. Finally, when he could stand, he began walking quickly back and forth in short paces, unable to see where he was going. His butt hurt, his hands hurt, his neck, legs, and back hurt—and suddenly he wanted very much to go home.

Feeling his way cautiously, he moved to the big doors and leaned his head against the crack where they came together. He could see the glimmer of a street lamp far away across the tracks and hear the distant noise of cars. He felt his way along the big doors until he came to the small walk-in door near the corner.

Hopefully he tried the handle, knowing all the while that he would find it locked. Misery gripped him, and tears came to his eyes, though he did not actually cry.

Again, moving carefully, cautiously, he worked his way around the wall to the little cage of the toilet near the other corner. He went inside and, standing on tip-toe, cupped his hands under the faucet to get a drink. Still feeling his way, he lowered the cover on the toilet, sat down, and rested his head on his hands in dejected, painful silence.

After a long while, stiff and sore, legs and feet tingling from sitting too long with his feet hanging, he went shuffling and stumbling through the black box of the warehouse, hoping to find the tunnel that contained his blanket. In several that he tried, he heard the scurry of tiny creatures, and once the high-pitched scream and the chi-chi-chi of an angry rat's teeth sounded somewhere near in front of him.

Patiently and painfully he explored until his hands finally contacted what he sought, the soft warm comfort of his wool blanket. He lay down, grasped the outside edge, and rolled, wrapping himself mummy-fashion in it soft comfort. He dreamed of a big warm house with soft carpet on the floor and a mother whose arms reached for him each time he came close. Strangely the woman in his dreams had his mother's body but Rosa's face, and though the face smiled, the eyes were constantly crying.

After a restless, uncomfortable, and eternally long night, Corky was finally roused by the sound of Otto rolling back the huge doors of the warehouse. He peeked cautiously from his hiding place and watched Otto until he finally went into the toilet. Then he silently stole out the door and ran for home as fast as he was able.

He found his mother, still fully dressed, asleep on the end of the sofa. She had a blanket wrapped around her legs, and for a moment she looked to Corky like an old woman, bearing little resemblance to the young lively person he was used to.

As he crossed the floor, she heard him and roused herself. She looked at him questioningly for a few seconds.

When he did not speak or come near her, she asked, "Corky, you okay?"

When he nodded, she got up, straightened her skirt, and went to the kitchen sink, where she washed her face and combed her hair.

This done, she turned to Corky. "I'm going to work. If you get hungry, you can come down to the diner, and I'll see you get something."

Without a love or a touch or a good-bye, she went out, closing the door behind her.

Corky threw himself down on the sofa, pulled the blanket around him, and cried himself to sleep.

CHAPTER 51

▼

The sun was already shining through the cracks of the boarded-up windows when Chimp awoke the next morning. Wash was leaning in the doorway staring at him with a scowl on his face. He sat up quickly, rubbing his eyes, and had to think for a minute to remember where he was.

"Good morning, Mister Wash," he greeted as he finally became fully awake.

"Well, I don't know about that," the old black man growled. "I din't sleep worf a damn las' night thinkin' 'bout this problem we got. Money is trouble, boy, an' lotsa money is lotsa trouble. I guess thass why I was nevah one to hang aroun' too long in one place. Man gets workin' reg'lar, gits a li'l money, an' right away got to figure some way to use it. Firs' thing he knows, he's all burdened up wif things an' stuff he can't carry, an' he's stuck forever where he might not want to be, an' the whole world peckin' an' grabbin' tryna take it fum him. If he just keeps the money, come soon or late, somebody goin' try takin' it away fum him anyways."

"But Mister Wash, if nobody knows I got it, except us, how can it be such a problem?"

"Looky here, son, you got to git through you head, an' right now, you might as soon try to hide a growed-up gator in you hip pocket as keep folks fum knowin' you got money. I knows! Whiskey Tom knows! An' ever' one o' them dudes jokin' 'round in front of Tom's place las' night knows by now. You tole them the minute you flash a twenny-dollah bill where no twenny oughta be. They knows what you got, an' they knows where you at. Oh, they don't know how much you got, but they's wonderin', an' if you hangs aroun' here long enuff, they's some that's ornery enuff to begin' checkin' you out. Bes' thing I can do for

- 277 -

you is see you off on another freight before they gits strong on the scent. By the way, you can quit callin' me mister right now. I'm jus' Wash."

Chimp thought about this for several minutes and then asked, "You really think someone is going to try to take my money from me, Wash?"

"If they even gits the idea you might have another twenny or so in you pocket, it's as sure as Saturday an' sunshine. Nex' time you git off in a strange place, when they's people about, the less money you shows, the easier it gonna be on you. Like me now. I got a dollah or two tucked by, case I can't find no other way I might buy somethin' to eat, but I don't gen'ally show even a dollah 'cep' in emergency, an' then I show it only to the guy that's got what I'm buyin". I don't nevah take out no more than it take to pay up."

"Well, Mister Wash...sorry, Wash, if you think all those people already know, and I've got no choice except to leave, at least I'm not going with an empty stomach again. I'm hungry. Let's go eat."

'Jus' not goin' to listen till it's too late, huh?" Wash replied.

"Well, like you said, I'm just a kid. I don't think grown men are going to take anything from me this early in the day. They might try after dark, but not now, isn't that right?"

"Okay, maybe you right. These black peoples anyways ain't goin' after no white boy in the middle of town in daylight, but the longer you stays, the better chance they is that you gonna be had. Take ol' Poker now. He jus' plain' hate white folks, an' he ain't no great ways different fum Morgan for bein' mean. He get wind of that load you carryin', an' you ass ain't worth a carnival token if the time is right. He ain't likely goin' after you while you wif me, but I ain't stickin' my neck out for you forever neither. I likes you, an' I admires you spunk, but I ain't so fond of you that I's lookin' to git kilt or crippled to keep the buzzards off'n you."

"Okay," Chimp agreed. "Thanks for helpin' me. Now let's go get something to eat. Since these men might cause us trouble, why don't we go to the other side of town and eat where nobody knows us at all."

Wash looked at Chimp again for a long moment. "Kid, you so green, somebody gonna take you for cabbage. Don't you know that dark town is the only place you an' me can sit at a table together?"

It was Chimp's turn to be amazed.

"What do you mean, Wash?" he asked.

"You really don't know, does you?" Wash asked in turn. "Black folks—niggers—ain't allowed in white folks eatin' places. I seen men spend ten days in jail an' get beat half to death besides, jus' for tryin' to go in a white restaurant. Nope, if we gonna have breakfus' together, it gonna be a loaf an' some fixins an' make our own or take a chance on my people. The damage already done. We might's well see if Whiskey Tom got some eggs an' coffee, an' we'll take up fum there wif you problem."

They left the little house and scuffled through the dust back to Whiskey Tom's. Tom was sweeping the porch when they came to the door. He immediately put aside the broom and led the way inside, after greeting Wash and ignoring Chimp. He went behind the bar and disappeared through the curtained doorway.

Wash and Chimp seated themselves at the same table they had used the night before. As soon as they were seated, Wash leaned over to Chimp and spoke very low.

"Gimme five o' them dollahs you got las' night, an' don't say nothin' 'cept if I asks you somethin' when Tom comes back."

Chimp complied, though he was puzzled about the strange request. Tom soon returned to the room, now wearing an apron, and strolled casually to their table.

"Have much business after we'uns lef' las' night, Tom?" Wash asked.

"Some of the boys come in fo' a while," Tom replied, looking nervously back and forth between Wash and Chimp.

"I don't s'pose you-all talked bout my frien' here, did you?"

"Well, not much," the bigger man replied, "'ceptin' Poker din't believe 'bout the kid getting' off on Morgan an' Jonesey like he said."

"Y'all din't talk none about money either, I s'pose?' Wash asked.

Suddenly Tom appeared very nervous. "I don't recall nothin' 'bout money, Wash," he replied.

Wash reached into his pocket and took out the five crumpled bills. He smoothed them on the table and laid them neatly fanned out in front of him.

"Tom," he said after a lengthy silence, "I know an' you know y'all talked 'bout money, an' I want to know who we got to watch. Now I'm willin' to pay this five for some useful talk fum you. If I don't git what I ask for, you gonna get paid in a different kinda coin, you know what I mean?"

Tom backed away a couple of steps and began nervously wiping his hands on his apron, staring hatefully at Chimp.

"He's jus' a kid, Tom, an' he come here 'cause I tole him to look me up. I done him a favor, an' he done right by me. He nevah had to come here a'tall, an' mos white folks wouldn't bothered, but he brung back my torch, an' he paid fo' my service, an' I ain't gonna sit by an' see him hurt. Now." He stood as he spoke, taking a step in Tom's direction. "Which way it gonna be?"

"Okay, Wash, ain't no call you an' me gittin' in a shitteree ovah no white kid. Ol' Poker an' Bailey sayin' they wants to know what you frien' got in that tow sack."

"An' you tole 'em the boy give you a twenny las' night, right?"

"Well, I guess it mighta come up, Wash, but I din't go to make trouble. I jus' thought it funny, a kid like him, runaway an' all, got that kinda money."

"He allus been a po' boy jus' like you an' me. His daddy die, an' his neighbors been hasslin' ovah what they goin' do wif him. He just takin' what he could fin' belong to his daddy an' lit out, same as you'n me prob'ly would. He a po' boy still, an' that's all you or any the boys need to know. Long's he's here, if they mess wif him, they messin' wif me. Save ol' Poker an' you an' Bailey a heap o' trouble to keep that in mind. Here's you five, an' that's for both speakin' an' not speakin', know what I mean? Fum now on, Chimp here, he just a man on the road, like me an' you an' mos' the rest of us been befo'. Now, how 'bout bringin' us some eggs an' hoecakes, an' it won't hurt none if you was to forgit we had this li'l chat when you talkin' to the boys."

Chimp had sat quietly listening to the two men talk. When Wash finished speaking, Tom wiped his hands nervously on his apron, tucked the five dollars in his pocket, and went into the back. As soon as he disappeared, Wash returned to the table.

Chimp stated in a questioning tone, "Whiskey Tom seemed like he was scared of you, Wash."

"Ol' Tom jus' a chicken, young feller. He back away fum trouble ever time. Lotsa men like that. If you talk straight at 'em 'stead of pussyfootin' aroun', they gonna eat crow, but jus' so's you know where I'm comin' fum, I may be on the road, but I got frien's in the right places. Tom knows I can tear down his shit-house if I sets it in mind. I think you don't have nothin' more to worry 'bout him."

"Does that mean I can stay on here with you for a while?"

"Not on you tin-type it don't. We tooken care of Tom, but the bag's open, an' dealin' wif Poker ain't like dealin' wif Tom. Tom a flap-jaw, an' I was just tryna hush him up for long enuff to get you clear."

"You mean you can't scare Poker like you did Tom, is that right?"

"You blame right, Chimp. Poker is a dangerous man, not much better than them two you was dealin' wif earlier. Oney thing 'bout Poker, he got a woman an' two kids, an' he live here. He ain't gonna foller you if you head out like Morgan and Jonesey might if they knew you was carryin' all that money, but long's you hang aroun' here, ain't neither one of us safe. He live purty good, an' he don't work. He slick as all gitout wif a deck of cards, but they ain't all that much to be made aroun' here. Poker Carl make crooked tracks no snake could foller, an' he got his own li'l pack of wolves too. No good invitin' trouble."

Just then Whiskey Tom came back with two plates of eggs and pancakes. He put them in front of Wash and Chimp, hurried to the kitchen, and came back with two cups and a pot of coffee. Chimp shook his head when Tom started to pour his coffee.

"I don't drink coffee, Mister Tom," he said. "Could I please have a beer like I had last night?"

"You payin', you drink whatevah you like, if I got it," Tom replied.

He soon returned with a dripping glass which he put in front of Chimp.

"You better start changin' you ways, you gonna make it on the road, kid," Wash advised when Tom walked away. "All this mister, please an' thank you make you show up like a snowball in a coal bin. You gonna hang out wif po' folks, you better start listenin' to they talk an' watchin' their ways. You soun's like you still sittin' at the head o' the class. People hears you an' right away starts wonderin' what the hell you doin' here. You big as a horse anyways. No way you can hide, an' you ain't half growed yet, or I miss my guess. Till you git this kinda livin' figgered out, bes' you do ever'thing you can to fit in. You too smooth and clean to be what you is tryin' to be."

They finished eating without further talk, and when Tom came to collect, Chimp tried to pay for both again. Wash objected.

"Tom, I'm payin' my own. The kid gonna need ever' cent he got till he gits straight on a few rules I'm tryin' to teach 'im."

He pulled out a silver dollar and clumped it on the table.

As Tom picked it up, Poker and another man Chimp had not seen before came into the bar. Poker stopped short inside the door and stared at Wash and Chimp for a few seconds, then went on to the bar, where they both leaned over and began a low-voiced conversation that neither Wash nor Chimp could hear.

When Tom came back to the bar, Poker motioned him over and spoke to him in the same low tone. Tom spoke briefly and shook his head as he glanced over at Wash and Chimp. When he saw they were both watching, he broke hurriedly away and returned to the back room, carrying the dirty dishes.

"The buzzards is flyin' lower," Wash commented to Chimp.

"What do you mean by that?" Chimp asked.

"It ain't ten in the mornin' yet," Wash replied, "an' Poker Carl ain't nevah been up befo' noon in his life 'less he had some kinda deal cookin'."

The door opened again, and two uniformed police officers came in. Both were white. They went directly to the bar and stopped only three feet from where Poker and his friend bent in low-voiced conversation. Both straightened and, facing forward, leaned against the bar watching the officers.

"Hey, Tom!" one of the officers shouted. "Git you big black ass out here."

Tom came hurrying through the curtained doorway once again.

"Gimme two jugs o' shine an' two glasses of beer. Put the jugs in the brim sack, an' fetch it out to the back seat of my wagon out there."

"Yes, sir, Mister Griffin," Tom replied, and he hurried to follow the order.

While Tom went about business, the two officers began looking around the room. When they saw Wash and Chimp sitting at the table in the corner, the one called Griffin frowned and turned to Tom as he came out of the back with the beer.

"What's that white boy doin' here, Tom?" he asked in a loud voice.

Wash immediately stood up and came forward, Chimp following.

"His daddy make that shine you buyin', Mister Griffin," Wash butted in. "He send this boy down here from Wes' Virginny to keep a eye on ol' Tom here for a few days. He say he wanta make sure Tom ain't waterin' down his shine an' give him a bad name. Me an' Whiskey Tom kinda entertainin' the young'un til his pappy come back. He on summer break fum school."

The officers turned to Tom for verification. "That right, Tom?"

"Yes, sir," Tom answered quickly. "His daddy don't trust no nigger to deal straight. Maybe you tell the boy I ain't sold no bad whiskey. If he hear it fum you, maybe he believe it."

The officer turned to Chimp and stuck out his hand. "I'm Chief of Police in these parts, boy, an' I git to sample lots of good whiskey. Youah pappy make some of the best. Ol' Whiskey Tom donate me a gallon or two here an' there to keep things peaceful like. Right, Tom? You tell youah pappy he don't hafta worry 'bout no shenanigans with One-Shot Griffin keepin' a eye out."

"Pleased to meet you, sir," said Chimp as he shook hands. "I'm Chimp."

"Hey, you don't soun' like no shiner's son. Soun' more like a goddamn Yankee schoolboy."

Wash interrupted again. "He been goin' to school up in Pennsylvania. That what make him soun' like a Yankee."

The officers both looked closely at Wash.

"Say, ain't you Henry Washington the fighter?" the younger one asked.

"Used to be," Wash answered. "Ain't nothin' but Wash, the travelin' man, these days. Old age creep up on ever'body soon or late. The kid hangin' out wif me whilst he in town."

"Look, boy," the big cop offered, "might be youah daddy an' me could do some business. I got connections 'round about, an' we could get more than ol' Tom handlin' his stuff. Y'all tell him drop by an' see me nex' time he come in. Meantime, you oughtn't be stayin' down here in Niggertown. Okay, you tend to business here, but I can find you a sleepin' place uptown with white folk, an' it ain't gonna cost you if you bring you daddy by. I'll be checkin' 'round, an' I'll let you know in a day or so. Okay?"

Chimp looked at Wash, uncertain what to say or do next. The last thing he needed was for the police to start checking into his affairs, and now he was caught up in a lie he could not get out of.

The police officer looked at Wash and laughed. "You needn't be waitin' on no nigger to approve youah affairs, son. This'n got a reputation for takin' care of his-self, an' I'm sure you pappy mus' trust him, but it just ain't seemly for no white boy to be livin' here in Niggertown. I'll find you somethin', an' I'll be in touch. See you aroun', you heah?"

Chimp nodded, and the two officers drank their beer down and left. Wash and Whiskey Tom immediately went into a low-voiced huddle at one end of the bar, and Poker and his friend did the same at the other. Suddenly Poker slapped his hand loudly on the bar, looked angrily at Wash and Chimp, and the two of them walked abruptly from the bar.

As Chimp watched, Wash shook hands with Tom and said, "So long, Tom. Sorry if I brung you trouble, but if you jus' play dumb, I think it'll all smooth out once we on our way."

He turned to Chimp. "Git you goods in hands, son. We ridin'."

"You mean right now?"

"You bet you eyeballs I mean now, an' we ain't got much time to jaw 'bout it neither. That cop worse than two Poker Carls, an' he smell bigger money than you carryin'. Ol' Poker dasn't touch you now that Griffin got his eye on you, but that don't mean Poker ain't gonna be trouble. He jus' the kinda guy that go lookin' for Griffin to tell him we bullshittin' him to throw him off. Poker knows you pappy's dead an' you runnin', an' he heered me lyin' to ol' One Shot. Bes' thing we can do is git on down the road 'fore the bees gits to buzzin'. Whiskey Tom makin us a couple of sanwidges, an' we gonna hole up till dark an' ketch us a southbound."

Chimp felt bad that he was causing Wash to leave his friends and his comfortable hideout, but at the same time he was very glad to have a companion on the road. He quickly gathered his belongings and came back to the bar where Wash waited.

When Tom returned with a paper-wrapped package, they both thanked him and were ready to leave when Chimp suddenly asked, grinning, "Y'all wouldn't have a jug o' pappy's shine I might git fo' the road?"

Tom and Wash both laughed at this attempt to mimic their talk, and Wash put in, "We better be travelin' light as we kin', son, an' you totin' a fair load already."

"Don't worry, I can handle it, an' I'd rather be with than without. I'll pay for it, and I'll carry it. Like my papa used to say, that's my ham and eggs."

"Okay," Wash replied. "It's you baby, an' it sure ain't gonna git any heavier as we go fum what I seen already. What the hell, Tom? Trot her out, an' we'll take her."

Barely thirty hours after his first stop, Chimp had a strong start on his education for the life he had committed to. He and Wash caught a southbound freight just after dark. They became fast friends and companions for many months. For a boy in his situation, Chimp could not have handpicked a more able teacher, friend, or protector.

CHAPTER 52

▼

The summer of 1943 was a warm one. Jan's and Bob's romance seemed to heat up with the weather. They had spent several nights away from the house recently, leaving Corky to take care of himself. Corky preferred this arrangement to having Bob hang around their house anyway, so he made no complaint.

He continued to do menial odd jobs for Rosa, but only on his own conditions. He did more for Otto and for the truckers on warehouse row. He made a little money, which he squirreled away either at home or in a convenient hiding place in Otto's warehouse. He seldom bought anything for himself other than a rare candy bar or other treat.

His mother kept him comfortably dressed, though most of his clothes came from Goodwill. Practically all of his food came from sharing the lunches of workers on the row or the more generous lunches and snacks that Rosa and Jan gave him at the diner. Rosa treated it as a normal part of Jan's wages and never asked for or kept an accounting.

In early August Jan came to work one morning very excited. She brought Corky along, and they ate breakfast together in the kitchen. When Rosa finished racking the donuts she had been frying, Jan called out to her.

"Hey, Mama, come an' sit down with Corky an' me for a minute. I got somethin' to ask you."

Corky looked at her questioningly but did not speak.

When Rosa had her cup of coffee and had seated herself, Jan exclaimed, "Mama Rosa, I'm so happy, I don't know what to do. Bob asked me to marry him last night, an' I want to, so much. We could move out of that raggedy little house into a real home, an' Corky will have a father, an' we can live like other people."

Corky jumped up from his chair and stared angrily at her.

"That creep ain't gonna be my father!" he shouted. "I ain't living in no house with him!"

Jan reached out and got him by the arm, though he angrily tried to avoid her grasp.

She pulled him close to her and said quietly, "Look, Corky, it ain't gonna be for a while yet. I can't marry him till I get a divorce, and I really don't know how long that takes. For a fact, I don't even know how to do it, but this is the only way we are ever gonna have any kind of life. You got a while to think about it, an' I know you'd like him if you just try."

She squeezed him tightly for a minute and rubbed his raggedy hair. Then she released him, and he turned and ran from the room, leaving his breakfast half eaten.

Rosa smiled at Jan. "Sweetheart, I'm really happy for you if you think it's the thing to do. Like they say, ya gotta strike while the iron's hot. Bob's a nice fella, an' I like him. Only problem I see is tryna convince ol' Corky. Bob's gonna hafta do the bes' sellin' job of his life to git the kid to come across. You can't let no li'l fella like that run your life though, so do what you gotta do. You ain't quittin' on me, are you?"

"Oh, no, Mama, you'd hafta run me out to get rid of me. One thing though, Bob asked me to go with him to Niagara Falls this weekend for about ten days. I know it kinda lets you down, but I never been out of Chicago except once or twice for a day. Would you mind? 'Cause if you do, say no, an' I won't go."

Rosa got up and hugged her. "Jan, I never had better help than you, an' I almost feel like you're my daughter. You ain't never took a vacation since you been here, so I feel I owe you that much. I can manage for ten days. Too bad ya can't git married first an' call it a honeymoon. Shouldn't take long to git shed of that other beer tank you was married to. Anyways, go on an' have a ball." Then, as an afterthought, she added, "Whatcha gonna do with Corky?"

"Jeez, Mama, I was hopin' you would see he gets enough to eat. Keep track of what it costs, an' I'll pay you. Otherwise, he can do for himself. He does anyway. I hardly see him anymore, an' he never asks or tells me what he does or where he is goin'. He can sleep at home, or here if you don't mind."

"You know I don't mind. You won't never find no one thinks more of the li'l pecker than I do. He's welcome here for eatin' or sleepin', Jan. You know me. I'm easy."

"Mama Rosa, you're wonderful. Don't know how the hell I could get along without you. Well, it's all set then, if I can persuade Corky to go along with it."

That night Jan caught Corky as soon as she got home from work. "Corky, why did you run off this morning? I wanted to talk to you some more."

"I don't want Bob living with us, an' I don't want to live with him either, an' I don't wanna talk about it!"

"Look, Corky," Jan replied in her most persuasive and patient tone, "we shouldn't have to live like rats in a hole. I'm never gonna be able to afford better on what I make. Besides, I love Bob. I want to live with him, and it will be better for all of us. Why can't you see that?"

"I just don't like him, an' he don't like me neither."

"Well, I didn't want to start a fight with you anyway. I just wanted to tell you something else. I would have told you this morning if you hadn't run off. Bob and I are going away for a few days. We are planning to leave this weekend. Rosa said you can eat there, an' sleep there too if you want. If you wanna stay here, that's okay too. Do you think you'll be okay if I go?"

"How long?" Corky asked curtly.

"It won't be long, honey, only about a week or ten days. We're going to Niagara Falls. Bob has to go there on business, an' Rosa said I could take time off an' go with him if you won't mind staying with her."

"It don't matter, I guess," Corky repled sullenly. "You'd go anyway if I said no or not—but I ain't staying at Rosa's house."

"No, Corky, you can stay at the diner or here at home. And Rosa said she's got work for you while I'm gone too, if you wanta make some money."

"Okay, Mom, but she better not try to lock me up."

"Don't worry, I'll talk to her. You will help her out if she needs help, won't you?"

"Long as she pays me," Corky replied.

On Friday evening Corky stood on the steps of the diner and waved, unsmiling, as his mother and Bob drove away. Bob had tried to give him a five-dollar bill before they left the diner, but Corky wadded it up and threw it in the corner. Rosa had picked it up and assured Bob she would give it to him later.

Jan voiced her disapproval of his actions toward Bob. She hugged him afterward and tried to give him a kiss, but he turned his face away.

"Be good, and mind what Rosa tells you," were her last words to her obviously unhappy and disgruntled son.

CHAPTER 53

▼

Ten days came and went, and Jan did not come back. After twenty days Rosa called the police. She reported what she knew and asked the officer if there was a way to locate them.

"Well," the officer replied, "people disappearing pretty reg'lar from Chicago. You ain't givin' me much to go on. A man and woman in a black car, no license number, no contract address or phone, gone to Niagara Falls, don't know if American or Canadian side. Seems like a woman leavin' her kid behind would give some kind of contact information. I'll put out a bulletin an' see what happens, but I ain't expectin' much. These people drinkers?"

"Not drinkers, or least not drunks," Rosa assured him. "Oh, they might tip a glass now an' agin. Jan now, she been workin' for me for several years, an' she ain't never missed a day, 'cept if she or the kid was sick. First time she ever been on vacation even. She tole me she'd be back in ten days. I know these people, mister, an' she ain't the kind to jus' run off. No way she wouldn't let the kid know if she was gonna be even one day late. I'm really worried. Maybe they had a accident or in the hospital or somethin'."

"Okay, lady, we'll make some inquiries. Sure soun's like somethin' ain't right. Gimme a couple days to check, an' I'll git back to ya. If I pick up anything, I'll let you know."

The officer drove off, and Rosa went back to working and worrying.

Thirty days passed, and the police told Rosa they had found no trace of them. They had checked hospitals, hotels, and motels all along the main routes and found nothing.

Corky accepted it stoically.

"They didn't want me around in the first place," he told Rosa. "They probably just left and ain't gonna come back at all."

School started, and Corky did not mention it. Neither did Rosa. She tried to keep him busy at the diner, and she fed him regularly and well. She did not pay him a wage as she had with Jan but gave him what she thought it was worth either as soon as the task was finished or at the end of the day.

When Corky made up his mind that his mother was not coming back, he began spending more and more time away from the diner. He did not want Rosa to get the idea she had any claim or control of him.

One morning late in September he arrived at the diner at about the same time as Rosa. She gave him some scrambled eggs and toast and sat down with him as he ate.

"Corky," she said when he was almost finished, "what if you mama never comes back? What in the world can I do about you? I don't wanna be bossin' you aroun', son, but you oughta be in school. You been wearin' that same shirt an' pants for over two weeks now. Somebody got to take a hand in seein' you git raised right. A feller your size an' age hadn't oughta be skinnin' aroun' all on his own. What you think we oughta do?"

Corky looked her in the eye steadily for a few moments. "I can take care of me if my mom comes back or not, and I think she ain't comin' back. What does she want with me when she got Bob? I'd just be in the way like always. Don't worry. I'll work for what I eat. You don't hafta pay me no more. Just let me know how much the food costs, an' that's how much I'll work. I can make money somewheres else."

"You poor l'il smart-ass stinker," Rosa barked, "I love you. I ain't worried bout the money. Hell, I'd feed you forever an' be glad if you was my boy, but we ain't talkin' bout eatin' here. They's more to life than eatin', an' you ain't got a steer's chance in a slaughterhouse without somebody sets you on the right path. Me, I got the old man to worry about. Him an' me, we're gonna close this place down someday an' go to Florida. I was plannin' to give the place to your mama, but if we can't find her, then what? I can't give no diner to no l'il peckerhead like you. Would you come an' live with me an' Carl?"

"I told you I can look after myself," Corky repeated.

He quickly drank his glass of milk and left.

That night when he was crossing the lot to go home, as he came in sight of his house, he noticed a car parked in front. All he could see was the back end of it.

His heart jumped as he thought, <u>My Mom has got back after all</u>.

He started to run, excitement building as his feet beat a tattoo on the hard-packed path he had worn through the lot. As he turned the corner, he could see the open door, but as he pounded up the steps, he suddenly noted the latch was broken, and wood splinters lay in the doorway. He stopped suddenly and peered cautiously in the door.

A big man in a brown suit was sitting at the table writing something on a piece of paper. He looked up at Corky.

"Where's your mama, boy?" He asked gruffly.

"She ain't here," Corky replied.

"I can see that for myself. I asked where she was, not where she ain't."

Corky decided to try to bluff his way through.

"She'll be here pretty soon," he said.

"You better be right, son, an' you better send her right down to see me. She's two weeks overdue with the rent, and this place don't look like nobody lives here. Dried—up dishes in the sink, no oil in the stove, no food in the fridge. You sure you ain't pullin' my leg?"

"No, sir," Corky replied, trying to be convincing, "I'm waiting for her to get off work."

"Well, okay, I'll wait another day or two, but she better bring me some money, or I'll hafta put you out. Tell her I'll get the lock fixed soon's I get the rent, okay?"

He put his paper pad and pencil in his pocket, walked out past Corky, and left without even closing the door.

Corky did not know the man, nor where to find him if he did decide to pay. He knew his mother paid rent every month, but he had no idea how much. In any case, he did not think he had that much money, so he just ignored the man's ultimatum.

Now he was being pressured from two directions. Rosa was worried, because she felt responsible in Jan's absence. He did not want to surrender his independence to do as he wished, particularly when it included returning to school. He had made up his mind he was never going to school again. He knew Rosa would insist sooner or later if he let her continue to feed him every day. Now, if this man made him leave the house he would have to stay in the warehouse or at Rosa's. He knew of no other choices at the minute.

"Oh, well," he said aloud to himself, "I'll just hafta wait and see what happens."

It was not long in coming. Two weeks after the man had demanded the rent, Corky came home in midafternoon, and another man had a pickup truck backed up to the side of the house and was standing on the tailgate nailing boards across the window.

Corky watched from a safe distance for a short while, then cautiously approached the truck.

"Hi, kid," the man said cheerfully. "What you want?"

"How come you're doin' that?" Corky asked.

"I guess the people livin' here ain't paid their rent, and the boss told me to seal it up. Gonna tear it down one of these days anyways, 'cause the railroad says it's sittin' on their property."

"Me and my mom live here, an' all our stuff's inside."

"Well, if that's true, you best tell her to git down to Mister Cain's office an' pay up, 'cause I got orders to seal it up tight all the way around."

"I can't," Corky said. "My mom's gone for a few days."

'Your mom is gone an' left a little feller like you on your own? Don't sound right to me."

"I ain't on my own. I'm staying with friends. How can this guy keep our stuff?"

"You ain't paid the rent. He got a right to anything left on the property. Best I can say is, I ain't lookin'. If they's anything in there you want, best get it quick, or it's gonna be gone for good unless you mama goes by an' pays up."

Corky went hurriedly inside and began gathering those things he could carry. He was both angry and frightened. Each blow the hammer struck sent quivering nails of anxiety into his brain as well as metal ones into the window frame.

His mother always kept some brown paper sacks folded in the space between the sink and the refrigerator. He put all his clothes in one sack. Then, with tears in his eyes, he began sorting through those things that were personal belongings of his mother.

He wondered what Rosa would say if he came to the diner with all these things.

I'll bet it's all she needs to make her think she owns me, he thought. If I got nowhere else to go, then she's gonna start makin' rules. If Mom comes back, she'll be mad 'cause I didn't take her stuff. What can I do now?

Tears flowed freely down his cheeks, and the beating of the hammer insisted, Get out! Get out!

He ran to the bushes a little distance from the house and hid the sack containing his few belongings. Then he turned and, with trembling hands and a lump in his throat, began sacking up his mother's things. One pretty skirt that he always like to see on her, he held momentarily over his face, breathing deeply the smell of her that still clung to the material.

Blinded by tears and sick with fear and worry, he secreted the two sacks of her things beside his own in the bushes and returned to the house. He looked around briefly and then decided he would probably need the remaining blankets on the Hide-a-bed. He clumsily folded one. Then, overcome with grief and loneliness, he fell forward on his mother's pillow, hugging it to himself, and sobbed hysterically for several minutes.

The pounding at the window suddenly ceased, and he heard the truck motor start. The door stood open, and he raised up in time to see the truck backing toward the front of the house. Soon the hateful sight of the workman, hammer in hand, was standing on the tailgate before the front window.

Corky thought of that other night, long ago, when a monster had stood there threatening him as he cowered on the couch, and as before, he suddenly became furiously angry. He went to the cupboard, pulled a chair over, climbed up, and opened the cupboard door. He seized the six plates stacked there and, timing his action to the beat of the hammer so the workman would not hear, dropped them one at a time to the floor.

For the next several minutes he repeated this action with every breakable object he could see in the little one-room place. As the workman closed off the last strip of light at the window, Corky took the broken bottom of a drinking glass and slashed the material on the sides and seats of the Hide-a-bed until it hung in shreds. He drove it one final time into the cover of his mother's pillow and left it sticking there.

Then he gathered the blankets under his arm and went out the door and down the steps.

"Get everything you wanted?" the workman called out to him.

Corky bent, picked up a small rock, turned, and threw it at the man. The workman ducked and suppressed the impulse to curse at the child. Thoughtfully he watched as Corky trotted away across the field.

"Can't say as I blame you, Red," he said aloud as he returned to his work.

Corky awaited his opportunity over the next several days, and one by one he secreted his salvaged belongings away between the paper rolls in the warehouse. He did not say anything to Rosa about not being able to return to the house. Afraid she would take some action to control his activities if she knew, he spent less and less time at the diner. He went there now only when he was hungry. He worked there just enough to compensate Rosa for what he ate to the best of his judgment. True to his word, he would not take any more money from her for the odd jobs she gave him to do.

As the weeks went by, the weather began to get colder, and the fall rains started. No word ever came from Jan and Bob.

Rosa continued to check with the police from time to time until she finally got the feeling that any replies they gave her were offered to pacify her. When their statements started to sound the same every time, she quit calling.

Her concern for Corky's welfare began to be more and more obvious. Each time he came to the diner, she tried to love and mother him, but he rejected her efforts at physical contact with obvious annoyance. He was not outrightly rude or physical about his withdrawal but made it obvious he did not welcome her handling and fussing. He began spending his small savings for food and avoided the diner except when he became very cold.

The warehouse, though heated minimally, became frosty and damp, and Corky was constantly chilled. Otto, aware that Corky was around every day now, still had not discovered that Corky was living in the warehouse at night. Everything the boy owned was stashed away between the rolls of paper, and he had become very adept at slipping in and out of not only the warehouse that Otto managed but others on the row as well, without the busy workers knowing he was there.

At lunchtime he would lean against a doorway or squat nearby while the workers ate. He learned to let the men know he was hungry without actually asking for food. He practiced this silent begging as long as he could find groups of men eating, and stored away fruit and other long-lasting items beyond what he wanted to eat at the moment.

Even though he had three blankets and a pillow, the tunnels between the paper rolls became drafty and cold with the change to winter weather. Inevitably Corky came down with a cold and fever. No attempt to bundle in his meager bedding would shut out the burrowing cold of the concrete floor on which he slept. Finally, half sick to his stomach and chilled to the bone, he buried his concern about Rosa's parenting and went to the diner.

Rosa was amazed by his pale and ill appearance and became immediately concerned about his health.

"Sweet Jesus, child!" she exclaimed, seizing his jacket sleeve with one hand and feeling his forehead with the other. "You look like a alley cat with diarrhea. Where th' hell you been keepin' anyways? You know if you're hungry or need somethin', you can come to Mama Rosa. I bet you ain't got no heat in that damn house, do you? For Chrissake boy, get in here an' eat a nice hot bowl of soup."

She led him into the kitchen and sat him down at the table. While he ate, she bustled about, making up the sofa with pillows and blankets. She stood close by and watched as he finished the soup.

As soon as the last mouthful was gone, she grabbed him by the arm again. "You want more, Corky?"

"No, I had enough," he replied as he stood and made a move toward the door.

Rosa would not release her hold on his arm.

"Now, goddamn it, you hard-headed li'l pecker," she said firmly, "you ain't gittin' away from Mama tonight. You got a fever on you, an' it's too cold for polar bears in love out there tonight. Now you git them things off you an' plunk yer ass under them blankets, or I'll do it for you."

Corky was too cold and miserable to argue. The warmth of the diner and the thought of a soft place to sleep were too much temptation. He momentarily swallowed his independence and meekly complied.

CHAPTER 54

▼

As they rumbled along on the train, Chimp and Wash chatted about each other and life on the road. Chimp told him about Sam and Piney and the hours he had spent with them, expressing hope that he might someday come across them again.

"Likely," Wash asserted, "plumb likely. If you keep on hoppin' the rails, you near certain to meet up somewhere. Particular if you follows the route they laid out. Peoples gits jus' like robins and ducks, long as ever'thing keeps goin' normal like. The main rail routes don't change all that much, nor neither the weather, so year by year, till Father Time ketch they ass, they follers pretty much the same track. Yar'masters an' inspectors kin set they clocks by some o' these bo's comin's and goin's."

Chimp laughed. "That's jus' what Piney said, that they made calendars by his and Sam's travels. Wash, what is a bo?"

"Jus' short talk for hobo. A hobo is a guy jus' like us that got no reg'lar home nor job an' jus' keeps movin' wif the weather. Mainly the ones they call bo's jus' lives and dies by the rails. They's lots of folks on the road. They walks, they hitch-hikes, steal cars, howevah they can do to make it fum here to there, but the bo's is a breed to theyself. Even got they own king, but he really don't rule nothin'. Fact is, the nothin'er he gets, the more likely it be that he goin' be king someday. It jus' kinda a family joke, 'cept the chosen guy really got respec' fum the rest of the bo's."

"So are we bo's, Wash?"

"Manner of speakin', I guess you is, more than me. I been knowed to walk ever' step fum Charleston to 'Lanta. Never ketch no bo doin' that. You ain't moved no way yet 'cept the train. Ain't nevah in my life seed no other bo wif two thousan' green in he's pocket, so I can't rightly say if that is no disqualifier or not, but you keep spendin' an' not makin', son, you gonna sure 'nuff qualify, faster'n you might think."

"What kin we do to keep fum gittin' in the same kinda mess we just left in the nex' town we gits to?" Chimp asked, trying his best to follow Wash's earlier advice and learn to talk like the people around him.

"One thing we gotta do, or you gotta, is not go flashin' you bucks aroun' like you done back yonder."

"Where we goin' now, Wash?"

"Mights well keep on rollin' on into Georgia now. They's a couple places twixt here an' there we could jump, but better to be on the safe side an' git as far fum ol' One Shot as we kin. If he wanta make trouble down the line, he shore could, but long's ol' Poker don't blab, we is safe for a few hours. Bes' we can do is git off in Georgia an' bum inta some li'l sharecropper town somewhere. Work aroun' a li'l bit till the heat's off. Cops ain't goin' lookin' far fum the rails noway."

"What good is my money if I can't spend it, Wash?"

"No problem bout spendin' it, Chimp. Jus' gotta be careful where an' when. Guys like you'n me can walk inta a bank an' ast em to change a twenny inta smaller stuff wif nevah a question. Show the same twenny in a backstreet bar, an' you got big trouble. Bes' you break a couple bills down at a bank an' use a dollah at a time. We finds a good leather man, pay you to spend a li'l sumpin' on a money belt an' keep the big stuff hid away insides you clothes."

"How long befo' we git to Georgia?"

"Oh, I'd reckon tomorra aftanoon we oughta be into Augusta. That's if they don't go shufflin' this empty inta a side yard somewheres along. They do that, we gotta ketch another ride or bum the road in."

"If we're gonna be that long, seems like we could have a drink or two an' enjoy the ride."

"How'd a kid you age git into drinkin' anyways?"

"Well, Papa always had beer an' brandy. He drank lots of it. I used to snitch a drink. Then I started snitchin' bottles when he was drunk. Then I got a job in a market where my grandma bought her groceries. They sold beer an' wine, an' I would buy it an' tell 'em it was for Papa. Then I'd hide it somewheres and drink it myself."

"You holds you likker purty good for a young'un, an' I like a drink myself now an' agin. You papa ever tell you it bad for you to be drinkin'?"

"He told me I couldn't have it at all. One time I got drunk, an' he really punished me, but I just like to drink. I don't like to get drunk."

"Soun's to me like you okay, but some guys gits to drinkin' an' can't quit. Soun's like you papa mighta been like that. Should be a warnin' to you. Don't let it git a holt on ya, or you gonna be like Morgan an' Jonesey an' lots more like 'em. They gits one drink, they gotta keep goin' till they pins is plumb knocked out."

While Wash talked, Chimp worked the cork from the liquor jug. He took a sip and passed it to Wash. For two hours they chatted, laughed, and got acquainted.

In this short period before the anesthetic of liquor and the rhythm of the road lowered them into the peaceful valley of sleep, the invisible arms of true friendship began to lock them together. The old man's philosophical humanity and Chimp's innocent ignorance, combined with their mutual loneliness, became a two-way bond of friendship that both would wear as long as they remained together.

CHAPTER 55

▼

For more than a week Corky ate and slept at the diner. He did odd jobs to pay for this accommodation but stayed only through the morning hours. He broke away and returned to the warehouse area as early as he could finish what Rosa asked of him. He usually came back to the diner only moments before she began locking up for the night. He still rejected any physical show of affection from her.

"Why'ncha c'mon to the house with me an' Carl t'nite, Corky? We can have a nice dinner an' play some checkers or sumpin'," Rosa said one morning as Corky was gathering the kitchen trash to go to the dumpster.

He gave her a cold-eyed stare for a few seconds, then shook his head, picked up the trash, and left.

Ornery li'l bird-turd, Rosa complained to herself. Sure wish I knew what th' hell I oughta do about him. I know damn well I oughta git the county folks in here, but that'd put his bony li'l ass on the run, sure as shit. His mama played hell dumping him here, but I don't even know is she 'live or dead, so I can't be blamin' her neither. Christ! What to do?"

On the ninth day of Corky's stay at the diner, he had faithfully done his chores, grabbed a hot doughnut from the batch that Rosa was cooking, and disappeared. Rosa thought he had left the diner.

Charlie came in for a cup of coffee just as she finished the doughnuts. She got herself a cup of coffee, brought Charlie a doughnut, and sat down with him at one of the small tables near the counter.

"Cholly, you'n me been buddies for a long time, an' I'd like to hear what you got to say about this here deal with Corky. Cops still ain't found hide nor hair of his mama, God bless her. Can't help but think somethin' awful musta happen to her, or she'd o' been back. Anyways, was you in my shoes, what th' hell would you do about the kid?"

Unknown to Rosa, Corky had not left the diner but had lain down on the end of the old sofa to eat his doughnut. As soon as he heard Rosa's growly voice mention his name, he was alert as a chipmunk. He slipped off the sofa and sneaked silently up to the doorjamb to listen.

"Tell the truth, Mama, I been thinkin' about that rascal my own self. He's a nice li'l guy. Seems willin' enough to help out an' all that, but a kid his age oughta be in school. He needs some kinda trainin' if he's ever gonna mount to a hill of beans. He oughtn't to be your worry though. Jus' cause his mama worked for you. Only right thing to do by my way o' thinkin' is call county welfare an' let 'em know. About the best you or me can do for him."

Corky's heartbeat picked up, and sweat broke out on his forehead as he heard the two plotting to get rid of him. Stealthily he slipped forward through the doorway and crouched down under the end of the counter just a few feet from where Rosa and Charlie sat.

"You'n me got some kinda telepathy goin' here, Cholly. I'd sooner have a boil on my ass than tell the kid, but what else I'm gonna do?" Rosa complained.

"Was I you, Mama, I'd keep it quiet as hell till I found out what county says on it. Sure as hell you'll put the li'l bugger on the run if he even thinks they're gonna shut him up somewheres."

Corky almost panicked and thought of making a run for the door at this point, but he silently held himself in check.

"Maybe you right, Cholly. Sure hate to pull a trick like that on the l'l pecker though. He gonna fight like a caged weasel if they try to take 'im away, an' he's gonna hate me the rest of his life, but I been cookin' the meat off this bone for two months now. I guess I gotta start the soup or throw out the water an' forgit it. God help me!"

"I feel for you, Mama. I know how hard it's gonna be, but I wouldn't stew myself too long about it. You know it's what you gotta do, an' someday I'll bet ol' Corky'll drop back an' thank you. Meantime, I gotta git this load into Detroit. See ya next week. Don't worry, it'll work out."

The big man threw some change on the table, gathered his cigarettes and lighter, patted Rosa's hand, and left.

Charlie had eaten only half of his doughnut. Rosa absentmindedly picked it up, soaked up the little coffee left in her cup, and stuck it in her mouth. She gathered the cups and saucers, wiped the table with a napkin, and returned thoughtfully to the kitchen. As she passed the end of the counter going in, Corky slipped quietly out between the counter ends, going in the other direction. As soon as he hit the street, he was running.

Rosa heard the door close as she was putting the dishes in the sink, and she returned to the counter. She looked around for a moment, puzzled.

"What th' hell? I mus' be hearin' things," she grumbled. "I coulda swore I heard somebody come in."

She wiped her hands nervously on her apron and stared thoughtfully at the phone, her pulse mounting. Then, nervous and dry-mouthed, she picked up the phone book and looked up the number for county welfare. Her hands trembled as she dialed the number.

When a voice finally came on the line, she clumsily blurted, "I got a kid down here got nobody, nor nowhere to go. I need somebody to come down here and talk about it."

After giving her address and phone number and receiving a promise from the receptionist that they would soon "have somebody down there," she hung up the phone and, with a lump in her throat and tears in her eyes, returned to work in the kitchen.

Corky went back to Otto's warehouse. He waited for an opportune moment when he would not be seen, slipped into the building, and like a hunted rabbit, crawled quickly into his burrow between the paper rolls, where he buried himself in his spare clothes and blankets. He stayed there all day and far into the night.

When the noise of the street finally died away, and the only sounds he could hear were the tiny creatures that shared his home with him, he crawled cautiously out. He had long ago learned to find his way about in the black cave of the warehouse at night. He went to the toilet, then sucked a drink of water from the sink faucet while lying across the sink on his chest and stomach.

With these basic needs satisfied, and too stiff and chilled to sleep anymore after the many hours of hiding out, Corky dragged the heavier of his blankets from the hole. He wrapped it about him Indian-fashion and began pacing back and forth to keep warm. When the gray light of dawn began creeping through the door cracks and dirty little windows, he returned to his hideout to wait until the rattle of Otto's key ring told him he was released from his self-imposed prison.

Over the next several weeks, Corky never left the warehouse except during meal hours when he slipped out to bum a few bites of whatever he could get from the workers. He watched, alley-cat cautious, for any stranger in the area. He watched particularly for anyone dressed in more formal clothing than the workers wore. If any such appeared, he would immediately hide wherever he could find a convenient hole. Small as he was, it was never difficult for him to disappear like a puff of smoke at any sign of danger or an unfamiliar face.

Soon he came to the point of being constantly hungry. Whenever his scrounging for scraps left him unsatisfied, he began slipping off to the Seven Eleven in late afternoon and spending his meager hoard of cash for cupcakes, candy bars, and an occasional loaf of bread or package of wieners.

He soon learned that regardless of where, or how supposedly safely, he hid these extra items of food, the rats, mice, and insects quickly found them. It often left him gritting his teeth in frustration to find he was spending his hard-earned cash to feed wild creatures. At first he would doggedly collect whatever rations they left him, eat what was not fouled, and ignore what was, leaving these scraps to be finished by whatever spoiled it for him. Often he got hungry enough to attempt cleaning the mouse dung from any larger pieces and soon schooled his stomach not to get queasy and his eyes not to search too closely for foreign matter in his food stores.

After many cold and hungry weeks, spring finally came. With the coming of warmer weather, he began to roam father and farther from the eight or ten-block area where he had spent his entire life. He quickly learned to recognize those other unfortunates, condemned as he to life in the streets and back alleys. He watched and listened and learned. Food was available from many sources if one got there first or was quick enough or strong enough to keep it once he had it.

He learned that larger cans that he found, especially if they had covers, made the difference between keeping what he found or sharing it with dogs, cats, birds, and wild creatures. Accordingly, he established caches in cans and jars over a wide area of South Chicago. He himself began to look more and act more like a wild thing.

He learned that sleeping outdoors in warm weather could be a pleasant experience. He also learned that in colder weather it was essential to have more than one alternative sleeping place. Many times when he thought he was already set for the night, some other human animal, bigger and stronger than he, would decide his choice of a spot was ideal and would take it from him. Other people became more and more something to be avoided.

From mice he learned that paper and cardboard made a warm if not thoroughly comfortable bed. From the birds, dogs, cats he learned of alternate food sources. From people he learned rejection. Clean and comfortable people looked the other way or brusquely brushed aside any request for money or food. Many of those like himself would attempt to take from him if he got too close or careless.

He talked with others only when necessary but, like many isolated people, formed a habit of talking things over aloud with himself. His money became something to use only when no other alternative existed. Then he spent it only for food or second-hand clothing.

Any useful item he found, he soon learned could be bartered with someone for something if he chose his target cautiously. He learned never to approach a group of street people carelessly, particularly with such a barter item in hand. From one person or two he could nearly always escape unscathed, but larger groups had too many hands and quick moves, resulting in loss of the prize more times than not.

It was better to find a lone target, or a legitimate business such as a loan company, describe what he wanted to exchange, and show it only after a deal had been tentatively made. The Goodwill and second-hand stores occasionally let him exchange one useful item for another, and on rare occasions he might make a cash deal.

He lived and learned and survived. Odd jobs were still available from the warehouse workers and truckers who knew him but became harder and harder to find outside of his familiar area. As he grew older, it became more and more difficult to find people willing to pay him for his efforts. Because of his shabby appearance and peculiar looks, he was treated with suspicion and hostility by most people with the means to pay for shoveling, sweeping, and cleaning tasks, which was about all he knew how to do well. Though willing and able, his sources of honest employment gradually disappeared.

One winter day more than two years after his exile from Rosa's protection, cold, hungry, and desperate, he went by the diner thinking he might bum Rosa for a bowl of soup or a sandwich. To his surprise it did not even look the same anymore. It had been repainted, and a concrete walk now led up to the wrought-iron steps that had replaced the rickety wooden ones.

When he opened the door, a little man in a too-large apron and a white cook's hat scowled at him from behind the counter. The inside had been redecorated and arranged so that nothing was recognizable anymore.

"What you want?" the man growled at Corky.

"Can I talk to Rosa?" Corky asked.

"Sure you can, if ya wanta bum your way to Florida to do it. If yer lookin' for a handout, just beat it, kid. I don't give nothin' to people what don't wanta work."

Corky turned dejectedly and returned to the sidewalk.

<u>There goes my last chance with anybody that's got anymore'n I do</u>, he said to himself.

He checked the garbage can at the back door and found enough meat and bread scraps to make it until morning. He stood there, shoulders hunched against the cold damp wind, and thought about the good meals and soft warm couch he used to be welcome to here. Dejectedly then, he turned and slumped away in the gray twilight, looking for some makeshift shelter to carry him through till tomorrow.

Over the years that followed, Corky never traveled more than ten miles or so from the spot where he was born. He often sat listening to groups of street people who talked about the places they had been and their exciting experiences in places far from Chicago. Some of the older people, particularly the drunks, talked of homes and families they once had and how good their lives used to be "before."

The older Corky got, the less he remembered of home and comfort. He listened with interest and envy to these people who had at least sampled a normal and comfortable life. He was like a child listening to a favorite fairy tale. Even into his thirties, whenever he heard people reminiscing about that nebulous experience call the 'good life," he would imagine himself into the situation and dream of a time when it would happen to him.

He often found magazines and catalogs, which he would thumb through, looking at the pictures. Since he could not read more than a few words, he simply daydreamed his way into the bedrooms, fireplaced living rooms, and fairyland kitchens he saw pictured there, but his constant search for food and shelter left only rare moments for such fanciful daydreams. The cruel reality of life in the street permitted only very short flights into fantasy before hunger or cold would beat him unmercifully back to face his hardscrabble world.

He daydreamed and wished about far-off warm and sunshiny places he heard about where one could pick fresh vegetables and fruit at his leisure and sleep without being cold—He never fathered the nerve to abandon the familiar and jump a freight to find it. To think of travel by any commercial means was as impossible as his dreams of living in his own house some day.

Corky hunted and gathered, scratched and scrabbled, occasionally stole, constantly ran, and on rare occasions fought to maintain the most meager existence. His fortunes had taken the best turn ever in the few weeks immediately preceding his chance meeting with Chimp.

CHAPTER 56

▼

Chimp and Wash stayed together for over four years.

In comparison to Corky's existence, Chimp's had been a walk in paradise. Wash was cleaver, experienced, and seemed to have friends everywhere. Chimp was an apt pupil, quick to pick up on any survival tips Wash might drop him. They rode the rails on short trips throughout the southland from the Florida coast to East Texas and from Louisiana waterfronts to the hills of West Virginia.

By the time he was fifteen, Chimp was six feet, three inches tall and weighed well over two hundred pounds. Like a great friendly bear, he accepted people at face value until they proved to be unworthy of friendship. Those who occasionally attempted to take advantage of them found themselves facing a bear but no longer a friendly one, as well as an experienced and dangerous fighter, in Wash. Chimp's strength and confidence grew with his size.

Together they worked stevedore or warehouse jobs both for the railroads and on the waterfronts. They did cleaning, woodcutting, loading and unloading, or gardening chores. Most often they worked as transient farm labor, not only because they liked this work, but it also gave them a ready source of free food. They picked fruit, cotton, peanuts, sweet potatoes, lettuce, and carrots as the seasons offered them. Never committed to one location or full-time work, they worked a day here and a day there, moving on when the mood hit them.

Chimp's hoard of cash never caused them further problem from the day Wash led him into a small leatherwork shop in Alabama where a talented young black man crafted him a smooth, soft, and comfortable money belt. From there they went to a small town bank and changed all of his money into bills no smaller than twenties.

From that day on, if they needed to spend anything from the belt, they always went to another bank with one or two bills in hand and changed these larger bills to ones, fives, and change. After two years he and Wash had made only small inroads into Chimp's bankroll. They lived on what they made from day to day. Chimp still carried nearly fifteen hundred dollars on his person.

Chimp continued to drink, mostly wine. Wash joined him only occasionally in an evening drink or two. Chimp drank all the time, finishing at least one bottle of wine, and often two, every day when it was readily available. Some places sold it to him, no questions asked; others required identification or outright refused him service.

These refusals caused him no problem, however, as Wash bought for him when he could not buy for himself, but always with the friendly warning, "you drinkin' gonna fetch you trouble one day, son."

Beer or wine in large quantity did not alter Chimp's manner or disposition in the slightest, and it took a truly abnormal amount or extremely strong drink, such as white lightning, to affect his coordination and balance.

As in his early school days, Chimp delighted in showing off his tremendous strength. By his fifteenth birthday he could lift and carry objects that it took two average men to move. He and Wash had many a laugh and often made a little extra cash by betting on Chimp's ability to perform some physical feat.

In those places where hobos gathered, like the sunny end of railroad depots or line shacks and at crossings and sidings where the trains normally slowed, there would usually be stacked extra sections of rail. A favorite test of strength among these men was to see whether anyone could raise the end of the thirty-foot rail section clear off the ground. Few men could do it alone.

Chimp could, and often did. Clasping both hands under one of these rails, he could raise it chest-high. Resting it momentarily against his chest, he could then shift his grip and boost it to arm's length over his head. Then, shifting slightly to one side of it, he would roar and push it away to come crashing down again as he stepped aside out of danger.

Chimp and Wash were an excellent working team. Had they any goal or wish to settle down, they could have taken Chimp's money and started a small enterprise of their own. Neither had the education to consider such an action, and both entertained an ingrown itch for travel that kept them transient and unburdened. Many people for whom they worked a day or two offered them full-time employment.

Wash would always refuse with a soft, "No, I reckon not."

They accepted their one or two days' wages, ate and drank well, and slept wherever night found them. Then they moved on to repeat the process in some other town and some other line of work.

Near the end of their last summer together, they were working in a Georgia lumber mill, moving rough slabs of pine out of the way of the saw. It was very hot and humid, and neither had taken a break for several hours. Wash had picked up an armload of slash and was walking toward the discard pile when he suddenly stumbled and fell.

Chimp threw down the slabs he had gathered and ran to the old man's side.

Wash was lying on his face, one arm outstretched, the other folded under him. As Chimp approached, it appeared that Wash was trying to push himself up on this one arm. His body tensed and strained with the effort. Chimp knelt beside him and gently rolled him face upward. His eyes were glazed, and every line of the strong old face bespoke pain.

"Somethin' wrong wif my leg, son," Wash mumbled.

His speech was slurred and unclear, and in spite of the heat, his skin was cold and damp.

Chimp was frightened and did not know what to do for his friend. He put both hands under his arms and started to lift him up, but Wash objected.

"Leave me lay, Chimp. My leg feel like it not there, an' my arm's dead too. Bes' git the foreman."

Chimp ran quickly to the foreman's shack.

"Sir!" he shouted, reverting to his school days' polite and correct English. "My friend has fallen down and can't get up. I think something bad has happened to him. Please help me quick!"

Without waiting for a reply, he ran back to Wash's side. His breathing was rapid and shallow, and he did not speak. His head rolled sporadically from side to side, and his silver-gray hair was damp and now sprinkled with leaves and saw-dust. Chimp raised him to a half-sitting position and began cleaning the trash from his hair and face.

The foreman walked up to where Chimp knelt, trying his best to make Wash comfortable and determine what was wrong. He hooked his thumbs in his bib overalls and spit a stream of tobacco juice from the corner of his mouth.

"Look to me like he done took a heart attack or somethin'," he stated mat-ter-of-factly. "Prob'ly ain't much we can do fer 'im."

"We gotta do something for him, mister. We can't just stand here an' let him die. He's my friend. Can't you get a doctor for him?"

"Ain't no doctor I know gonna come call all the way out here in this heat fer to help no nigger that prob'ly gonna die anyways," the foreman said, still unconcerned.

"You mean you won't help because he's black, is that right?" Chimp snapped at him.

"Ain't none o' my concern noways," the little fat man stated gruffly. "You-all jus' one-day help, not reg'lah employees. If he gits medical help, it on you-all, not me."

He turned and started to walk away. Before he had gone three steps, Chimp was in front of him, holding a handful of his overalls in his left hand and a big fist under his nose.

"Mister," Chimp stated flatly, "right now there ain't nobody here but you an' me, an' if you don't get something started to git my friend a doctor, you are going to need one worse than him."

The red-faced foreman paled a little at the threat. He knew immediately that the boy meant what he said, and he did not argue further. He walked quickly toward the mill with Chimp close at his side. He whistled shrilly at two black men who were loading fresh-cut lumber onto a wagon pulled by two mules. A second team and wagon was tied under a tree a few yards away.

"Rube," he said to one of them, "take thet spare team an' tote thet ol' nigger yonder into town to the doc. Make sure Doc know I ain't payin' no bill on 'im though. Take this'n here wif you too. He don't work here no more."

He turned abruptly and walked away.

Chimp was too concerned about Wash to deal with the man further, so he turned his attention to Rube.

"Hurry, please," he implored. "I think my friend might have had a heart attack, and I don't want him to die."

He ran back to where Wash lay. When Rube stopped the wagon alongside, Chimp picked up the old man and laid him gently in the bed of the wagon. After running to the corner of the mill where they had left their packs, he retrieved them and ran back to where Rube had already turned the team and started for town.

Without pausing, he jumped into the moving wagon and urged Rube, "Hurry it up, mister. I'll pay you a full day's pay if you get him there alive."

It was a long three miles to the doctor's office, and Rube ran the mules most of the way, while Chimp sat in the bed of the wagon supporting Wash's head and shoulders to protect him from the bumps.

Chimp ran into the office, where a lady in white uniform and a thin, sad-faced, middle-aged man stood beside a desk in conversation.

The man turned, scowled at Chimp's rough and dirty appearance, and looked questioningly at the nurse.

"I'm a doctor," he said finally. "What can I do for you, young man?"

"The only friend, only family, I got is out front in a wagon, and I think he is having a heart attack. Can you help me, please?"

The doctor started for the door.

"Bring my scope and the little bag," he said over his shoulder to the nurse.

They walked rapidly to the wagon.

As soon as the doctor saw Wash, he came to an abrupt stop. "What are you trying to pull on me, young fella? I thought you said this man was family."

"To me he is family," Chimp stated flatly, "and I want you to take care of him like he is family too."

"I'm sorry. I am not equipped to take care of black folks here. You will have to take him to the county sick house," the doctor said. "I'll see him there soon as I get through here."

He turned and started to walk away just as the nurse came running out with his equipment.

"What if he dies on the way, Doctor?" Chimp asked. "We have already hauled him several miles. I've got money, and I'll pay you to take care of him right now."

Cash customers were hard to come by for a Georgia country doctor.

"Well, okay," the doctor agreed reluctantly, "but we can't take him inside. I'll do what I can for him right here."

Wash had been lying on his side in the wagon, and as the doctor rolled him onto his back, he began calling Chimp's name in an almost incoherent whisper. As the doctor unbuttoned his shirt and began listening to his heart, Chimp climbed into the wagon and knelt on the other side of him.

When Wash called his name, Chimp replied, "right here, Wash. I ain't leavin' till they git you taken care of."

"Listen, boy, you gotta hit the road agin. I heered you tellin' 'em you got money. Cain't no good come of it."

Wash squeezed Chimp's hand and fell silent again.

The doctor completed his brief examination and turned to Chimp.

"Your man's heart is a little irregular but strong. His heart isn't the problem. Looks to me like he has had a partial stroke of some kind. That left hand is pretty weak, and the left side of his face is slack. Probably a stroke."

He wrapped up his stethoscope and began putting away a few things he had used. "Bring him to the county sick house and leave him. I'll check him out some more later. Come on in the office, and I'll make you a bill and give you a little something to keep him from hurting."

Inside, the doctor sat down at the desk, selected a carboned pad from the top drawer, and began writing.

When he finished, he looked up at Chimp. "That'll be twenty-five dollars for the call and admittance at county. You got that kind of money?'

Chimp looked around nervously, then unbuttoned his shirt. He opened a small zipper on the side of his money belt and pulled out several bills.

"Don't worry about the money, Doctor," he said. "You worry about lookin' after my friend."

He flashed a couple of one-hundred-dollar bills as he carefully selected a twenty and a five from the handful he held. Then he carefully put away the rest.

"Understand, kid, often there isn't a hell of a lot that any doctor can do for a stroke victim. We can make him comfortable and feed him and hope he recovers. Some medicines help a little, but mainly they remain partially crippled after. I'll do what I can. What's your address, so I can get back to you?"

"We're jus' passin' through, Doctor. We don't have no address, but I'll be around. You won't need to come lookin' for me long as my friend is sick. I ain't leavin'."

"Well, get him down to the sick house, and I'll call on him this evening. Here, give him one of these every four hours or so."

He handed Chimp a vial of pills, put the money in a box on top of his filing cabinet, and disappeared into the office.

Chimp hurried out to the wagon. "Rube, do you know where the sick house is?"

"Yessuh," the black man answered. "It ain't that far, but Mister Hargis jus' tole me bring him to the doctor, an' we been. He gon' be on me like a red-ass ape if I don't git back soon."

"Look, my friend can't walk. I'd carry him on my back if I knew the way, but I don't, and you do. I told you I'd pay you, an' I will. Let's go!"

Chimp climbed back into the wagon. Rube cracked a whip over the mules' backs, and they started with a jerk. Chimp sat down beside his old friend and, grasping one of Wash's hands in his, he leaned back against the wagon box.

"Please, God," he said, "don't let him die."

Within fifteen minutes they arrived in front of a long low building, which at one time long past had been painted white. Strips of peeling paint stuck out from the dry cracked boards like dead leaves on an autumn tree. Rickety wooden steps led up to the front of the building, where a sour-lookin, thin black woman in a white smock leaned against the open doorjamb, fanning herself with a small, dirty white towel.

Rube pulled the mules to a halt. "Here you is, sir. Was it me, I'd ruther they kep' on goin' right ovah to that graveyard yonder, but maybe he'll come aroun'. Some does."

Chimp stared in shock at this awful-looking place where he had brought his friend. Then he jumped from the wagon and pulled Wash gently to the tailgate.

"How much does ol' Hargis pay you a day?" he asked Rube.

"Tain't much, jus' three dollah, but don't worry bout it. I nevah seen no white boy have such a care fo' no ol' nigger befo'. You keep it. He gonna need it."

Chimp insisted and forced the three dollars on Rube, though he obviously did not want to take it.

"Here then, lemme h'ep you tote 'im in. Least I kin' do," he said.

They picked up Wash and advanced on the forbidding woman, still fanning herself in the doorway.

"You got a doctor paper there?" she barked at Chimp as they approached the steps with Wash.

"Yes, I have it," Chimp replied.

"Tote 'im in here, an' put 'im on a empty bunk den."

She stepped aside to let Chimp pass, then immediately resumed her place in the doorway when they were inside.

As soon as Chimp stepped in out of the sunlight, the smell of the place hit him like a hammer. He gasped, and his eyes watered, but they laid Wash on an empty bunk. Rube made a hasty retreat, and Chimp heard his shout and the crack of his whip as he drove the mules away.

He made Wash comfortable, then straightened and began to look around. There were twenty bunks in the long barracks-like room, ten on each side. A wash basin and toilet stood in plain sight in the back corner. Nine elderly black people, men and women, lay sweltering on gray-striped straw mattresses. Most wore little or no clothing. What clothing they owned lay scattered on the floor or hung in disarray on the head or foot of the wooden slat bunks. A gray-white sheet was draped across each bunk or dragged on the floor alongside.

Behind the door, where the nurse still leaned, stood a small stove with four lids and an overhead warming oven. Beside it a huge old oak cabinet half blocked one of the six windows, three on each side of the room. A pot of something that smelled edible steamed on the back burner. Beyond the few feet of open space in front of the stove, the odor of food began to mix with the acid smell of sweat and urine. Once past the first four or five bunks nearest the door, the stench became unbearable, particularly to someone like Chimp or Wash, who were used to living all their time in the fresh air.

Low moans, uncomfortable coughs, belches, and snores chorused through this nightmare hall. It looked and smelled to Chimp like the waiting room to hell. For the first time in several years, he bowed his head as tears of frustration and anger welled in his eyes.

After this brief exploration, he returned to Wash's side.

"God, Wash," he whispered, "I can't leave you in this place."

Wash had been only semiconscious when they carried him in. To Chimp's surprise, he was now awake and heard his anguished whisper.

"It'll be okay, Chimp. Maybe I'll be all right in a day or two. No need you hangin' by in this place. It don't smell like no flower garden in here, but it serve for now till I git me some rest. Go ahead, boy. Find you a spot to flop an' come by tomorra. Ol' Wash ain't out of it yet."

CHAPTER 57

▼

Reluctantly Chimp left the sick house, suddenly aware of how frail and weak his old friend looked. Wash had always seemed very strong and capable.

This almost instantaneous change from total freedom and apparent robust good health to invalid dependency and confinement in this' place' brought home to him as no other experience could the fragile state of the human condition. He felt alone and abandoned again, as he had on his flight from Pennsylvania several years before. It seemed unfair to him that those he loved always became victims of illness or death, leaving him on his own.

The old thirst was suddenly upon him, and he walked rapidly to the liquor store in the little village. They had been in this area for only two days, so he had no idea whether they would sell to him. He decided the bold approach would serve him best, so he walked directly to the counter and carelessly threw a twenty beside the cash register.

"Gimme a bottle of brandy," he said gruffly.

The clerk looked at him questioningly for a moment, then picked up the money.

"Any brand in partic'lar?" he asked.

"It don't matter none, jus' so it ain't rotgut. I'm drinkin' it all myself."

The clerk adopted a "What-the-hell-do-I-care?" expression and turned to the shelves behind him. He selected a short fat bottle, which he started to put in a sack.

"Don't bother," Chimp said. "I'm startin' on it right now."

He reached for the bottle.

"Look like you jus' bought you'self a headache for tomorra. Hope you have a jumpin' good time t'nite," he said as he handed Chimp the change.

Chimp was in no mood for chitchat. He took his change and the bottle. As soon as he got out the door, he broke the seal with his thumbnail, pulled the cork with his teeth, and spat it noisily into the middle of the unpaved road. Standing there on the board sidewalk of the dusty Georgia street, he tipped back the bottle, and gulped down about a third of the hot smooth liquor.

Briefly he considered getting something to eat, but the warmth of the liquor began to burn in his stomach, and he decided not to dull it with food. After adjusting his bindle under his arm, strap across his left shoulder, he scuffled through the dust toward the small river that skirted the east side of the town.

A huge old willow tree laid it's umbrella of shade over a grassy section of bank and all the way across the ribbon of slow-moving greenish water. Chimp settled himself between the gnarled roots and leaned his back against the rough-barked tree, staring blankly across the expanse of fields, fences, and trees on the other side of the river. From time to time he would sip the liquor, and as the sun sank behind him, he drifted in and out of a drowsy, drunken stupor, staying awake only long enough to take another pull at the brandy.

The heat of the sun on his face woke him the next morning, the empty bottle still in his hand. He had slid down the bank during the night, and the heel of one boot rested in the water. The moisture had soaked up his pants leg so that the whole back side of his pants was wet.

His mouth felt and tasted like some road crew had extended the dusty street through it while he slept. His head throbbed, and he was terribly thirsty. He thought briefly of quenching his thirst with the river water and was leaning forward to do so when the belly-up body of a rotten fish went floating slowly by in front of him. He nearly gagged, then caught himself and struggled to his feet.

He could not remember when he had felt so bad. Then he thought of Wash alone in the shabby sick house. His concern for his friend took his mind momentarily from his own misery. He stumbled to his feet and half walked, half jogged back to the ramshackle little town.

He did not see many people moving about. The grocery store, the only one in town, did not open till eight o'clock, according to the faded sign on the door. It was only six-thirty, and he did not want to wait until eight o'clock for something to eat. What's more, his thirst was still bugging him.

The smell of fresh bread was strong in the air, so he followed his nose down the block, sniffing as he went. When he reached the corner, he saw the bakery sign halfway between him and the next corner. A lady was coming down the block with a white paper sack of something in her hand. As she passed, the unmistakable smell of warm doughnuts passed with her.

The half-mile walk from the river had gotten his blood circulating again. The butterflies in his stomach had become rumblings of hunger, and it struck him that he had not eaten since yesterday morning. He hurried to the bakery, where he bought a dozen sugar doughnuts and a loaf of still-warm bread.

Outside again, he leaned against the wall and devoured several of the doughnuts. Then he was thirsty again. He wished the liquor store was open but knew the hours there, and they did not open until eleven.

When he came back to the single-north-south street, a stoop-shouldered, white-haired man was moving racks of fresh fruit and vegetables from inside the store to the empty spaces on either side of the steps. He stood watching for a little while until the man set up a three-legged stand and began carrying out small dark-green watermelons and stacking them in the stand.

"How much for a melon?" Chimp asked eagerly.

"Ain't open for business yet," the old man growled.

"Can I help you set up? I'll take a couple of those melons when we're through."

"I got no handouts for no piss-ant bums," came the surly reply.

"Look, you crabby old bastard, I ain't lookin' for somethin' for nothin'. I'll work for it or pay for it, don't matter to me, or if you don't go for that, I'll jus' take it an' go, an' there ain't a damn thing you could do about it. Might be better not to make me mad."

Chimp opened his bag of bakery goods and took out another doughnut. He grinned at the bent old man, bit off more than half the doughnut, and began chewing.

"Sure, I guess I could use a li'l h'ep," the store owner said thoughtfully as he looked Chimp up and down. "Ya gotta git outta here before the ladies start comin' though, 'cause you don't look nor smell none too purty. Might be bad fo' bi'ness."

For the next half hour Chimp fetched and carried, with the storekeeper standing by giving sharp, curt orders. When the outside display was completed to his satisfaction, the old man looked quizzically at Chimp.

"How come a hustler like you is bummin' it? You know somethin' 'bout groceries, an' you a better worker than lots I seen. Might be you could git reg'lah work hereabouts."

Chimp was rather surprised by the man's change of attitude, but he was used to this way of life and could not even consider full-time work with Wash laid up.

"No, I reckon not," he replied, echoing Wash's familiar reply to the same proposal.

"Wal, you earnt y'self a couple them melons you was wantin'. H'ep y'sef, an' should you set yer head to stay, I 'low I could steer you to sumpin' steady."

Chimp thanked him and picked up two of the head-sized melons. Putting one down on the step, he took the other in both hands and cracked it across the porch rail. He broke it in half, pulled the heart out of one half with three fingers, and stuck it in his mouth. Then he picked up the whole melon and put it in his bindle. He tucked the folded top of his bakery sack over his belt and, with a broken half melon in either hand, headed down the street in the direction of the sick house to share his goodies with Wash.

The doctor had been in to see Wash twice—once the previous night, and he had just left a few minutes before Chimp arrived. Nothing about the sick house had changed in the least. The same smells emanated from the stove and the back of the room to mix in nauseous confusion somewhere near the middle. Wash lay in drowsy semiawareness on the bunk. He turned his head and put on a half smile when he saw chimp approaching.

"Why you hangin' 'round, Chimp? Bes' you should git on wif livin; an' fo'git ol' Wash. I ain't goin' nowheres for a spell, 'cordin' to the doc."

"C'mon, Wash, you know I can't leave till I know you gonna be okay. I'm gonna go talk to that doctor an' tell him I want you out of this place. There's gotta be better than this, an' I got the money to pay for it."

"You an' that damn money gonna be the death of you yet," Wash replied. "How long you think it gonna be 'fore that Rube or that doctor tell someone about the kid wif a sock fulla cash 'roun' his middle? They be sniffin' 'roun' here like a bear on a honey tree in no time at all. How long you think it been since that doctor called in on a ol' nigger in the sick house more'n once a week? I seen the look on that house girl's face when he come by again this mornin'. What you think she gonna think when he come in here lookin' these old bones over twice in one day an' ain't come near these other wretches. She gonna know the name of the game is ol' dirty green dollah. Bes' you take you bindle an' ketch the nex whistle out. Ol' Wash gonna do or gonna don't, whether you here or not."

This lengthy speech wore the old man out. His head fell back on the pillowless mattress, sweat streaming down the sides of his face.

"Are you hungry, Wash?" Chimp asked, trying to change the subject.

"I s'pose I could do wif a bite. It gotta be better'n what they brings you in here. We gits chicken soup an' pone for breakfas', pone an' chicken soup for dinner, an' lef'overs for supper, 'cordin' to that guy yonder." He nodded toward a skinny old man leaning on his elbow in a bunk directly across the room. "I tried a li'l bit las' night, but I ain't got hungry much yet. Hard to think about food wif the smell of this place in you nose."

"I got some fresh doughnuts an' bread an' a piece of watermelon outside with my stuff. Why don't I carry you out under the trees, an' we'll have a snack?"

"Soun's good to me, leastwise the fresh air." Wash tried to push himself up as he spoke. "Chris', I can't believe I'm so weak, Chimp. My lef' arm ain't lis'nin' to me at all, an' my leg the same. One side works, and t'other don't."

"Hey, don't strain yourself!" Chimp exclaimed. "You know I can carry you."

He walked to the other side of the bunk, slipped his arms under Wash's body, lifted him from the bed, and started for the door.

The woman hurriedly left her place by the door, exclaiming, "What goin' on here? You cain't take him fum here 'less the doctor says so."

She stopped with her arms crossed, directly in front of Chimp.

"Don't worry, we ain't leavin'. I'm takin' him outside for a little fresh air. I'll bring him right back. Now get the hell out of my way, or we'll walk right over you." Chimp spoke with authority.

Still objecting, the woman stepped aside. Chimp ignored her complaints and went out the door and down the steps. He laid Wash under a big tree in the yard and did his best to make him comfortable.

For the next two hours, Chimp talked with Wash, handing him small pieces of watermelon, fresh bread, and doughnuts. Some he put into Wash's still-useable right hand; other pieces he put directly into his mouth. At one point he went back inside, got a grimy-looking drinking glass from the attendant, and caught a glass of water from the rusty old pump beside the building. He drank the first glassful himself, then took one to Wash.

"Look to me like this jus' a place they brings you to die," Wash remarked gloomily. "Sure don't see no smiles in there, an' the smell wuss'n a stock yard in August. Don't know what I'll do if I can't git up an' about right soon."

"Don't be worryin' yourself, Wash," Chimp replied. "I'll be comin' by every day an' take you out for some fresh air, an' I'll try to git the doctor to move you to a real hospital instead of this shithouse."

"You jus' barkin' at the moon, boy. Tryna git a black man in a real hospital in Georgia gon' do you jus' about that much good too. I 'preciate what you tryna do, but let it lie, Chimp. I ain't really sick. Doc says this happens to lotsa guys that spent their younger days fightin'. Ketches up wif you when you gits older. I'm more'n sixty, an' I've had it better than most, time to time. Thing 'at really itches me is the thought of layin' here in this pesthole waitin' to die. I ain't feered o' dyin'. It's the waitin' that's bad."

"Hey, boy, the world is fulla frien's. Gener'ly you treat a man like a frien', he'll be one. You'll never have no trouble there. You done changed a lot since first I seen you. People looks to you for help now. When I firs' met you, you'd ask the devil hisself for advice, but you come a long way. You'll do fine. Bes' you should grab the nex' train out an' forgit ol' Wash. I ain't likely goin' nowhere but yonder."

Wash nodded his head toward the weed-grown field of headstones and crosses that stood about fifty yards from the sick house.

"I ain't leavin' long as I can help you." Chimp insisted. "I don't care what it takes. I can work for money. The money don't matter. Better I should spend it to help you than have somebody knock me on the head and steal it. You wait, I'll get that doctor to find someone to take you in their house if you can't get in no hospital."

"Jus' as well bring me back in," Wash replied finally. "Getting' out of there for a li'l break make me feel better even if I ain't. You been one of the bes' frien's I ever had, but I see it no good talkin' no more. You gonna do it your way, no matter. Well, who knows? Maybe ol' Wash ain't all that helpless after all."

When Chimp had carried him back inside, Wash lay quietly looking at him for a while.

Soon he stuck out his hand and said, "Thanks, son. Keep them rails hot, an' mind them yard bullies. Wash gonna be thinkin' 'bout you. God bless."

"I told you I ain't goin' nowhere till you're better. I'm goin' to see that doctor right now and git you out of here."

Chimp shook the old man's hand.

'Okay, kid, whatevah you say, but maybe if you was to leave me a hunnerd or so, I could do my own talkin', an' you could be on your way. Maybe a li'l cash might get me a clean sheet an' a pillow or somethin' decent to eat too. How 'bout it?" Wash smiled and winked at Chimp.

"You know you can have anything I got, Wash," Chimp said.

He unzipped the money belt and handed Wash a hundred-dollar bill and several fives and ones. "If you talk to the doctor here, and I get him at the office, and we both show him money, maybe he will help."

Chimp buttoned his shirt, shook Wash's hand again, and left.

"See ya tomorra, kid," Wash called after him as he turned away.

Chimp went from there directly to the doctor's office. The nurse was there, but the doctor was out. She told him the doctor probably would not return today. Because he was making calls all over the area.

Chimp returned to town and bought a bottle of wine at the liquor store. This time he did not set out to get drunk but took only a small drink, recapped the bottle, stuck it into his pack, and went looking for something to eat.

Wash wasted little time when Chimp left. He called the nurse over and held out a five-dollar bill to her.

"What you spec me to do fo' that, Mister Moneyman?" she asked.

"Go on, take it," Wash said. "It's yours jus' for listenin' to what I got to say."

The nurse examined the bill suspiciously and stuck it in her pocket.

"I'm an old man," Wash told her. "I really 'preciated gittin' out in the sunshine today. I know it ain't in the rules, but if you wanta make a li'l more money, it gonna be easy to do."

"Okay," she said, "what you want fum me?"

"You evah made twenny bucks in one day in you life?" Wash asked.

The girl shook her head.

"Okay," Wash went on, "I'm gonna give you twenny jus' to give a friend a message. You know that Rube what brung me here yesterday?"

"Yeah, I know him."

"Tonight when you gits off, you gonna find him. You gonna tell him ol' Wash got a hunnerd-dollah bill fo' him if he come by here wif his mules after dark tonight an' take ol' Wash fo' a li'l ride in the moonlight."

"You plumb crazy, nigger. You dizzy as a tree-hung possum. What the hell you gonna do out in the moonlight, crippled like you is?"

"It cain't make no nevah mind to you what I does out there. You want that twenny or not?"

"Well, okay," she said finally, "but a sick man like you oughta be layin' up in the bed 'stead of gallivantin' out, peekin' at the moon."

"I knows a mojo woman hereabouts can conjure up a spell fo' me when they's a good moon, if you got to know," Wash said with a smile. "An' I don't want you tellin' no one but Rube neither, or I'll have her mark on you whilst she's whuppin' up a cure fo' me. Now git that message to Rube, an' there'll be twenny dollahs right here under the mattress fo' you in the mornin'. When my frien' come back tomorra, you tell him Wash said he'll be ridin' wif him on the twelve-twenny. He'll know what I means."

Two hours after dark, Wash heard the rattle of harness and the creak of Rube's lumber wagon. Soon Rube was standing by Wash's bed in the darkness.

"I think you mistaken, mister," Rube began. "That woman say you wantin' to go fo' a ride in the moonlight. This here the dark of the moon. Full moon done gone near two week ago."

"You think you can git me fum here to you wagon, Rube?"

"Sure can," he answered, "but I cain't hang out no moon fer you."

"Look, Rube, I jus' can't stan' bein' cooped up in this place. I'll sleep lots better in the fresh air. All's I wants fum you is to get me down by the river where's I can hear the poorwills an' the frogs a'singin' an' get some fresh air jus' fo' tonight. It worth a hunnerd bucks to me. I cain't spend it no other way, the shape I'm in."

"I sure unnerstan' why you cain't sleep here," Rube answered. "I'll swing you legs offa there an' hold you weak side, but you gonna hafta he'p me some. I ain't no hoss like that kid you run wif. Where he gone, by the way? How come he ain't doin' this fo' you?"

"Oh, he been worryin' an' carryin' on 'bout me ever since I got in here. I told him to go git hisself a bottle of wine an' a night's sleep an' come back tomorra. I told the nurse to tell 'im come get me come sunup."

Rube raised Wash from the bunk and half carried, half dragged him until he got him in the back of the wagon. It was only a ten-minute ride to the river.

When they got there, Wash told Rube, "Find a spot where the grass plenny soft an' the bank run steep to the water, so's I kin hear them frogs singin'."

Rube walked away in the darkness, and Wash lay quietly humming "Rock of Ages" to himself.

Presently Rube returned and said, "Look like a good spot jus' a spit an' a holler down here."

He jumped back on the wagon seat and turned it around. The river was a silver ribbon in the darkness, and the boom of a bullfrog's song came vibrating across the water. Soon Rube stopped the mules again. He jumped down and came back to Wash. As their hands came together, Rube heard the unmistakable crackle of money and felt a bill being pressed into his palm.

"You cain't tell in this dark whether or not that's a hunnerd," Wash said, "but you knows I cain't git away, the shape I'm in. If I'm lyin', you knows where to find me."

Rube helped Wash from the back of the wagon and laid him as gently as he could in the soft thick grass of the riverbank.

"You sho' you wants to stay here all night? I kin come an' fetch you back later. Jus' say the word," Rube offered.

"Nope," Wash replied cheerfully. "You earned you money. I'll be fine."

They said goodnight, and Rube climbed into the wagon and creaked away into the darkness.

Wash lay there for half an hour listening to Mother Nature's beautiful night song. Then he dug the heel of his good leg into the soft damp earth and began pushing his crippled frame toward the steep bank. When his hand fell downward over the edge, he carefully pushed his whole body straight with the bank until he lay poised on the edge. Again he rested a few minutes, listening and breathing deeply of the sweet fresh air.

Suddenly he chuckled softly.

Who the hell ever woulda thought ol' Wash's last free ride would be on the water? he thought as he pushed himself over.

When his body hit the water, he kicked out strongly with his good leg, thrusting himself outward and downward into the current.

CHAPTER 58

▼

Chimp went the next day to see Wash, and after getting Wash's message about "ridin' the twelve-twenty," he knew in his heart that further investigation would be useless. Nevertheless, he went to the sawmill and talked to Rube.

"I knowed they was somethin' funny 'bout him wantin' to stay all night on the riverbank. You think he kilt hisself for sure, huh?"

Rube expressed his regret at having helped Wash destroy himself and offered to return the money. Chimp refused, saying that Wash had a right to give the money however he thought best.

Chimp went several miles downriver, checking both banks for his friend, but found nothing. Not wanting to get involved with the authorities, he went to the doctor and told him that he was taking Wash somewhere to see if he could not get better care. He paid the doctor's bill and caught a northbound freight shortly after midnight that night.

He had claimed Wash's bindle from under the raggedy bunk in the sick house and told the matron they would not be back. Before he got on the train, he sorted through his and Wash's things, disposing of what was of little use and keeping the most useful things in both packs. He replaced everything into one pack and threw away the oak staff he had been carrying ever since he had taken it from Jonesey several years before. He kept Wash's flashlight, razor, canteen, and knife, but he threw away most of his clothes, because they were far too small for him.

Then he paid another call at the liquor store, bought two bottles of wine, and headed for the train yard. Here in this small town, the yard consisted of only two tracks, the through line and a siding spur, and an old whitewashed depot. He sat behind the depot for several hours waiting for a train.

The first one that arrived sped right on through, never slowing sufficiently to hop on. The next one slowed to a stop, and the crew began unloading sacks of produce, grocery items, and mail. They dropped two empty cars on the siding and picked up a flatcar with lumber.

It took Chimp nearly half an hour to find a boxcar he could get into without being seen, but finally he made it just as the train started to move. Once aboard, he opened a bottle of wine and settled down for a long ride. He had no definite goal in mind except to eventually arrive in California for the winter.

With Wash gone, his thoughts turned again to Piney and Sam and the possibility of joining them.

His search lasted far longer than he had hoped. After more than twenty years of crisscrossing the country, north to south and east to west, he never found them again. For the first few years he occasionally met other hobos who knew of them, and he was fairly certain they were still alive. For the last five or six years his inquiries all brought negative responses until he had finally ceased his quest.

Over the years he had come upon several old-timers on the road, burying a partner or brother of the road in some lonely spot with nothing but a rusty coffee can or a hand-tied stick cross to mark the spot. This always put him in a melancholy mood, and he would reflect momentarily on whether he might be better off to settle down in one spot and stay. He wondered whether his friends might lie in some such lonely spot, and whether anyone had ever found Wash and given him a decent burial.

Many times he made friends with whom he spent a few days but never again found as close a friendship as he had with Wash. His fortunes were up and down as the seasons came and went. After leaving Georgia by himself that first time, he worked very little for many months, traveling as constantly as he could catch rides. He ate and drank on his hoard of cash until one frosty morning, upon examining his money belt, he found only one twenty-dollar bill remained. At this point he hocked the belt for four dollars in an Oregon pawn shop and caught a train heading south to California.

By his twentieth year Chimp was six feet, seven inches tall and weighed nearly three hundred pounds, and he never began the daily shaving habit that most American boys start early. The only grooming he ever did was to occasionally trim back the point of his beard into a rounded shape and snip the straggly ends from his hair to keep it about shoulder length.

At forty years old, he had never been to a barber as long as he had been on the road. His hair and beard were rich dark brown and curly, and the large brown eyes sparkled with the joy of living.

He worked when he had to and otherwise did exactly as he pleased. He continued to drink his daily bottle or two of wine and made friends everywhere he went. He would share anything he had with anyone and always took the part of the underdog in any chance altercation that might occur with people on the road or the streets. He spent the night in jail on occasion but was usually released the next morning to go his carefree way.

Corky was the smallest man Chimp had ever met in his transient existence, and perhaps his sympathy for the underdog was what drew him to Corky at the outset. He had worked his way up the east coast to New York and was moving gradually westward, intending to spend the winter in California as had become his habit.

On the morning he met Corky, he made the instant decision to befriend this diminutive, ugly elf and try to persuade him to travel to California also. He had been alone for many weeks and was in the mood for companionship.

As for Corky, he was immediately impressed by Chimps size. He had never met so big a man in his entire life. He had never had a friend except Rosa, and that had been very much a one-way relationship. The only other person with whom he had ever formed any kind of personal relationship was his mother, and that had been so short and so long ago that he did not know how to act toward a friendly demeanor such as Chimp's. Corky was awestruck. He was afraid of the big man but drawn to him at the same time.

For the first time in his life someone had come right out and said, "I want to be your friend."

It was a new and confusing sensation that set his whole being into conflict. To gain a friend after all these years of loneliness was beyond his immediate comprehension. The fact that this person was big enough to squash him like a bug with either hand or foot worried him, while at the same time the rest of his senses said, <u>Accept him. He's real</u>.

After his initial raucous introduction, Chimp clomped his way to a large boulder a few yards from Corky's castle and sat down. He opened his pack and brought out a third of a loaf of hard brown bread. He tore off a large chunk, put it in his mouth, and followed it with another swallow of wine.

"You got anything to eat, li'l feller?" he asked Corky. "'Cause if you don't, you're plumb out of luck. I got nothin' left excep' this here hunk of bread."

"I got a little," Corky replied cautiously. "Enough for me."

"You still scared of me, ain't you?" Chimp grinned at him. "C'mon and sit down here an' tell me 'bout Chicago. I ain't been here but a couple times, an' then only for a night or two. How long you been here?"

"All my life," Corky answered but volunteered nothing further.

He was still apprehensive about this giant stranger who had moved into his home and now was trying to pry into his personal life.

"You want a hunk o' this here bread?" Chimp asked, still trying to break the ice.

"No, that's okay. I have my own."

"Well, don't be so goddamn standoffish there. Le's have a li'l snack an' bat the breeze a while. I ain't gonna eat ya. How come you been hangin' 'round here all yer life? There's better places than this."

Chimp wiped his mouth with the back of his hand and grinned again.

Corky went to the spot where he had hidden the food he had found that morning and took a tomato from the sack. It had a large brown spot on one side. He took out his knife, trimmed away the brown, and returned to stand in front of Chimp. He took a bite from the tomato but still said nothing.

"What the hell ails you? Corky—that's what you said, right? Ain't gonna be much of a conversation if I'm the only one talkin'. I ast ya how you come to hang aroun' Chicago all yer life?"

"I don't talk to people much," Corky confessed. "Fact is, I don't really know any people."

"What you do, come out here in the bushes an' bury yer ass in a brush pile an' let the world go rollin' by? That right?"

"It's all I got, an' nobody bothers me here, least till now," Corky replied.

"Hey, if I'm buggerin' up yer life here, I kin git on down the road. You can go on playin' groun' hog long's you like. No skin off my nose."

"No, I don't mind," Corky put in quickly. "Only most times when people come talkin' to me, they're tryna take somethin' away from me. Thass why I don't talk to people much."

"Well, I got everything I need, "Chimp replied. "Don't need to worry none 'bout me takin' your stuff. Some guys used to try that shit on me, but no more. I can always git what I need without pickin' on no li'l guy like you. Anyways, how come you stay here for so long if you got no friends or nothin'? Must be a helluva place to be in winter. Don't you ever think about goin' to California or Texas or Florida, where they got sunshine in the winter?"

"I think about it, and I've heard people talk about it, but I never knew if it was true. I know what's here, an' I git by. I got 'nother tomato over there. You want one?" Corky asked, half hoping the offer would be refused.

"Now, thass more like it," Chimp said. "You startin' to sound like a neighbor now, 'stead of a grouchy-ass groun' hog. Sure, I'll take a tomater."

Taken by surprise, Corky went immediately to his sack for another tomato.

"You want me to cut the bad off it?" he asked as he held it out to Chimp.

"No, I got a knife my ownself," Chimp replied. "How come you buyin' rotten tomaters anyways? Whyncha git good ones?"

"I don't buy nothin'. I never got no money to buy nothin'. I used to get jobs sometimes but not much no more. Mostly I scrounge. I git them tomatoes and sometimes grapes an' lettuce an' apples an' stuff like that from the dumper by the grocery stores. I git something nearly every day. I git stuff from restaurant trash cans too, if the dogs and cats don't git it first."

"Hell, I got to work sometimes. Them wine bottles don't git no rotten spots. If they was throwin' them out, they'd never git to the trash can anyways, 'cause guys like me would ketch 'em 'fore they hit the can. I can almost always git a days work if I need it though, an' I don't look for it if I don't need it."

Chimp took another drink, then asked, "How far is it to a grocery or liquor store? This here's the last of my wine, an' I got to have another for tomorrow."

"Can't say how far," Corky replied, "but I know where it is, an' I can run there in fifteen minutes, but I bet you can't. Might take you half an hour."

"Nice afternoon. Wanta take a walk down, an' you can show me where it's at?"

Corky was fascinated by this friendly giant, and he readily agreed. He quickly put his food he had gathered into the box he kept for that purpose within the castle and returned to Chimp. Together they strolled through the September sunlight toward the warehouses in the distance, Chimp talking and Corky listening. Occasionally Corky volunteered some information, direction, or comment but kept most remarks to one sentence.

As the scene changed from warehouses into residential and small businesses, Chimp asked again, "You mean to tell me you been here in Chicago all yer life?"

"All my life," Corky asserted.

"This is a pretty big place," Chimp stated. "How far is it to them big buildings I see over yonder?"

"Don't know," Corky replied. "I never been there."

"Christ, din'tcha ever git curious to see how big they really is, or how far away?"

"Too many people," was the terse reply. "People always been trouble for me."

"I wanna see somethin' or know about somethin', I go look for myself. No shit, I been in every big city in America. Some I jus' passed through, others I stayed much as a month sometimes. You gonna git some real surprises when we head for Californy in a few days."

Corky looked at Chimp in shocked amazement, and his heart did a flip-flop.

"We?" he almost shouted. "What you mean, we?"

"Don't git yerself all in a sweat there." Chimp laughed. "I thought you might like to see somethin' besides Chi-town fore you die all by yerself in a brush pile. Here you live all yer life in Chicago an' ain't even seen Chicago. Time you learn somethin' 'bout the rest of the country."

"But how would we get there?" Corky asked, still excited.

"You mus' be blind well as short an' ugly," Chimp stated. "You lived all your life beside the railroad, an' you don't know how to get somewhere. Don't you never wonder where them trains goes to or comes from? By tomorra mornin' you can be five hundred miles from here. Train that goes outta here every mornin' is called "The Five Hundred," 'cause it goes five hundred miles to Minneapolis in five hundred minutes. Did you know that? You got a dozen rides a day goin' right by your door. All you gotta do is reach out an' grab it. Don't cost you nothin'."

"But what would I do with all my stuff I got back there?" Corky asked, as though he had a houseful of furniture.

"Old friend I had one time told me if I can't carry it, I don't need it, an' he was right as rain," Chimp offered. "What you want to hang aroun' here for when the snow blowin' 'roun' yer ass? If you go where the sun shines, you can flop your ass under any tree, wash yourself in a river or even the ocean, an' pick fresh fruit from the trees and melons from the field. Most times somebody will even pay you to do it, but they's never no need to go hungry."

By this time they had come to the business area commonly known as skid row in the old dilapidated area of most big cities. It contained third-rate restaurants, run-down hotels, burned-out buildings, and empty weed-grown lots.

Corky stopped in front of a large glass-fronted building with steel bars inside the windows and a flashing sign creaking in the breeze out front. The windows were soot streaked and difficult to see through. Two ragged drunks pushed out of the double doors in front of them, arguing over which of them would open the bottle of wine they had just purchased.

Chimp reached out in a remarkably quick grab for so big a man and seized the wine from the drunk's hand. In one quick motion he spun the top off the bottle and stood looking at the two derelicts for a moment with the bottle poised half-way to his lips as though to drink it.

"Goddamn, mister, it took us all day to bum enough for that wine. At least give us a drink," one of them complained, almost in tears.

"Hell, men, I was only helpin' settle the argument."

Chimp laughed as he passed the bottle back to the man. He slapped a big hand on each of their shoulders and went inside, Corky following.

"You sure had them worried," Corky said. "I bet you could have kept it, an' they wouldn't be able to do nothin' about it, huh?"

"Sure, they'd a spent a lotta time bitchin' and moanin', but they wouldn't dare touch me if I was a mind to keep it. I was just funnin' with them though. If I steal anything, it gonna be from the man that still got somethin' left. Those guys got nothin'. I know what it's like to want a drink an' there ain't none. Speakin' of which, where's the wine in this place?"

"Don't know," Corky replied again. "I ain't never been in here before."

"Damn, I can't believe the stuff you don't know. Wait'll I get yer nothin' li'l ass on that westbound. Can't wait to see yer eyes bug out when you see them farms out there, an' the prairies, an' the deer an' antelope over there on them Montana slopes. When we get to Californy, we'll spend a few days right between the carrot fields an' the orange orchards. You can eat till it comes out your ears, an' you won't be cuttin' out no rotten spots neither. So fresh you can smell it half a mile away."

"I ain't said I was goin' nowheres," Corky pointed out, not quite sure whether Chimp actually meant to take him along and half afraid to find out.

"You goin'," Chimp said emphatically, "if I have to pack yer bony li'l ass in my pack an' tote you outta here. You goin', all right! What the hell you got to stay here for?"

By this time they had found the wine, and Chimp picked out two bottles of cheap wine. Now he was looking at the shelves of brandy. He picked a bottle off the shelf and held it up to the light.

"Now this here's the real ham and eggs," he declared. "Sometimes I git a little long on dollars or fed up with this poison," and he indicated his wine bottles, "I buy a bottle of this. This here is sweet enough for grandmas an' little kids. I git this when I got somethin' special to celebrate. You oughta taste it sometime. I bet this won't make you sick."

He patted it lovingly as he replaced it in its niche on the shelf. They paid for the wine and left.

By this time it was almost full dark, and they started back toward Corky's brush pile. Chimp stopped at the *Seven Eleven* along the way and bought another loaf of bread and two cans of sardines.

When they were only a few feet from the castle, Corky suddenly stopped.

"Ain't nobody ever stayed with me before," he declared apprehensively.

"Don't think two of us gonna fit, is that it?" Chimp asked. "Or you still worried about me?"

"Don't know," Corky said again. "It ain't real big."

He fidgeted nervously, suddenly embarrassed.

"Well, don't worry yourself," Chimp said, patting him on the shoulder. "I can hole up out here in the bushes. I'm used to it."

He turned and started to walk away.

"No, wait!" Corky stopped him. "I think it's big enough for two of us. It's just I ain't had nobody even want to talk to me before, let alone live with me. I jus' wish it was a better place, like a house or somethin'."

Chimp laughed his hearty bellow again. "You problem is yer near civilized from stayin' one place too long. Give you a li'l money an' somebody to come home to an' bullshit with, an' you'd wanta start improvin' the place. Like my ol' friend Wash used to say, if you can't carry it, ya don't need it. Hell, a few more days we gonna be on the road to Californy anyways."

When they were settled down in Corky's primitive hideout, Chimp opened another bottle of wine and some sardines and began munching on what was left of his old dry bread.

"Late as the season is gittin', I better find a few days work before we bag outta here," Chimp said between bites. "I ain't got but a few bucks left. Here, you want one o' these sardines?"

He passed Corky a sardine on a chunk of bread.

"Jeez, that tastes good," Corky explained. "I ain't had nothin' fresh outta a can for months. I got a hell of a time to git money to buy stuff. Nobody wants to hire a little shit like me."

"It ain't little that's got you. It's ugly that's your problem. What happened to yer eye anyways? I think civilized folks'd get nervous jus' tryin' to figure which way yer lookin'."

"What the hell you got to talk about?" Corky said indignantly. "You're big enough to scare a locomotive right off the track, an' I don't see nothin' so pretty about you neither."

Chimp laughed heartily at Corky's show of spirit, and for the first time in many years, Corky found himself laughing as well.

"I got a hunk of cheese I found. It's got some mold onto it, but it's good if you shave it down a li'l bit. Ya want some?" Corky offered.

"Why not?" Chimp said. "Anyways, you never said yet about yer eye. What happened to ya?"

"I think it's always been like that," Corky replied, red-faced. "It don't bother me none, so I don't think about it."

"No, I guess not," Chimp said. "I s'pose it's like me bein' so big. I ain't never been able to bum anything like some guys I met. Nobody thinks I need help with anything, jus' 'cause I'm so big, but everybody wants me to work for 'em, jus' to see what I can do. I had a friend one time could talk a old woman out of her Sunday hat. He could make more money in a hour bummin' in the street than I can make in a week of workin'. That was up in New York. I think he was like you, been there all his life. Couldn't blow him outta there with dynamite. Hell, people comes chasin' me down the streets sometimes tryin' to git me to work for 'em, but the same guys won't spit out a nickel if I bummed 'em for it. You ever wonder how come we're different from other guys? How come one guy lives in a house an' has a wife an' kids, an' us here hidin' in a brush pile today an' ridin' a boxcar to hell an' gone tomorra?"

"I don't know," Corky replied. "I look at pitchers in magazines an' catalogs I find sometimes, an' I pertend the places I see in there are mine, but then I git to thinkin', I don't even know what some of them things I see in there are for, so I'm prob'ly better off here. Least there ain't nobody makin' me do what I don't wanta do."

"I thought about it a lot, friend," Chimp said. "It's funny, but I always come aroun' to jus' what you said. Always somebody wants you to do what you don't want doin'. I walked away from many a good job, an' some good friends too, 'cause they gits to pullin' me this way an' that to where I got to do things their way or git the hell down the road, so I seen a lotta road in my life. Be times I find a nice warm place, a easy job, an' a good friend, I find myself thinkin' I should stay. Then suddenlike I git the itch to feel the train wheels bumpin' under me, an' come midnight I'm a hunnerd miles away in a cold boxcar kickin' my ass for not stayin'."

Corky listened and commented little. It was pleasant listening to the big man's voice droning on about places he had been and people he had left behind. One word that he heard often in Chimp's stories stuck in his brain. A warm drowsiness came over him and somehow each time the word was used, it caused a sensation of happiness to buzz through his skinny body. The rest of the words became a   meaningless   frame   supporting   that   single   oft-repeated   word—friend...friend...friend—until he was fast asleep.

CHAPTER 59

▼

The next morning when they awoke, Corky was quick to warn Chimp about not disclosing their hideout.

"Let me go out first an' check around," he said. "Sometimes them railroad workers go by here on their little car, an' I don't want nobody to see us comin' outta here. If they knew we lived here, they'd probly burn it down."

He crept cautiously out, raising his head slowly and peering this way and that to see that there was no one else nearby. He looked much like the ground hog Chimp had accused him of being.

Soon they were both standing outside. It was a sunny day but frosty. The green grass crunched as they walked, and the tops of the willows were starting to drip as the sun peeled the frost from the upper branches. They both relieved themselves in the nearby bushes, then returned to the big rock where Chimp had sat the night before.

"Well," Chimp said suddenly, "we leavin' for Californy today, or we gonna wait for the snow to start blowin' up our ass?"

"Hell, no," Corky replied forcefully. "I can't leave yet."

"Why the hell not? It ain't as if it was gonna take you a week to pack. For what I seen, you could drop a match on this pile an' walk away an' be no better nor worse than right now."

"I just don't know if I wanta go anywheres. This place is the best I've had for a while, an' we could make it better, an' bigger too, if you'd stay an' help me."

"First thing I tole you was I ain't hangin' 'round here. Ain't nothing like sunshine to keep you warm in winter. I ain't liked snow since I was eleven years old an' ran off from Pennsylvania. Once I found sunshine all year down south, I ain't standin' around shiverin' in the snow for nobody."

'Well, okay," Corky replied, "but maybe you could help me fix it up anyways. Then if I don't go, least I'll have a better place."

Scheming ahead, Corky thought if he could get the place more comfortable, he might be able to persuade Chimp from moving on, thus taking the pressure off of him to move from these familiar surroundings. Chimp, on the other hand, was reluctant to help, because he knew Corky would not move if he got too comfortable. Simultaneously, neither wanted to displease the other for fear of jeopardizing their new relationship.

"What the hell you think you can do to make this place better anyway?" Chimp asked suddenly.

"You mean you'd help me?" Corky asked, surprised.

"Depends on what you got up your sleeve."

"A while back I found a whole waterproof tarp offa one of them semi's layin' by the road one mornin'. I drug it away out in the weeds an' covered it over. I slept under it a couple times in summer, an' it's nice an' dry, but it's too far away an' too heavy for me. I can't git it here by myself. I thought if you could get it here for me, we could pull the branches offa here, cover the metal parts with the tarp, an' maybe prop it up a l'il bit with boards an' put the brush back, so it won't leak no more, an' be warmer too."

Even though staying around here longer did not appeal to Chimp, he was curious how it would turn out, and he thought if he managed to please Corky now, he might be more inclined to go along with his wishes later.

"What the hell? It's only September, maybe early October, probably a few weeks o' good weather yet. I can git to the coast in a couple days anyways. Where is this thing you found?"

"No good goin' there now," Corky declared. "We got to do it at night so's nobody sees us. Them railroad guys see us, they'll burn us out for sure. Prob'ly gonna do it anyways sooner or later. I know where they's an ax inside a warehouse down there." He pointed. "I can steal it today. Then if the tent is too big for what we got, we can cut some more of this brush an' cover it over."

"Soun's like you been plannin' this for a while," Chimp observed.

"If I coulda got the tarp here, I woulda had it already done."

"How far away is it?"

"See them warehouses way over there? Well, that's near where I used to live when I was a kid an' still had a house to live in. It's pretty close to them warehouses."

"Christ, that's near a mile off. How heavy is this thing anyways?"

"It's heavy," Corky replied. "I could barely drag it by pullin' one end an' then the other."

"Can't be too tough," Chimp answered, feeling the challenge in Corky's tone. "We'll git her down here if it takes all night."

During the rest of the day they strolled in the sunshine over a large part of Corky's territory, ending up near sundown in the warehouse area where Corky had lived nearly all his life. Corky showed him the boarded-up house where he had been born, now unpainted, rotted out, and near fallen down.

As they walked down warehouse row, one of the workers on the dock called out to Chimp.

"Hey, big fella, you lookin' for work?"

"What you got in mind?" Chimp asked.

"I got two carloads of bales to load out tomorra, an' I need some good strong help."

"What kinda bales we talkin' about?"

"Rags. 'Bout a hundred-twenty a bale."

"You got a hand truck, or do I hafta stiff 'em?"

"I'll truck 'em to the dock, but the cars is low-boy. We'll hafta stiff it from the dock onto the cars, least till we get up to dock level."

"How much?" Chimp asked.

"Give ya fifteen if we finish it all tomorra. Otherwise, ten dollar a day till it's done."

"I'll do it if you find somethin' for my li'l buddy here. He cain't handle the heavy stuff, but he's a good odd-jobber."

'Place ain't been swep' out in a month a Sundays. Think you can sweep out this whole warehouse whilst me an' the big un load?" he asked of Corky.

"Sure I can," Corky replied.

"How much?" Chimp asked.

"I already tole you, ten a day, fifteen if we finish in one day."

"No, no, how much you givin; my buddy?"

"Couple bucks, I s'pose," the other replied.

"Five," Chimp said.

"Looks kindly puny to me. You sure you can hack it?"

"Tell you what, mister. You don't take him, you don't git me," Chimp stated sharply.

"Okay, done," the dockman said, eying the wine bottle sticking from Chimp's coat pocket. "See you in the mornin', seven-thirty, an' no drinkin' on the job!"

CHAPTER 60

▼

Darkness was beginning to settle over Southeast Chicago as Chimp and Corky arrived at the spot where Corky had hidden the tarp. It was heavy canvas material, grommeted on both edges and ends, fifteen feet wide one way and about twenty-five the other. It weighed at least a hundred pounds. Corky had folded it into about a four-foot square and covered it over with grass and leaves.

Chimp seized the edge of it and stood it on edge with one hand.

"Tell ya what," he said. "Let's unfold it, fold it once longways, an' then roll it up. Then I can toss it on my shoulder an' tote it home in no time."

In about forty-five minutes they were back at the brush pile.

"I'm gonna have a bite an' a sip of wine," Chimp said. "Then we'll git this thing rebuilt."

After lunching on odds and ends they had within the shelter, they fell to moving the branches. Within about twenty minutes the truck fender and board floor lay exposed. Chimp selected three short pieces of two-by-four and, using the ax that Corky had swiped from the warehouse, sharpened one end of each piece. Slanting them outward away from the fender, he drove them into the ground at the three corners of the floor not covered by the fender. Each stuck up about thirty inches to three feet high.

Then, working together, they spread the tarp over the corner posts, the fender, and the sheet metal lean-to, then staked it down with small forked sticks through the grommet holes. When they were finished, they had a slope-roof tent about ten feet square. It nearly filled the depression in which it sat.

Working quickly then, they covered it back up with the branches, hiding it as best they could. The branches did not fully cover this larger area as they had the previous one.

"Soon as it gits light," Chimp said, "we'll have to cut some more brush an' cover it better, else them gandy dancers gonna notice. It looks lots bigger than before. Just hope nobody notices before we git it all covered up like we want it. They may notice anyway, with fresh green stuff on top, but if they don't notice in the firs' couple days, no sweat, they probly ain't gonna notice at all."

Feeling quite satisfied with their efforts, they crawled in and settled down for the night.

The next morning Chimp was awake at daybreak. Corky still slept soundly on his pallet under the fender, so Chimp crept cautiously from the shelter and began gathering sticks and branches from the bushes 'round about to cover the exposed canvas. Soon he had a sizable pile next to the shelter and began arranging them over the top as nearly as he could to the way it was before.

Soon Corky wakened and joined him. Before long, after cutting a few more willows and gathering more dead branches, they had the shelter concealed as completely as before.

"If I'm gonna work all day, I gotta have more than a few scraps for breakfus'," Chimp told Corky as they finished laying the branches. "Where is the closest eatin' place?"

"We can either go to the diner where I used to work, or we can go to Seven Eleven and get more bread an' wieners an' stuff if you got money," Corky replied.

"The diner it is, Corky," Chimp said. "I gotta have some hot coffee with mine, an' I can't git that at no Seven Eleven. Today it's gonna be the real ham an' eggs."

Corky's astonishment must have shown on his face as he watched Chimp put away six eggs with hash browns, two large slices of ham, six slices of toast, and several cups of coffee.

"Couldn't eat that much on your hungriest day, I'll bet," Chimp said, laughing, when he looked up and caught Corky watching him.

"I wouldn't believe anybody could eat that much in one meal. Hell, that's enough for me for a whole week," Corky replied. "I got plenty with two eggs an' toast. Not much use us workin' if we gonna spend it all on one meal."

"It won't cost that much," Chimp ventured. "They never know what to charge for one meal like that, so they cut it down pretty much. If I got it on three plates, we couldn't afford it, but on one it won't be that much."

Ten minutes later it turned out Chimp was correct. When he got the bill, Corky's was a dollar twenty-five, and his own was three dollars.

They were a little late when they got to the warehouse, but the dock manager was so pleased to see them that he did not even mention it.

"Sure hoped you'd show," he said to Chimp. "Think we gonna git this load out today?"

"If you can haul it out here in one day, I'll git her loaded." Chimp assured him. "Got a pair of gloves I can use?"

"I got several pairs in there, some not in much good shape. Doubt if they'll fit them mitts of yours, but yer welcome to try 'em."

After trying several pairs, Chimp found one pair that, although ragged, he could pull on with some difficulty.

By the time he found the gloves, the dockman had already brought out several bales of rags on the fork lift. Though they were big and bulky, they were no problem for Chimp. Standing down on the low-boy, he could still reach the top of the bales. He was so strong, he could flip the bale from the dock to his shoulder, turn, and in three quick steps flip it down again on the outer edge of the car.

Meanwhile, Corky had started his sweeping task and was making good progress. The dockman was amazed that Chimp could move three bales into position on the flatcar before he could run the fork lift into the warehouse and return with three more. By noon they had loaded one car, banded the load securely to the car, and started on the second one.

When the dockman took a break for lunch, Chimp tried again to persuade Corky to go to California within the week.

"Didja see the lading ticket on them cars?" Chimp asked him.

"What's that?" Corky asked.

"The lading ticket, thass what says where the load's goin' to. This stuff's goin' to Minneapolis. I could leave a hollow spot in the middle o' this second car, an' we'd have a nice warm place to ride, an' nobody'd even know we was there. I can find out what time she's due to be picked up. We could be here half hour before an' pile on. Tomorra night we're halfways to sunny Californy."

"But we jus fixed up the place this mornin'," Corky objected. "We can't leave yet."

"Easier to read you than a carnival billboard, Corky. You jus' lookin' an' lookin' for somethin' to keep us from goin', ain'tcha?"

"No, I just ain't made my mind up yet. I'd like to go, but I ain't never been nowhere but here. Least here I know where I can git somethin' to eat, an' I got more places to stay if I hafta too. Besides, I got my stuff, an' I don't got a pack to carry it like you got. Don't know if I'd wanta carry it around all the time like you do neither."

"You know you're gittin' windy as hell, Corky." Chimp grinned. "That's the longest speech you made since we met. But it all says the same thing. You tryna find ways not to go instead of thinkin' on the good things thass gonna happen if ya do go. C'mon, git offa yore ass, an' let's ride this baby outta here tomorra."

"No," Corky said emphatically. "It's still warm enough here, an' I ain't ready yet."

"Okay," Chimp replied, "but don't say I din't tell you when that snow starts blowin' down yer neck in a couple weeks."

The fork lift came out of the warehouse with more bales, and their conversation ended abruptly. By three o'clock it was apparent to the dockman that they were going to make the one-day agreement.

"Take a break for a few, man," he called out to Chimp. "I gotta call the shipper on this load an' let 'im know we're gonna be able to tie 'er down this afternoon."

"When's it goin' down the line, mister?" Chimp asked.

"Oh, probly tomorra now. I doubt if we can git a engine in here to switch it out today anymore," the man replied. "The front office ain't gonna want doin' the paperwork this late."

Chimp smiled to himself and thought about working on Corky all night if necessary to catch this comfortable ride out. He was sure that by this time tomorrow they would be on their way to the sunshine and warm waters of California.

Just when Chimp was positioning the last few bales, a short fat man in a gray business suit drove up. He got out of his car and watched as Chimp and the dockman finished off the load and strapped it down. When they were done, he held a brief conversation with the dockman and then approached Chimp and Corky where they stood waiting for their money.

"Name's Abe Goldstein," he said as he stuck out his hand, first to Chimp, then to Corky. "Hell of a day's work youse guys put in here loadin' my stuff."

"Don't mind workin', long's I git paid an' don't hafta stay too long in one place," Chimp replied.

"On the road, eh?" the man asked.

"Jus long enough to git from here to there." Chimp laughed.

"Got a deal fer ya, if you'll stay long enough to finish it," Mister Goldstein offered. "I watched you tossin' them last few bales there, and I got some more stuff I need moved. Take yuz maybe two weeks or so if today is any sample."

"What kinda work we talkin'?" Chimp asked.

"It'll take two of yuz," he said. "None of it ain't real heavy, but some of it's too big for one guy to handle alone."

He took out a notebook and scribbled an address on it. "This here's an old hotel, the Great Northern. It's about ten blocks from here. I'll met yuz there inna mornin' around nine-thirty, ten o'clock, an' I'll explain then. You can look 'er over, an' if ya decide to do it, I'll pay ya whatever he paid you today till the job's done. Okay?"

"He give us twenny bucks for today," Chimp said in a questioning tone.

He doubted that Mister Goldstein would pay that much when he knew he could get other men to do it for half the price.

"I need this junk moved in a hurry," Goldstein said. "I don't mind puttin' out a buck if I get my money's worth. You do that job well as you done this here, an' I might throw in a li'l bonus."

"Let's do it, Chimp," Corky put in. "You said you needed a few bucks before we go, an' now we don't even need to look. If it takes a week, we'll have enough."

"Okay, Goldstein, I ain't sayin' for sure we'll do 'er," Chimp agreed, "but we'll meet you in the mornin' an' look 'er over."

CHAPTER 61

▼

The dockman had paid them a few minutes after Mister Goldstein left. They walked to the liquor store, and Chimp got two more bottles of wine and drank half of one bottle in front of the store. From there they visited the Seven Eleven and picked up some odds and ends of food.

Corky objected to Chimp's free spending on some snack things.

"I can git food most times without spendin' good money on it. Why don't we save our money? You can go back an' rest, an' I'll scrounge around till I git enough for two of us."

"No good havin' money if you don't spend it," Chimp said, remembering Wash's lectures. "'Sides, I'm not real sure I like where you git some o' that stuff you eat. Anyways, you git too much saved up, an' somebody'll be tryin' to git it away from ya anyways."

"I wanta check a couple places 'fore I go home," Corky said. "Nobody much but me picks up the fruit an' veg'tables from the dumper at the market, an' they ain't nothing wrong with that stuff 'cept a spot or two. If you're so fussy, you don't need to eat it. I seen somethin' at the Goodwill I wanta check on too. I wanta see is it still there."

Together they walked to the grocery store, where they found some spotted but edible apples and tomatoes. Then they went to Goodwill. In the back of the store, hanging from a rusty nail on the wall, was a kerosene lantern. It was rusty and old, and the price tag said two dollars.

"I been wantin' that ever since I built my place out there," Corky declared. "This is the first time I felt I could spare the money to get it."

"You git that, an' you're gonna hafta spend more money for kerosene to put in it. "Sides, ain't no way you put somethin' like that in a travel pack. Leak a li'l bit, an' everything ya got is screwed up. Ain't nothin' I'd wanta travel with."

"Well, we ain't travelin' yet, are we?" Corky shot back. "You bought what you wanted. I'll spend mine how I want too."

Corky bought the lantern, and they stopped at a station and filled it on the way back to the castle. While they sat chatting inside the tent that evening, the lantern spread its cheerful light in their makeshift room. When they had been there about an hour, it became quite warm as well.

"See, Corky bragged, "now we got a comfortable place, nice an' warm, an' we don't hafta feel our way around in the dark in here no more. We got it jus' as good as people livin' in them big houses, an' it's all for free, 'cept the kerosene."

"I bet if we stayed here all winter, you'd find it ain't all that good," Chimp pointed out. "Much heat as that things puts out, you git much snow, an' this hole we sittin' in soon be full o' water from snow meltin' off the top of this brush pile. Don't know about you, but I ain't much on sleepin' in mud puddles."

"Prob'ly we wouldn't burn it that much to melt snow. Blankets keep me warm enough sleepin'. Nice to have it jus' to get the chill off an' have a li'l light sometimes."

As before, the conversation was back and forth—one trying to convince the other to leave and the other doing his best to defend staying. Neither was quite willing to bring up the third possibility, that of going their separate ways. Though critical of each other, some strong bond of comradeship held them together. Finally they both fell asleep, the issue unresolved.

The next morning they were up early. The routine at the diner was the same. Chimp ordered a breakfast that two ordinary men would have had difficulty finishing. Corky had the same order of eggs and toast he had enjoyed the day before.

"I think this is the first time I ate a hot breakfast two days in a row since I last seen Rosa," Corky declared.

"Yeah," Chimp joked, "keep on feedin' you reg'lar an' buyin' stuff for that castle, an' you'll be wantin' a two-piece suit like that Goldstein feller. Won't that be the real ham and eggs? Corky in a suit. No way I'd ever git ya outta Chi-town then. You'd be wantin' to move uptown. You gonna be too good to hitch a freight away from here."

When they finished eating and Chimp had leisurely enjoyed a fourth cup of coffee, they paid the bill and asked the cook how to get to the address Goldstein had given them. About a thirty-minute walk found them standing in front of the building where they were supposed to meet. They were at least thirty minutes early. Together they began to examine the place.

It was a red brick building with weathered double-oak doors in front. Glass crosshatched windows, so dirty it was difficult to see through, decorated the upper half of the doors. Chiseled letters in the brick above the door read, <u>Great Northern Hotel, October 1902.</u> To the right of the doors was a plate-glass window that, like the door, was soot-stained and dirty, making it difficult to see in. Chimp rubbed a spot with the sleeve of his coat and peered in.

"Christ!" he exclaimed. "This guy mus' be in the salvage business. This whole floor is fulla junk. They's stoves an' sinks an' cabinets an' Christ knows what all in there stacked clear to the ceilin'. I bet he wants us to load that shit outta here."

A narrow alley separated this building from the next one. Dead weeds, bottles, cans, cardboard boxes, newspapers, and trash of all kinds littered the alley, which was only wide enough to walk through. They walked through to the wider alley that ran behind the hotel. Two iron fire-escape ladders ran up the back of the four-story building, with a platform at each story. Single doors with no outside knobs led into each floor from these platforms. Several windows in the back were broke out, and glass littered the alley.

Across the alley from the hotel, another old building had burned down. Parts of the foundation still stood, and two old car bodies had been dumped into the cavity where the basement used to be.

As Chimp and Corky looked, they heard voices. Looking around the abutments remaining of the burned building, they saw two men, both very drunk, arguing over whose turn it was to go for more wine. Both were dirty and ragged. As they watched, one of them walked to the nearest car body, flopped down in the rotted back seat, and rolled laboriously onto his back.

"Screw you, Joe," the other man said. "If I got to go again this time, I ain't comin' back."

"You'll be back," the other mumbled. "You been pissin' like a wounded skunk every time it's your turn for ten years, but you allus comes back. Now git yer ass down the road. I'll be right here waitin'—an' don't you open her till ya gits here neither."

Corky and Chimp looked at each other for a moment, and Chimp said, "Bet I know what you're thinkin', Corky."

"What then?" Corky asked.

"Same thing as me," Chimp replied. "We ain't got it bad at all compared to some guys. Right?"

"I been runnin' on nothin' lots of times," Corky said thoughtfully, "but they ain't never gonna find me dead in a alley like those guys gonna be one o' these days."

"Only difference 'tween them an' us," Chimp stated, "is they quit thinkin' a few years back. The booze does all their thinkin' for 'em. I drink 'cause I like it. They drink 'cause they gotta have it. When drink starts to be the why for everything I do—an' it could happen, I s'pose—I think I'd rather be dead."

"Well, that guy is prob'ly waitin' for us out front," Corky said, changing the subject. "All I know is, I ain't gonna be found in no alley with rats an' empty wine bottles. This place give me a chill."

He turned and walked up the alley, Chimp following. Abe Goldstein drove up just as they returned to the street.

"Hey, glad to see youse guys," he called as he stepped form the car. "I hope yer ready to work, 'cause there's plenty here for a while. I tried to get guys to do this before, but they always take a look an' back out, or either they work half a day an' walk out on me."

He unlocked the door as he talked. "I got this place an' the lot behind, an' she's comin' down to put up a new building, but first I got to git all this crap out so the contractors can salvage the doors and windows, hardwood, toilets, marble, electrical, and stuff. There's forty-five rooms in this place. Some is nearly empty, some ain't. Other guys that started the job just moved stuff from upstairs to here, then got drunk or tired an' quit. Then I been stackin' stuff in here for years too, thinking; I might sell it or use it sometime. Like I told youse earlier, I'll pay you twenty a day till she's done. I got a trucker gonna park his rig in the alley back there. He ain't gonna do no loadin'. That's on youse guys. Everytime you git the truck full, you holler for him, an' he'll haul 'er away and bring the truck back.

"I want everything that'll move outta here fast as you can git the son-of-a-bitch clear. Fast as you can handle it. You see anything in there you want, it's yours. Keep it, sell it, give it away. All's I want is to git it empty. If ya wanta fix one room up an' stay here till ya git her done, hey, knock yerself out. No need to carry no more of this shit down them stairs neither. The fire escape doors all open from inside. Just pack it to the fire escapes and dump her over. Mind you don't hit this guy's cab. I don't want no damage bills to pay, but everything that moves, including the carpets, goes out. We all clear on what I want?"

Chimp and Corky agreed that all was understood, and then Mister Goldstein took them on a quick tour of the building. Several rooms on the upper two floors had already been emptied except for a few odds and ends. The rest on the second floor and first floor, including an office and small lobby, were still much as they had been when the hotel was operating.

Vandals and derelicts had used and misused the place for several years. Broken windows and leaky roofs and pipes had contributed to its decay. Chairs and mirrors were the main items that might be considered still useable of the furnishings that remained.

"So what you think?" Goldstein asked. "You gonna do it?"

Corky and Chimp looked questioningly at each other, and Corky nodded at Chimp.

"Okay, you got a deal," Chimp told him.

"Plan out how you wanta do it," Goldstein told them in final instruction. "Everything that move gotta go. I got a pawn shop down the street right on the corner of the next block. Yuz got any problems or questions, lemme know."

Just as the conversation ended, the truck driver came up the steps. Mister Goldstein told him where to park the truck. Chimp and the two of them made arrangements for contact to remove the junk as it was loaded.

When the truck was positioned and Mister Goldstein and the driver had left, Chimp said, "I bet we can make a few extra bucks with some o' them chairs an' mirrors. Go pick out a couple good ones an' bring 'em down while I make a sign, an' then we'll start haulin' this crap out."

Chimp took a piece of plywood that was lying on the floor and, using a grease pencil he found, scribbled a <u>FOR SALE</u> sign boasting, <u>Meers—$2.00</u> and <u>Chairs—$4.00</u>. He placed the sign against the wall on the sidewalk with a mirror on one side and a chair on the other.

"Any luck at all, we'll pick up a buck or two to git by till ol' Goldstein pays off," Chimp told Corky.

"Looks to me like most of the work gonna be right here on the bottom floor," Corky observed. "I ain't gonna be able to keep up with you noways, so why don't I git as much of the small stuff as I can out of here, and you start with the bigger stuff? You don't touch nothin' you think I can handle, okay?"

"Sure," Chimp replied, "but what you think about what he said about stayin' here in this rat trap, Corky? We'll be right here, so's it will save time. I seen a couple mattresses up there look pretty good. Ain't they a mission or somethin' like that close by? Maybe we can eat there for nothin' sometimes if we donate some of this stuff. That way we won't have to go back and forth so much."

"I know where the mission's at, an' it ain't far, but I ain't never ate there. Too many people, an' they always stare at me. I don't like eatin' with no crowd of guys around."

"We'll ask the driver when he comes back. Maybe he knows a good eatin' place handy to here. Truckers always knows the good ones, but I don't see no difference between eatin' places an' the mission. They's still gonna be people around."

"Don't wanta eat in no mission. They make you sing an' say prayers an' stuff, from what I hear guys talkin'. I'd rather hunt my own. I can git by."

"Hey, you can pick shit with the birds an do just fine, small as you are. Man my size gotta eat," Chimp retorted. "Anyways, we can work that out later. We'll quit early tonight an' check aroun'. Maybe we'll find somethin' suits us both. Might be they's a market aroun'. We could buy somethin' an' bring it back here."

That settled, they returned to planning the work.

"I'd rather work together than one on bottom an' one on top. I like somebody around to bullshit with," Chimp said. "If that trucker does what he's sposed to do, we oughta be able to finish the bottom in two, three days, then jus' work our way up."

Though it was a big truck, it took them only a little over an hour to load the first load, and they found the driver sitting in the sunshine on the sidewalk when they finished. He immediately left with the load, and it was nearly an hour before he returned.

By the time they had loaded the next load, Chimp began to complain of hunger.

"It ain't hunger that's gonna git me," Corky stated loudly. "My ass is draggin' already, an' we only jus' started. Look at me. I'm wet as if we was workin' in a thunderstorm."

Chimp had hardly strained himself at all thus far. Still, he had done at least three-quarters of the work.

"Don't try keepin' up with me, Corky. I ain't never met a man yet could do that," Chimp answered. "You git tired, take a break. No need you bustin' yer ass. We gonna git paid twenny a day for a couple weeks anyway, so take it easy, okay?"

They loaded out four loads that first day. When the trucker said that he would not be coming back until the next morning, Corky sank gratefully into a broken-down overstuffed chair and closed his eyes.

Chimp watched the truck disappear up the alley and then turned to where Corky sat in a half stupor.

"Le's go get a couple bottles of wine an' sumpin' to eat, man. I'm starved!" Chimp bellowed, apparently fresh as when they had started that morning.

"You go ahead," Corky said. "I'm soakin; wet, an' I feel like somebody beat me up. I ain't used to workin'. Maybe I'll go find somethin' to eat later."

"C'mon, Corky, you ain't gonna goddamn chicken out on me, are ya? I could eat the south end of a northbound skunk, an' I know they's at least half a gallon of wine got my name on it. Let's go. You'll feel better if ya got a coupla drinks in ya."

"You know I don't drink. I tole you before. Jus' lemme have a little rest here." Corky stood. "I'll be on one of them mattresses we laid out up there for a while. Maybe I'll get somethin' to eat later."

"Okay, have it your way," Chimp said, "but don't look for me to crap out at five o'clock ever' night till we finish this. I got things to do. I'll see you later. I'm gonna lock this front door. If you want out before I git back, yer gonna hafta use the fire ladder."

"See ya, later," Corky mumbled and went shakily up the stairs.

CHAPTER 62

▼

Chimp returned to the hotel several hours later. He had eaten an enormous but plain meal of soup, mashed potatoes, baked beans, and pork at the mission. He had found it with little difficulty. He had also surrounded nearly two quarts of wine after dinner while chatting with several men he had eaten with at the mission.

He had taken no notice when darkness came. Humming some ancient tune his father had sung to him many years before, he stumbled up the stairs to the room he and Corky had selected earlier. The night had grown chilly, and the air in the unheated old hotel was damp and drafty.

He heard Corky moaning and mumbling as he came into the room. He struck a match and saw his little friend curled in a tight ball on the naked mattress, shaking and shivering as though in a spasm. He bent and shook him by the shoulder. It took several minutes to rouse Corky sufficiently to get him to talk.

"Whatsa matter, kid?" Chimp asked solicitously. "You was curled up like a newborn calf there. You okay?"

"I think I'm frozen to death," Corky said. "How long I been sleepin'?"

"Four, five hours anyways. Din't even go out for nothin' to eat, huh?" Chimp responded.

"Christ, no, I don't think I can even stand, let alone go huntin' the streets for food. If I go out there in the wind now, I'd damn well die. Christ, it's cold."

He flopped back on the mattress and, tucking his hands between his knees, curled himself in a knot again.

"Hey, ya l'il shit, ya gotta git up outta there an' move aroun', or you gonna be sick. We got work to do tomorra. Don't crap out on me, or I'll hafta finish it by myself, an' it'll be goddamn December 'fore we can bag it for Californy."

However, no amount of coaxing or agitation could persuade Corky to move. Chimp, worried now, went from room to room tearing several sets of dusty rotten drapes from the windows. He returned to the room and covered Corky with several layers of these. Corky sneezed and coughed at the dust but remained half asleep and cuddled himself gratefully in this warm cover.

Chimp was still concerned, because Corky had not eaten since morning. They had both gotten drinks of water at a service station across the street during the day, but Chimp knew men should eat more than two eggs and toast if they were going to work, so he went back to the street. He found an all-night diner, bought a hamburger and fries and a cup of hot coffee, and returned and made him eat.

By morning Corky's clothing had nearly dried, but he still complained of the cold. An unpleasant chill gripped him, and he was so stiff and sore, he could scarcely move. After much badgering by Chimp, he was finally persuaded to leave the hotel for breakfast.

"Keep on like this, we gonna hafta shake ol' Goldstein' down for some more eatin' money 'fore the first week is out," Chimp commented. "I ain't got but a few bucks left right now. You got any?"

"Jus' change," Corky said as he hunched his shoulders and shivered.

Chimp threw a big arm over his shoulders and gave him a quick squeeze. "Hang on there, fella. We git to pitchin' that junk on the truck again, you'll warm up pretty fast. A good breakfast gonna do you good too."

CHAPTER 63

▼

Each day went about the same and each night found Corky damp, exhausted, hungry, and uncertain of whether to eat or sleep first. Most times he would opt for the sleep, and Chimp would go out to eat and bring something back for Corky.

The problem with this procedure was that Corky was so tired and chilled by the time Chimp returned that he would eat little of the rough food before falling back and covering himself with the makeshift blankets Chimp had provided.

In the mornings he would suggest that they go back to the castle and get his jacket and blankets after work that night, but when nighttime came, he would be too tired to go, so he would delay the trip until tomorrow, "when I feel better."

Each day the amount of work Corky was able to do got less and less, and Chimp soon found himself doing more and more. He did not complain and encouraged Corky to rest as much as he would. In spite of Chimp's objections, Corky continued to try to keep working. He developed a hacking cough that wracked his body and hurt his chest.

Mister Goldstein came by every couple of days to check on their progress and complimented both of them. Whenever he was there, Corky would hustle around and try to pretend nothing was wrong.

When they had been at it for ten days, Chimp asked Goldstein abruptly, "What the hell date is it anyways?"

"It's October fourteenth, an' it looks like youse guys gonna finish in another four, five days if you keep on at this rate. I'm surprised you got that first floor empty already. Good job!"

He shook hands with Chimp to emphasize the compliment.

"Mister Goldstein, you reckon you can pay us a few bucks?" Chimp asked. "We run plumb out."

"Sure, I'll pay you part. How about a hundred bucks? I ain't payin' you up to date an' I'll tell ya why. I done that before, an' the bastards'd take the money an' run, an' I'd hafta find somebody else. Sorry, maybe youse guys ain't like that, but I gotta have this done, so I ain't takin' no more chances."

"No sweat, Mister Goldstein. We jus' need somethin' to eat on."

"Matter with yer buddy there?" Goldstein asked suddenly. "He's lookin' a li'l pekid."

"Ain't used to workin' this hard, an' ain't eatin' right neither. Thass why we was needin' some money," Chimp replied.

"Christ A'mighty, whyntcha holler if yer broke?" Goldstein demanded. "I ain't no goddamn Simon Legree, ya know. I ain't runnin' no goddamn chain gang here. Jus' let me know. Knock off here right now for an hour, an' I'll buy youse guys a meal. Workin' man gotta eat!"

"No, we'll eat after if ya can pay us something"," Chimp objected. "We wanna git this done much as you do. We're leavin' for California soon's we git done."

Goldstein insisted that they take a break and took them to a side-street diner, where he treated them to the best meal either of them had eaten for a long time.

Afterward Chimp remarked to Corky, "I don't know about them other guys, but I couldn't walk out on a job for a man like that. Nice if everybody treated people like he done us today."

"Nobody ain't never done nothin' like that for me neither," Corky replied, "an' even after you told him not to. I'll finish this if it kills me."

"An' then we're pickin' up our shit from the tent an' makin' it for California, right?"

"I was thinkin', if they ain't gonna take this thing down right away, maybe we could talk him into lettin' us stay here till spring. Maybe, if we do the job right," Corky said in a tentative tone.

"Goddamn, I thought we had this all settled!" Chimp yelled angrily. "Ain't nobody I know goin' to California in the springtime. That's the time you wanta be movin' north to git away from the heat. You jus' don't know how goddamn hot it gits there in summer. If you ain't goin' with me, open your yap an' say so, an' I'll quit plannin' for two of us. I'll jus' hey my ass down the road tonight."

Corky was suddenly worried by Chimp's angry tone. He hastened to assure him that he still planned on going. Now that he had found a friend after all these years, he could not stand the thought of being alone again.

"Don't git mad, Chimp," he pleaded. "I was jus' thinkin' of, if the weather got too bad to leave. I'm gonna go. I jus' don't know when yet."

"I'll tell you when," Chimp said. "They ain't no such thing as weather too bad to leave. There's weather too bad to stay, an' when this job's over, I'm leavin' next night. If it's rainin' snot or snowin' baseballs, I'm leavin'!"

"Okay, okay," Corky apologized. "Sorry if I said the wrong thing. I'll go."

Chimp grinned and slapped him on the back. "Okay, let's git this crap outta here. We been screwin' aroun' too long."

Though he felt weak and sick, and his chest felt like someone was sitting on it, Corky followed Chimp up the stairs.

They had finished the second floor, except for the carpets. Chimp made a brief inspection of each room on the second floor.

"Tell you what, Corky. You ain't in no shape to be liftin' a lot of stuff. Why don't you take that end room down there, an' start this way rollin' up them carpets. You git em all rolled, an' I'll come back down an' pitch 'em out."

Corky agreed and began immediately. Chimp went up the stairs to begin removing the remainder of the heavy things from the third floor.

Corky's part, though not heavy work, was slow, tedious, and dirty. Some of the carpets were stuck to the floor in places and required some effort to push or pull them hard enough to get them loose. All were stained, worn, dirty, and most were damp, at least in spots.

A heavy odor of mildew and dust permeated each room as be began moving the ancient fabrics around. He worked on his hands and knees, and the rising dust clogged his nostrils and irritated his lungs. This sent him into heavy, abrasive spasms of coughing. Soon sweat was streaming down his face, and his clothing became damp and uncomfortable.

Corky worked steadily, though slowly, and had started on the fourth carpet without a break. He was finding it more and more difficult to continue. His throat felt hot and dry, and a weak, sick feeling invaded his stomach. He had rolled this carpet about three turns, almost in a trance, when he felt something slip under his hand as he crowded the roll forward. He glanced down, suddenly stopped working, and gasped in astonishment.

He looked to his right and left, jumped to his feet, and stepped over the roll onto the open carpet. Seizing the outer edge of it, he hauled it forward with a burst of energy he would not have thought possible a few seconds before. He looked again.

"Holy smokin' balls!" he cried aloud, echoing a favorite expression of Rosa's from long ago.

"Chimp!" he shouted, "Jesus Christ, Chimp!"

He turned and ran from the room and up the stairs, calling loudly for his friend with every step.

"I'm right here, ya li'l fart. What's all the hollerin' fer?" Chimp stopped him at the head of the stairs.

"Christ A'mighty, Chimp, come an' see," Corky sqeaked as he turned and ran down again.

As Chimp entered the room, Corky stood there pointing in unbelieving amazement. On the bottom of the carpet, stuck there from years of dirt and moisture, was row on row of dirty brown and yellow money. All were small-denomination bills, mostly ones and fives, but an occasional ten and twenty sprinkled the neat array of money.

Chimp stood staring in silence, mentally trying to estimate the amount of this fortune they had suddenly fallen heir to.

"That shit ain't fake, is it?" he questioned at last, beginning to doubt his senses.

Corky picked up the bill that had originally slid under his hand and examined it.

"It ain't the right color," he said, "but it sure looks real to me."

He handed it to Chimp, who looked it over and started to crumple it. A piece broke off and fluttered, leaflike, to the floor.

"If it's real, it been there for a long time to git faded out that way," Chimp said. "I wonder if it's still good. Sufferin' Christ, there must be hundreds of dollars there."

He repeated Corky's move and pulled the carpet back farther. Still more rows of bills appeared.

"Shut the goddamn door, Corky," Chimp said suddenly. "If that old Jew sees all this money, he's gonna go back on what he said about us keepin' this stuff, an' we don't want that trucker nosin' in here neither. What we got here is ham an' eggs, Corky!"

Together they began peeling the bills from the carpet and stacking them in piles by denomination. Some came away from the carpet readily, but others tore or broke in several pieces.

"Sure wish I knew for sure if this stuff's any good when it's all broke up like that," Chimp said worriedly. "Maybe we oughta check it out before we go to all the trouble. No use gittin' our balls all in an' uproar if it ain't no good. Tell you what. Take one o' them tens that's all broke up an' go to the diner an' try to spend it. Git some doughnuts an' coffee or a samwidge or somethin'. If they take it, we'll know it's good. I'll stay here an' watch."

Corky ran full speed to the diner in spite of the pain in his chest, his illness suddenly forgotten. He went to the counter and confronted the large middle-aged woman behind the register.

"'Scuse me, ma'am," Corky gasped. "If this ten's any good, I want some coffee and doughnuts."

After a close examination, she reached under the counter, picked up a roll of Scotch tape and, fitting the pieces together, taped them.

"Looks good to me, my man," she said. "What happened to it anyway?"

"I don't know," Corky said. "I found it. I'd like to get four doughnuts and two cups of coffee then."

"Wherever you found it, it been there a long time," the lady mused. "Might wanta go back an' look again. Might be some more."

"Thanks," Corky said, "I'll do that."

He took his sack and the clean new bills she gave him in change and left hurriedly from the diner.

By the time he got back to the hotel, Chimp had finished peeling the last of the bills from the carpet.

"More than four hundred here, near as I can figger," Chimp told Corky. "They musta took it, or you wouldn't have no sack of stuff, huh?"

"Right," Corky exclaimed. "All's she did was tape it together an' put it in the register.

"Okay," Chimp replied. "This gonna be your job for the rest of the day. Go back an' find a store that sells this kinda tape an' git a couple of rolls. I'll stay here till you git back an' keep an eye out. Then you can tape all them torn ones, an' we'll sack it up an' bring it to the bank an' trade it for good stuff. That way folks won't be wonderin' every time we drop a bill on 'em. Christ, you know what? With the hundred we got already from Goldstein, an' this, we could fergit it all an' hit for Californy tonight."

"I told you I ain't leavin' till the job's done," Corky objected. "This guy done us right. Ain't many people looked out for me in my life, an' I'm gonna do it right."

"Yeah, Corky, I guess you're right. We'll just hide it away an' take it with us. We can live like kings for a couple of months on that much in Californy. Maybe I'll have time to look for my ol' friends Sam and Piney if I don't hafta work all winter."

During the rest of the day Corky pieced together and taped the money, which he put away in a paper bag. He rolled a few more carpets, while Chimp outdid all previous efforts and nearly completed work on the third floor before the driver announced it was his last load for the day and he would not be back until morning.

CHAPTER 64

▼

Over the next few days Corky did not accomplish much. In the last two days he vomited his meals on two occasions and was constantly thirsty.

Chimp tried several times to persuade him to take some of the money and go see a doctor.

"You might have pneumonia or some damn fool thing," Chimp said. "You found the money, an' if you crap out, I'm gonna hafta spend it all by myself. Why not use some of it to git well?"

"I ain't goin' to no hospital. Them kinda people always start tellin' ya what to do an' wanta shut ya up somewheres. I'd be all right if I could jus' git warm," Corky replied.

He worked in spurts and spent the rest of the time asleep on his mattress or whatever soft surface he could find to collapse on when his chest began hurting so that he could not longer work.

For the last two days the weather had turned cold, wet, and windy. Corky could not go out without becoming chilled again. Then he would shiver and shake in his makeshift bed until the chills passed. He lost weight steadily, which he could not afford to do.

Finally Chimp took matters into his own hands. "Look, you li'l peckerhead, if you ain't goin' to the doctor, at least we're gittin' you some warmer clothes."

He physically dragged Corky to a clothing store, over his loud objections, and bought him a waterproof jacket and a pair of wool long johns. Corky hated the feel of the woolen underwear but appreciated the unaccustomed warmth.

"I been wearin' them things winter an' summer for about ten years now," Chimp confided. "Have to take 'em off once in a while to warsh 'em, but I don't never git cold long's I wear 'em. They'll itch ya fer a while, but you fergit that by an' by."

In spite of the new clothing, the constant chills continued, and the pain and congestions in Corky's chest got worse.

The day before they finally finished the job, the temperature dropped to the midthirties, and a cold wet wind began to blow.

"Looks like we gonna beat Ol' Man Winter outta here by about a step an' a holler," Chimp told Corky when they began pulling the carpets from the top floor. "Sometimes tomorra Goldstein gonna pay us off. With what we got, we gonna live it up in the California sunshine like no bo ever done. Once we git there, you can lay in the sun an' let Mother Nature cook that cold outta yer bones. Cheer up. Tomorra night we hit the rails south."

"I ain't never ketched no train before," Corky said anxiously. "I don't even know if I can do it."

"It's easy," Chimp said confidently. "I oughta know. I musta rode five hunnerd trains off an' on. Only fell once."

"You fell?" Corky exclaimed, fear apparent in his voice.

It seemed to him that Chimp could never have failed at anything he tried to do. Chimp's confession, meant to indicate that the chance of error was small, did not encourage Corky as Chimp had intended. It only emphasized the possibility of disaster to Corky.

"Don't worry yer bony li'l ass there," Chimp said, hastening to correct the impression. "I was half snockered an' tried to catch a fast train on a dark night. Dumb-ass thing to do. Knocked me ass over kettle as they say, but I was just scratched up a li'l bit."

"Anyways, I thought you said we was going west, not south," Corky said, still worried.

"Hey, I thought the way you been drag-assin' aroun', we better git to warm country quick as we could. You gotta git to the sunshine or a hospital, ya got yer choice. Much money as we got, we can take the long route. We'll go south first, git yore buns thawed out a lot quicker, since we got plenty eatin' an' drinkin' money."

"Okay, I guess," Corky finally conceded, "but you're gonna hafta show me how. I ain't never even seen anybody hop a train."

"From what I seen, the main yards mus' be at least ten miles from here, so if we ain't gonna ketch 'er on the fly, we'll hafta walk or take a cab to the yard. The goddamn bulls gonna be watchin' the yard too. If they ketch us, we prob'ly spend the night in the Illinois state hotel instead of ballin' outta here. Most o' what I seen down by your place ain't movin' that fast. We'll make it fine, you'll see. Tomorra we should be nearly done. We can grab our loot from ol' Goldstein, go back to the place, pick up our stuff, an' ketch the Southern Pacific between ten and midnight."

"But I don't have nothin' to carry my stuff in," Corky objected, still half hoping he would find a way to back out.

"Horse shit," Chimp exclaimed. "I forgot. You shoulda tole me when we was buyin' that other stuff. Maybe Goodwill got a duffle or a packsack laid by. If they ain't, we'll hustle down an' buy a new one soon's we git paid off."

Corky went to sleep as soon as they quit working, and Chimp went for the street as usual. He went immediately to Goodwill, where he found a small backpack in good condition for seven dollars. Then he went to the liquor store and bought two bottles of brandy instead of his usual wine. Only then did his mind turn to food. After a meal sufficient for two ordinary men, he ordered bread, coffee, and a container of mulligan stew for Corky, then returned to the old hotel.

He woke Corky with some difficulty and spent several minutes persuading him to sit up and eat. Corky was so white and ill-looking that Chimp almost decided to delay their departure and force Corky to see a doctor. Corky drank the coffee and nibbled a few spoonfuls of the stew while Chimp stood by sipping on his bottle of brandy.

When Corky started gagging a few minutes later, Chimp said, "C'mon, git up outta there, an' I'll git a cab an' bring you to a hospital. You gotta see a doc."

Corky rolled over with his back to Chimp and pulled the old drapes tightly around him. Chimp grabbed him roughly and turned him back in spite of his weak struggles.

"You ain't gittin' no better, an' you need some kinda medicine. You can't git it without you seein' a doctor," Chimp insisted.

"Ain't nobody lockin' my ass up," Corky said sullenly. "Teachers, police, and doctors always wanta lock you up an' change you into somethin' else. I'd rather be dead than be locked up an' hafta do what somebody else thinks I should."

"They can't lock you up without you say it's okay," Chimp said. "Couple more days freezin' yer bony ass here, an' you ain't goin' nowheres but six feet under."

"Don't care," Corky croaked. "Ain't no whitecoat gonna lock me up an' stick needles in me."

"Have it yer way," Chimp agreed finally, "but we gotta git outta here tomorra, or I'll hafta carry yer ass to the doc whether or no."

CHAPTER 65

▼

Chimp was up at daylight that final day. Doing his best not to wake Corky, he began moving the last few items of furniture and the carpets on the fourth floor close to the back door. By the time the trucker arrived, everything that remained was stacked in the hallway or on the fire escape.

When the trucker stepped out of the cab, Chimp hollered down to him.

"Hey, Bill. Don't go runnin' out on me. I got the last of 'er settin' right here behind me. Ain't gonna take an hour till this job's done."

"Okay," the driver responded. "I'm only going to eat, and I'll be back in a few."

He waved and went away down the alley.

Chimp seized the rolls of carpet and the remaining furniture items with the vigor of a hurricane and soon had the final pile aboard the truck.

By ten-thirty in the morning on the first of November, 1969, Chimp and Corky had the money for their efforts in hand and were ready to leave. Goldstein had inspected their work and was pleased. When he paid them off, he added a fifty-dollar bonus.

"If you was to stick around, I could use a good man on the strippin' crew. Probably give you regular work at a good wage if you want it."

"Couldn't use my li'l buddy though, I guess?" Chimp questioned.

"Hey, don't git me wrong. Not tryna insult the li'l fella none, but I'm a businessman. I gotta have men that can cut it all day every day. This young feller can't handle the kinda job I gotta have done. Besides, 'pears to me his health ain't none too good. I pay good wages, so I can't take on sick people. Too expensive."

"Well, I was only seein' what you'd say anyways," Chimp replied. "We're together, an' we stay together, come fight, freeze, or footrace. Anyways, when a man starts workin' reg'lar wages, he's stuck in one place fer good. Ain't gonna happen to me. Thanks all the same."

They shook hands with Mister Goldstein and left. During the three weeks they had worked, they had sold several chairs and mirrors. This, together with their wages and the money they found, gave them more than six hundred dollars in cash. Chimp kept it tucked away in his overcoat pocket.

When they were back on the street, Corky grabbed Chimp by the arm and looked up at him like a small boy begging his father for a candy bar.

"Hey, Chimp, how much do you s'pose a new pair of boots costs?"

"For you, li'l buddy, I don't care a rat's ass how much they cost. If you want 'em, you gonna git 'em."

"God, Chimp," Corky rasped, "I ain't had new boots in my whole life. I always thought if I ever got the money, I'd git new boots."

"We got the money now, kid. Let's go to a shoe shore an' git you some." Chimp grinned. "Anything else you been wantin' all yer life?"

"Yeah," Corky replied, and for the first time in many days he also smiled.

"If it ain't too big to pick up an' carry," Corky replied, "but I already got it."

"Jesus Chris', what we into now? What you talkin' 'bout anyways?"

"I'm talkin' about you, Chimp. If I died right now, I could feel good about it. You're the only friend I ever had in my life, and I can't figger how come I got so lucky all at once. Only two things I ever really wanted, a good friend and new boots, an' it all come true at once."

Chimp wrapped a huge arm around Corky and raised him momentarily from the sidewalk in a one-armed hug. "You the greatest, li'l buddy. Even if you are ugly enough to puke a buzzard. I love ya. I tole you the first time I seen ya we was gonna be great buddies. Listen, ya wanta split up the money now, so's you can spend yer part any way you want?"

"Nope, Chimp." Corky smiled again. "I know you'll treat me fair, an' it's a lot safer for you to have it than me. Jus buy me some boots, okay?"

An hour later Corky was the proud owner of brand-new genuine leather boots. His ragged and torn old tennis shoes, he dropped in a streetside trash can as soon as they left the store.

They went to the diner, where Chimp stuffed himself on a sirloin dinner with several side dishes, and Corky ate a bowl of hot soup and a glass of milk, which was all he felt like eating. Afterward, they went to a small grocery, where Chimp bought several junk food items they could carry in their pockets and eat on the train. Their final stop was at the liquor store for another bottle of the best brandy they had.

"Tonight we gonna have a li'l celebration 'fore we wave good-bye to Chi-town, Corky," Chimp said as he paid for the bottle.

Arm in arm they walked from the hustling industrial area to the outskirts of South Chicago and the brush pile that Corky had so proudly called home for several months. They had to stop a few times for Corky to rest. His breath came in ragged sobs after they walked for only a few minutes, and his chest felt like someone had thrust a hot knife into his lungs from both sides.

Chimp made one more attempt to persuade him to see a doctor and get some medicine before they left.

"Hell, no, Chimp, I got me a friend, an' I got my mind made up to leave. If I went to a doctor, I know he'd lock me up for a while. Then we'd have no money again, an' I'd have to make up my mind all over again about leavin'. If I still need a doctor, we'll go when we git somewhere that's warm."

As they walked and talked about the great times they would have in the California sunshine, the skies turned grayer. A cold northwest wind began whipping dust, papers, and trash along the street around and ahead of them.

"Yep," Chimp remarked, "we gittin' outta here jus' one jump ahead of Ol' Man Winter, Corky. Chris', I hope it don't snow till we git well down the road."

CHAPTER 66

▼

Finally they arrived at the brush pile. It was midafternoon, and nothing had been disturbed since they had left it several weeks before.

Just before ducking down to enter, Chimp took an anxious look around at the weather and the area.

"Kind of wish I'd made better note of damn daytime train schedules," he observed. "If I know the next one comin' down was southbound, we'd be on 'er 'stead of waitin' till night. I know the ten-thirty-five tonight is Santa Fe, but it look like the weather gonna be really shitty. We'll hafta huddle up to keep warm for sure. Can't be sure of gittin' inside a car on a movin' train. Gonna be a cold ride, l'il buddy, you can bet yer ass on that. If we miss tonight, we'll walk to the yard early mornin' an see can we duck the bulls to git on a boxcar or a stock car. Lot warmer than draggin' the wind on the outside."

As soon as they were inside, Chimp lit the lantern.

"Might's well be warm as we kin long as we're here," he said. "Why don't you pile whatever you gonna be totin' there by your pad, an' I'll pack 'er away for ya. Jus' hang onto what yer gonna wear. We'll wrap our blankets in yer slicker till we git aboard. Then we can break 'em out an' use 'em Indian-fashion. Don't want you wearin' no raincoat if I gotta pick you up on the fly. Too slick to grab onto, particular if it's rainin'. If we hear a rattler goin' by before dark, I'll show you how easy it is. Meantime, you better try an' get some sleep. I'll pack everything, yours an' mine."

Chimp finished the last few swallows of the open brandy he had been drinking on earlier, then opened the expensive one he had purchased that day.

"Ya oughta try a nip of this. It'll warm ya up an' help ya sleep too," he told Corky.

Again Corky refused, so Chimp had another long drink himself.

"It's gonna be cold, Corky. This stuff here helps warm yer innards. Even if you don't like it, ya oughta try it before we git aboard."

By this time Corky was half asleep, so Chimp did not bother him any further. At about five-thirty he heard a distant whistle warning the crossing traffic of a train approaching. Quickly he roused Corky.

"C'mon, buddy, I'll show you now in the light how we git on this thing. You don't hafta do nothin' but watch."

A few minutes later they were standing along the track, watching the train pick up speed as it pulled out of the city.

"She'll be doing twenty miles or so when she gits here," Chimp said. "You go up the track there about fifty feet an' watch careful. It's real easy. I've done it a thousand times."

Corky did as instructed. Chimp stood on the grade about three feet clear of the track and waited. When the engine and several cars had passed, Chimp picked an approaching car and turned his left side toward the moving train. When the ladder of the target car was about fifteen feet from him, he lunged forward and took about ten running steps. As the ladder came even with his shoulder, he reached out and up with his left hand and grabbed a rung of the ladder well above his head.

The speed of the train raised him off his feet, and he kicked downward and swung himself forward as his feet left the ground. With the smoothness of long practice, his left foot found the bottom rung of the ladder as his body swung inward toward the car. Simultaneously he grabbed another rung halfway between his feet and his left hand with his right hand and within five seconds was securely balanced on the ladder.

As he breezed past, Corky he shouted, "Keep watchin' while I git off!"

He rode a few feet farther, then shifted his hands downward till he was half-crouched at the bottom of the ladder. When he was over a fairly smooth level area, his feet turned sideways on the bottom step, and he suddenly let them slide off, swinging his right arm outward for balance. As his big boot struck the soft gravel, he pushed away from the car with his left hand and was running alongside, kicking up gravel and leaves as he fought to stop and keep his balance at the same time. When he came to a stop, he turned and walked back to Corky.

"She's movin' a li'l bit fast for what I like, but ya see how easy it is. Tonight we'll walk down that way half a mile. That way she'll be movin' slower. Not hard at all, see."

Corky agreed that it looked east, but he still had strong misgivings about his own ability to follow Chimp's lead in this adventure.

"Only thing, I ain't near as strong as you, Chimp, an' I'm kinda shaky too. Sure hope I don't miss, 'cause then you'll be gone, an' I'll still be here with nothin'."

He sounded worried.

"Don't worry yer old red head, feller," Chimp reassured him. "I ain't runnin' out on you. If you miss yore grab, I'll drop off, an' we'll try again. Better yet, we'll start about fifty yards apart. I'll be first on. Then I'll stick my leg behind the ladder an' hang out to the side. You grab the same ladder as I go by, jus' like I showed ya. I'll grab you same time an'help you git aholt. Once we're both on, I'll show you how we can move around an' find a place to ride that's out of the wind. It'll be easy, you'll see."

As they watched the train roll out of sight, a fine mist of rain began blowing in on the cold north wind. Both of their hair and faces were wet when they crawled back inside the warmth of Corky's castle.

"Looks like we picked a bad night, kid," Chimp said when they were again settled inside. "One thing, them freights move right out once they git outta the city. Mostly they don't slow down except for big towns either. By mornin' we'll be a couple hunnerd miles south of here. You'll see how quick it warms up. Man, am I lookin' forward to some sunshine. I'm gonna grab some sardines an' bread here, an' another taste of this brandy, then maybe I'll ketch a li'l shuteye too."

Corky ate a few bites of the odds and ends Chimp handed him, but the chills would not leave him, no matter how he bundled himself in his blankets. They left the lantern on for additional warmth. His stomach was upset, and he was worried about this new adventure that was rapidly approaching.

All his life he had taken the path of least resistance and lived by following the same routine over and over in his small world. The thought of everything being new and different scared him as much as the thought of trying to catch a flying freight train on a dark wet night, so he could not go back to sleep, but lay and listened to the steady snoring of his big companion and worked himself into a nervous frenzy until a violent headache joined the other ills that plagued his skinny body. He was sore, miserable, cold, and thirsty, and frantically worried that Chimp's golden adventure was going to turn into dark, uncertain disaster for both of them.

It was Corky, not Chimp, who sounded the alarm that it was time to be stirring around if they hoped to catch the train. Chimp insisted they leave the lantern behind and had already packed everything neatly in their two packs except for their blankets and Corky's new rain slicker. He rolled these up compactly with the slicker as an outer wrapper and slung this over his shoulder with a leather strap from his own pack.

"Okay, you ready, kid?" Chimp asked finally. "We gotta git on outta here. Can't be more than a hour till train time. I shoulda bought me a watch. Could save us some time standin' around in the damn rain."

He dragged both of their packs close to the crawlway entrance. Then he turned once more to Corky who had thus far silently followed Chimp's preparation instructions.

"Hey, Corky, shall we burn 'er down 'fore we go? Might be okay to watch for the train near a fire."

"No!" Corky cried out. "Hell, no, what if somethin' happens an' we don't ketch the train? Besides, I might not like California an' want to come back when it's summer again."

"Jus' won't let go right up to the las' minute." Chimp laughed, shaking his shaggy head. "You gonna make a hell of a hobo if I gotta pry ya loose from every place we stop. Okay, le's hit the road."

He took a final pull at the brandy bottle and stuck it deep in his overcoat pocket.

Chimp gave a startled whistle as he crawled out into the stormy night. "Holy shit, Corky, colder'n a witches tit out here."

Corky came crawling slowly out behind him. The wind was blowing about thirty miles an hour from the northwest and driving a steady, stinging rain horizontally at them. The cold bit into his skinny frame as soon as he stood up.

He shivered as he voiced his objection. "God, Chimp, we're gonna freeze to death in this. Let's wait for a better time."

"I tole you before, li'l buddy, when it come time for leavin', ain't nothin' gonna git in my way, an' that's what I meant. It's a shitty night, all right, but we'll make it. She'll git better down the line."

He seized both their packs and headed away down the tracks.

Corky hunched his shoulders and, with hands rammed deep in his pockets, shuffled along behind. They had gone only about a hundred yards down the track when the unmistakable piercing, one-eyed beam of the train light rounded the turn about a half-mile away.

"Okay, Corky," Chimp said, giving final instructions, "you stand about here, jus' clear of them tracks. I'll run down here a few yards an' ketch on as she passes. We'll git on about the middle. That way we can look a few cars both ways an' maybe find a way inside outta this horse shit weather. When ya see me latch on, move in close an' grab the same ladder. I'll grab you same time. No sweat, you'll see. Don't be scared, 'cause ain't nothin' I ever got a firm hold on ever got away from me. Y'all set now, right?"

Corky nodded, and Chimp went at a jog a few yards down the track. As the first few cars of the train <u>clickety-clacked</u> past Corky, he could not see a thing, because he had been watching the headlight for several minutes. As his eyes readjusted to the darkness, he saw Chimp make his lunging rush for the ladder and saw his big frame blend with the side of a boxcar as he pulled himself up.

What Chimp had not reckoned on was the wind chill. The temperature hovered right at the thirty-two-degree mark. Though it still was raining, the moving metal cars were several degrees colder, and the surface was coated with a rock-hard eighth of an inch of ice. His powerful left hand locked on the targeted rung of the ladder, and his feet swung free of the ground with the ease of long practice. The slippery surface was unanticipated.

As Chimp's foot hit the near side of the ladder rung, his boot sole slipped violently across the iced surface just as he put his full weight on it. As his toe hit the opposite side of the ladder frame, it slipped off. Simultaneously the wind whipped the tail of his coat behind and around the ladder. As his foot came off the ladder, the full weight of his three hundred plus pounds came down sharply on his left hand. He could not hold onto the icy rung.

His overcoat tied into the ladder just long enough to swing his great bulk back in toward the rapidly accelerating train car. Right in front of Corky, Chimp hit the ground, and Corky could not have told which was the more bone chilling sound, the agonized roar of his big companion as the massive train wheel amputated his right arm halfway between the hand and the elbow, or the awesome <u>crunch</u> as the end of the steel ladder on the next car entered Chimp's left temple and tore a four-inch channel through the top of his skull.

Corky stood in shock, watching the dim flicker of light play across his dead friend's body as the murderous machine <u>click-clicked</u> past and out of sight in the darkness. He stood there for ten minutes, wet, sick, horribly shocked, and desperately alone.

Then, hardly aware of what he was doing, he seized hold of Chimp's clothing and began tugging, rolling, pulling the huge body toward the brush pile. His concern and shock gave him a strength he would never have thought possible. Still, in his weakened condition, it took him nearly an hour to bring the body next to the brush pile.

The rain soaked his clothing from the outside, and his sweat soaked it from the inside as he worked and struggled. He did not notice the passage of time, nor did he notice when the rain suddenly changed to a driving blizzard. Sticky wet snow piled across his shoulders and made Chimp's clothing slippery as well as wet. Still he struggled on until at last he had Chimp right at the entrance to his castle.

Realizing that he could not hope to drag Chimp through the small opening, he took the time to remove enough of the branches to enable him to roll the body inside. Then he went back out in the driving snow and carefully rearranged the cover of branches to hide the entrance as before.

Once back inside, he attacked the task again, pushing, tugging, and rolling the big body until it lay stretched out on his own pallet beneath the fender. Only then did he stop and dig around in his pack until he found some matches and lit the lantern.

Then he took the only extra shirt he had, approached Chimp again, and carefully cleaned the gruesome mess from his friend's face and beard. He did his best to straighten the clothing and great wool overcoat to make him appear as lifelike as possible. As he pulled the tail of the coat from under the body and laid it straight over Chimp's legs, his hand came in contact with the bulk of the brandy bottle in the coat pocket.

Slowly he worked the bottle from the wet clothing and held it up to the light, it was nearly half full. Kneeling down, he pushed, poked and pulled Chimps body around so it lay on the right side, hiding the blood-soaked piece of an arm. Then he folded his shirt to hide the gore on it and laid it clean side out, hiding the wound in the skull.

Gently he patted the brown bearded face, and for the first time, tears came to his eyes. He sat back cross-legged on Chimp's pallet and placed the lantern beside him. He sat quietly crying for a few minutes, then reached out and picked up the brandy bottle. He opened it and took a drink. To his numbed surprise, it tasted good, and he repeated the action.

Suddenly a thought struck him, and he took the lantern and crawled back out into the storm. For half and hour he searched up and down the track until he found the amputated arm, half buried in snow in the middle of the track. Blindly he stumbled back to the retreat. He hid this grisly remnant behind the body and returned to his former position.

Again he opened the bottle, and this time he flipped away the cork. Soon the warmth of the brandy numbed his pain and grief, and the deadlier warmth of hypothermia deadened the rest of his senses.

When he finally tipped the bottle and found it empty, he pushed it aside. Slowly, painfully, he crawled drunkenly forward and lifted the upper edge of Chimp's coat. Holding tightly to it with his left hand, he squeezed his skinny, pain-wracked body in against that of his friend with his back against Chimp's chest. He tugged the coat forward to cover both of them as much as he could. Then he reached up, grasped Chimp's left arm, and pulled it across his body. Taking one big finger in each hand, he pulled Chimp's hand to his chest.

During this final ritual of love for his friend, the lantern flickered and died. Almost immediately frost and ice began to build on his wet clothing. As the snow began to drift across the top of the brush pile, and consciousness began to fade, brilliant sunshine flooded his mind, and bright green palm trees and corn fields stood waving before him in the sun-soaked fields. The last earthly sound that Corky heard was the mournful whistle of the two-o'clock Northern Pacific heading west out of Chicago.

"Ham and eggs, Chimp," he whispered as he faded away.

EPILOGUE

▼

On the tenth of June, 1970, a bright orange crew car putt-putted up the track in southeast Chicago and pulled to a stop near a big pile of brush close to the right of way.

The gandy-dancer crew off-loaded, laughing and joking among themselves. Swede Hanson, the crew boss, singled out one of them.

"Jack," he said, "take four of these guys and get some brush hooks and a chain saw off the tool cart. Clear this strip of brush out of here. Just pile it on top of what's already there."

"When you get it all stacked, dump a li'l gasoline on it an' burn 'er up. There's enough dry stuff there to make the whole thing burn jus' fine. A bulldozer's gonna be in here this afternoon to smooth this whole strip for that new warehouse project. Me an' the others gonna be back in a while. We got some ties to change down the line."

A mile-away, a fire-department crew was readying their equipment to burn down an old tool shack that someone had converted into living quarters and used for a home for a while. It was dilapidated and boarded up, and was being burned to make room for part of the same project for which Jack and his crew were preparing.

As Jack's crew stood watching the brush pile burn, one of the men came up with a dirty slicker-wrapped bundle.

"Looky here, Jack," the man said. "Some bum lost his bindle, looks like."

"Just throw it on the fire, kid," Jack replied. "It's probably loaded with crabs an' such. Best get rid of it."

0-595-31404-X

Printed in the United States
18569LVS00002B/4-39